Where A Little Rain Comes Down

God Bless

Where A Little Rain Comes Down

By

Tammy Wiens

They do not direct their deeds towards turning to their God,
for the spirit of harlotry is in their midst,
and they do not know the Lord.

Hosea 5:4 NKJ

To order additional copies of this book, contact:
Xlibris Corporation
1-888-795-4274
www.Xlibris.com
Orders@Xlibris.com
41232

CHAPTER 1

RAIN

The small girl huddled under the table listening to them talk. That wasn't unusual, but today the conversation was different. She held fast to the table leg as she tried to understand.

"And what, pray tell, am I supposed to do with a twelve-year-old girl?" the man asked, staring intently at the woman.

"Whatever you like!" the woman pleaded. "She could earn her keep."

"You realize what you're suggesting is selling your daughter and for what? A quick fix? Star, this is cruel; the child doesn't know me. Put the child out there yourself if that's the future you want for her—then she'll earn her keep and keep you supplied." He moved to get out of bed and retrieved his clothes.

"Johnny, you could give her a better life—a better clientele." Star argued, letting the blankets fall, revealing her nakedness, but she took no notice. "You know with me, she'll be old long before her time or dead. I know you don't want that! Haven't I always been there for you? You know Star will welcome you with open arms anytime!"

"Yes, and all it costs me is a hit or two." Johnny sighed. "She's so young; she needs her mother!"

"I've done my best by her! Now it's either you take her or she goes out there," Star said, pointing at the street outside the window. The street where Johnny knew all too well what awaited the child.

"It goes against my better judgment," Johnny finally sighed. "Star, don't be coming begging her back. You leave her, she's mine."

Star nodded her head in understanding. Johnny handed her the small packet and she stood to head toward the door. The child ran from the under the table grasping her small arms around her mother's waist, sobbing in fear. Star gently pulled the child to her, grasping her small face in her hand to gaze one last time into her eyes.

"Honey, you have to stay here!" she stated. With one last quick motion, wiping the tears from the small face, she hurried out the door.

The child ran after her mother but Johnny caught her, holding her tight. She cried out, begging her mother to come back. It was no use. She collapsed against the man she knew only as her mother's friend and wept.

It took an hour for the child to stop crying but her eyes wouldn't leave the door. Her mom would come back! She had to! There was a desperation in the set of the jaw that told Johnny this one wouldn't accept that her mother could actually abandon her like this. He hated this part of the job. He slid into the seat beside her.

"What's your name, child?" he asked, making sure to keep his voice gentle. He already knew but it was a good opener.

"Rain," she said, sounding detached from her being.

"That's a pretty name," he replied. "Well, Rain, you're going to stay with me from now on. Your mom can't take care of you anymore."

She turned her face to him, looking him in the eye. Today he looked kind but she knew he could change very quickly. She had witnessed it many times.

"You can't make me do anything I don't want to," she told him. "I won't be like her."

He looked at her. She had a face that shone with purity, but it was obvious that she had long ago been robbed of innocence. It broke his heart to know that one so young had to understand things so far beyond her. He knew he was a part of the business that put these youngsters in this place, but he had always made it a policy to make sure his girls were over eighteen. Even so, they looked too young now that he was growing older. He was getting too soft for this whole business! But then he had always been soft!

He had always kept his own children in the dark about his lifestyle until they were grown. To them he was Dad—the man who bounced them on his knee and helped them learn to swing a bat. It was only once they had grown old enough to understand that he had revealed the truth to them. His son had always admired him and quickly decided to become part of the family business. Johnny taught him all the tricks of the trade and he learned well. His daughter had taken a very different view! She was appalled and quickly disassociated herself from her family, choosing to fight against him and trying her best to shut him down. Undercover cops swarmed his every move as she revealed his secrets to the world of justice. He wondered what she would do when she actually stood on the other side of the courtroom telling the judge to send him to jail. He shook his head. He loved his children no matter what they felt about him. He had kept them fed and clothed and they couldn't deny that.

Pulling himself out of his reverie, he looked back at the child beside him. Rain was obviously wise to her mom's reality, but something about her still held sweetness. He looked into her eyes closely—she looked clean. It was a rare thing for a woman of Star's reputation to keep her child away from the drugs that were so accessible, but then

Star was a selfish one. She probably didn't want to waste a hit on a child! He shook his head. He was getting too old for this business! What would make him accept this child except foolishness? He took her by the hand gently and led her to the stairs.

"I'll show you your room," he offered.

Rain followed him. She knew her mother wasn't coming back and to run away from here was a guarantee that she would be working the streets. Maybe she'd be able to get on his soft side and avoid what seemed to be her destiny.

Johnny showed her to a bedroom that was beyond anything she could imagine. It was a mansion in comparison to the one-room apartment she lived in with her mother. This one bedroom was larger than their whole place.

"This is all mine?" she questioned.

"All yours!" he smiled. He knew what was going through her mind. The rooms were designed to be wonderful—just one of his traps to get his girls to be cooperative. "Here you'll have the best of everything!"

She looked up at him with a wary look.

"Nothing in life is free!" she reminded him.

He didn't have the heart to tell her he knew exactly what she meant. For a second, he let the guilt wash over him. She could already read his mind and his objectives. He showed her the closet and left. When he looked back in on her an hour later, she was fast asleep. He let his hand sweep through her hair, not sure what he would do with her.

And the question kept at him while he avoided answering it. Rain had spent six months with him before he even let it be known that she couldn't just stay with him forever. His other girls were already getting upset. He decided to put her to work as a courier.

Johnny smiled at the girl when she walked in the door. She was like a breath of fresh air in his life. They both knew he wasn't the man he once was and somehow she assuaged the pain of the lost relationship with his own daughter.

"You make all your deliveries?" he asked sternly.

"Yes, Johnny," she replied, with a sparkle in her eye. She knew he was just doing business and the sternness was part of the act—the part he played with all his girls.

He smiled at her and invited her to join him for dinner. She quickly took her seat. They enjoyed the meal in silence, lost in their own thoughts. It was only after they finished that Johnny spoke.

"Rain, my son is coming and he's . . ."

"Mean?" she asked, as a chill ran through her.

"He's not aware of your existence," Johnny said, taking her hand gently in his. "He's taken over most of my business. I only have a few of my favorites around these days—the rest are all with him."

She narrowed her eyes, not liking where this was going.

"He's very free with enjoying the fruits of his labors," he said and took a deep breath. "You've become a young woman in the year since you arrived here and my son may see you as a great asset to the business."

She stared at him. "Are you giving me to him?"

"No, Rain, I just want you to be aware of his lack of control. Just stay away from him. Do your work and be the wonderful girl you are, but keep out of his way."

Rain bit her lip. She would choose death over prostitution and, so far, with Johnny, she'd managed to avoid it. She prayed this son wouldn't be able to override his father. It often happened that way—the younger would push the elder out of the castle and the elder would disappear into the shadows. She had to avoid him.

Rain heard the doorbell about two hours later. She watched the two men from her vantage point on the stairs where they couldn't see her. She felt pangs of jealousy at the kindred spirit that obviously flowed between them. This guy was competition. Until now, she was the only one she knew of who could put the smile she now saw on Johnny's face. She followed their every move like a cheetah on the prowl.

"Son, it's so good to see you. How's business?" Johnny said, taking a seat.

"Great, absolutely wonderful!" Johnny Jr. smiled. "I'm raking in the cash and enjoying every minute."

"So why this talk of expansion?" Johnny asked, tilting his head slightly.

"Because I can," the son replied. "The dancing girls don't put out and a lot of my clientele want a closer touch. I have to please my clients!"

"You know that this will put you into a new relationship with the law! Do you really want this?" Johnny pleaded. "It is so much easier when you just keep away from them. The dancing is paying the bills."

"I've thought about it and I got it cased."

"You aren't even twenty and you got it cased!" Johnny Sr. sniffed. "We all got it cased at twenty! Foolish kid. I can't stop you, you don't need cash, so why are you here?"

"I realize the importance of wisdom that comes with experience."

Johnny laughed and kicked back into the chair. "Wisdom hey? Rain, bring us some drinks!"

"Rain?" Johnny Jr. asked with a curious look on his face.

Rain scurried from her hiding place to the kitchen to grab the tray she had prepared earlier. She wondered why Johnny would tell her to keep out of this man's way and then put her right in his line of fire? She shook the thought aside knowing Johnny would be upset if she didn't appear on demand. Rain entered the room balancing the tray of glasses and drinks while her eyes looked this newcomer over carefully. He was a carbon copy of his dad—handsome, charming and dangerous.

"Here you are, Johnny. Do you need anything else?" Rain asked, knowing every second of scrutinizing she did was matched by this newcomer.

"No, we're fine." Johnny smiled, grabbing a drink.

"Then I'll head to bed," she said, setting the tray down and hurrying out of the room.

Johnny Jr. watched her leave with a thousand questions in his mind but one summed them all up. "Who is she?"

"One of my girls had a kid and left her in trade for a snort. She works for me and I supply her mom."

"Her mom just left her?" Johnny Jr. asked, still staring at the spot where she had stood. "Do you have her working?"

"She's a child," Johnny replied, waving the thought away. "I know what you're thinking and you can forget it. She's too genteel for your type."

"You just keep her around and what; she does odd jobs for you?" Johnny Jr. asked, unable to believe such a commodity was not earning her keep.

"I can trust her. That's worth a lot in my business and that's your first lesson—find people you can trust."

Johnny folded his arms across his chest, letting his son know there would be no more discussion about Rain—at least not today. The son tried to hide the smile that the thought of Rain put on his face, but he failed. Johnny grimaced, knowing all too well what his son was thinking!

The next morning Rain hurried to prepare breakfast—a regular event in her life. She was busy buttering the toast when he came into the room.

"Good morning!" Johnny Jr. greeted her with that smile that she knew all too well.

She looked up at him, shuddering at the sight.

"So you live here with my Dad?"

She pushed herself to the other side of the table making sure to put some distance between them.

"Yes, I live here!" she told him, every hair on her body telling him to leave her alone.

He smiled, reaching across the table to grasp her hand. She pulled away quickly.

"Nervous?" he asked.

"Get away from me!" she warned.

Johnny Sr. pushed himself into the kitchen. Rain was never late for breakfast! He looked from his son to Rain.

"Am I interrupting something?"

"No, Johnny!" Rain said, picking up the tray and hurrying to the dining room.

"What did you do?" Johnny Sr. demanded when she was gone.

"I was just trying to be friendly!"

"Mmmm—back off that one!"

Johnny Jr. didn't miss the malice in his dad's voice. He nodded. Rain would have to be a project for another time.

Rain sighed with relief when the goodbyes had all been said and Johnny Jr. was gone. Johnny went on and on about the wonderful visit while she nodded silently, trying hard not to disagree. Her true feelings would remain deeply hidden to protect her from upsetting her meal ticket.

CHAPTER 2

Johnny sat in the den with a group of his best informers listening to the latest word on the street.

"She's very careful but she's being watched. Johnny, they know she lives here!"

Johnny sighed, knowing exactly what this meant. Rain was in danger of being discovered and she would lead the law right to his door. Armed with all this new information, he debated his options as he sat on the step waiting for Rain.

It was a short day and Rain was glad she could head back to the safety of the house. She knew that several of her regulars had been arrested in the last few weeks and feared every transaction would bring the law tumbling down on her head. She moved quickly through the gate leading to the house and saw him.

"What's wrong?" she asked, worry lining her young face.

"You're being watched," he said in a whisper. "I have to pull you off the street."

"And do what?" she asked.

"We'll think of something. Maybe if you lay low this will all quiet down!"

"I'm gonna have to work the street?" she cried, letting the fear swallow her up as the tears fell in streams down her cheeks.

"Rain, I'm sure there's another way," Johnny said, taking her into his arms. "Let's just calm down and think this through."

Three months later, Rain was still not working and she could tell Johnny was frustrated that narks still tailed her everywhere. Having turned fourteen the week before, Rain had wished she could forever remain a child, but looking in the mirror, she knew that was not the case. She had seen many girls who looked much younger working the streets, and it seemed that would be her destiny. But it was more than just the selling of her body that scared her. It seemed that the only way these girls could face themselves in the mirror was in a drugged stupor, and she didn't want that for her future. She needed a way to escape! She thought of running away, but she knew they would find her—and then what? At least now, Johnny trusted her and let her stay at his house.

She went about her day's chores watching every movement around her as she headed to the store for groceries. They were there! It was like she had a private bodyguard with the narks always on her tail. She grabbed the groceries she needed and headed back to the house.

She got home to find a car that had a familiar look to it even though she was sure she had never seen it before. It had to be him! She almost turned back into the street but remembered they were out there and that would look suspicious. She trudged into the house, heading to the kitchen to put away the groceries before going to greet the guest. Rain stopped at the closed door that led to Johnny's office. She didn't like what she heard through the wall.

"Pop, she needs to leave here. I've heard they follow her everywhere!" Johnny Jr. said in a tone that sounded too gentle to be true to Rain. "I could take care of her."

"She's just a child!" Johnny Sr. stated. "She's not ready for the lifestyle you live."

Rain prayed he would stay strong.

"Pop, she's the daughter of the streets. She can handle it—besides, you have no choice. Are you planning to just have her stay here freeloading until you die?"

Rain could hear Johnny Sr. sigh. She shook with fear that he was starting to soften.

"I know I've gotta cut her loose and that letting you take her would be the best."

"Yes, that would be best!" She could almost see the smile on his face.

"I'll agree to this only if you can make me a promise!"

"A promise?" Johnny Jr. asked, wondering what strings this girl would come with. He couldn't very well refuse his dad!

"You must promise not to put her out on the street!"

Rain shook her head. He was selling her out.

"Pop, that's asking too much."

"I realize you'll want her to work, just not the street. Only the best clientele—keep her safe! Don't hurt her more than is necessary."

"Pop!" Johnny Jr. protested.

"Promise me that!" Johnny Sr. demanded. Rain could hear movement.

"All right, Pop. I promise the best clientele for the genteel Rain." Johnny agreed gasping like his air was being cut off.

Rain slipped away from the door and headed to her room. The tears flowed down her cheeks. All the time she'd spent here and it was worth nothing. He'd sold her for a promise.

Rain cried all night, thinking her pillow swallowed up her tears, but one look at Johnny Sr. told her he had heard. She knew he knew she'd eavesdropped.

"We knew this day would come, child, but he has promised to take care of you." Johnny's eyes filled with tears as he spoke. "He's promised!"

"His promise is worth spit! I won't do it!" Rain wept.

"He will not break his promise to me!" Johnny argued. "He'd rather die than have to look at me after breaking a promise!"

"You know what he'll do!" she said, turning to face him, hoping her eyes could plead her case better than her tongue.

Johnny knew he had to stay strong—there were things she didn't know. This really was the best thing for her.

"Rain, one word of advice; don't anger him. He has a bad temper."

"Ready to go, Girly?" Johnny Jr. asked, sticking his head through the door.

"Please, Johnny!" she pleaded.

The older man stood and left the room. He couldn't bear to listen to her pleas—this was best.

Rain said nothing. She grabbed her suitcase and threw in a few necessities. Soon they had made their way to the car. Johnny Sr. stood at the door, waving goodbye, wanting to pull her back into his arms and hold her, keep her with him. Tears stung her eyes but she would not wave goodbye. She would not look back. Johnny had betrayed her—she had fooled herself into believing he cared but she would not make that mistake again.

Johnny Jr. started the car, giving his dad one last wave before pulling away. He knew it was the girl his dad wanted some recognition from but it wasn't happening. They drove in silence until they pulled out of the city.

"So Rain, my Pop tells me you're not to into the bedroom stuff?" Johnny said, while changing lanes for the third time in what Rain saw as a futile attempt to get out of traffic.

"I'm not going to pretend I like you so you don't need to pretend you like me. I know what you're planning and you can forget it. I'm not interested."

"How can you know what I'm planning? You a mind reader too? Maybe you've been talking to the wrong people and leading them right to the house? Did you think I might just be driving you off to dump your body in the nearest river?"

"You already passed that. I would never have betrayed Johnny, but obviously your loyalty is not quite so deeply rooted." Rain spat the words. "I know Johnny would have taken care of me himself if he thought I was backstabbing him."

"You're pretty smart!" Johnny Jr. smiled. "I made Pop a promise and I'll keep it as best I can but I'm not like my Pop. I won't have you just mixing my drinks and bringing me my slippers. There are girls who would pay me for that honor. You'll work where I tell you and do what I tell you."

"I won't work the street!" Rain defiantly declared. "You'll have to kill me to get me to do that and I don't want none of your stuff. I don't snort, shoot or smoke and I don't plan on starting."

"I guess we'll see, won't we." He looked over at her. He hadn't spent much time with her and hadn't realized how strong willed she was, but wills could be broken. He would have her in the palm of his hands by the time they got to their destination!

They let the silence settle over them, enjoying the scenery for the next hundred miles. For Johnny, this was a strange thing and he soon found himself bothered by the lack of noise. He turned the radio on, humming along softly while he tapped his fingers on the steering wheel in rhythm to the music. Rain enjoyed listening to him, finding his voice pleasant. He looked over at her and smiled when he caught her tapping her foot. She turned quickly to return her gaze outside to a world she never knew existed. Land covered only with nature and the odd house for miles and miles. It enchanted her.

He pulled the car to a stop at a stop sign and turned to her. They were in a town that to Rain only existed in dreams. She stared at the white picket fences that seemed like something out of a television show.

"Want to get some lunch? I'll buy."

"I don't want anything from you—not lunch, not a job, nothing!" Rain declared.

"Suit yourself. I'm going in there," Johnny said, pointing to a small cafe, "and having a meal."

He stepped out of the car and she considered making a break for it but there was no way she could outrun him and there wasn't a soul around. Reluctantly, she followed him inside and ordered a hamburger.

"I would like separate bills," she told the waitress who was staring at Johnny with gaga eyes.

"See, I could have her if I wanted," he boasted, that annoying smile pasted on his face.

"So let me trade her places and see if she's still so willing." Rain shot back.

"We got a three-day drive here, girl," Johnny tried to explain. "Are you planning to cheer up and be friendly at any point? Cause if you're not, I'll just take what you hold so dear and then you'll have no more reason to protest. The ladies say I have the touch."

"The touch of death! If you have any ideas of sharing my bed, you had better buy a hammer."

"A hammer?"

"To hit yourself in the head with to make you forget the pain you'll be feelin' everywhere else."

He shook his head at her. He liked her—she was feisty and creative! He'd heard many things but never that. They ate their meal, once again letting silence dominate.

"I think you ought to know, I've dealt with your kind before and I've always come out on top," Johnny said, pulling himself to a stand. "Come on, let's hit the road."

Once back in the car, Rain wondered why they were driving three days. It seemed rather foolish when a plane would be so much faster.

"Why didn't we take a plane?" It slipped out before she caught herself.

He looked over at her, surprised to hear her voice in a tone not dripping with hate.

"I'm delivering the car for a friend."

"It's stolen?"

"No, it's carrying some special cargo. Don't ask because the less you know the better if something goes wrong." He smiled at her as he pulled up to the stop sign.

She hated that smile. He thought he was so smooth. She smiled back, seconds before she opened the car door and leapt from the now moving vehicle. He slammed on the brakes and ran after her. She pumped her legs as hard as she could, making her way down the street. She careened her way down an embankment, wishing she wasn't wearing heels. She lost the shoes and ran until she came up against a fence. He was upon her before she could tear her sleeve free from the barbs. He held her tight, dragging her back to the car huffing and puffing with the effort.

"You're hurting me!" she whined, as he slammed her back into the car.

"Try that again and I'll kill you!" he whispered to her in a deadly cold voice.

"Why can't you just let me go? I've done everything your dad asked and made him a lot of money. My mom's habit has to have been covered for a lifetime by now."

"Rain, you forget that Pop put you up all these years; provided a roof over your head, clean sheets and all these fine clothes. Did you think a charity was paying for all that?"

"Then let me go back to what I was doing. I was good."

"Yeah and that's why you had narks on your tail all the time. Face it Rain, you were born to give a man pleasure—every man that asks." He pulled into a small roadside hotel.

She didn't need to look at him to know what he was hoping to gain here. He would be begging for that hammer if she had her way!

He hurried to get a room, leaving her alone in the car with a warning that she had better still be there when he got back! She felt forced to oblige but was already plotting how to handle the upcoming attack. He pulled her from the car and pushed her into a room. Much to her surprise, it was clean. He took a deep breath.

"So Rain, how we gonna do this? There's only one bed!"

She couldn't see his face but knew he was smiling. She hurried to the washroom to hide in there but he anticipated this and jammed his foot in the door. She wedged herself in the small space between the door and the tub pinching his foot hard. She sat rigid.

"Come on Rain, let's not make it so hard. I promise I'll be gentle." He gritted his teeth as the door's pressure squeezed the circulation out of his foot.

Tears filled her eyes. How many times had she heard a man say those same words to her mom? She knew they were lies—all lies.

Johnny knew he could out muscle her but something made him stop. He pictured her soft doe-like eyes and all the pain he saw there, and decided he would lull her into a false security—then he would carry the hammer. He had, after all, made a promise.

"Okay, Rain," he said, trying to sound gentle. "You win, just release my foot and I'll leave you alone. Your virginity is safe."

She didn't budge.

"Rain, let me get my foot out of the door!" he repeated, now feeling slightly agitated. She still didn't move. This time he added a lot of color to the request, yanking hard on his foot. Finally, after ten minutes of cursing at her, he managed to work himself free. The door slammed shut. He grabbed the doorknob before she could lock it.

"I give you my word of honor I'll be a perfect gentleman tonight," he coaxed while pushing hard against the door. Nothing. "Fine, I'll do my business outside!"

He lay in the bed wondering how he would get her out of the bathroom, realizing she could remain in there for days. He pulled himself out of the bed, pacing the floor. He had never encountered this type of dilemma before. He decided to try pushing on the door again. It opened. He shook his head when he found Rain was fast asleep on the floor crunched into the most uncomfortable looking position. He gently reached for her in an attempt to lift her, waking her in the process. She became a wild tiger kicking and scratching. His anger consumed him as he grasped her around the waist and dragged her to the bed.

"Look," he cried, adding some colorful names, "I've had it! If I wanted you, I could take you right now. I'm going to let you go and you're going to lay nice and still."

He released her and she sprang from the bed like a dolphin going for a fish treat. He grabbed her before she could make her way back to the bathroom.

"I'm not going to touch you!" he promised, pulling her back toward the bed. "At least not tonight."

She caught him hard between the legs, crumpling him to the floor. He moaned in agony. She finally stopped struggling, watching him crawl on the floor in pain. A smile broke across her face.

"Okay," he said, struggling to pull himself onto the bed, "let's just go to bed."

"I'm not sleeping with you."

"You're really trying my patience! Get in this bed right now."

"No." she declared, not liking his tone at all. She was trapped like an animal. The tears came as the sense of hopelessness took over.

"Rain, get in this bed!" he yelled. He turned to her and saw the tears. He let his demeanor soften. "I won't touch you!"

She eyed him up carefully trying to decide if she should trust him. In the end, she realized her choices were limited and gave up the fight. She laid herself on the very edge of the bed on top of the covers. He looked at her thinking this looked just as uncomfortable as the bathroom.

"That's how you gonna sleep?"

She just closed her eyes and tried to shut out everything around her—especially him.

Morning came and she was still lying fully clothed on top of the covers. Johnny tapped her awake offering her a cup of coffee and some donuts. He wasn't surprised when she refused.

"I took the money out of your purse. Take the stinking coffee." He smiled.

"You took my money?"

"Just enough for breakfast. How did Pop ever trust you?"

"He treated me kind and I returned the favor."

"I could've had you last night but I refrained. That has to be worth some brownie points."

"No!" she told him. She had no intentions of ever trusting this man.

"Fine! Let's go. I want you to know this is the worst trip I've ever taken in my life and it better improve or I'll be needing something to cheer me up."

The threat was well understood.

They traveled in silence, both lost in their own thoughts. Rain knew he had counted her money and knew she couldn't go very far on her funds. He would use that against her but what could she do?

They didn't stop to eat—only grabbed a few snacks when they stopped for gas. It was getting dark when he finally spoke.

"Rain, we'll be stopping at another hotel tonight and if you're determined to pay your share, this one's on you."

"Fine!"

He stopped at a much nicer hotel than the first night. She stepped into the lobby and came back to direct him to the parking spot for the room. She handed him a key. He stepped out of the car and opened the door assuming she was following him.

"See how nice . . ." he looked around but she had vanished. He heard a door slam and he knew—she got them each a room. He laughed—she got him!

She met him at the car the next morning. He smiled at her.

"Very clever. Just remember tonight we'll be in my back yard. In fact, we'll be in my house."

"But it's only been two days!"

"We drove a little further than I'd planned yesterday. I figured there was no reason to stop early since all we'd be doing is sleeping!"

She glanced at him, wondering what that meant!

CHAPTER 3

Rain was exhausted by the time they pulled up to a house that appeared to be very large and had to be expensive. The large part appealed to her. There had to be a way to find a hiding place where he couldn't find her. She let him guide her to the door where they were greeted by a room of women. Rain saw her chance to slip away as Johnny's attentions were diverted to the rush of women ready to give him a proper welcome home. She hurried to find an escape looking back only once to make sure she wasn't being watched.

Rain found a secluded space in the pool house where she curled up and went to sleep. The whole trip had been too much and her body was worn out. She would need every ounce of her strength to endure this place and more than she had in her to survive long term.

"Ladies, it's wonderful to be home!" Johnny said, pushing his way out of the mob. "Did anyone see the girl I brought with me?"

Most of them shook their heads, but one stepped up.

"She wandered down that way," she said, pointing down toward the pool. "She new blood?"

"She's new but she'll need a little encouraging. Sissy, you don't mind taking a little bird under your wing, do you?" Johnny said, caressing her chin gently.

"Forget it, Johnny. I ain't no babysitter."

"Just try to get her calmed down. She's still a virgin."

"Where'd you pick her up?" Sissy moaned. "On the front step?"

"No, she's Pop's pet. I wish she could see I'm really helping her out."

"So how long she gonna be virgin material?"

"I'm planning to change that tonight!' he informed her and then looked around. "Did someone declare a holiday? Get ready for work, ladies."

Johnny searched the whole house without finding her. He knew she hadn't escaped, but where could she be? He was having many second thoughts about letting Rain join his household.

"She's gotta come out some time," Sissy sighed after they finished searching the entire house for the third time.

"I guess, but this just tears me. She made the whole trip hell and now this."

"Sir," a small voice said.

"What?" he yelled impatiently, swinging around to see the pool boy.

"I heard you were looking for a young lady and I saw someone in the pool house when I went to put away my cleaning gear."

"Andrew, you're getting a raise!" Johnny shouted as he hurried to the pool house.

"Hello, Sleeping Beauty!" he shouted.

She sat up erect, all thoughts of rest gone from her head.

"I believe we have a date in my bedroom because your quarters are a bit cramped." He grabbed her hand hard and pulled her, fighting and screaming, up to his bedroom. The other girls laughed at her antics.

"Don't touch me!" she threatened.

"Look around," he said with a wave of his hand. "You have no place to run or hide. Accept this already."

Her demeanor changed and she smiled at him sweetly, "Of course, you're right. I must just accept this."

"See, was that so hard?"

They heard the yell all through the house. Rain scrambled out of the bedroom and bolted for the pool. Johnny limped out after her.

"I'm going to kill her!"

"What she do?" Sissy asked.

"Can't you tell?" he growled. He stared in disbelief at the small figure making her getaway. "Someone grab her, she's climbing the fence!"

Andrew, the pool boy, made his way around other side of the pool to the fence where Rain had already scaled to the top. He jumped and managed to snag her foot, bringing her down with the force of his weight. The two crashed to the ground. The fall stunned him, but she was up and on the run. Johnny was still limping but his anger had taken over. He and Andrew sandwiched the girl between them, leaving her two options—jump into the pool or try to scale the concrete wall.

"Okay, Rain, we've had some fun, now let's just settle down," Johnny cooed softly.

She stared at him and he found himself starting to hate that calm demeanor her eyes gave her.

She was trying to anticipate their move but waiting just allowed them to move closer. She quickly dove into the pool. Andrew dove in after her. Johnny moved quickly, trying to meet her at the corner. She beat him and was once again at the trellis fence. 'Climb,' she ordered her tired body. Johnny hurried over and lunged for her legs. She caught him with a kick in the chin. Andrew now dragged himself from the pool and moved to help Johnny. At last, between the two of them, they were able to subdue all of Rain's appendages. Both men held tight while they took a moment to gain their breath before attempting to get the girl back to the bedroom.

Johnny handcuffed the girl to the bed and sent Andrew to get him an icepack. She lay motionless on the bed. The icepack arrived and he shut the door, locking it and making sure he took the key.

"No woman has ever done that to me before and you've managed it twice!" he complained. "It's going to be very hard to keep that promise to Pop with you."

She lay silent, just staring at him.

"Close you eyes already!" he bellowed at her, adding some colorful words to the command. She didn't move.

The icepack brought some relief from the pain the initial well-placed kick brought on, and Johnny felt that perhaps he still possessed all the necessary tools to have a family. The girl had no fear of attacking that area! He looked at her and she still had not moved, but her lips had taken on a blue tone from the cold. She was still dripping wet and her hair stuck to her in a mass around her face.

"I am going to take off the handcuffs and take you to the shower and warm you up." he told her.

She watched him move slowly toward her, glad that her earlier behavior was having an effect on him. The key was inserted into the handcuffs and soon he was carrying her to the shower. She waited for him to try to remove her clothes but he didn't—he had no idea what a smart decision that was. The warm water almost burned at first but after the initial shock, she welcomed the warmth. The fight was gone out of her so she let him dry her hair. As with his father, she found herself wondering how he could be so gentle one moment and a complete monster the next. Right now, she needed this personality. She fell against him and cried softly. It was an inescapable truth that this man was her only refuge, the only shoulder she had to cry on when she couldn't go on. He was both her worst enemy and best friend.

"I don't suppose you'll let me take off the wet clothes?" He asked. She pulled away.

He changed the sheet, always keeping a wary eye on her. She was a beautiful girl and he knew with a little make-up, she could pass for eighteen or twenty. Her skin was smooth and clear with a tanned hue. Her hair was long and blond but surprisingly thick and coarse. He wondered if maybe she dyed it but quickly dismissed the idea. He didn't think she spent more than five minutes on her appearance a day. He lifted her, towels and all, onto the blanket that she quickly wrapped around herself.

"You look like a cocoon!" he laughed. "I'm going down for some supper. Would you like something?"

She shook her head no.

"Suit yourself."

He left, letting her know he was gone with the click of the lock.

Johnny headed downstairs knowing this one would be hard to explain. He wasn't happy to see his right hand man sitting on the couch with Sissy waiting to hear him boast about his conquered kingdom.

"So you get it done?" Sissy asked when she saw him make his way down the stairs. Tommy sat on the couch smiling. "Of course he did. He's Johnny!"

"Actually, I didn't." The gasps were audible. "She's different."

"Johnny, you can't let a girl have that kind of power. She'll bring this whole place down!" Tommy cried out. "Let me have a crack at her."

Tommy smirked with confidence that he'd accomplish what Johnny had failed to—an attitude that didn't sit well with Johnny. Maybe he should let Tommy enjoy the girl's company!

"I made a promise to Pop," he sighed. "No rough stuff with this one."

"And I hear she adheres to the same law." Tommy laughed. "Maybe that's why the job didn't get done. The family jewels still bruised?"

"You are replaceable, Tommy," Johnny warned. "Just leave the girl to me."

Rain didn't want anything to eat, but Johnny brought up some soup anyway. She was still shivering in the wet clothes, towels and blankets when he came back with the tray. She hated the pity she saw in his gaze. She was glad when he turned to leave as quickly as he came. But he stopped at the door.

"Sissy," he called, "do you have any flannelette pajamas?"

"You must be kidding!" Sissy shouted back.

"I am not!" Johnny replied. "If you don't have any, get some. Now."

He returned to her side and began spooning the soup into her and, much to his surprise, it went down. Sissy delivered the pajamas and Johnny debated getting her into them. He could ask Sissy, but she wasn't too happy with the newcomer. He knew this would be his job no matter how much he dreaded it.

"Rain, we have to get you out of these wet things. Now I don't want any kicking or screaming, we're just going to do this."

He struggled, pulling off the wet things. She was still shivering so he carried her now naked body back to the shower. He repeated everything—toweling her off, wrapping her up, but he added the pajamas. Once again, he changed the sheets and took a blow dryer to the mattress. He shook his head when she didn't protest any of this. He lay her down and crawled under the covers beside her. Soon he heard the rhythmic pattern of sleep come over her breathing. He lay in the darkness trying to figure this girl out!

The rays of sunshine splashing on his face told him it was morning. He turned to see her still lying exactly as she did the night before.

"Good morning, Rain." No response. "Well, still not talking? I'll make you a deal, you act civil and we'll go down for breakfast. Act otherwise and we'll just stay put."

He threw on a housecoat, offering her one. She refused. He shrugged, grabbing her hand and pulling her down the stairs. The pajamas probably covered more than the housecoat anyway! Sissy and Tommy greeted them as they walked into the dining room.

"Ah, the lovebirds!" Tommy quipped.

"That's enough, Tommy!" Johnny warned. "Sissy, get her some clothes."

"I don't want her kind of clothes!" Rain hissed.

"Oh, you can still speak!" Johnny sang in mocked praise. "Sissy knows the kind of clothes you'll need for your new job."

"I'm not doing it with you or any of your slimy friends."

Tommy and Sissy waited for his hand to send her across the room but it didn't happen. Instead he just smiled.

"Remember that little talk we had upstairs?" His face smiled but his voice spoke a different sentiment.

He sat her down by the table where every setting had a cup of orange juice already poured. She took her orange juice and tossed it in his face. Sissy and Tommy held their breath. Johnny felt the anger creeping up his neck but he just grabbed a napkin to sponge off the juice. Rain wasn't finished. She grabbed the plate and hurled it at him, followed by whatever she could grab. Johnny deflected the barrage of objects, hoping that the table would soon be cleared. Tommy and Sissy pushed away from the table and cleared out of the room. Finally, the objects stopped flying and Johnny dared to put his hands down.

"That was fine china. How are you planning to pay for it?"

She glared at him. "You already owe me more than that for liberties you've taken."

"Excuse me? I own you. You work and give me the money. I don't pay for your services. Does a farmer pay his cow for milk?"

"I'm not a cow and you don't own me. Not yet."

"I get it now. If I conquer you, I truly own you."

She stared at him. The eyes were still calm but the body was rigid. If that was the deal she wanted, he was willing. Let the games begin.

CHAPTER 4

LANCE

Lance and Bryan Hawkins stared down at the ground looking as remorseful as they could. Arthur Hawkins stared at his sons in disbelief. It wasn't often they pushed the rules this hard.

"How many times have I told you two to stay away from this creek during spring thaw?" he asked, staring them down even though neither boy had the courage to look their father in the eye.

"Lots," the two boys responded in unison.

"And do you think your mom and I tell you this to spoil your fun?"

"No."

"So what got into you two—playing down here?" he softened his tone, knowing they wouldn't respond if they felt it would get them into more trouble.

Lance and Bryan stood silently, knowing there was no excuse good enough to justify their actions. They knew very well that they were being careless and disobedient. The question now was did they just face the music or did they try to soften the blow with some story that sounded plausible, making their transgression sound less vial and intentional?

"We disobeyed," Lance relented, opting for the truth. "We wanted to play at the creek and we decided to do it even though we knew it was wrong."

Arthur grabbed the muddied hands of his boys and pulled them back to the house. Dottie took one look at her boys and knew what had happened and what was about to happen. Her heart went out to them but there would be no interference on her part in this ritual. In this house, disobedience had consequences.

Arthur opened the cupboard of dread as the boys called it and he pulled out the heavy belt. They could squirm and cry but that just made everything worse. Lance went first, biting back the tears. Bryan hated having to go second, allowing him that opportunity to hear the smack of the belt on the skin, knowing all too well what it felt like. In moments, Arthur reappeared to fetch Bryan, leaving a teary-eyed Lance to wait for the final chapter of this saga.

"Now you two head to your room." Arthur ordered when the spanking was done. They headed down the hall to their room without questioning his authority.

Bryan sat silent while Lance, who needed to discuss everything, went on and on about the episode.

"We should have stayed on the bank. We shouldn't have gone in the water. I think Dad would've just given us a good talking to if we had just not been in the water. If we try this again, we'll stay out of the water!"

"We did wrong!" Bryan concluded and then added his last thoughts, hoping to end the discussion. "It doesn't matter if we were on the bank or in the water—Mom and Dad told us to stay away from the creek!"

Lance nodded in agreement, shifting his position to try and lighten the sting on his derriere.

"They were down by the creek?" Dottie asked.

"I couldn't believe it myself, especially after the drowning last week." Arthur sank heavily down into his chair.

"I hope this will cure those ideas or I'll be tying them to this house!" Dottie declared. The sting of the strap was nothing in comparison to the loss of a life.

Arthur and Dottie took a moment to pray together for wisdom on how to handle the situation. Arthur took out his pocket watch and nodded. It had been an hour and it was time to have a talk with them about the matter. He pushed open the door to his sons' room.

"You two understand why you received a spanking tonight?" he asked as he seated himself on Lance's bed.

They nodded. Tears shone in the man's eyes. He didn't like disciplining his boys, but it was better than losing them to the creek. He'd seen the gut-wrenching agony of the family that suffered that fate a week earlier.

"You know it hurts me to have to punish you both but willful disobedience can't go unattended. You know we love you too much to let you put yourselves at risk like that."

The boys went to their father and threw their arms around him.

"We're sorry! We won't go down there anymore!" Lance promised.

"I love you both and I forgive you." Arthur gathered them into his arms and kissed their cheeks gently. "Now go apologize to your mom."

"Yes sir." They hurried from the room. Another teary scene followed in the kitchen.

"Boys, you have someone else that needs to hear apologies," Dottie reminded them.

They both bowed their heads and offered their apologies to their Lord and Savior. Lance lifted his head and smiled. Bryan followed suit.

"Now don't you both feel better?" Arthur asked, smiling at them.

The boys nodded. They knew the incident wouldn't be brought up again unless they repeated the crime.

"Now go wash up for supper!" Dottie smiled.

Being eight and nine was tough sometimes as these two could confess to—there were so many things that were so much fun but alas, also forbidden. Lance and Bryan hurried to wash their hands, not risking any more acts of disobedience this day.

After supper, Arthur pushed his chair back from the table and announced that he needed to call a family meeting. The boys looked at each other wondering if this would involve the incident at the creek. But that matter was closed, wasn't it? Their ears perked to hear what this could be about.

"As you know, I had a very important meeting today," Arthur said. "I met with some men who have been looking for a place to set up a farm that would help some of the people in the city who have made a mess of their lives. The program is new and well, not very orthodox. It would mean we'd always have people around. We'd build them a separate home and it would just mean lots of things would change."

"So they've accepted our bid for sure?" Dottie asked, nervously straightening out the tablecloth as she spoke.

"Yes, David thinks it's a great idea and even the police think it might be good. They're even talking about having the bosses and workers meet to work out a new respect for one another. I've dreamed of doing something like this for a long time but it will change all of our lives, so I feel we all need to be together on this."

"So we'd be helping people?" Lance asked.

"Yes. People who've had a lot of bad things happen to them." Arthur nodded. "These are people who've not had good families, and they've been born into a life where they have to do things to stay alive—things that aren't very nice. It's going to be a big job showing them there are better ways."

"Will you still tuck us in?" Bryan asked, not comprehending exactly what they were voting on. "Are you still going to be our mom and dad?"

"Of course. It would mean I'd have my office right here but I'd have more to do. We'd have a staff around, too."

"It will mean more rules!" Dottie informed them. "And you would have to adhere to them!"

The boys glanced at each other nervously. That didn't sound good when they couldn't even follow the ones they had now.

"What is it exactly we would be doing?" Lance asked, realizing even at his young age that this decision they were making would have long-reaching effects.

"We'd be bringing girls here that have been forced to sell their bodies and sometimes their souls and trying to help them see that God still loves them."

"Just girls?" Bryan sighed, thinking that sounded awful.

"Well, in the beginning just girls!" Arthur smiled. "Later, we'd like the boys to come, too. Now before we vote, let's all commit our decision to God."

They all bowed their heads to pray. Lance searched his soul. He wanted to do the right thing but the thought of new rules . . . he sat very still listening to a voice that seemed to say he needed to do this. His head remained bowed long after the others had raised theirs. At last, he made his decision.

"So what do you think?" Arthur asked, curious what might be going through his eldest son's mind. "Who says 'yes'?"

Arthur smiled when they all agreed this was a good thing for the Hawkins family. He wouldn't have gone any further without a unanimous vote.

The machines arrived three weeks later. The boys were thrilled. Watching the giant earthmovers build wonderful piles of dirt was like waking up to one's wildest dreams. The men worked until five and after that, the dirt piles were fair game. All the neighbor kids rode their bikes over to join in the fun.

"What exactly are you building here?" Hawkins' neighbors asked.

"Some housing," came the evasive answer. David, the project leader, had told them to keep things under their hat until it was certain. No use stirring up trouble for no reason, but the questions kept coming.

"For who?"

"Some people that need to have a farm experience!" Arthur would smile with a twinkle in his eye.

These answers worked for a while but then things started to escalate.

"I've heard that you'll be bringing city youth out here!" one neighbor accused.

"Not exactly, Bill." Arthur responded. He wasn't lying but he wasn't giving him the whole picture either.

"So who?" Bill asked, knowing Arthur's love of ministries that included the outcasts of society.

"We're opening a home for women of the night who want to make a lifestyle change." Arthur responded, tired of beating around the bush. Bill knew him too well anyway.

"Excuse me?"

"Don't worry," Arthur smiled, heading back out to the barn in an effort to make light of what he had said. "They'll be contained to the yard here."

"And how can you be sure?" Bill asked, staying right in step with the man.

"These are girls who have fallen into the wrong lifestyle. Not grown women, but girls. From what I understand, most of them are fourteen and under—hardly hardened to the lifestyle—kids actually."

"I don't know, Arthur." Bill shook his head with concern. He liked the Hawkins family but this was a bit out there; even for him.

"We are planning a town meeting to advise the area and tell you about other similar programs," Arthur told him. "I think you'll see this will be fine. Bill, you and I have been on church council together for years—you know we need to love them all."

"Love 'em from where they live. Why bring them here?"

"We're talking about young girls here. Why are you so afraid?"

Bill worked his jaw hard trying to stay calm, not daring to say more. Arthur watched and knew they were in for a bumpy ride.

Two weeks later, after a heated town meeting, the whole area wasn't so sure they wanted this type of facility in their backyard. Worst of all, they felt Dottie and Arthur had tried to sneak it in.

"I assure you, all measures will be taken to insure everyone's safety!" Arthur shouted, trying to be heard above the negative ranting.

"You can't really promise that!" a lady shouted back.

"Nothing in life is certain!" Arthur replied. "But this I know: these girls deserve a chance and I'm going to give them one!"

It was the last word he gave but the arguments against this idea kept coming. Most of the arguments were emotional nonsense, but a few of the things actually held some merit. Arthur took these to heart, deciding he would review anything that did offer constructive criticism. The rest he would ignore. It was almost morning when he finally returned home to Dottie who sat by the bed on her knees, deep in prayer.

"You've brought me safely home!" he smiled, pulling her into his arms.

"And what of our home for these girls?"

"Our safe haven will go ahead," he stated, "although, not exactly with all of our friends and neighbors giving us their blessing!"

She bit her lip. They knew this wouldn't be easy, but just how hard would it be?

Arthur and Dottie expected things to be rough for a time but they hadn't anticipated the boys having to defend them. Dottie knew things were getting bad when the once over-talkative Lance grew quiet, often retreating to his room right after school. She prayed.

Lance and Bryan stepped off the bus to the taunting that had been following them around the playground for the past few weeks. Lance kept his head down followed closely by Bryan. They had been taught to keep the peace and they were trying. Today an especially pushy Joe Murdoch decided he was going to teach these jailhouse builders they weren't ready to deal with the likes they were planning to play house with. He shoved Lance hard, sending him sprawling into the dirt. Lance took a deep breath, fighting to keep his temper under control. He pulled himself back up to a sitting position. Joe took the opportunity to kick him hard in the back. Bryan cowered, praying he wouldn't be next but Lance lost it. He grabbed a handful of dirt and tossed it into Joe's eyes before he leapt to his feet, fists swinging. Joe wasn't prepared to meet a Hawkins face to face—everyone knew the Hawkins boys were not allowed to fight! But today, Lance didn't care what the rules were or what punishment would follow. He swung again and again until the teacher dragged him off the now bloody Joe who was weeping like a baby.

"What's going on here?" Mr. Jackson, the principal, asked.

Lance stood by the teacher's desk refusing to say a thing.

"Lance, I asked you a question!"

"What difference does it make what I say?" Lance finally roared. "They all think they can hurt us and bug us because of the place we're making for those poor people! Think they're so much better than that trash we are planning on making our friends! I'm not going to this school anymore and no one can make me!"

Lance ran from the room. Mr. Jackson shook his head. He had known the Hawkins boys were getting teased, but he had no idea things had gotten this bad. He picked up the phone.

That evening, Arthur didn't mention the call from the school but called a family meeting after supper.

"Boys," Arthur said, as the family gathered in the living room, "is something on your minds?"

"Dad, are we setting up a jail?" Bryan asked.

"No, Bryan. What would make you think that?" Arthur asked.

"I watched them putting the walls in those houses," Lance responded. "They look like prisons inside."

"Boys, remember when I told you to stay away from the creek?"

"Yeah," they said, nodding their heads.

"Well, sometimes people get too close to the running water and get swept in."

"Like that boy that drowned?" Lance questioned.

"Yeah, like that boy that drowned but not everybody gets drowned."

"What happens to them?" Lance asked.

"The current grabs them and tosses them around and then they finally reach the shore."

"Do they get hurt?"

"Sometimes."

"So what happens to them?"

"Well, if you got taken down the creek, you might not know where you are when you manage to get to shore."

"I'd just follow the creek back," Lance piped in.

"That would be smart but you know how the creek connects to the river and the river connects to bigger rivers and finally you end up in the ocean."

"The ocean? You could never get out of there," Lance exclaimed, his eyes getting wide.

"You couldn't make it home either." Bryan added.

"It would be hard, unless someone came and rescued you." Arthur said, hoping they could see the logic in his story.

"I guess they could help you get back home." Lance said slowly.

"Yeah, they could help you get back home," Arthur agreed. "These houses are for people who have sort of fallen in the creek and been dragged to the ocean. We're rescuing them."

"So why do they need prisons?" Bryan asked again.

"The houses aren't prisons. I know they look like prisons but we aren't bringing the people that we want to rescue here to be locked up. Remember when we caught that fish and we wanted to throw it back but it kept flopping around so we couldn't help it back in the water."

"Yeah, he was really slippery." Lance laughed at the memory.

"He got guck all over me!" Bryan commented with a sour look on his face.

"Well, he'd have flipped further away from the water the way he was going, but we caught him and tossed him back."

"Then he swam away," the boys chimed together.

"Well, these people we're bringing here are flipping around the shore like that fish. They don't realize that what they're doing is going to hurt them, so we have to help them back into the water. Sometimes that means locking them in their rooms for a little while and making sure they can't hurt themselves in there. They don't want to hurt us or anyone else. They're just scared and trying to figure out a way to get back to safety."

Bryan and Lance looked at Arthur in confusion.

"I know this is pretty tough to understand, but just remember you will not be in any danger." Arthur smiled. "Now how about telling me what happened at the school this morning?"

Lance hung his head.

"He was just defending himself, Dad!" Bryan announced. "Joe hit him hard and started kicking him! He had to fight back!"

"You know we don't approve of fighting," Arthur sighed, looking at Lance. The boy looked sick with it all. "But this time, I think you had to defend yourselves!"

Lance stared at his father in shock. Surely he heard wrong.

"Now, I don't want you making it a habit, but I think you had to do something to open up the eyes of the adults around here. I talked to Mr. Jackson and from now on, things should be better. Now, go have some fun and get those long faces washed away with some good old fashion dirt!"

The boys were satisfied and ran off to play. Dottie watched them go, feeling guilty that they had become entrenched in this battle.

"We are doing the right thing," she said, trying to assure herself that was the case.

"They'll grow to be better and stronger in the end!" Arthur reassured.

"I know this is a noble thing, Arthur, but do you really think our boys need these lessons? It wasn't until I saw how close these buildings are that I thought about it. What if they seduce our boys?"

"Dottie, they will not have that much to do with the boys and I don't think that Dave will send us any women looking to remain in the industry. This program is for those trying to get out."

"What about the men?"

"We aren't even certain at this point that there will be any men. Dottie, this building project is going to take two years at least before we actually see people coming here and I think that will give us the window we need to prepare the boys and the neighbors. In the end, God has this in His hands. We've prayed and felt His leading. We have to trust!"

"You're right Arthur. We have a lot of time to prepare and we just need to keep on trusting."

Dottie cleared the table, still wondering if she was sure about it all, but they had prayed and this did feel right. She couldn't let the enemy have a foothold this early on—they would never make it at this rate!

One year later, the buildings standing on the Hawkins yard were just part of the scenery. Because it was privately funded, things went at a casual pace. Arthur and Dottie worked hard to make the interiors look homey, and the boys had lost their interest in the dirt piles. There was also the matter of building fences and cultivating fields. They always had chores to keep their minds off the complaints that were slowly fading.

"Dad, why can't the girls pick all these rocks?" Lance complained as they moved slowly down the field, clearing the area of rocks and other debris.

"Because we need these fields ready for planting next spring. Don't worry, the girls will do their share of work around here," Arthur replied, smiling at his son. Lance could be so cooperative, but he could also be the loudest complainer.

"I hope so. What will they be like?"

"You've seen girls before."

"Yeah, but not city girls. All the girls around here look like boys with longer hair."

"I think that's what these girls are going to look like."

Arthur ruffled the boy's hair thinking how short a time it would be when his oldest son would understand exactly what these girls were about. He hated to think about that loss of innocence. He hated to think that some of these girls might stir other ideas in his young mind.

CHAPTER 5

Lance and Bryan waited impatiently for the bus carrying the first girls to arrive. Dottie had shooed them from the window a dozen times already and now she just gave up.

"I see it, Mom!" Lance cried.

"Here they come!" Bryan piped in.

Arthur and Dottie took a place behind their sons to gaze out the window, watching the bus make its way up to the house. They knew it carried six girls between the ages of twelve and seventeen. Dottie had gasped in horror when she heard a twelve year old was among the group. Arthur could see the mother hen mentality take hold even as he described them. These girls would be covered with love if Dottie had anything to say about it.

Dave used the bus trip as a means of getting to know the girls a little better. It was an interesting mix of ages and ideas, and to his surprise, a fairly quiet trip. The girls scarcely reacted even when he announced the destination was in sight. Now he stepped out of the bus and stretched, making sure everything was ready for the guests before inviting them off the bus to see their new home. They stepped out, each carrying a small case. Those cases held all the belongings most of these girls owned—or were allowed to bring here. No flesh-revealing clothes were allowed. The Hawkins family rushed out to greet them.

"Dottie, Arthur, sorry we're late!" Dave greeted, holding out his hand for the ritual shake. "Lance, Bryan, here to help, are you?"

They smiled shyly looking the newcomers over carefully. They were definitely all girls! No boy would wear that much makeup.

"Why don't we step into the conference room and outline the rules and get the girls settled after that," Arthur suggested.

They moved silently down to the conference room located in the same dorm where the girls would be staying. Lance and Bryan watched them go, knowing this event did not include them. They watched them disappear before turning to laugh at the made-up faces.

In the conference room, everyone found a seat. The girls all looked nervous.

"First of all, I'd like to say 'welcome.' My name is Arthur Hawkins and you may call me Mr. Hawkins and this is my wife Dottie Hawkins and you may call her Mrs. Hawkins. The lovely lady at the end of the table is Marnie Schaeffer and you will call her Miss Schaeffer. She will be your dorm mother for the next six months.

"Do you want to go over the names?" Dave asked, looking at Arthur.

"Yes, let's go around the room and you say your name and age and maybe something about yourself." Arthur agreed.

"I'm Melanie," said the smallest of the girls. "I'm twelve. My mom died from an overdose and I don't know my dad. You can call me Mel."

"I'm Deb. I'm fourteen and I want to be real successful here."

"I'm Lacy. I'm seventeen and I'm real nervous about being on a farm."

"My name is Janie. I'm fourteen."

"My name is Sue. I'm Janie's best friend. I'm fourteen, too.

"My name is Kaye. I'm fifteen. This is the first time I've ever been out of the city."

Arthur and Dottie smiled. They wouldn't remember all the names right off but before long, these girls would be like family.

Dave cleared his throat. "I've explained the rules but, just as a reminder, you all have a nine o'clock curfew. At nine, you are in the dorm. Bedtime is ten. No dating. No makeup after today unless the Hawkins' or Miss Schaeffer says it's okay. You must keep up your studies. You do what these three people tell you."

"Yes, Mr. Evans." the voices chimed.

"Well, I'll be on my way. Good luck, girls. Good luck, everyone."

And so the first six had arrived.

Within two weeks of their arrival, Mel proved to be spirited. She wasn't about to let her less-than-perfect beginning in life hold her back. She worked hard at her classes and in the fields. It didn't take long for her to be drawn to the ever thinking and talking Lance. They would challenge each other as they moved down the long rows of the garden. The two became fast friends.

"Mom, can Mel come over here ever?" Lance asked, as he grabbed an apple out of the basket on the table.

"Of course. It's no different than when you have any other friend over. She just needs permission from Miss Schaeffer."

"She looks so sad sometimes. She says that some men hurt her but Mr. Evans rescued her so she didn't get hurt like some of the other girls."

"Yes, Mel was very lucky to meet Mr. Evans when she did." Dottie agreed as she worked at the sink peeling potatoes.

"When are they going to put people in the other place we built?" Lance asked.

"Well, when Mr. Evans finds someone to go in there. I think right now we need to just get used to the girls."

Lance shrugged. He didn't see the good in building something and then not using it. He decided he would start praying for men to fill the place.

Getting used to the girls was easier than any of them imagined. Dottie took them under her wing and mothered them all. Arthur became very protective, and Lance and Bryan felt like younger brothers. This first group was very carefully chosen and Dave warned them that the next ones may have more difficult pasts and longer periods of time spent in the ugly society they came from. It was important to make this first group successful, so they had been very carefully chosen.

It was also decided that this first group would remain exclusive for six months. The girls got along well helping to minimize activity that may involve police or counselors outside the farm from having to get involved. These girls actually had a chance for a life with a foster home if they could get into a solid home first time around. Dave knew some of the future residents may go back to the very place they were rescued from, but he would not let that be the case with these!

Dave came back at the halfway point. He was amazed at the change in the girls. The once pale, shy, beaten creatures had blossomed into smiling cheerful helpers.

"I think we have a chance here!" Dave told Arthur. "These girls have done much better than we could have hoped. I wasn't expecting anything this good!"

"Yes, but as you've pointed out, these girls were very carefully selected. What happens when we fail?"

"I'm sure it will happen but I'll screen every candidate carefully. I see the boys have adjusted well."

"I think Lance is destined to carry on this work," Arthur said thoughtfully. "He has such a good way of talking and dealing with them. You'd never know he's younger than them."

"I noticed Bryan has a way, too. Different than Lance but he gets them to trusting him," Dottie added, not wanting any favoritism building.

"Arthur," Dave said, looking nervous as he spoke. "I've met someone and she'd like to come out here and meet you and Dottie."

"Is this a colleague or a love interest?" Arthur asked, smiling as he spoke. It was about time a woman caught this guy!

"A colleague that I'd like to make a love interest," Dave explained. "She's a lawyer and has a real passion for this ministry. I think if you're really serious about filling that other building with these men that sell human dignity, she's the one to get it going."

"I'm sure she understands many things that I don't," Arthur admitted. "Bring her down next time you come and we'll talk."

"I asked her to drive out this afternoon!" Dave smiled, glad he finally got one up on this man.

Lori Ross made her way down the road, hoping she had followed Dave's directions. She had just made the grade and got a good position as a prosecution lawyer. She hoped she would do some good with this new position, but it seemed to those around her that she was on the wrong end of the game. She thought just the opposite. She turned onto the driveway and smiled when she saw the facilities.

They watched the small blue car pull up. Dave smiled widely as he watched her approach the house where they sat having lemonade on the porch. He stood to meet her, pulling her close to him as he made the introductions.

"Arthur, Dottie, I want you to meet Lori Ross."

"Welcome!" Arthur smiled at her.

"The pleasure is mine!" Lori smiled back, offering him her hand.

He took the hand offered him gently. Something about the girl told Arthur they would be very good friends. It wasn't very far into the conversation that he knew this woman needed to be a part of this place.

CHAPTER 6

Lance blew out the candles on his cake. At fifteen, he was tall and handsome.

"What you wish?" Mel asked with her eyes sparkling.

After completing the program on the farm, Arthur and Dottie took her into their home, officially adopting her. She was now a part of the Hawkins family and a most annoying sister that the boys loved dearly. She was also the only one of the six original farm rehabilitation residents still here. She felt it was her honor to throw Lance the surprise birthday party after all this family had done for her.

"If I tell you, it won't come true," he teased.

"You probably wished Dad would tell me to do all the weeding by myself!"

"That's pretty close!" he laughed.

"You two stop discussing wishes and cut that cake!" Bryan urged. He also had grown and at fourteen was almost as tall as his brother. "You should have probably wished for saving from an untimely death after eating this cake Mel baked!"

Mel punched Bryan lightly on the arm, making a pouty face at such an unfair comment.

"Alright already!" Lance smirked, "I'll cut the cake if I can get the knife to go through."

Dottie and Arthur smiled at the friendly banter. They could never have dreamed this would be their life. The houses were housing twelve girls and four men. So far, the successes had outnumbered the failures and only two of the many had returned to their former life. The boys were both just as involved with the project as they were. Then there was Mel. She fit right in at school and church. People who didn't know them before assumed she was their firstborn and to them, she was.

The birthday party was a hit. The cleanup was like pulling teeth. Dottie smiled at how Lance, Bryan and Mel could put together these things but never cleanup after.

"You three can get in here and help. Dave's coming with a bus load and that means we'll have plenty to do tomorrow without this." Arthur's input assured the job would get done. Dottie was glad it came from him—it was good to let him be the bad guy sometimes.

Three groans escaped from the three teenagers. They pulled themselves up and got at the task. Why did fun always have to include this part?

Lance waited at the bus stop for the new arrivals the next morning, excited about the prospect of getting to know some newcomers. It helped to know that one of the passengers was actually a pimp. He'd met plenty of boys who sold their bodies, but this guy sold other people's bodies—this was a whole new level of the game. He strained his eyes to see into the bus windows to see if the guy stuck out like a sore thumb. He hardly even heard his dad greet them as he let his eyes take in the group.

"Welcome. As you know you're all part of a new program," Arthur explained. "You'll be going through daily sessions together here, working through the pain that you have caused each other."

Dave started them toward the conference room where they would go over the rules. Lance stared at Ricky B as he called himself. He was as easy to pick out as Lance expected. This guy was all attitude and it was going to be interesting to see if he could keep the act together over the next few months.

Lance's first chance to actually meet the man came the next evening while he was doing his work at the men's dorm. He saw Ricky B sitting at a table staring out a window.

"Want a magazine?" Lance offered.

"No," came the curt reply.

"I got some interesting ones today," Lance continued. "Last month, all I could offer was some knitting thing—I don't know why people give us gift subscriptions to that all the time . . ."

"Kid, are you hard of hearing?" Ricky demanded.

"I just thought you should reconsider," Lance shrugged. "It gets pretty long in here with nothing to do. Guys like you have a hard time adjusting to the long nights at first."

"Do they?" Ricky growled. "So if you're so concerned, why not bring me something I can really cuddle up with?"

Lance laughed. "Yeah, right. Fat chance."

Lance moved on, taking a second glance back at the man. He made up his mind that the guy was more talk than action.

CHAPTER 7

RAIN

For six months, Johnny played the game, letting Rain set the pace. This was fine for Rain but it wasn't doing much for the rest of the household. Tommy was starting to feel like Johnny was losing his touch, and Sissy was feeling like she was being dethroned. Before Rain's arrival, she had occupied the coveted place of Johnny's bedroom and now this brat held that place without even giving anything to earn it. Sissy decided she needed to have a talk with her boss.

"Johnny," Sissy smiled, "it must be getting very hard for you. You know I'm here waiting, ready to relieve all the tension that must be building." She draped herself around him.

"Sissy, stop it!" he complained. "I've got work to do."

"I bet you wouldn't say that if she came to you!"

"I think you're forgetting your place here." Johnny replied, his voice cutting like broken glass.

"I'm forgetting my place? That little wench runs you. I recall a time when you enjoyed us girls, but now—what you saving yourself for; that day when she comes to you?"

"You are that close," he said, holding up two tightly pinched fingers.

"I come here offering you my services and you threaten me?"

"Fine, Sissy, I'll get Tommy to move you downtown."

"What? Johnny, this is ridiculous. I'm your girl. I'll give you everything you want."

"I'd already decided this before you even came in here today. You think you wield too much power here. I think some time in the trenches will remind you who you are."

"No, Johnny, I know you're the boss. What you do with that tramp is your business. Don't do this!" Sissy pleaded, retreating to a corner of the room, curling into a ball like a scared worm. How come Rain wasn't heading down to the trenches?

"Tommy can move you this afternoon."

Sissy left the office completely in shock. Rain would have to pay! Somehow, someday she would pay for this!

Sissy ran to Tommy after her encounter with Johnny, giving him the whole story and shedding crocodile tears as she spoke. Tommy massaged her stiff muscles softly.

"I know, doll, that brat is going to undo this whole setup."

"What kind of spell did she cast anyway?" Sissy demanded, pushing his hands away.

"I wish I knew. I've even wondered if he's got real feelings for her. Six months and he ain't been with anyone but her and we both know nothing is happenin' there."

"Maybe she damaged him when she first came." Sissy said, remembering that first day. "I ain't ever seen anyone do Johnny that way before!"

"I don't know anymore. I just don't know!"

Johnny couldn't concentrate. Another night spent with Miss Cool had left him physically ill. He should've just taken Sissy up on the offer and relieved the tension, but that would mean she won. He knew sending her away hadn't been fair but the temptation was too much. He wasn't about to let Rain use his needs for physical pleasure against him. He could last as long as her, couldn't he?

Rain looked in the mirror, hating her reflection even though men stopped and stared wherever she went. She hated the idea of turning fifteen, knowing every day made her older and Johnny more impatient. She knew the day would come when he wouldn't put up with her protests anymore. She had to get out of this place, but how?

Tommy headed toward Johnny's office after dropping Sissy off. It wasn't a job he enjoyed doing but he knew better than to argue with the boss. He couldn't believe he did this to Sissy. No one was safe if Sissy got done like that! He was getting worried about his boss and his ability to handle the responsibilities that he had. He knocked on the office door thinking maybe a heart-to-heart was in order.

"Busy?" Tommy asked, entering the office—Johnny's sacred place.

"Yes, but I can't concentrate," Johnny replied, stretching. "What's up?"

"It's this Rain business. I'm getting worried about you. You have to take her—your reputation is starting to suffer!"

"Then that makes two of us that are worried. You know, Tommy, she has a way of making you look bad no matter what you do."

"Just grab the 'you know what' and do her. I'll do it for you if you can't."

The expression on Johnny's face let Tommy know he had maybe spoken a little too strongly. He deflated into the corner of the room.

"It's something about her," Johnny replied, after letting Tommy feel the full wrath of his gaze. "I mean, all the girls count on us to protect them and make sure they get their pay. I mean, we keep the johns in line. Most of my girls just work with the escort service and seldom even get to the hotel room. Old men that can't even get it up wanting some pretty young thing on their arm comprises two-thirds of our clientele right now. I've broken them all in personally and never cared if they cried. If they dared talk back, I smacked them. Rain has broken half the dishes in this house and I've never laid a finger to her. What's happening to me?"

"I know your Pop made you make this promise and maybe that's upsetting you?"

"Maybe. Maybe."

A month later, nothing had changed. Tommy sat in the dining room shaking his head while Johnny and Rain had it out once again. To everyone's relief, the phone rang, interrupting the war.

"Hello." Johnny said, making sure to keep an eye on Rain while he talked.

"Johnny, its Lori." He rolled his eyes at the sound of his sister's voice but she kept talking. "Dad had a heart attack. They don't think he's going to make it. You better get up here."

"What?" She had his full attention.

"Get over here and he keeps asking you to bring Rain. I hope that makes sense to you."

He hung up the phone.

"What's wrong?" Rain asked, keenly aware of the mood change.

"Rain, Pop had a heart attack. They don't think he'll make it. He's asking for you."

She was up and ready when he pulled the car up to the house. This time they took a plane, and soon she was sitting beside the man who was both her best friend and greatest betrayer. She tried to hold back the tears, but seeing Johnny Sr. looking so frail broke her heart.

"Rain," he whispered, "is he taking care of you?"

"Yeah. I'm fine, Johnny. I wish I was still here with you. I could've taken care of you!"

"I'll make him promise on my deathbed that he won't hurt you."

"Don't talk about dying—you can't die. You're the only dad I ever had and I don't want you to die." Tears flowed down her cheeks.

"We all have to go, child," he said, gently taking her hand in his.

Johnny Jr. pulled her away from the bedside. He wanted a chance to talk to his dad before he died, too.

"Johnny," Johnny Sr.'s voice was weak but still rang with authority. "You promise me you'll take care of the girl—take care of Rain."

"Pop, I have been. Believe me, I've sacrificed for that girl."

"Take care of her, Johnny. Promise me."

"I'll take care of her, Pop. I promise."

Johnny closed his eyes and fell asleep. Johnny Jr. stared at the shell of the man before him, feeling robbed. Not once had he said, "Good job, son" or "I love you"—just Rain—take care of Rain. He shook his head and let the tears flow.

Getting home after the funeral left Rain empty. The only person in the world she felt loved her was gone. She felt completely abandoned. She fell into a deep depression that took the spirit out of her. She could tell even Johnny was worried. She lay beside him needing to feel needed, loved by someone. Unknown to her, he had similar feelings with the loss of his father. He moved toward her and this time, she didn't push him away.

The next morning in the shower he wondered if he had dreamed it or had she really submitted to him? He stared at her still sleeping form and knew it had been real, but was it a one-time thing or the new standard?

Rain woke up alone but heard the shower. He would come in the room soon feeling victorious and in fact, was. How could she fight this? It had been a moment of weakness. She heard the water turn off.

"Good morning!" he said, walking from the shower draped in a towel. "How about a second running of last night's feature?"

She spit at him.

"I see. So what was that last night, cause I think you enjoyed it!" he smiled, his eyes sparkling as he spoke.

"I just felt sorry for you and let you have some comfort. That's not conquering."

"I have your virginity, and that was your flag. I captured your flag."

"If you think that's true, just try to make it happen again."

He was angry. He owned her and she knew it. He moved toward the bed and the lamp flew at him, crashing to the floor. She jumped from the bed, grabbing things from the dresser and hurling them at him. He grabbed the blanket to deflect yet another attack. He pushed in closer until he had her cornered and out of ammunition. He wrapped her in the blanket. She fell against him crying.

"Why did he die?" she sobbed.

"This isn't going to work. You're not going to use your tears and make me feel sorry for you. I am going to have you." The words of promise to Pop rang through his head. "No way, Pop," he shouted. "She has to work and this is what my girls do!"

He picked her up and carried her to the bed, kissing her hard. He waited for her to fight, wanted her to. She lay limp beside him just staring at him, her eyes glistening with tears.

"There you go with those eyes. That's the start and then you make the words echo through my head. It won't work." He pulled her toward him and once again kissed her hard.

It hurt, not at all like the night before when he had been passionate and gentle. The image of her mom flashed in her mind except her face was where her mom's should be. She couldn't just let this happen. She clawed at his face, pulling out hair by the handful. He grabbed at the hands that moved like lightening bolts.

"Yeah, fight, Rain, fight." He said, laughing at her effort.

The blanket was still wedged between them. He tore at it but she broke loose, and he felt her hand slap him hard across the face. He laughed harder.

"Think that hurt? You'll have to do better than that!"

"Get off of me!" she screamed. He laughed all the more.

Johnny didn't give up and Rain felt defeated. How could she have been so weak? She had the power until she showed some tenderness to this monster. For him, this was a victory that would get money coming in; for her, it was the loss of everything.

Tommy listened outside the door, a smile spreading across his face. 'Go boss' he cheered silently. He waited in the dining room for an hour before Johnny emerged.

"Need some coffee?" Tommy asked nonchalantly.

"Sounds good to me!"

"She fight?"

"Like a tiger."

Tommy smiled. Rain came down to the kitchen a few minutes later, made her way to the coffee and poured herself a cup. Tommy snickered at her.

"Looks like the ice princess has been melted!" he laughed.

The rage inside Rain spilled over. She walked over to Tommy and put on her sweetest smile.

"And now you think it's your turn?"

Tommy smiled. She returned the gesture and let the coffee pour on his lap. He stood up fast, screaming and clawing at his pants.

"What did your mama teach you anyway?" Johnny screamed at her. He grabbed her by the hair and pulled hard. "That won't happen again."

Tommy glared at her an hour later. He had sustained a burn where no man wants a burn and somehow, someday she would pay. Rain nursed the bruises left by Johnny's fists. She had the same thoughts for Tommy that he had for her. But Johnny was the man who owned the majority of her rage. He had promised never to hurt her and the dead would come back to haunt him.

With his victory in hand, Johnny began to lay the groundwork to get Rain to the place she belonged. He was a businessman and making sure men who wanted a pleasant evening with a beautiful girl got one was his business. He left Tommy to deal with the street working end of the business. Now Rain needed to join the ranks of one of Johnny's girls. He chose the client carefully, knowing Rain had a tendency to be unpredictable. The beating had slowed her spirit but he knew it was far from broken.

Rain stared at the reflection in the mirror, hating it. Even though it had been almost a year since Johnny's victory, this was her first time actually working for him—a fact that was not lost on all the other girls. She looked like her mom and over the last week felt the same emptiness she saw in her. He had won and something inside died.

"Rain, are you ready?" Johnny asked, knocking lightly on the door. "Tommy will take you to the meeting place."

"If he tries to touch me, I'll kill him." Rain warned.

"He's a long time client. He just likes a pretty girl to show off while he's in town."

He walked into the room. She looked beautiful and at least five years older.

"I was talking about Tommy!" She softened her demeanor. "I hate this. How old did you say this guy is?"

"He's a grand gentleman and he's about seventy."

"And you want me to just snuggle up and act like I'm loving every minute with him?"

He pulled her up to him and smiled. "Just be your sweet self. Think of him as Pop."

"What if I can't do this?"

"You'll make yourself do this or you'll be sorry."

The night was so boring. She escaped to the bathroom as often as she could. Three times she tried to run off, but Tommy's smiling face greeted her each time. She scoped the place and realized there were two more exits that led into the hotel area from the banquet room. She had an idea. Stealing into the lobby, she purchased jeans and a tee shirt. She moved quickly to the bathroom and changed. Tossing the dress out the window, she ran to the kitchen and pushed open the delivery door. Freedom at last! She ran down the street.

Tommy watched the client make his way to the car alone. He searched for her but he couldn't see her anywhere.

"Where's the girl?"

"You tell me," the man glared at him. "I paid for the full evening and she hasn't made an appearance for the past hour and even when she was there, she wasn't."

"I'm so sorry, sir. She's new and I tell you what. You can have a freebie next time you're in town. In fact, I'll take you to the hotel right now and send someone who wants nothing more than to make you happy."

The man smiled. "I guess I could accept that."

Tommy hurried the man to his hotel making sure Sissy would meet them there. The man smiled his approval but Sissy was livid.

"She did this!' she whispered, before she made her way into the hotel with the man. "I have to fix Rain's messes now?"

"Just make him happy! Rain will get hers when Johnny hears about this!" Tommy grinned as he spoke. She had messed with business this time and even Rain couldn't escape Johnny's wrath for that! He grabbed his cell after he made sure Sissy got to the room.

"Hi, Johnny, we got a problem. She bolted."

"Bolted? I thought you had your eyes open there?"

"I don't know how she slipped out. I had guards all over the place. I got Sissy settling things with the client!"

"Meet me at the hotel and we'll find her. Oh, and tell Sissy this has earned her back into the house!" Johnny slammed the phone down, cursing as he made his way out the door.

Rain had never walked in a park in her life. She was awestruck by the trees. She touched them and smelled them. He would come soon and she supposed he would find her. Where could she really run? She didn't know anyone else in the whole world. She sank down on the grass and waited for him.

Johnny found the dress and shook his head. He should have figured she had a stash of cash somewhere. So what would she be wearing? He walked around to the back of the building and saw the park. The idea that she might just have just walked across the street to this park nagged at him. She had talked about the trees during the road trip, and he was surprised by her reaction to nature. He walked to the path and saw a blob leaned up against a tree in the distance.

"You're in a lot of trouble!" he said as he approached her.

"He was a disgusting dirty old man."

"He was your client and mine. He paid for you to be his escort and now Sissy is in his hotel room doing what you refuse to do to save your butt."

He ran his hands through her hair gently. She felt bad but Sissy did these things willingly enough. She was only doing what she had told him all along she would.

He sat down beside her trying to figure out what to do next. He could beat her but sometimes the gentler touch was more effective. Johnny stared at the dreamy look in her eyes as she gazed at the pond in the park. His mind went into gear.

"Why don't we go to the mountains for a few days?" he offered.

"Why would we do that?" she asked, eyeing him suspiciously.

"Cause if we stay here and I don't beat the living crap out of you, Sissy will. I'm bringing her back to the house. I never intended to leave her out there long—just wanted to make sure she remembered who was boss around here."

"Yeah, you're the boss," Rain sighed. Sissy would probably be getting back more than just her place in the house—the bedroom was probably included in the deal. Where would that leave her?

Johnny was weary and it was nice to be at the cabin. It was even nicer to have Rain actually enjoying something for a change. Three days here and she seemed relaxed. She was totally awed by the mountains and the lakes like they were some great discovery never before seen by mankind. She was so innocent and childlike in so many ways but she was only sixteen.

As far as his business went, she was a nightmare but she entertained him. Two years and he still hadn't conquered the spirit that drove her and many times wondered if he really wanted to. But the reality was he had to!

At the house, a storm was brewing. Tommy couldn't believe that Johnny would treat this insubordinate to a mountain retreat after her behavior but Sissy wasn't surprised. Rain had cast a spell that didn't seem to be wearing off.

"I hope he's at least doing her by now." Sissy complained as they waited for Rain and Johnny to return from the mountains.

"Oh, yeah. He looks pretty satisfied these days, Sissy." Tommy said, raising his brows to measure her reaction.

"With the little prude, I doubt it!" Sissy sneered. "He's just forgotten what a real woman is like but I'll make sure he's reminded."

"You might be right but she's been in his bedroom while you were on the street. She's at the cabin and you're here."

"You know, Tommy, not one of the girls would mind if she had a little accident. You know, slipping in the pool or falling down the stairs. We could make it worth your while."

"I work for Johnny," Tommy said, glaring at the places she was heading with these kinds of thoughts. "Sissy, don't bite the hand that feeds you. Accept that she's bewitched him and I'd be glad to take Johnny's place if you think you have that much to give."

"You know, Tommy, we don't really need Johnny at all. You're holding things together here. Where's the boss?"

"Right here, Sissy!" Johnny said, pushing his way through the door.

"Johnny!" Sissy gasped. "We were just talking hypothetical! I didn't mean . . ."

Johnny hit her hard and when he quit, she lay moaning on the floor.

"Understand, Sissy, I'm the boss." He whispered. "Tommy, get her out of here."

Rain watched the whole scene. She knew that was the beating Sissy thought she deserved, and she did by the way things normally worked around here. Johnny sat at the desk like nothing out of the ordinary had taken place.

"He used to beat my mom like that!" she whispered to the air. "I would watch and he would laugh and tell me to take a close look because someday it would be me."

"Go to the other room, Rain. I have work to do." Johnny ordered.

"She was just like Sissy, letting him hit her over and over like she thought she deserved it," Rain continued, frozen to the spot where she stood. "What did she do? Not fluff up his pillows the way he liked or brought him the wrong drink because she wasn't a mind reader. And then he would push her out the door and tell her if she didn't want more of the same, she had better bring in a good haul. He never let her keep anything. She had to stay because he had everything."

"She couldn't leave because of her habit and that's what Sissy needs, too. That's how the business works, Rain," Johnny explained. "You've been spared because I have a soft spot for you and I promised Pop. Don't go thinking this is going on forever. I get tired of the same plaything day after day. Get my drift?"

She turned to him, meeting his cold stare with one of her own.

"Yes, perfectly."

She left the room walking straight and tall even though inside she hated everything about her life and wondered if this existence was better than not existing at all.

CHAPTER 8

"Happy birthday, Rain!" Johnny greeted as he made his way to the bed from the shower. "What do you think you would like?"

"Freedom," she sighed.

He looked at her, knowing that in the years since she came, the girl had turned into a woman; a very sad, unhappy woman. He wished just once he could make her smile, but her wishes were not the kind he knew how to give.

"You know that isn't what I mean. I think a promotion is in order. I mean, you're seventeen now."

"I go out with all your disgusting clients. I bring all the money to you. Why does it always have to be more?"

"Cause I own you!" he reminded her, bending over to kiss her cheek.

"You think I'm going to put out in here and out there you're crazy."

"I can find someone else to fulfill your duties here. I'm not monogamous, you know. We aren't married!"

Her eyes closed as the pain of the truth of his words penetrated her soul. No, they weren't married and no one would ever desire that commitment from her. She returned her gaze back to him, trying to find some way to even the hurt.

"You'll never be satisfied again if you send me out there!" she warned with no enthusiasm.

"Got a bit of a high opinion, don't you?" he laughed.

"Fine. I'll sell myself!" she relinquished.

He looked her over carefully. Lately there had been no spark in her eyes, no life in her voice. She was starting to scare him.

"Rain, I've known you far too long to believe you would just submit. I'll escort you tonight. He's playful but the girls say he's not into anything terribly strange."

"Whatever," she sighed.

He couldn't let himself look at her. He hated watching her die and he knew that was exactly what was happening—he was killing her. His mind replayed his Pop's words—keep her safe, keep her safe! He was failing but there was no other way to go—she had to work to earn her keep.

Johnny seldom dropped off the girls himself, but with Rain he made exceptions. He smiled at her, kissing her gently on the cheek before pushing her out of the car. He'd never admit it, but he hated the idea of another man's hands on her delicate body. "Business is business," he whispered to himself.

The client was younger than most of the ones she saw, and that made things a little less awful. Moving to the hotel went smooth and then came the moment. Rain felt herself die inside while the man enjoyed himself. She closed her eyes and pretended she was back in the mountains.

Johnny welcomed her back smiling.

"So that wasn't so bad, was it?"

She dropped her head in his lap and cried. He stroked her hair gently, knowing there was nothing that would sooth the pain.

So life became that. Rain did as she was told and each day brought her a little closer to totally losing herself. She couldn't look in the mirror anymore unless she had lots of makeup on, and even then, she hated the image she saw.

Johnny watched the transformation and smiled. He was winning her soul but that nagging little voice in the back of his mind wondered at the cost. He still didn't let Tommy touch her even though his heavy had requested many times to taste the forbidden fruit.

"Tommy, she hates you!" Johnny explained.

"That just makes it so much more fun!" Tommy replied with an evil grin on his face.

"I'm sure it does, but I'm still enjoying her."

Tommy stared in disbelief that his Boss would stick with the same girl for three years. In the back of his mind, he kept hoping something would bring about a change of heart. He would make sure that his first opportunity would be her last. Things had changed since she came and no one but Johnny liked the changes.

CHAPTER 9

Johnny drove Rain to her destination.

"This is a real generous client, Rain. Make him happy and you'll make me happy, and you might even get a small bonus."

"Whatever."

He looked at her, a crease of worry forming on his brow.

"Not feeling good tonight?" he asked, stroking her back affectionately.

"No worse than usual."

"You just do what you need to do in there tonight. Don't get smart or cocky or get that attitude going." He kissed her roughly making sure she understood the gesture.

She pulled away and made her way to the meeting place. She was dying inside and if something didn't change, she would be her mom and then there was nothing left to live for. She had thought about killing herself but she didn't want to die—but then what else was she doing but just that?

Rain was quiet during the meal. It was a business luncheon and the client did enough talking that she could be silent without seeming rude. Then he stood to leave and bid her join him. She closed her eyes as she pushed away from the table.

"So you want a night cap before we head up to the room?" he asked, grinning.

"I don't drink," she replied, her mood growing even more sullen.

"Really? That's quite a shock. Most of the girls in your profession prefer to be loosened up before we reach the room."

"I'm not most girls in my profession."

The taxi pulled to a stop and he flashed a wad of bills while he paid the driver. Her eyes stared at the cash with a hunger—not for the money exactly but what it could afford her. For one moment, the Rain of old breathed and an idea formed in her mind, but the control Johnny now exercised quickly quieted the voice in her head.

The man took her arm and led her through the hotel lobby. She was surprised to find that he stayed in an apartment instead of just a room. He led her to the overstuffed sofa.

"Rain is a very interesting name," he commented, settling on the sofa beside her.

"I've always thought it was a lack of a name. Just an object." she droned in a monotone voice. How would death feel she wondered as she tried to concentrate on his words.

"I don't know, rain can be pretty; romantic even." He slid into the seat beside her.

His breath smelled of alcohol and she hated the way his hands were beginning to roam. She couldn't do this. He moved closer.

"Are you sure a drink wouldn't help you relax?" he asked, when she pulled away. "You seem a little tense."

"Actually, I need to use the washroom. Could you direct me?"

"Of course," he said, pulling away, recognizing the tactic as a stall. He would have to ask why they had sent him a first-timer when they knew very well he liked a woman with some experience.

She hurried to the washroom and threw up. She grabbed the cell phone from her purse and dialed Johnny.

"I can't do this," she cried, as soon as she heard his voice.

Johnny rolled his eyes. He knew she wasn't acting right earlier.

"Yes, you can!" he ordered. "Just close your eyes and picture me."

"Very funny. I've already thrown up once."

"Rain, what's up with you today?"

"I want to die, Johnny."

He could hear the tone of her voice and knew this wasn't just a game. The words were the death throes of one with nothing left to fight for.

"You've done this a hundred times. Once more won't kill you." He said gently.

"I'm tired of it all. I'm getting out of here."

"Rain, you walk out of that hotel and I'll make sure you don't walk for a long time." He hung up.

She splashed water on her face while images of the brute hitting her mom circled through her mind. She took a deep breath and moved back to the couch.

"Everything all right?" the man asked, suddenly wary of her.

"Fine." she said, pasting a smile on her face.

"Good, now how about we have some fun?" he pulled closer to her as he spoke.

"Yes, some fun." Her voice was devoid of emotion as she once again seated herself beside him.

The man turned on the radio and an old time dance tune came on. He pulled Rain up to her feet and they danced together. She kept his wine glass full as they swayed together. By the third song, she noticed he was beginning to stumble. The wine bottle stood nearly empty. She waited patiently for the inevitable. He collapsed on the couch and poured the last of the liquid into his cup.

"Alright, Honey, let's do the horizontal tango." He winked at her as he drained the glass.

Rain could feel her heart pounding in her chest. She couldn't do it—not tonight, not ever again—even if Johnny killed her. Just then a lively tune struck it's melody over the small speaker of the radio as the announcer encouraged everyone to get up and jitterbug.

"Just one more dance. I love to jitterbug." She cooed, putting more expression in her words than she had for the entire evening.

She had no clue how to jitterbug but the man smiled and complied. They moved around the room where she led and now she almost had it in hand. She grabbed the bottle and brought it solidly crashing on the man's head. She grabbed the wallet, pulling out the cash. She counted out her fee and stuck the remainder into her pocket. She hurried out of the room and out the front door, moving quickly toward the car where Johnny waited for her.

"You're done already?" Johnny asked, eyeing her suspiciously.

"Here's your money." She slammed the bills into his hand. She could never get the lie by him so she avoided the question.

He slipped the bills into his pocket and shrugged.

"Are you getting in?"

"I just need some fresh air," she begged. "You know I won't run—I have nowhere to go!"

He looked at her, scared to leave her alone, but he also knew Rain was in a strange mood and it wouldn't be beyond her to make a scene.

"You are planning to get home tonight, right?"

"Where else would I go? Like I said, I have nowhere else."

"Okay," he complied. "Rain, I'm worried about you."

"You don't need to be!" she told him and then whispered to herself. "You don't care about anybody, so why should you worry about a no-good whore?"

Johnny drove away against his gut instincts. He'd give her an hour.

Rain walked through the streets, looking at the buildings, wondering what it would be like to work inside like normal people. She heard something, and peering down a back alley, spotting what looked like a person lying in the garbage. Curiosity pushed her forward until she came upon a man who had been badly beaten, lying on the ground among the garbage.

"You need help?" she asked.

He looked up, blood staining his face, his eye swollen shut.

"Yes, I need some help," he said, trying to ascertain her intentions.

Rain went back to the street and hailed a taxi. The driver took one look at her and was on his guard.

"Please, there's a young man here that needs help. He's hurt. I'll pay you well if you'll take him to the hospital."

The driver tapped his fingers on the steering wheel trying to decide if she was just looking for a way to rob him or if she was telling the truth. He swore under his breath, knowing if the girl was lying, this could cost him his life, but if she was telling the truth, he might be a hero. He jumped from the car and followed her into the back alley where there was indeed a man crumpled on the ground, moaning in pain. They carried him back to the car and set him in the back seat.

"I'll give you a hundred dollars and you take him to the hospital." Rain said, looking the man in the eye as she spoke.

"You give me a hundred dollars and I'll take him wherever you like," the driver smiled. The hospital would only be a twenty-dollar trip at best.

"I'd like you to take him to the hospital." Rain repeated as if not understanding the man's words.

The driver sped off with the money in hand. Rain watched the tail lights disappear. She could hardly comprehend that she was able to help someone else without a bed involved. Something new and strange awoke inside her—a good feeling within her being. She smiled.

Rain finally made it home two hours after Johnny left her. He was livid. Then he saw the blood on her dress.

"What did you do?"

"I helped someone. I proved that I'm human and I helped someone. I'm not just an ordinary prostitute. I could love if I was ever given the chance." Her eyes filled with tears as she spoke.

"Rain, you can love every man you're with," Johnny said, with a wave of his hand. "They love you."

"That's not love!" she said, shaking her head. "I mean something else. Nothing I've ever felt before!"

She was talking strange again! He would prove to her about love and stop this nonsense.

"You can sleep in the spare room tonight and see if that feels like love!" he growled. "I gotta get some rest anyway, thanks to you."

"Yeah, so much love you have for this ordinary prostitute."

He shook his head. Ordinary was not the right word for Rain. He lay awake late into the night. From the time she phoned to the time she came down the stairs didn't jive. He couldn't bear it any more. He burst into her room and shook her awake.

"What happened up there?"

"Up where?" she asked, still groggy with sleep.

"In the hotel. It's been going around in my mind and something isn't right here."

"You know what happened up there."

"Stop lying to me. What happened?"

"He drank too much wine and he passed out. I took my fee and left, thinking he wouldn't remember what had or hadn't happened anyway."

"You didn't do it?" he growled.

"What? Was I supposed to force myself onto an unconscious man?"

He laughed in disbelief. "You didn't do it. He paid for sex. You took the money. This man is a long-time client, and you probably just turned him away from ever coming back. And tell me how is it that this man who has been a client for three years and has never passed out does so when he's with you?"

"I didn't drink and he drained the bottle so quickly." she explained, knowing Johnny was even now holding his temper back.

"I see."

What should he do? He grabbed her and pulled her to his room and threw her hard on the bed.

"He passed out, Johnny!" she cried, realizing as she said it she sounded just like them—the girls she hated.

He wanted to believe her but it just didn't sound right. He lifted his hand to strike her.

She wouldn't just be beaten and take it quietly—she wasn't becoming them—she had felt something else. There was something left to fight for. She kicked hard into his gut, pushing him back into the dresser. He smiled, happy to see the old spirit back. She hurled her body off the bed and rolled onto the floor while he lunged forward only to find he was grasping at air. She moved to the bathroom fast, slamming the door and turning the lock.

"You can't stay in there forever!" he called to her. No response. He could wait her out. Yes, he might even enjoy waiting her out.

Tommy sat wearily at the door waiting for Rain to emerge. Johnny entered the room, having had to shower in another room since his bathroom was occupied.

"It's been three days, Johnny. How do you know she's even still alive?"

"She's alive. I've heard the water." He said loud enough for her to hear.

"So Tommy, what have you heard?"

"I told you. She hit him over the head with a bottle and robbed him."

"And how much did she take?"

"He said a thousand dollars." Tommy was weary of this game.

"Just the fee, hey!" he yelled, pounding on the door. "Where is the money, Rain?"

"I don't know!" she screamed back. "I took my fee."

"You know she took it," Tommy sneered.

"Yes, I know she took it. I want to know where she put it." Johnny's jaw was clenched together so hard his neck hurt.

"You gonna do something this time?"

"Oh, yeah. When Rain finally exits my washroom, she will be very sorry."

"So why not break down the door?" Tommy asked, like the answer to this little problem was very simple.

"Cause she's gonna come to me!" he growled, leaving the room in a huff.

Four days in the washroom and Rain knew she had to get out. He wouldn't find the money and until he did he couldn't totally convince himself she took it. She had heard him with someone else. It hurt to know she could so easily be replaced, and it brought home the truth that she was expendable and probably more of a liability than an asset. He might kill her. She listened. He was snoring. She took a towel and shattered the window. She worked quickly, letting herself out and using the towels as a rope, dropped down on the ground.

She knew he'd hear the glass and that if she went for out running him, he'd have her for sure. She secured a ceramic lawn ornament in her clutches before dropping to the shadows waiting for him to arrive. And he did. She watched him move forward slowly, calling her name, making his way up the lane. She sprang up behind him, slamming the gnome over his head. He dropped like a stone. She took off.

She could hear someone behind her, closing in fast—Tommy. She glanced back, but it wasn't Tommy—it was Johnny. Blood ran down his scalp where the ceramic figurine had caught him. He should have been out cold. It provoked her, causing her to lose her concentration. She slipped and fell. He was on her. She pulled another weapon out of her pocket—a razor that she pulled roughly across his bare chest. He let out a howl of pain and as she tried to work herself free, she could see he wasn't about to let her go. He wrestled the razor from her hand and was just about to run it across her face—on those eyes—when Tommy caught up to him.

"Not the face! Not out here!" Tommy screamed, grabbing the razor.

They pulled her up and dragged her back into the house, kicking and screaming all the way. Throwing her on a chair, Johnny looked at her, trying to decide what to do. He wiped the blood from his forehead. She had gone too far this time.

"Tommy, go get a hit," he ordered, knowing this would hurt her more than a thousand strikes with the fist.

"No, Johnny," Rain begged, her eyes growing wide with fear. She wouldn't go down this way.

Tommy smiled and hurried to the kitchen, thinking he would make sure this would be the first and last time Rain used drugs.

"Don't do this, Johnny," she begged, hoping he would move closer to her. A plan formed in her mind. "Anything but drugs."

Johnny stepped toward her. "I'm sorry, sweetheart, but you've asked for this."

She needed him closer. "Please, Johnny."

She changed her demeanor to one she had seen many times on the other girls. She moved toward him in a sensual manner. She saw the smile of conquest spread across his face—she had counted on his ego and it worked.

Tommy heard the bloodcurdling scream and came running.

"She blinded me! The 'you know what' blinded me!" Johnny screamed, clawing at his eyes.

Tommy hurried back to the kitchen and fetched a cold compress for Johnny. He returned quickly—they always had compresses in the freezer to keep the swelling down on the girls after a beating.

"Where is she? Tommy, where is she?" Johnny howled, his eyes still burning like fire. He pressed the cool relief against them but his desire at the moment was revenge.

"I don't know. I can't see her."

"Find her!" Johnny ordered. "Find her so I can kill her!"

Tommy was suddenly urgent in his search. He just had to find her and the problem of Rain would be a thing of the past. But he had to hurry—he had to hit while the fire was hot.

Tommy walked back into the house the next morning empty handed. Johnny sat at the kitchen table looking worse for wear. His eyes were still red from the substance Rain had tossed into them, and his head was swollen where she impacted him with the ceramic figurine. A white bandage could be seen out the top of his shirt—all injuries caused by Rain.

"I got the spies keeping their eyes out. We'll find her." Tommy said, shifting his eyes from Johnny's injuries.

"Find her?" Johnny sneered. "And then what? Drug her? Beat her? I should've just let her stay with the clients she could handle. Pop made me promise and she knows it!"

"You should've never let her run you." Tommy accused.

"I promised Pop I'd take care of her. Tommy, he chose her over me. My father chose some whore's child over his flesh and blood and made me promise I would take care of her."

This was news to Tommy. He knew the old man had asked for Rain but had no idea Rain had gotten any favors above Johnny. So she did have a hold over him! Now he really did need to get this woman out of the business permanently or they would all drown in her flood of grief.

The girls headed out to do their business and Tommy took everyone else out to hunt for the missing Rain. Johnny didn't know what was wrong with him. Either he was coming down with the flu or she had gotten to him deeper than he ever imagined a woman could. He felt chilled and feverish. He spent most of the day in bed. It was evening when he finally dared to head downstairs to grab something to soothe his aching head. He walked into the kitchen and there she sat beside the counter looking more dejected than he had ever seen her before.

"I have nowhere to go," she said simply. "I won't ever give you any trouble again, Johnny."

"And you think I want you?" he said.

"I guess it don't really matter. I'm dead either way."

He walked over to her, pulled her up to him and she fell against him crying. He couldn't even have her run away and disappear.

"You know I don't believe you for a second. You're just running from the beating you know you deserve."

"Whatever," she sighed, pulling away from him.

He pulled her back, holding her face tightly in his hands. He stared into her eyes and saw she was right. The life he loved was gone but he felt it was just the moment. She would regroup.

Tommy walked in later and sighed when he saw her sitting on the sofa beside the boss once again. She was worse than a cat—it seemed nothing could get rid of her. Johnny had fallen in a way no man in his position could afford to fall.

CHAPTER 10

LANCE

Lance stared at the rows of peas awaiting him that would be followed by carrots. He hated weeding carrots. He procrastinated, taking time to watch the men being moved to the gardens. He smiled at the thought of the man in the leather jacket bending over and pulling weeds.

"Lance, come over here," the men's guard requested.

He shrugged, glad to oblige if it meant not weeding.

"Can you teach this new guy? I have a feeling he doesn't know a pea from a cucumber much less a weed and I have a matter that needs settling in the dorm."

Lance nodded. Watching a novice could maybe even make a bad job fun. He hurried to Ricky's side

"What are you doing here?" Ricky greeted.

"I get the pleasure of instructing you in the art of weeding."

He could see the eyes roll.

"If you don't fill your quota, you stay out here until you do," Lance told him.

"And what would a quota be?" Ricky smirked.

"Three rows."

"Rows?"

"You see that way over there," Lance asked, pointing to a fence on the far end of the field. "That would be the end of this row."

"But that's . . ."

"A quarter mile."

"No way."

Lance didn't argue. Instead, he showed the man the difference between a pea and a weed and headed to the next row.

"That's it?" Ricky asked.

"And you have to keep up with me," Lance taunted.

An hour later, Ricky was sweating profusely, his leather jacket cast aside. Lance was enjoying every minute.

"Hey Ricky," Lance called, "how come you're way back there? I don't want to be here all night."

He could hear the growled response.

He couldn't wait for Ricky—he had homework to do. He chuckled as he passed Ricky, still hard at work.

"You'll get the hang of it," Lance encouraged.

He hurried into the house where Dottie already had the table set. He'd never get his homework done before supper.

"Where were you?" Dottie asked.

"Mark asked me to help that new guy get the hang of weeding. He's a slow learner."

Dottie nodded. "Well, hurry up and get your homework done."

He didn't waste any time. He still had his regular chores at the dorm.

Lance couldn't hide the grin as he set the fresh towels down at Ricky's door. The man was already in bed.

"Kinda early to head to bed, isn't it?"

"Get lost," Ricky replied.

"How about a nice magazine to curl up with?"

"I'm positive you have a hearing problem."

Lance shook his head. He was about to go to the next room when he noticed some papers on the night table.

"You're supposed to have those filled in already."

"I'll get to it," Ricky said, with a wave of his hand.

Lance looked at the man and it hit him. He probably couldn't read very well—it wasn't an uncommon problem around this place.

"Ricky, if you want help with those, I have a minute."

"Why would I want help from you?" His defensiveness confirmed it for Lance.

"You wouldn't be the first and I find it's easier to admit you can't do it to me than to guys like my dad."

Ricky considered this for a moment. At last, he pushed the papers toward Lance.

"I can do it," Ricky informed him. "It just takes me a while."

"Well, if you want some pointers, just ask."

Lance read the questions and Ricky gave his answers. Soon the forms were filled in.

One of the things Ricky had to put up with was daily sessions with the ladies he had put into the business. It was a time when he had to listen, nod and admit his crimes.

He wasn't allowed much of a chance to defend himself. Lance could always tell when the session had gone badly. One day, Ricky seemed especially upset.

"Hey Ricky, you look down," Lance greeted.

"I'm sick of this," he admitted.

"Of the program?" Lance asked to qualify the statement.

"The broads. They accuse and I have to just take it. They forget all I did for them. Not one of them would be here without me."

"Yeah, a regular savior, aren't you?" Lance mocked.

"I should've known you'd side with them."

"I don't side with anyone," Lance replied.

"Really? So tell me, what do they do for them to get them out of here?"

"I'm not totally sure—mostly counseling."

"Do you see me getting any counseling?"

"I don't have much to do with all that."

"Well, I'm getting nothing. You know, I had no intentions of letting any of this get to me—I was going to do my time and get back to business."

"But?"

"I'm nothing, but it's all I know. I can't read, write. Who's going to hire me? And this place is doing nothing to change that."

"So talk to Dad."

"They don't listen. It's all about the dames."

Lance had to get going but Ricky had sparked an idea. He'd talk to Bryan.

That night, Lance approached Bryan with his idea.

"You want to do what?" Bryan cried. This was the zaniest idea Lance had ever come up with.

"Ricky needs to learn how to read. If you help out with the chores, I can take some time with him."

"Dad won't like this."

"Well, Dad can't know," Lance warned. "Ricky's a little sensitive about it all. I don't think he wants this spread around."

Bryan was Lance's only hope—if he didn't agree, the plan was a bust.

"He really can't read?"

"Not very good."

"Dad will be very angry if he finds out."

"Not if we succeed. I have to show dad that I can do more than drop towels at the door. I'm tired of getting all the dirty jobs."

Bryan agreed with that. But what other jobs was he talking about?

"I want to work with them—you know, talk to them one on one," Lance replied as if he heard the question. "Get to know them. Then maybe we could get out of weeding now and then."

Bryan was hooked with the thought of getting out of weeding. He would be an accomplice.

CHAPTER 11

Teaching Ricky proved to be a little harder than Lance first thought. Suddenly, he was sneaking out to spend a few minutes here and there with the man, lying to his parents about his comings and goings. His own grades began to slip and the inevitable visit with his Dad followed.

"So?" Arthur asked. The word said it all.

"I've been letting things slip," Lance admitted.

"I can see that. What I want to know is why?"

"Too many things on my mind."

"Well, clear that mind. Lance, I know you want to be a counselor. If you want to get into that field, you have to have the grades. It's very competitive."

Lance nodded. He'd make sure to pull things up this next semester.

That's when he came up with his next brilliant plan. He'd teach Ricky his material. That way, he could keep up with his work *and* help the guy out.

Lance knew that Ricky's stay at the farm would be totally dependant on his reviews that occurred every three months. Dave and his dad would assess Ricky's progress and decide if the farm was of any benefit or if another facility would better fit his needs. The first meeting went well but for some reason, Ricky was worried about the second one.

"You're still listening to the women," Lance shrugged after hearing of Ricky's misgivings.

"But have I got any further than the last time? It all gets a little monotonous after a while," Ricky explained. "How many times does a guy need to hear what a jerk he is?"

"By what I hear on TV, all his life; if he's married, that is."

Ricky laughed.

"I don't think you need to worry," Lance encouraged.

"Your dad can see through stuff," Ricky fretted. "He'll see I'm not feeling this like I should."

Lance knew all too well what sixth sense Ricky was talking about. He didn't get much passed his dad either and he'd had plenty of time to practice. Ricky might be right to worry about this meeting but he had no time to work out a plan of action. Mark would be coming to take Ricky to the meeting and he couldn't be found here.

"I know you are supposed to be here and things will work out. I'll be praying for you," he stated as he headed towards the door.

Ricky hoped that would help.

Lance couldn't get Ricky's comments out of his mind. Why wasn't the program for the pimps more comprehensive? He decided to head to the conference room to see if the meeting had started. Maybe he could do something for Ricky and all the others who came to the farm.

"Lance, what are you doing here?" Arthur demanded when he spotted him.

Lance winced, knowing he was not allowed around the conference room on evaluation days. His dad needed to concentrate and found family interruptions upset the flow.

"I need to talk to you," Lance explained.

"About what?" Arthur demanded. "I have things to do here."

"Ricky."

Arthur's eyebrows rose in surprise.

"We talk sometimes," Lance said, the words tumbling from his mouth. "Ricky isn't getting enough personal counseling. He needs more help to keep him out of the business when he leaves here."

"Is that so?" Arthur replied.

"He needs to state his side now and then," Lance explained.

Just then Mark walked in escorting Ricky into the conference room.

"Do you feel we're not supplying you with adequate services?" Arthur asked, turning to Ricky.

Ricky glared at Lance, upset that he had brought any of this to the attention of Arthur. Now he'd have to say something and that might be taken as complaining. He didn't want to be seen as a complainer!

"I just feel like I do a lot of listening but never get to say my side of it all," Ricky shrugged. "I'm not all bad."

Arthur nodded, taking in the meaning of the words beyond what they said on the surface.

"Lance, I think you have things to do," he stated, pushing his son out of the conference room.

Lance headed towards the house feeling he'd done the right thing. Ricky would get more consideration but he might be paying for his interference. Dad would know something was up and sooner or later, he would have to fess up.

Arthur sat stern-faced behind his desk, staring at Lance's report card. Lance couldn't hide the smile.

"What you think?"

"You've done well. Looks like grade 11 wasn't a problem for you. It's good to see you putting some time into your studies."

Lance left the office where he found a glum looking Bryan.

"I take it you didn't get real good grades?" Lance sighed.

"It's doing all these chores," Bryan lamented.

Lance let the guilt wash over him. It seemed that they would have to come up with a new system.

CHAPTER 12

Lance always wanted the dorm residents to have some time at the house, but with Ricky, he had waited. At first, it was because he didn't want it to slip that he was helping the man with his reading. Then it was because his Mom wasn't comfortable with him, but as he began grade 12, it hit him that Ricky had been at the farm a long time.

"Mom, can Ricky come to the house?" he asked, deciding he couldn't beat around the bush on this one.

"Honey," Dottie sighed, "Ricky is kind of a wild card."

"Everyone else comes to the house," he reasoned. "I think if you'd actually meet him, you'd like him."

Dottie wasn't sure but then again, she didn't like to exclude anyone from the privilege of experiencing family life.

"You know he wants to adopt again," Bryan murmured.

"What makes you say that?" Dottie questioned.

Bryan quickly realized his mistake. He had to think fast.

"He wants to adopt them all," he finally replied.

"That's true," Dottie admitted but something told her there was more to this idea.

Dottie finally gave in to Lance's pleadings, and Lance hurried outside to let Ricky know.

Lance was out of breath by the time he got to the dorm. He took a second to slow down before heading inside.

"What are you doing here?" Ricky greeted him.

"I've got great news. Mom said you can come to the house."

"And why would I want to do that?"

Lance froze. That wasn't the reaction he was expecting. Most people were glad for the change of scenery.

"It's proof that you're doing good."

"I see," Ricky smiled. "So when is this big event?"

"I'm not sure. I didn't ask."

That Saturday turned out to be the day. Lance waited impatiently by the conference room door while Arthur laid out the rules. At last they emerged.

"I'll give you one last piece of advice," Arthur smiled at Ricky. "Don't let this young man get you off course."

Lance shrugged. It had been a while since he got himself into hot water. He didn't see he'd have any problems today.

Lance introduced Ricky around the room. Ricky politely greeted them one by one.

"So Ricky, how long are you planning on staying anyway?" Mel asked, ignoring Lance's warning glance.

"It's looking more and more like jail would've been shorter," Ricky replied.

Arthur rescued him, guiding him toward the dining room where a meal waited.

"Lance, could you say grace?" Arthur asked.

The boy didn't hesitate, thanking God for the food and Ricky's presence. His head came up and his eyes fell on Ricky. He could see the confusion. But the moment passed and everyone dug in.

After supper, Ricky watched everyone jump up and pitch in. He dutifully took his plate to the kitchen.

"Pretty nice here, isn't it?" Mel commented.

"A lot like where I grew up," Ricky replied.

"You grew up in a place like this and ended up as a pimp?" she cried out.

He laughed. "My mom was like Mrs. Hawkins but my dad was a tyrant. I couldn't take the beatings. Lance told me they took you in."

"Seems like I've always been here now."

"You're pretty lucky. These people are pretty special. I guess a part of me wishes I had something else that made me stand out besides being able to control women."

Dottie was listening in and felt her heart soften toward the man.

"Oh Ricky," she cried, throwing her arms around him. "You have special qualities too."

It was completely spontaneous, nothing unusual to anyone but Ricky. He felt the love seep through his body like electricity. He couldn't move even after she released him.

It was only later, when Lance was escorting him back to the dorm that he had a chance to talk about it.

"She just hugged me," he ranted. "It's no big deal, but man, it felt funny."

"My mom's hugs have a strange power," Lance admitted.

"You can say that again."

"It's like her arms are attached to God's and you feel them both when they wrap around you."

"I have to admit, I kind of never believed in God but after that hug, I'm not so sure anymore."

"You don't believe in God?" Lance cried out.

"Not really."

"Even after all the Bible studies?"

"I can't understand half the stuff in there."

Lance took a deep breath. This was as serious as it got. He had to have a talk with this man.

"Ricky, God sent his only son here to earth for you. How much more does He have to do?"

Ricky stared. This kid was not getting this.

"I don't believe there is a God."

"Really? Then explain to me why men have died for Him? If He wasn't who He said He was, why did they keep preaching after He died? I'll tell you why: because He rose again. Fishermen. Not some weak-minded, namby-pamby guys. They went out and proclaimed it."

Ricky couldn't help but agree that Lance's argument had some merit.

"And why do people use the name of Jesus in vain? Why not Mohammad? Because that name has power. It's all around you—how can you not believe?"

Ricky was silent. Lance had a way of making things so clear.

"God loves you and that hug you got tonight felt the way it did because He wants to show you just how much."

Lance turned on his heel and marched out of the dorm. He knew Ricky would have to digest what he said, but he wasn't letting this guy not face the truth.

The next time Lance went to see Ricky, he could see by his expression that he had questions. He smiled, glad school was done. He had some time.

"So if this God is real, why do bad things happen?" Ricky asked, ignoring the nicety of greeting his guest.

"God doesn't tell people how to live. He wants us to choose. If we choose Him, He shows us what to do to make the best out of life. He doesn't force anything."

"Where was He when I was a kid begging Him to show Himself?"

"He was there. How hard did you look?"

Ricky smiled. "Not very. It was much easier to build a business."

"Can't blame Him when you don't heed."

"How do I know He'll forgive me?"

"Because He says He will. His Word is good."

"Okay," Ricky replied, trying to hide the emotion building. "Will He?"

"Yes, He will. He loves you."

Ricky nodded, not trusting his voice.

"You just need to ask Him for forgiveness and accept it. You know you're a sinner."

"That I do," Ricky squeaked. "So how do I pray?"

Lance led him in a simple prayer. Ricky looked up.

"I don't feel any different."

"But you are," Lance assured him. "You are."

The next day, Lance showed up with a cupcake topped with a candle. Ricky shook his head upon seeing it.

"What's this?"

"Your birthday cake—spiritual birthday, that is," Lance announced.

Ricky laughed, accepting the cupcake.

Another party followed when he announced his new birth at his next counseling session. Ricky was a little overwhelmed with the attention.

Lance didn't let him forget it all summer and the fruits of the effort were showing; Ricky was softening.

"I hear you're facing the tribunal again," Lance greeted.

"And I hear you're back in school." Ricky smiled with satisfaction—he finally knew something about Lance that he shouldn't.

"So you think that you'll get out this time and avoid our sessions?"

Ricky raised his hands, "They've gotta see I've changed a bit."

"That you have," Lance agreed. "But I don't think you're walking out of here yet."

"You heard something?"

"Not exactly," Lance said, with a hint of conspiracy. "See, I know that no one leaves here until they've been brought out of this place and put back into civilization."

"What?" Ricky sighed with frustration.

"You ain't been civilized yet," Lance told him, doing an imitation of Huck Finn. "We gonna civilize you." [1]

Ricky laughed, shaking his head. "So how do you do this civilizing?"

"Escorted trips to town. You'll start taking some courses on household management. I'm guessing they'll give you some career counseling."

Ricky couldn't help but let his face droop. He'd never get out of this place.

"Don't worry," Lance chirped. "I know it sounds like a lot but it doesn't take that long unless, of course, you're a complete moron. You aren't, are you?"

"I listen to you, so I'm beginning to wonder."

Lance laughed, checking his watch. "I gotta get ready for school. Don't sweat it—I'll be praying."

Lance asked about the meeting as soon as he stepped in the door after school. Arthur explained all the rulings, knowing Lance and Ricky had a special relationship.

---

[1]   Huckleberry Finn by Mark Twain

"So how long before he'll be able to get off the farm?"

"It will be a little while. Ricky still struggles with his treatment of women. We'll be going very slowly."

Lance nodded.

"Now, you need to get at your homework. Let Ricky deal with his problems."

Lance nodded, heading to his bedroom. He would spend about half an hour there and then head out to hit the books with Ricky. He couldn't let Bryan's grades slip again so his only part in this would be to keep the whole thing a secret. Lance would give Ricky the books and answer questions while doing his chores.

CHAPTER 13

The year went by like the wind. Soon it was graduation time. Lance had something else on his mind. Ricky had done the work—he should graduate with him.

"Lance, you blow me away," Ricky laughed when Lance announced his intentions. "You're supposed to be looking for a girl to take to the prom—not worrying about an ex-con."

"I got a girl," Lance shrugged.

"You do?" Ricky replied. "How come I haven't heard about this?"

"She's a great girl. We plan to go to the same Bible school to study counseling."

"And you haven't mentioned this?"

"I'm not sure about, you know, girls. I really feel God calling me to a mission field that doesn't make for a great family life."

"I know you're pretty passionate, but there are other things in life."

Lance shrugged. He didn't want to talk about it. God would lead.

"Now about this grad idea," Ricky continued. "Lance, I'm twenty-seven years old. I've only learned to read over the last three years. I haven't ever written an exam. How do you think I can graduate?"

"I'll figure it out," Lance decided.

Lance hurried back to the house, praying all the way. He knew what getting Ricky to graduate with him would involve and he'd have to face the music. But this was for Ricky!

He remained silent during the meal. Dottie and Arthur glanced at each other, knowing this wasn't normal. They didn't press, knowing if Lance had something on his mind, he would share it when he was ready. Arthur moved to his office after the meal and it didn't take long for him to hear the knock at the door.

"Dad, I have to confess something to you," Lance said solemnly as he took a seat in Arthur's office.

"Confess something?" Arthur asked, worry creeping all over his face.

"I found out Ricky never finished high school and so I've been tutoring him. He's doing real well. Actually, he could hardly read at all in the beginning."

"I see," Arthur replied slowly. "When did this tutoring take place?"

"That's the confessing part. Bryan's been doing some of my chores and I've been working with Ricky."

"I see," Arthur sighed. He and Dottie had discovered this little secret some time ago but had decided they would see if the boys would come clean.

"I know I've disobeyed, Dad," Lance said quietly but then added with enthusiasm, "but Ricky has worked hard and if he could take the exams somehow, he could get his diploma, and then he could get some schooling and get a profession."

"Lance, I'm glad you helped Ricky and I'll talk to him about this tomorrow, but you disobeyed. I'll have to talk to Mom about this," Arthur's face was grave as he spoke. "Have you finished your chores?"

"No, Sir." Lance replied, knowing he would reap the rewards of his disobedience. He couldn't understand why he was punished even when what he was doing was helping someone else!

"Go do them and no sloughing them off onto your brother. I'll be needing to talk to him, too."

"Dad, can Ricky be here when you and Mom deal with this?" Lance asked before leaving the office.

"Lance, this is a family affair!"

"I know, but I just want him to see how things are dealt with around here."

"Go do your chores." Arthur shook his head and thought about Bryan's words— maybe Lance actually did want to adopt Ricky.

Ricky sat uncomfortably in the Hawkins' living room wondering why the late night summons to the house. He was spending more time here all the time, but this felt different—something was up. Bryan and Lance didn't dare look up and Arthur looked grave. Had he done something wrong? Dottie joined them, letting Mel finish up the dishes. She was more than happy to have the chore instead of being in the discipline room. Arthur locked his gaze on Ricky.

"Ricky, Lance tells me you've been working at completing high school?"

That's what this was about!

"Well," Ricky stammered. "I've been working with Lance but I'd hardly call it completing high school."

"Lance feels you should write the exams and I've arranged for you to do just that if you want."

"I don't think I'm ready."

"Mr. Baxter is going to come in and evaluate you, and if he feels you're ready, the option is yours."

"Thanks, Mr. Hawkins," Ricky nodded. "Couldn't this have waited? I mean, it seems kind of overboard to bring me into the house after dorm hours."

"No, Ricky. This isn't all we brought you in here for," Arthur replied, now turning to his sons. "Now the real business of the day and the reason you're here will begin.

I know this might seem strange, Ricky, but the boys wanted you to be here because they are in some trouble."

Ricky glanced over at Lance who looked at him, shrugging slightly. Ricky didn't know what to make of it all. Arthur let his gaze fall on his boys for several moments before continuing.

"Do you two have anything to say before we tell you what we've decided?" Arthur finally asked.

"I'm really sorry, Dad," Lance nodded.

"Yeah, I'm really sorry, too," Bryan echoed.

Dottie's heart went out to the boys, but she admired their honesty—at least they disclosed their lie.

"You two disobeyed willingly and, as you know, that cannot be dealt with in this house with a blind eye. So Mom and I have decided that you two will clear those thirty acres south of the house before you go to work with Dave."

"The whole thirty acres?" Lance squeaked. Bryan went pale.

"The whole thirty acres!" Arthur repeated emphatically. "Lance, I want you to know that if you had come to us and asked if you could do this, in all likelihood we would have said yes. Now you did this the dishonest way and have reaped a reward that I'm sure you agree will tarnish this good deed for all involved."

"Yes Sir," Lance replied, not really believing the part about them saying yes to this whole thing two years ago.

Arthur and Dottie nodded and left the room.

Bryan let his wrath rain as soon as his parents left. Lance had done him in again.

"Just like the creek!" Bryan whined. "I get involved with one of your schemes and get myself into more trouble than I need."

"It's only thirty acres!" Lance shrugged. "How bad can it be?"

"Thirty acres of rock bed. Have you forgotten the first fields and how bad it was?"

Ricky watched them curiously. Arthur and Dottie came back in the room and the boys fell silent. Lance rose slowly and threw his arms around his Mom.

"I'm sorry, Mom," he said softly.

She hugged him and whispered in his ear softly. Ricky knew exactly what she was saying. Then Bryan repeated the process. Ricky was moved and thought it was a beautiful family ritual, but it wasn't over. Lance then moved to his dad and threw his arms around him.

"I'm sorry, Dad," he cried and then pulled back.

"Lance, you're heading out on your own in a few months and I hope you see that I'm just trying to make you into a good man. I love you, son."

"I love you, too, Dad. I should have asked."

Then it was Bryan's turn. He hugged his dad and made his apologies.

"Bryan," Arthur said, looking at the boy intensely, "you followed like a puppy instead of taking a stand. You, too, are almost a man and you need to follow your heart. You can't let someone else pull you into things you know you shouldn't do!"

"I did follow my heart!" Bryan muttered, knowing the earlier tongue lashing he gave Lance would have to be recanted. Lance would make sure of that! "It may have been Lance's idea but I did it because I thought it was a good one."

"Don't let him get you into these messes. You have to be strong in your own skin! I love you, son."

"I love you, Dad."

Ricky watched with tears in his eyes. The boys left the room and Dottie hurried back to the kitchen.

"Arthur, it seems a might unfair that they tried to do something nice and get such a harsh punishment." Ricky responded.

"If a man," Arthur said, looking Ricky in the eye, "knew his neighbor was starving and had plenty of food to give but went and robbed the store for his neighbor, his intentions would be good but the method would be wrong. Lance has a good heart and he truly wants to help. I just want him to understand that the method has to be the right one."

"I guess that makes sense, but I feel bad for getting them in trouble. Would you mind if I helped with that thirty acres?"

"Not a bit!" Arthur smiled. He then turned sober "Ricky, Lance has this notion of you graduating with him."

"So he's told me. He's a pit bull when he gets his mind on something."

"You can graduate without the ceremony but it might help town people see this place a little more positively if you stood to receive the diploma."

"I'll think about it," Ricky sighed, not letting on that he had already thought about this a lot and he didn't want to think about it anymore. But he knew it would be there, nagging him all the time.

Arthur had the boys up bright and early the next morning starting work on the thirty acres. Lance couldn't believe he was making them get up at six to get a couple of hours in before school in addition to a couple of hours after school. Weekends would be totally enveloped by this task. Ricky stood right beside them, accepting his part in this whole situation gracefully.

Lance and Ricky were working on moving a big boulder while Bryan filled a wheelbarrow with smaller ones that had already been loosened. They used the time to quiz each other for the upcoming exams that Ricky had finally agreed to take while Bryan whined.

"I can't believe Dad is making us do this by hand!" he complained.

"He must really want this lesson engraved into our memories." Lance quipped, actually taking a moment to listen to his brother's laments.

"I can't believe I said I'd help you two." Ricky said, grunting with the weight of the boulder.

"I'm sure glad you did!" Lance groaned, wiping the sweat from his brow while balancing the boulder against his back. "We should be finished before grad now—that is, university grad."

"University," Ricky scoffed. "What if I don't measure up—what if you not only did all this behind your parent's backs, but failed to teach this lug nut anything?"

"You'll do great!" Lance smiled. Ricky wasn't so optimistic.

Mel, Lance and Ricky stood on the steps waiting for Dottie to snap a picture of them dressed to the nines. Mel was a year older than Lance but they were in the same grade so they got to share this moment along with Ricky who passed all his exams.

They headed to the ceremony where Lance and Mel had dates waiting for them. They tried to convince Ricky he needed an escort but he declined.

All too soon, the formalities began. Ricky heard his name called by the Master of Ceremonies and made his way to the stage. He really thought this speech thing was a bad idea and as he moved to the stage, he felt these thoughts were quickly becoming facts. The audience didn't look any happier about this than he felt.

"Good evening, ladies and gentlemen, fellow graduates, esteemed teachers." He tried to locate Lance, knowing he would be down there cheering him on. He wasn't disappointed. "I came here almost three years ago, very messed up and unable to cope with life within the rules society deemed acceptable. Today I stand here with my high school diploma—a first step to becoming part of the society that once eluded me. I would not be here if it weren't for the love and caring the Hawkins family and staff at the farm have given me. I'm not proud of what I was, but it will be a reminder of how far I have come and that I have the strength to overcome and keep moving forward. I have to say a special thanks to Lance and Arthur for hanging in there with me and for Dottie and her special hugs. To Bryan and Mel, for sacrificing and just sharing. To Mr. Baxter for getting me ready for this moment. Most of all, I want to thank the Lord for healing and blessing me so much. When I was not loveable, He sent someone to love me and that has made all the difference. Thank you,"

The crowd erupted into applause and Lance stood to give him a hug as he made his way back to his seat. Ricky smiled.

Sitting in her seat watching in awe sat Dottie. The full measure of the accomplishment of her son was just beginning to set in—her boy was gifted! How had Lance reached this man so completely? It had to be a special blessing from God, a gift that would be an asset to the farm in so many ways.

CHAPTER 14

RAIN

Six months passed and Rain did not regroup. She cooperated, never protesting anything. Everyone else thought the change was good but Johnny knew better. She was dead. She didn't fight anymore or even protest things that she should fight and protest. Her eyes were silent orbs that peered out from their long lashes that drooped in a manner that gave her a sad dog appearance. He put her back with the clients that just needed an escort for functions where showing up alone was awkward. If she was as unenthusiastic in the client's bedroom as she was in his, he didn't want to put them through it.

Tommy had approached the Boss on many occasions, knowing the girl hurt business. He was sick of hearing about promises to dead men. She wasn't just pulling herself down but Johnny was starting to lack flare. The phone rang and Tommy talked for a few minutes before hanging up.

"Johnny, we got a snag this weekend."

"What's the problem?" Johnny asked, not looking up from the spreadsheet he was studying.

"The client we set Rain up with has decided he would like more than the usual."

"So get another girl," Johnny replied, suddenly finding the conversation more interesting than the numbers.

"They're all booked up. You know, there's that big convention in town."

"I'll talk to her," Johnny sighed.

"Talk to her?" Tommy spit out. "How about tell her?"

"Back off, Tommy."

"I'm tired of backing off. She's killing us and I think we need to get her onboard or get rid of her altogether."

"I'll talk to her!"

The finality in Johnny's voice let Tommy know he had said enough. Tommy stormed from the room, shaking his head. He had to get rid of this problem.

Johnny looked at the girl and wondered if Tommy was right. She was becoming more of a liability all the time. She was beautiful but so unpredictable.

"You realize you're going out tonight?" he asked, staring at her still sitting in a housecoat.

"I'm not feeling very good," she said, not even taking the time to look at him as she spoke.

"That's nice, but you have a client."

"I know. I just took some medicine and I should be fine in a second."

"Are you using?" he asked, unable to believe that could be the case. He grabbed her face to take a good look into her eyes. He hated looking in those eyes that once vexed him and now broke his heart.

"No," she protested, pulling away from him. "I just really don't feel good."

"I came to tell you your client phoned and upgraded his package."

"Great!" she sighed. Her whole body slumped in defeat. "I'm just not up for this!"

"He asked for you specifically and you're going. I'll be waiting for you downstairs."

Getting dressed was a slow painful process. Rain chose her outfit carefully making sure it was the most modest thing in her closet. She did her hair without the aid of a mirror as well as her make-up. She just couldn't look at herself anymore. She moved to the car slowly. Johnny smiled approvingly as she slipped beside him.

"You put that together pretty quick. I would never have imagined that the little kid I met at Pop's would be this beautiful woman beside me."

"Stop, Johnny. I'm not beautiful. I'm nothing—just rain—an object. Not even worth a name."

She was scaring him. Every time she spoke as of late, the words always seemed to be saying she was garbage and everyone knows what you do with garbage. Pop made him promise to protect her and he was starting to wonder what Pop knew that he didn't.

The man was younger than any client she had ever had before. He was good looking and she tried to make her mind believe that he could be pleasurable. The evening went smooth enough and then they headed to the hotel. They entered the room and the man pulled back his jacket revealing a gun. She froze with fear.

"Something wrong?" he asked smiling.

"You have a gun?"

She knew ignoring it would have been better, but something fascinated her about the close proximity of the object in question. She longed to touch it.

"Yes, I use it in my profession." he said, quickly hiding the weapon from view.

"Tommy hired you to kill me?" she asked.

"No, Lori hired me to find you." he told her.

"I don't know anyone named Lori." she replied, completely perplexed by this man.

"Well, she knows you and she hired me to find you. I'm a PI. I don't really want the bedroom favor. I just thought it would buy us a bit more time."

"Time for what?" she asked, her heart pounding hard with fear.

"Lori is Johnny's sister and she's been looking for you. Your mother passed away some time ago. She left you some things, and Lori said she'd get them to you. It has been one big job finding you."

"She knew I was with Johnny." Rain eyed him carefully. His story wasn't adding up.

"Yes, but she didn't know where Johnny was. I've tried every escort service in town looking for one with a girl named Rain."

"What does Lori have to do with my mom?"

"Well, uh, I was under the impression that you were aware of your mom's occupation."

"She was the same as me," Rain said, looking down as the shame washed over her.

"Yes, with the father instead of the son."

The announcement hit her like a brick. Johnny Sr. owned her mom. Somehow she'd blocked that truth from her mind. She'd let herself believe that he was just one of her regular johns. It was all there, but she didn't want to see it.

"That can't be right." she stuttered.

"I'm sorry, miss, but it is right and that's why Lori really wants to meet with you. Is there any way to arrange a meeting?"

"Why doesn't she just come to her brother's house?"

"She's a lawyer. It didn't seem like a good idea to show up there and tell him she had to talk to you."

"Oh!" Rain knew Johnny wouldn't appreciate any of this. "Tell Lori that it's too late and I'm no longer around for her to make good on her promise to my mom. Just tell her I'm dead!"

"I can get you out of here," the man said quietly.

For a moment, a longing passed through her eyes but then they returned to their lifeless state. He wished he could light the fire that he saw spark.

"Maybe my body but for my soul, it's too late and, to be very honest, it's too late for my body, too."

"Rain, don't let him take these things from you. You're a beautiful girl and I think if you got out of here, you'd see life has a lot of promise."

He stood to fetch her some of the documents Lori had asked him to leave with her. She reacted quickly. Rain smiled as he fell to the floor. He wasn't dead but he would have one great big headache when he woke up. She grabbed the gun and cradled it softly. It was much too late to escape any other way and, knowing for once in her life that she held the power, Rain smiled.

Johnny listened to her story.

"I'm telling you it was a cop."

"How can you be sure?"

"I saw his ID and his gun. I smashed a vase on his head and ran."

"Are you sure it was real?"

"Yes. It was very real."

Johnny didn't know what to do. A cop and Rain assaulted him. This didn't look good. He might have to talk to Tommy and admit he was right—Rain was becoming poison to him and his whole organization.

CHAPTER 15

Over the next few days, Tommy and Johnny met several times, trying to come up with a solution to the Rain dilemma. Johnny couldn't face the truth even though he knew very well what the best solution was. Tommy felt it was time to take matters into his own hands.

Today the argument had been heated. Johnny couldn't kill her! He had promised Pop. Tommy felt it was time to override the boss.

A few rooms away, Rain shook even with the warm water from the shower raining down on her. She was just a bad omen. She knew Johnny wouldn't understand, but she had to free him of her curse. He couldn't live with killing her so she would have to do it herself. She had a plan.

Johnny kissed her softly as he let her out of the car to go do some shopping. He never could figure out how many outfits were enough for a woman. Today's request for a ride to the shopping mall had come out of nowhere, but thinking maybe she was starting to pull out of her funky mood, he had agreed.

"I'll pick you up around five," he said, leaning over to check her over one last time. She seemed okay.

"I'll be here," she said, careful not to smile as she spoke. He would be suspicious if she did.

He looked at her eyes and he saw the clouds. He pulled away. She had been so sure the last john was a cop and Johnny had decided he had to confirm that. If it was a cop, they would be watching her, so he decided to get Tommy to follow her. He picked up his phone to get his man on the job.

"Tommy, I just dropped her off at her usual place. Keep me posted on her activities."

"Sure thing, Boss." Tommy smiled. He dropped the phone with a smug look. Oh yeah, he'd keep him posted; right until she fell head first off a bridge.

Rain hurried to the spot and grabbed the money that she had stashed there so many months earlier. She smiled with glee that it was still there. She felt under her jacket and felt the bulk there. She roamed through the stores feeling a presence that disturbed her—someone was watching her. She snuck into a store she wouldn't normally visit and watched—Tommy. Her heart raced. She hurried to another store and purchased some clothes of a style he would never recognize her in. Her first thought had been to just kill herself, but then she decided she was going out with style. Rain Patterson was going to have one big bash before leaving this miserable world, and she couldn't let Tommy interfere. She had to come up with a plan.

It was five and Johnny could see no sign of Rain or Tommy. He tapped impatiently on the steering wheel, trying to decide what to do when the phone rang.

"What do you mean, you lost her?" he yelled into the receiver.

"She just vanished!" Tommy repeated.

"Where are you?" Johnny demanded.

Johnny hit the steering wheel with his fist in frustration. Did the cop get her? She could destroy his whole empire.

He hurried down the street hoping to spot her. Two hours later, he had searched the entire area and was now expanding the search. He drove his car slowly down the street and spotted someone that looked like her, but the clothes. He looked closer; it was her! She made her way into a busy pizza shop. Minutes later he saw Tommy definitely following her. He didn't want to believe it but he knew what he was seeing. He picked up his cell.

"Hey Tommy, I've searched this whole shopping area and I can't find her. You had any luck."

"Sorry, Boss. Haven't seen her."

The pain of the betrayal was acute. Johnny debated whether to shoot the man where he stood, and then another thought hit him. Maybe Rain and Tommy were working together? He couldn't believe that. He had heard the rumblings behind closed doors about Rain and he saw this for what it was—a ploy to rid the organization of a problem in a way he didn't approve of.

Johnny couldn't just let Tommy take out the girl he had promised his Pop to protect. He didn't have time to plan, so he stormed ahead into the restaurant where he realized that his leather jacket stood out like a sore thumb in the sea of denim. He didn't have time to consider that right now as he headed to the back of the busy establishment where he spotted her. She was looking down into her coffee cup, her brow furrowed in thought, as he approached her. It was only now that he thought about her reasons for being here—this wasn't a place he could see her visiting on a regular basis or ever before. He moved toward her slowly, careful not to disturb her train of thought before he was right beside her.

"Rain, don't run," he said softly. "I need to talk to you."

Her head shot up in surprise. How did he find her?

"What are you doing here, Johnny?" she asked, trembling as she spoke.

"What am I doing here?" he asked, taking the seat across from her. "I think maybe that should be my question."

"I can't hear you." she said, pointing at her ears.

His mind went back to Tommy. Maybe talking here wasn't a wise idea anyway. He looked around debating how to get out of this place without alerting the man he knew was seeking the head place in the business. He could make this all look like an accident, especially with Rain involved. He finally pulled Rain into the kitchen where he knew there would be a delivery door. He cautiously stepped out into the back alley, still pulling Rain behind him.

"Rain, I have to talk to you!" he repeated but a movement in the corner of his eye caught his attention. He reached for his gun!

It all made sense in a moment—this place was secluded and she had earned this end, but she wasn't going this way! When she saw Johnny reach for his gun, she made a split-second decision to get the first shot. Her free hand grasped the gun hidden under her jacket and, before she could consider the ramifications of what she was doing, she pulled the trigger. Tommy stared from his vantage point, his gun aimed on her, as Johnny crumpled. Rain ran. Tommy shook the initial shock off and re-aimed, pulling the trigger. She felt a sharp sting in her shoulder but she wasn't stopping. Tommy ran down the back alley passed Johnny who was struggling to get up. Flying around the corner, she collided head-on with a customer just leaving the restaurant. The force twirled her around at the precise moment Tommy squeezed the trigger.

Johnny stared in horror as he watched Tommy aim the gun. He lifted his own weapon, squeezing the trigger with the last bit of energy he could muster.

CHAPTER 16

LANCE

Lance, Ricky and Bryan got the rocks moved. Lance headed to the university and Ricky headed out to find his new life. Before they knew it, three years had passed. The farm was no longer a big part of Lance's life as he did his best to become a social worker who would really make a difference. Summers were spent working with Dave on the front lines—a place Lance loved being.

Lance was headed home for the weekend; the first time in almost three months and he was looking forward to the break. He was just heading to the door when the doorbell rang. 'Great, this will probably wreck my plans,' he thought as he swung open the door. He couldn't believe who greeted him on the other side.

"Ricky, what are you doing here?" he cried, wrapping his arms around the man.

"Can't an old high school buddy drop by?" Ricky smiled, pulling out of the bear-like grip.

"Very funny—but it has been three years."

"Yeah, I know, but I've been busy."

"Yeah, I know how that goes. I have a phone, too. So what are you doing here?" Lance asked, pushing Ricky toward the kitchen with a wave of his hand.

"Looking for a best man."

"You're getting married?" Lance asked, the joy showing in his face.

"I am. I'm also looking for work, but that will happen, too."

"The job should come before the wedding."

"My fiancé has a very good job and I'm fresh out of school. I'm a bona fide counselor now but I haven't got a job yet."

"Well, I'm just on my way out to the farm. Maybe we could get together when I get back? My Mom will kill me if I don't show!"

Ricky laughed. He knew very well Dottie would do no such thing but she might find a nice big potato field that needed hoeing!

"How long you planning on staying?" Ricky asked.

"I have to be back at work Monday." Lance sighed. "Don't get me wrong, I love my job, but I really need a break so I thought going to the farm would be nice for a change."

"What are you doing these days?"

"Working with Dave. It's pretty interesting."

"I bet. I don't think I want to be that close to the old life."

"Don't blame you. I'd guess you'd still know some of these people."

"I might, even though I hope not." Ricky laughed and then went back to the subject of the farm. "Could I drive up with you or would that be asking too much—or maybe you already have a driving companion?"

"That would be great and no, this guy is single and loving it," Lance replied, getting the full jest of the question. "Bryan's the guy with the girls."

Ricky shook his head. Single and loving it he couldn't quite fathom, but a ride up to the farm with his old friend would be a treat.

Two hours later, they could see the familiar buildings come into view. Ricky rolled down his window, taking in a deep breath. He could smell home. Lance laughed, thinking he hadn't laughed this much in a very long time.

"It hasn't changed," Ricky smiled.

"It has and it hasn't. Dad's had some problems with some of the residents. Tougher cases are not responding like the early easy ones—guys like you with weak minds."

"Ha, ha!"

"Just joking!" Lance smiled but then grew serious. "He's been working like crazy because the men's dorm guy quit and he's been filling in. Dave's spent a few days out here helping out, too. The worst part is the guy that quit spread a whole bunch of lies about the farm, telling people there had been many escapes and knife fights and whatever he could think of to say to justify his being unable to cope with the position."

"So is that what's brought you out here?"

"No. I miss Mom's cooking but I imagine I'll help out. Truthfully, I'm a little burned out right now but you know the problems don't go away just because you're tired."

They pulled into the yard where Lance brought the car to a stop in front of the house. For Ricky, this was a strange place—he had spent all his time here living in the dorms and they dropped dorm residents off at a different spot—he liked this better. Dottie ran to greet her son and when she saw Ricky, had a hug for him, too. Everyone was excited to see him and he felt like he had come home. Arthur was noticeably absent from the greetings, letting both men know things were definitely bad.

Arthur let the lines of worry creep onto his face. There had been some problems in town with some of the program graduates. Dave stepped in quickly and had the culprits placed in a different facility, but the townspeople were upset. In the ten years that the farm had been in operation, this was the first time the townspeople felt they were risking the safety of those around them. They argued that the teens coming here now where of a different breed than the earlier ones. In some respects, they were right. The early participants in the program were all very short-term residents of the red light district, but the newcomers were lifers. Arthur would have been able to quiet these complaints until the unthinkable happened. The man in charge of the men's dorm decided to quit—something perfectly within his rights, but in the process, he spread many lies about the operations of the farm. He had come highly recommended but it was obvious he had been a wrong choice early on, complaining about everything! But now the dilemma faced Arthur; who would they get to replace him?

"Arthur, could I talk to you," Ricky asked, after knocking lightly on the open office door.

"Ricky!" Arthur cried, standing to greet the man. "I thought I heard that you were visiting! Come on in, have a seat. I always have time to talk to an old friend."

"I think former resident is a more accurate description but I like this friend stuff!" Ricky replied. He then looked at Arthur. He could feel the sweat on his palms and his mouth was suddenly dry. "I've heard about you needing a new man for the guy's dorm and I'd like to apply."

"Are you serious?" Arthur asked, suddenly looking at the man a little more closely. This man would be perfect for the position.

"Very. I know I don't have any experience in my field but I have the papers that say I can do the job. You know I understand the guys you deal with because I was one. I guess I'm seeing that as both my best asset and biggest detriment."

"Truthfully, I haven't had very many applications come in and there isn't one that I wouldn't consider at this point. In fact, Ricky if you're truly serious, I'll give you a fair shake!" Arthur shuffled some papers nervously. He knew he had to mention the part of the job that made most applicants flee. "You know this isn't a great paying job?"

"I'm aware of what goes on here and how tight the budget is. I lived here for almost four years, Arthur, and I was a businessman before I came. I couldn't start until after the wedding but if that's okay, I'd really like a chance to give back to the place that has given me so much!"

"Ricky, you don't need to sell yourself to me! I'd give you the next shift if you could take it. This is an answer to prayer!" Arthur said, not ashamed of the tears forming in his eyes. "I was beginning to think we'd have to shut down the men's dorm. You have no idea how much I needed you to be here today!"

"God knew!" Ricky smiled.

Arthur pulled Ricky from the office to the main house where Lance, Dottie and Marnie, the women's dorm mom, were visiting.

"I'm sorry to interrupt, but I have an announcement!" Arthur boomed, his face shining with joy.

They all turned to listen.

"This guy here is our new men's dorm manager!"

They all cheered. Ricky lifted his brows in doubt. He hoped he did this job half as well as they all seemed to think he could. Even with his practical knowledge and education, he was feeling a bit overwhelmed with the whole thing! Lance moved to shake his hand.

"I knew God had a reason for me running into you!" he cried, not letting the handshake be good enough. He pulled Ricky into another bear hug.

"You know!" Ricky grunted at Lance who was still wrapped around him. "You have got to take lessons on hugging from your Mom! You're crushing my bones!"

Lance released him, grinning from ear to ear. Ricky gave him a friendly cuff on the shoulder. He used to be bigger than this guy—skinny kid was how he thought of Lance, but that had changed.

Lance wandered around the farm Sunday afternoon remembering all the good times this place had held for him. Arthur saw him and headed out to join him, finding him deep in thought.

"I hope it's a good memory!" Arthur said, clasping his arm around his son's shoulders.

"Very!" Lance smiled. "Dad, it's harder than I ever dreamed it would be! I mean, I love my job but some days, you can't win."

"I know how you feel! We did our best to shelter you and Bryan from some of the harder things around here! Maybe we shouldn't have!"

"I'm glad you did. But this place is heaven compared to where I work! It's unbelievable what people will do to each other!"

Arthur nodded but let his son continue.

"I laugh out loud when I hear people talking about the cruelty they see in hunting and farming. They spend millions of dollars on campaigns for animals and right in their backyard, people are doing things a farmer or a hunter would never dream of doing to an animal; and the victims are people. Usually young people—children being made into victims of unspeakable crimes. We just close our eyes and go on living."

"Lance, I know you love every one of them but son, you can only do so much. You have a gift that the enemy would very much like to take away. Don't let him!"

Lance looked up at his dad understanding what he was saying. His heart broke with each one that walked away, and usually they did. They'd come for a session with him and then walk out the door right back to the place they had just run from.

"Pray for me, Dad!" Lance whispered.

Arthur did just that.

CHAPTER 17

A week later, Ricky drove back down the familiar road. This time he had a very special someone sitting beside him. He never dreamed any woman would even consider him as a mate, but this angel beside him saw some good where he still struggled to find any. She glanced out the window as he pointed out the farm in the distance.

"So that's the place that made the difference in the man I love?" Sarah smiled.

"And it's the place I hope to do the same in other lives," Ricky responded.

Moments later, they pulled up to the house where Arthur and Dottie greeted them. Sarah smiled as she received her first famous Dottie hug. Ricky had been right about that! The woman would be a millionaire if she could figure out how to bottle that. They moved into the house to a feast and chatter. By evening, Sarah felt like one of the gang, wrapped firmly in the Hawkins blanket of love. They, in turn, very much approved of this wonderful young woman Ricky had chosen to make his mate.

As much as they all wanted this to be a pleasant evening, Arthur and Ricky did have some business to discuss. Ricky looked over at Sarah, knowing the poor woman had only just met these people and here he was abandoning her with them.

"Are you sure it's okay to just leave you?" Ricky asked, looking worried.

"Ricky, I love these people already. They're your family and will be mine too, very soon!" she said and then pointed to the door where Arthur waited. "Go."

He smiled at her before he made his way out of the room. She was a treasure.

"He's so kind!" she said to Dottie as the men left.

"Yes, Ricky is one of our greatest successes. I know we never officially made him one of our own but he is!" Dottie smiled. "Lance was right—they all become our children!"

Sarah looked at the woman and saw so much love and understanding. She took a deep breath as she gazed around this home. Her heart longed for a home just like this after she and Ricky were married. Married—Ricky. Sarah's thoughts once again drifted to the fears she had been trying to push down for several weeks now, but the closer they got to the day, the more afraid she became. Dottie saw the cloud come over the girl's face.

"Is something wrong?" she asked gently.

Sarah looked over at the woman. There were some things she needed to discuss with someone, and maybe this woman would be the right one. Sarah knew beyond a doubt she couldn't talk about this with her own mom and the pastor didn't seem like the right person either.

"Dottie, I know I haven't known you very long but I need to talk to someone," Sarah said slowly, as if testing the waters to see if she could really open up to this almost stranger.

"Of course, Dear. What is it?"

"Ricky and I will be married in two weeks," Sarah stammered, "and I'm having doubts about the wedding night."

"Doubts?" Dottie asked, not quite sure what the girl meant.

"I'm a virgin and Ricky, well, isn't." Sarah blushed.

"Oh Sarah, you're not the first one to ask me about this. In fact, my soon to be son-in law had the same question!" Dottie replied, leaning in as if conspiring. "I've never known exactly what to say, so I asked my daughter how she felt about this. Know what she said?"

"No," Sarah said, feeling lighter already. This woman was the perfect person to ask about this!

"She said 'but Mom, I've never made love to anyone in my life.' Of course, I looked at her and told her I knew she had been with a man. She told me she had been with men but never made love to one. Sex yes, love no. I'd hazard to guess it would be very much the same with Ricky."

"I hope so, but it's still scary because he'll know what to do and I won't."

"This is something like so many things in marriage that must be learned. He may have some approaches that he's used and may use them with you but truly, it's something the two of you will have to discover with each other. Now, I know some of Ricky's history and I pray he's much more passionate with you! It may be that you are the better lover of the two of you—who knows?" Dottie said, gently patting Sarah's shoulder. "Now, when are you free so we can give you a bridal shower?"

Sarah smiled. The words had hit home—she didn't need to worry about these things. She pulled her date book out of her purse to see when she could have the honor of letting this woman arrange a bridal shower for her.

The wedding was beautiful. Arthur and Dottie both wiped away tears. Mel and Paul stared dreamy-eyed, thinking about their own upcoming nuptials. Bryan thought about Lance having to wear the monkey-suit all day, and Lance just enjoyed watching his friend look so happy.

"So you next?" Dave teased Lance, finding him finally relaxing at the reception.

"Married to my work, Dave!" Lance reminded him. "Bryan will be walking the aisle long before me."

"Work is okay but it will never love you back like a wife."

Lance laughed. "What do you think it will be like for them sleeping together for the first time?"

"And you're not thinking about getting married?" Dave laughed now. "I don't think men who don't want to ever get married let that be so high on their mind!"

"I mean, will he compare her to the others?" Lance said in his defense.

"No, because he'll never have experienced anything like it before in his life!"

That was probably true, Lance decided. And he would never experience the bliss. His job took up every minute of every day and he doubted any wife would put up with that. They all cheered as the couple drove off an hour later, each with their own thoughts about the night ahead.

CHAPTER 18

It was good to be back at work. At least, Lance thought so! He had taken a few days off for the wedding, giving him the breath of fresh air he needed to get back to the old grind. He really enjoyed the work and his co-workers. As long as he could remember, he had dreamed of working with Dave and now he did. Dave's wife, Lori, would come in and help out once in a while, too—another pleasant face to have around, although she and Lance seemed to be cut of the same cloth and both knew how to scheme and get into trouble. Actually, everyone at the center was wonderful, even the clients, most of the time anyway. He tore into his files with a new vigor until he was interrupted.

Lori stood at the door of Lance's office looking at him with that look that he knew would soften hearts made of stone. She only used it when she really wanted something, and usually she reserved it for Dave.

"Lori, that look should be for Dave and Dave alone!" he reminded her as she approached his desk. He knew she was up to something, but what? His curiosity was getting the best of him as usual.

"Lance, I really need a favor and I don't want Dave involved."

"This sounds bad on every level!" Lance smiled. "What is it?"

"I've kept something from Dave and now something has come up that will have an impact on our marriage."

"I hope you don't want me to talk to him and tell him." Lance said giving her a look that said that was going too far.

"No, nothing like that," Lori said, making sure to keep her voice hushed. "Lance, I have a brother."

"And Dave doesn't know?" This seemed pretty big.

"Dave doesn't know and there's more. My brother is a . . . a"

"Oh my!" Lance whispered, his eyes twinkling with mischief. "He's a . . . a."

"Yes," Lori nodded, "and there's more. My dad . . ."

"More?" Lance said, in mock disbelief. "How could there possibly be more?"

"Stop it!" she said, punching him in the arm. "This is serious!"

"I'm sorry, Lori. I can see this has you upset! So what about your dad?"

"My dad was kind of like a mini-mob boss."

Lance couldn't hide the surprise with the announcement. She was really sharing some dark stuff that he couldn't believe Dave didn't know.

"I was so ashamed of my family and I just never told Dave. Now, a woman that Dad favored, if you get my meaning, died and I was named in her will to find her daughter that she gave to my dad in exchange for drugs. The stuff is sealed and is to be opened only by the girl."

"And this girl is where?" Lance asked, still unable to believe she hadn't told Dave any of this. How did these two make this marriage work with these kinds of secrets?

"She's with my brother who is a you know what, working for him, but I have no idea where he is. I was wondering if you could get the word out that I'm looking for her."

"What is this girl's name?" Lance sighed, not liking it that Dave didn't know all this. His co-worker needed to come in for a session.

"Rain Patterson."

"Rain? Like as in water?"

"Yes!"

"Okay—Rain Patterson, I'll put out the word. Lori, you have to know Dave will hear about this if I do this! You're going to tell him, right?"

"Of course. I just have to find the right time."

"How about today?"

"I will tell him," Lori assured him. "Just let me do it my way, please."

Lance sighed. He could make some inquiries. He had never heard the name, but around here that meant nothing. There were many unknowns around this building alone. The urban jungle had many more nameless prisoners!

"I'll do this but you have to come clean with Dave. I will be checking up on this!"

She nodded, making more promises that he had no choice but to accept as good.

After Lori's visit, Lance glanced through his appointment book checking to make sure he hadn't missed anybody. It was a ritual with him. He glanced at the name of a young girl who had been coming to see him for quite some time but hadn't shown up for her scheduled appointment. He debated whether he should make some inquiries on the street or just leave it. Then he remembered his promise to Lori. He threw on a jacket and headed out the door, calling out to Dave that he was stepping out. The air was a bit crisp and it was later than he thought. He strolled down the street, talking to some of the familiar faces and making sure to inquire discreetly about Rain while keeping an eye out for his absentee client. It was easy to upset the apple cart in this precarious place and destroy years of work with one careless word.

Some boys were shooting hoops, so he tossed a few with them. Lance saw it as a friendly game and enjoyed his time with them. He glanced at his watch, surprised to find he had been gone from the office for almost two hours. He had to get going.

"Good game, guys. I gotta run," he said, walking toward the gate of the fence that surrounded the hoops.

The boys looked at him and he knew he had done something wrong, but what?

"Is there a problem?" he asked slowly.

"You owe us for the use of the ball and the court," one of the boys declared.

"Oh, I'm sorry. I have no cash on me. I'd gladly bring some . . ."

Lance didn't bother finishing his explanation but turned and ran instead as the boys made it clear they didn't accept excuses. The thundering of shoes behind him told him they were closing in. He felt a strong hand jerk him around, bringing him to a dead stop. He threw his arms up to protect his face only to have a well-placed kick in the stomach drop him to the ground. Next, he felt the force of a very strong punch snap his neck back until his head seemed to touch his back. The beating continued with a force that brought Lance praying for death. He felt a sharp blow to the back of his head. The world turned black before his body slumped to the pavement. The boys dumped him in a garbage heap and ran off laughing.

Lance woke up in pain, lying in a back alley among the garbage. He tried to move and pain shot through his body in every direction. He was in big trouble deep in the middle of a city where no one stopped to help a stranger. He moaned in agony as he tried to somehow move himself, and then through the haze of his double vision he saw her. It didn't take much imagination to figure out her profession, but at this second Lance wasn't fussy—help was help. She looked him in the eye before disappearing from his sight. He didn't let it bother him that she left, thinking he'd have to figure this out for himself; but she returned. She even brought help and soon he was on his way to a hospital in a taxi. She paid the driver a hundred dollars to get him to the hospital—what would that cost her? He knew her type, and her pimp wouldn't be very happy to hear she gave away a hundred dollars to help a stranger. It left him wondering who she was. He knew the chances he would ever know were slim but two things he did know: people could be kind, even the most unlikely ones, and God did hear and answer prayers. This could only be seen as a miracle!

Dave headed over to Lance's office to see if he had returned. It seemed he had been gone for a very long time! It wasn't unusual for Lance to work late, but he usually stayed in the office once the sun went down and always checked in with Dave or one of the other employees. He hadn't done either tonight. Dave grabbed his phone and called Lori to tell her he would wait around the office a little longer. He grabbed a pile of files and got busy.

He didn't even look up again until the pile was gone. He glanced at the clock and shuddered! It was almost midnight and no Lance! Something was wrong. The phone rang and Dave shuddered with relief as he listened. He dropped the phone back on its cradle and hurried to get to the hospital.

"Lance, what happened?" he demanded as soon as he entered the room, but then froze in his tracks, not sure he had the right room. It was only when Lance responded that he was sure the bruised figure on the bed was his coworker.

"I made a stupid mistake," Lance groaned, still finding every word used too many muscles. "Doc says I'll be fine."

"Dottie's going to have my head!" Dave ranted. "You know you're supposed to have someone with you when you roam the streets. This is why!"

"I know, I know. I just wanted to see a client and her address is really close to the center and things went very wrong."

Dave sat down beside the bed, knowing his pacing would upset Lance further. They had all done the same thing a hundred times, so he had no right to be too preachy now.

"Do your mom and dad know?"

"Yeah, I got the nurse to call them before she called you." Lance sighed. "I'm really sorry, I screwed up!"

"Don't sweat it! Let's just be thankful you're alive!"

Lance still wasn't sure about being thankful for that. There wasn't an inch of his body that didn't hurt!

Dottie and Arthur walked into the hospital room about two hours later, gasping in horror at the bruises on Lance's face.

"Oh, Lance!" Dottie cried, wanting to hold him in her arms but not sure where she could even touch him without hurting him.

"Mom," Lance whispered, "I'm fine!"

Arthur looked his son over and knew that was a lie. They didn't use that many bandages on someone that was fine!

"Are you sure you're okay?" Dottie asked, thinking the same thing as Arthur.

"I'm fine, Mom. Just a couple broken ribs and some bruises."

"How many is a couple?" Arthur asked.

Lance refused to say.

Arthur and Dottie could see he needed some sleep, and they wanted to get the real scoop from the doctor. They would make the doctor answer their questions that Lance was avoiding. Dave invited them to stay with him and Lori for the night that was quickly vanishing with all the excitement. They decided they could talk to the doctor in the morning and took Dave up on his offer.

Dottie and Arthur went back to the hospital early the next morning to talk to the doctor. Dave and Lori went to work, but Lori couldn't concentrate. She knew exactly why Lance was out on that street and she couldn't shrug off the guilt. She headed to the hospital during her lunch hour. She was glad to find Lance alone in his room, Arthur and Dottie having gone to the cafeteria for lunch.

"I'm so sorry, Lance. This is my fault," she let the words tumble out of her mouth quickly before the tears took over.

"No, Lori, I should've gone earlier in the day and I did stupid things that Dave has warned me about not doing. It didn't have anything to do with what we discussed."

She pulled herself together. He didn't need some weepy female who needed her guilt assuaged today.

"Did any of this at least lead to something?" she asked, grabbing a hankie from her purse.

"Sorry, no one has heard of Rain and they all said Johnny has high class clientele and doesn't run the street. His top man does, though, but she's not with that group."

"Now I feel really guilty! You got hurt for nothing. I hope my PI has better luck."

"You hired a PI?"

"I'm using some of my inheritance that I swore I'd never use to pay for it. Dad made Johnny promise he'd care for the girl and I know he'd try to keep his dad's dying wish. At least, his name came up as familiar."

"I hope your PI does better than me in many ways," he sighed, trying to shift into a position that didn't hurt.

Lori reached out and twisted his hair gently between her fingers. She loved this guy too much to ever put him at this much risk again. She knew better!

CHAPTER 19

Lance and Dave were swamped at the center. It seemed like the whole city needed something from them, and they all needed it yesterday. Lance's bruises had long since healed and he only had a small scar above his eye to show off. The ribs were another story altogether! They refused to stop hurting, but he knew Dave couldn't handle things by himself. But it was all getting to be too much. He didn't even see Bryan when he arrived—he was so deep in papers and files.

"Hello," Bryan called.

Lance's head shot up. Help. Before he knew what happened, Lance had Bryan too busy to know what way to turn.

"How do you guys do this day after day?" he asked during a brief break. He had learned on day one that these guys did not take lunch hours—they took lunch minutes!

"One call at a time," Dave laughed.

"I'm glad I have my sights on the saner pace at the farm."

"Yeah, sane pace at the farm, my foot!" Lance shook his head. "Weeding and more weeding and rocks to pick."

"You loved it there and still do." Bryan said, knowing his brother too well.

"I confess, I love weeding acres and acres of vegetables!" Lance quipped. "Actually, Dad and Mom think I should come visit for a while and get my ribs healed up. I don't know why they'd think working in the garden would help that process, but they do."

"Maybe that's a good idea. You certainly could use the break. Have you taken any days off since you started here?" Dave's question was sincere. "You even had files in the hospital."

"Do you take breaks from your wife?" Lance asked, also serious. "I love the work and I'd go insane taking a day off for no good reason. Besides, what would you do without me?"

"Look, big brother, if you don't take care of yourself, you're going to end up needing this place instead of working at it." Bryan straightened himself to tower a full three inches over Lance. He knew it annoyed Lance when he did that.

"Stop that big brother stuff," Lance scowled.

Bryan laughed. "Just remember who's bigger now and how you used to say the bigger man has the power."

"Well, you better think about how that size of yours can defend me from Mom. You know Mom will have just as many files on my bed with all of her pet projects as what I take home from here."

"And you love taking in all the strays!" Bryan shot back.

It felt good to take the moment to reflect, but the moment was over. The guys packed away the lunches and went back to work, but the smiles remained as each one envisioned different memories of Lance's antics.

Lori walked in and wondered what all the smiles where about. They all smirked as they passed it off as 'guy bonding.' She wasn't asking any more.

"Well, if I'm not allowed to know, can my sweet husband please go to the car and bring me the boxes from the back seat?"

"Of course, will I need help?" Dave asked in return.

"No, there are only two and you can put them in the back office." He smiled at her, pecking her lightly on the cheek as he passed. Once he had disappeared, she talked fast.

"Tomorrow is Dave's birthday and I've booked us in the pizza place on the corner. Dave doesn't know and he'd better be surprised when we walk in. Lance, you're getting him there at seven. Got it?"

The brothers smiled—Lori was at it again. Dave came back with the feeling that something was up but left it alone. He headed back to his office. Bryan joined him, thinking it was a lot less crowded than Lance's paper-covered nightmare.

Lance could see Lori had something else on her mind, too.

"Sorry, Lori, the name hasn't come up."

"I keep hoping my brother will wake up, but he doesn't."

"Did the PI come up with anything?"

"He found her and she stole his gun. He got a real good headache out of the deal. He said he almost felt like he reached her for a second but then she hit him."

"So why not pick her up on that?" Lance asked, throwing a pile of papers into the garbage.

"The poor guy feels like an idiot for letting her get the best of him. Says he never saw it coming and she just smacked him in the head in the middle of the conversation. He's hoping to find her and get it back without having to make it a big deal. Why would she steal a gun?"

"Let me see," Lance said in a mocking tone. "She's a prostitute—what could she do with a gun? Well, she could shoot her pimp or a john or herself or whoever she hates the most at the time of pulling the trigger."

"She could kill Johnny!" Lori gasped in horror.

"We see it all the time here. Some girls just lose it. Johnny might not be the nicest guy in the world, especially if his dad showed him the ropes. Usually the next generation is worse than the previous."

"My dad wasn't into the rough stuff—drugs, yes, but not the pimping end of things. He ran a legitimate business—an escort service. I don't think Johnny's doing any different."

"And what truck did you just fall off of? Come on, Lori. Rain is a product of the street life and I doubt it was all above the law."

"My dad sent me to the university, knowing I'd be a lawyer. Why would he do that if he thought I'd have to arrest him?"

"I didn't know your father but I've met many like him. The girl's life is ugly and the boys, well, they enjoy the fruits of their labor. Even the ones who claim to be above the law have some skeletons in the closet."

"This is my family you're talking about!"

"And the sooner you get real about them, the sooner you can help them."

"I've already figured out what to do with them if I ever get the chance—I'll get them into a program like the farm. I know Johnny isn't keeping true to Dad's standards."

"Lori, if you do get them into the system, there's no guarantee they'll be fit for a program, but I promise I'll do my best." He stopped, debating how much more he should say. "Lori, if we find them, you may not like the story they tell."

"I know," Lori said, looking down. "I'm really sticking my head in the sand."

"I'd pull it out," Lance advised. "Experience tells me Daddy wasn't a saint and brother, from what I hear, can be quite a devil."

Lori left, hating to have to face the truth, and Lance knew it. He'd have to have a few more heart-to-hearts with her. This had to be dealt with.

The office was busy the next day. Dave had two girls phone him with thoughts of suicide before office hours even officially began. Lance found his thoughts constantly going back to how he was going to keep Dave until seven and then convince him to leave. Lori took care of the first problem. She phoned to let Dave know she would pick the boys up at school and drive them to an out-of-town game that they had forgotten to tell them about—another part of the scheme. Lance wished he had kids to use for an excuse.

By five o'clock, Dave and Lance were the only two people left in the office. They bent their heads over the numbers on the sheets in front of them, wondering how to make the annual budget look better. Lance glanced at the clock for the tenth time in the last minute. At six-thirty he still had no idea how to get Dave to the pizza place.

"You seem distracted" Dave said, surprised to see Lance so jittery. It wasn't like him.

"Just trying to figure a way to make this whole thing work."

"I know what you mean. I think this is the only job where people take regular pay cuts but never quit."

"You think that's the answer again?"

"I hope not. Lori's job covers our expenses, but I wish I could contribute like a man should." Dave looked glumly at the facts in black and white. "Every year we get more kids in here but not a lot of new givers. The donations just aren't keeping us afloat."

"Well, we have another week before payday. Maybe something will turn up. I'll make do with whatever as long as I can head to Café Evans every so often."

He knew what Lance was offering and Dave didn't want to consider it. Lance earned his keep around here! They put their attention back on the budget.

The clock ticked away the minutes. Ten to seven and Lance had to get him to the pizza place—but how? What reason could he possibly give for suddenly being so generous and offering to take his friend out for pizza when he knew he wouldn't be getting a paycheck that would cover his basic expenses? He tapped nervously with his pen on the desk, thinking hard.

"Dave, I need to talk to you about something!" he finally announced.

"So talk." Dave said, wondering about Lance's strange behavior.

"Why don't we go have a bite at the pizza place? I'd feel more relaxed talking there."

"You'd feel more relaxed talking at the crowded pizza place than in my private office?" Dave said, furrowing his brows in question to Lance's conduct tonight.

"Actually," Lance stammered. "I'm really hungry and food helps me talk."

"What's going on with you tonight?"

Lance swallowed hard, trying to think what would get him over to the pizza place.

"There's a girl waiting at the pizza place that I want you to meet. I'm sort of sweet on her." It wasn't totally a lie. He really did like Lori but not quite the way he was inferring now.

Dave laughed. The thought of Lance being sweet on a girl was outrageous enough, but actually being asked to meet her was too much. He threw on his coat.

"Why didn't you just say something? Any girl that would catch your eye has to be pretty special! Let's go."

Lance whispered a prayer for forgiveness for the lie as they strolled across the street to the pizza place. Dave stepped in the door to be greeted by "Happy Birthday!" He nearly fell over with surprise.

"You guys! How did you do this? Lance, you dog! A girl. I should've known."

"I finally succeeded in surprising you!" Lori laughed, wrapping her arms around him.

The festivities began. Everyone laughed and told stories about Dave. Lance listened but he had heard most of the stories before. A girl came in and made her way to the back of the restaurant. Lance let his curious eyes follow her. There was something vaguely familiar about her but he couldn't put his finger on it. She had the look and his heart went out to her. It was his turn to tell a story. His attention went back to the party. Soon he had them all roaring with laughter, at Dave's expense, of course.

CHAPTER 20

COMING TOGETHER

Lance couldn't figure out why he was feeling so out of the party mood. He glanced away and saw the girl still sitting at the far table. His eyes were drawn to a man who entered the restaurant. He was definitely not a regular and had all the fixings of a pimp. He strolled through the place looking at every table until he spotted the girl. He hurried to her. She didn't look happy to see him. The party once again demanded his attention. Things were starting to wrap up. Dave was giving his thank-you speech. He glanced at the table where they had been, but now they were gone. Another one had slipped through the cracks!

The party was dispersing. Bryan opened his wallet and sighed.

"Hey, brother, I got you covered," Lance called to him, remembering how broke he always was during his student years. How broke he always still was.

"Thanks, I appreciate it," Bryan told him.

Lance tossed some bills on the table and headed toward the door behind his brother. The others had already gone out, leaving the brothers the last to leave. Lance pushed open the door, letting Bryan slip out ahead of him. He had just let go of the door when a small bundle of energy slammed into Bryan, nearly bowling him over. Bryan's face went from a smile to surprise as he found himself whirled around by the force. Lance hadn't even totally figured out what had happened when he heard the distinctive crash of gunfire. He saw Bryan jerk as the force of the bullet hit him, crumpling him to the ground, engulfing the small figure beneath him. His eyes rose for one moment to see the shooter fall. His brain couldn't make any sense of it until he saw the red stain spreading over Bryan's shirt.

"Bryan! Bryan!" he screamed.

Dave and Lori turned just in time to see Bryan fall. Lori gasped, too stunned to move, but Dave took control. He pulled Lori back to the spot where Lance still stood stunned, completely in shock.

"Lance, let's lift Bryan off the girl." Dave ordered, pulling Lance out of his haze.

He bent over quickly to help Dave, letting his training kick in so he could function on auto-pilot. They rolled Bryan over and Lori lost it.

"Rain! Oh my God!" she screamed.

"Someone call 911," Dave instructed, trying to keep calm.

A third victim stumbled out of the back alley also covered in blood.

"I shot Tommy," he whimpered. "I shot Tommy. What have I done?" He collapsed beside Tommy's body.

"Johnny?" Lori cried, rushing to the figure.

"I've shot Tommy!" he repeated, looking straight at Lori.

She couldn't stand to listen to his moaning. She reached over to pull him away from the body that represented all that was evil in her world. She pulled back when she felt the warm dampness of the blood soaking through his jacket.

"You're bleeding," she sobbed. "Oh my God!"

Two more people from the center rushed over to help Lori with Johnny. A police car pulled up, and the officers began the job of assessing the scene.

"How come my wife seems to know these people?" Dave asked Lance while he tore at Bryan's shirt.

"Uh, Dave, meet your brother-in-law and one of his girls."

Dave's fingers froze.

"What are you talking about?"

"I'm imagining there aren't too many girls named Rain and Johnny would be Lori's brother. She's been getting me to help track them down." He wished this was coming from Lori's mouth.

"My wife has a brother?" Dave replied, unable to comprehend all the other implications.

"I think you'd better discuss this with her," Lance suggested, turning his full attention back on Bryan.

The ambulance arrived. Rain had to get out of here but there were too many people. She tried to stand but there was always someone to push her back down. At last, she saw an opening. She half pulled and half crawled through the moving bodies. She was almost there when two shoes planted themselves firmly in front of her.

"Hello, Rain. I suppose you used my gun in this little fiasco?"

She let her gaze move up from the shoes to the casual khakis, then she saw the shirt and finally she was gazing into the cold steel stare. There was no mistaking the man—the guy she stole the gun from. She let her head drop. The game was over.

Dave, Lance and Lori waited patiently in the hospital waiting room. Dave was quiet—too quiet—while Lori felt the need to come clean.

"I'm sorry, Dave," she cried. "I should've told you. I wanted to tell you but every time I tried, I chickened out."

"But you told Lance?" Dave hissed in a low angry whisper.

"I went to him as a counselor to ask him how to tell you all this. I've been trying to tell you, but I didn't think you needed all this on your plate with all the stuff at the center. I was wrong."

"That's not how you put it to me," Lance interjected but Lori's dirty look quickly silenced him.

"Your brother is a pimp and Rain is . . . ?" Dave demanded to know.

"I don't even know," Lori cried. "I guess she's one of my brother's girls."

"May I suggest something?" Lance bravely interrupted.

"What?" both Lori and Dave asked, glaring at him.

"I would suggest," Lance said slowly, "both of you calming down and Lori telling this front to back. Then you can ask questions, Dave."

"Don't you dare throw some psycho-babble drip at me!" Dave replied.

"Dave, you are not going to solve anything while you're this angry and Lori—you and I need to have a little talk about honesty before you continue."

Dave stormed from the room, not willing to have his own methods applied to himself. Lori shook her head but remained.

"Honesty," Lance said, nodding his head, "is the best policy."

"I didn't lie!' she defended.

"You did not come to me as a counselor. You asked me to find Rain for you—a little different, I would say."

"Oh, stop your holier-than-thou ranting!" she shot back, leaving the room.

"I'm going to see if they know anything yet," he said to the empty room before making his way to the nurses' desk.

There was no new information on Bryan's condition. He wandered around for a few minutes before returning to the waiting room where he found Lori sitting alone.

"You know you have to come clean," he said, taking the seat next to her.

"And I will—my way in my time."

"As long as you don't misrepresent the facts," he encouraged.

"I don't even know the truth," she sighed. "I'm sorry I yelled at you."

"I wish you were sorry you lied," he replied in all sincerity. "I would gladly help you with this but then it truly would be in the parameters of my job. I won't put up with lying."

"I'll think about it," Lori decided out loud. She wasn't sure she could come clean. "Do you think they'll qualify for the farm program?"

"I don't see how that's going to be possible," Lance admitted. "They were both involved with the shooting and they both used guns. I talked to Officer Coop and he says that nothing's for sure yet, but Johnny did murder Tommy and Rain shot Johnny. The stolen gun is a whole other issue. I'm not sure we can get them out of going to prison for years under these circumstances."

"I have to try. He's my brother! How could he do this?" Lori replied, pounding her fist into her hand. "I can't believe he let things get this out of hand! Is she one of his girls? And Bryan, how is he? Why did he get into the middle of this mess?"

The questions came fast and it took Lance a moment to digest it all.

"As for Bryan, the doctor told me the bullet lodged in a bone and that was a good thing. They don't feel it did any real serious damage but we won't know until he comes out of surgery."

"I'm praying. I feel so responsible for all this!" Lori sighed, rising from her chair before he could address any of the other questions. "I guess I'd better go find Dave and start trying to make this right."

Lance followed her lead, standing beside her.

"I think if I were you, I'd just back off at this second, but you do have to be honest with him. You two can't work out anything if you lie to him," Lance said, gently putting his arm around her. "He might need some time but he never stays mad forever."

"I know, but it's hard!" She tried to let her body language tell him she was planning to do just that but her words conveyed something different. "I can't even accept the truth. How can I help Dave understand?"

Lance knew how she felt but the truth was best. He would give her a chance to realize that before pushing too hard on the issue. He decided he would give her some time to figure out the best move.

"I've gotta move around," he announced.

He glanced toward the room he had seen them move Rain into. The nagging feeling that he had met her before continued to persist and he had to have a better look. He pushed open the door slowly. She was sleeping so he could get a good look without her knowing or getting excited about his presence. He stared at the childlike face and it hit him. The girl who got him into the taxi—she was the girl! Nurse Maggie pushed her way into the room.

"One of yours?" she asked.

"Not yet but with a bit of luck she soon will be!" Lance replied, feeling suddenly like he owed her something—his life. "What can you tell me?"

"You know I shouldn't do that," Maggie said, trying to look like they weren't having this conversation.

"But you always do."

"Well, Mr. Hawkins, this young lady came in here with a gunshot wound that was non-life threatening. Her tox screen came back clean, but she had taken some cold medication and she has a cold. No bruises or scars like most of them have."

"Wow, that's far better than I could've hoped for!" Lance whistled. "I was thinking she'd be one step from the grave."

"I thought you didn't know her?" Maggie said, wondering if Mr. Lance Hawkins had just lied to her.

"I don't. I just know of her." Lance explained. "She's connected to Lori's family somehow and Lori asked me to find her. Well, I did but I didn't know it was her. She's the girl that stuck me into the taxi and had me sent up here, so I guess I owe this little lady."

"Well, isn't it a small world!" Maggie sang. "So will you be able to help?"

"It'll depend on what happens with this shooting. She was both a shooter and a victim. I need to hear the story and if I get some honesty, I'll go from there."

"What a mess!" Maggie said, shaking her head.

"You got that right! I just can't believe a girl that's been out there all her life isn't on drugs and she doesn't look beaten. I wish just one of the ones that walk into the center looked as good as her."

"You know, Lance, when they don't show physical signs, they've been abused in other ways, and sometimes those scars are much worse than physical ones."

"I know—I'm not naïve, Maggie! But for Lori's sake, I think this is easier for the short term. It also helps convince a judge of a second chance."

Rain opened her eyes and wondered where she was. The two people talking beside her were not familiar and she didn't like waking up to unfamiliar places and people.

"Hello there, Miss," Nurse Maggie greeted when she saw Rain's eyes open.

"Where am I?" Rain demanded, her eyes looking around wildly.

"You're in the hospital."

"Hospital? No, I'm not supposed to be here. Johnny will kill me."

She had this nagging feeling—her memories started coming back. There was a shooting.

"Where's Johnny?" Rain tried to sit up but the sedative made her head spin. She slid back down onto the pillow. "He'll kill me for sure this time!"

"Whoa there," Maggie said gently. "Let's just take this all a little slower. Let me check this wound of yours and then maybe Lance here can talk to you a bit."

Rain let her eyes fall onto Lance. Something about him disturbed her even though she didn't know what it was. She once again started to struggle to get out of the bed.

"I've gotta get out of here!" she cried.

Maggie tried to get her back down but Rain was not cooperating. It was becoming a battle.

"Maggie, can we have a few minutes?" Lance said quietly.

"Of course!" Maggie allowed, realizing she wasn't getting anywhere.

The nurse left the room and Rain abandoned her efforts to get up—her head was spinning too fast. She retreated back to the safety of the pillow. He watched her curiously.

"Hi, I'm Lance. You remember me?" he finally asked when he was sure she was going to stay put.

She forgot her present situation just long enough to look at him—really taking him in this time. He was tall and slender but not skinny. There was some bulk to his frame. He must lift weights or work hard. His face seemed familiar but she couldn't place it.

"I'm the guy you put in the taxi and sent to the hospital," he said, seeing the confusion in her face. "You know, the guy lying in the garbage pile."

"Oh you." She could see the outline of where the bruises had been now.

"I wish I'd known who you were that night and maybe this whole mess could have been avoided. But now that I know who you are, I've wanted to say thank you for saving my life."

"You know me?" she asked, ignoring the gesture of gratitude.

"No, just of you. Lori—Johnny's sister, has been looking for you and she asked me to help. She has something from your mother that she wants to give you."

"Get away from me!" she cried, pulling the blanket tighter around her chin.

"I'm sorry, I thought I was giving you good news," Lance told her, praying he hadn't scared her away. "I'm not here to hurt you or anything. I actually want to help you, and so does Lori."

For him to identify with Lori was scaring her. The last time she got pushed from one place to another in this family, it cost her everything, so what would it cost now?

"Why would you want to help me?" Rain asked, her eyes burning into him.

"You saved my life and I'd like to return the favor," he replied purposely leaving out any more mention of Lori. It seemed to make her edgy.

"I'm nothing worth saving, so save yourself the time."

He looked at her with compassion, hating to hear her talk like that. He wanted to talk more but Brad Coop came in the room. Rain took one look and knew this was a cop. Her whole body tensed.

"Hi, Lance, I heard she was awake." Brad smiled, hoping to put the young woman a little more at ease.

"Yep, she's awake," Lance sighed.

"She one of yours?"

"Not yet!" Lance stated but the look said that was going to change.

Brad smiled at him. He'd have to tread softly or he'd have Lance barking at him. He was known to get attached to his charges. He turned to Rain.

"Hello, Miss Patterson, I'm Officer Coop and I need to ask you a few questions."

"Why did you ask him if I was one of his?" Rain asked, trembling with fear. Maybe this Lance was another Tommy but this had to be a cop. "What's going on here?"

"Lance is a counselor at the center," Brad explained, realizing his mistake with terminology. "He helps girls like you get out of bad places. Lance just seems to take extra good care of anyone who comes to him, so we all think of him as the great protector and father of those he helps." He glanced at her to see if the mistake had been cleared up before continuing. "Now, what's your story? Why did you have a gun and why did you use it?"

Rain felt defeated. As far as she knew, she'd killed Johnny so Tommy would be hunting her. She had no place to run or hide so she decided the truth would be the best.

"I stole the gun from a client. I think he was a cop or something and I didn't like him. I hit him on the head with a vase and took his gun. I figured if a cop was taking me up to the room, I must be in trouble. I didn't want Johnny to have any more trouble from me and I didn't want Tommy taking care of me. I was getting out." Tears filled her eyes as she spoke.

For Lance, this was a good sign as he listened.

"My plan was to just once be a person that people looked up to and said 'now there's a lady!' I robbed a client a few months earlier and stashed the cash. I was planning to take the money, dress up nice and go to that real tall bank building. I was going to open an account and visit with the manager. He would call me Miss and mean it. Then I was going to take that gun and end it all."

"But you didn't do that?" Officer Coop replied, wondering how that plan turned into the shooting he was now investigating.

"No. Tommy found me and then he led Johnny right to me. I thought Johnny was going to kill me! I'd never have shot him if I had seen Tommy. I just saw him go for his gun."

"Tommy or Johnny?"

"Johnny."

"So you shot Johnny because you thought he was going to shoot you?"

"I didn't know Tommy was there. I shoot and then realize Tommy's got me in his sights. I run. I don't even know what happened after that."

"But you felt you were defending yourself when you shot Johnny?"

"I'm not claiming anything," Rain sighed. "I'm just telling it like it happened. I just want to have a chance to be a lady before I die."

Officer Coop glanced at Lance. It sounded and looked to him like this one needed a little Hawkins' care.

"I don't think killing yourself is the answer here," Lance suggested. "I know you've got good things to offer the world."

She glared at him. He didn't know who she was and he had no right thinking he did.

"I know what you think I have to offer!" she spat at him.

Brad laughed. The change in temperament was so fast both he and Lance were taken by surprise.

"Look, Miss," Brad said, hoping to get her attention back on him, "do you know who shot you?"

Rain glared at Lance for another moment before turning her attention back to Brad.

"Tommy, I guess."

"Tommy?"

"Tommy doesn't like me much and I guess he figured getting rid of me would get Johnny's heart back into the business. If Johnny hadn't shown up, this would have all ended the way it was supposed to."

"The way it was supposed to?" Brad repeated.

"Me dying so Johnny and Tommy could ride off into the sunset."

"So Tommy was there to take you out?"

She nodded.

"Tommy shows up to take you out—a problem in the organization—but Johnny doesn't let him and actually shoots him!" Brad said, thinking out loud. "So why did Johnny not let his top man take you out, and then shoot him to defend you?"

She started shaking. "Is Tommy dead?"

"I thought you knew," Brad said quietly.

"They're both dead?" Rain cried, obviously upset.

"Johnny survived but Tommy didn't," Brad explained.

Rain felt sick—now Sissy would be coming after her and she didn't fear Johnny at all. She'd probably kill them both."

"We won't let him hurt you," Brad promised.

Rain let out a sick laugh. "Johnny won't hurt me! It's Sissy that will."

Brad looked at Lance to see if he knew who Sissy might be. He shrugged.

"You don't remember anything else?" he asked, confused by the dynamics here. He was going to see if forensics had all the gun action figured out to see if this girl was on the level. It didn't make sense to him. Top guys like Tommy were hard to come by where girls like Rain were expendable. Why did Johnny shoot Tommy?

"Not really," she sighed.

"Well, I'll be back to see if that pretty little head remembers anything else," Brad told her. He rose to leave. "She's all yours, Lance."

Lance made sure they were alone before addressing the issue that had him most concerned.

"Should I assume you plan to end your life?" Lance said, looking at her face carefully.

"I gave away my soul so I figure its time to pay up."

"I don't think that's true and if you let me help you, I can help you see that you didn't give it away, just misplaced it. What makes you think you can afford the price anyway?"

"Where were you four years ago? Then it was lost but now it's gone."

Nurse Maggie strolled back in the room. "I have to give the patient her meds."

"Drugs?" Rain cried, looking so crushed in spirit, it broke Lance's heart. "Figures I stay clean and end up getting hooked in the hospital."

"Not drugs, Honey, meds," Maggie explained. "The doctor is trying to keep you comfortable. That slug you took in the shoulder is going to be mighty sore and I know that guy that fell on you! He's no light weight."

"Yeah, drugs. Johnny tells them all the same thing. This will make you feel better—make you forget that you're nothing, worth nothing!" her voice was filled with bitterness.

Maggie gave Rain the shot quickly, thinking the faster she got out of there the better. Rain didn't bother to struggle, thinking it was futile. Lori would have her destroyed anyway. Maggie smiled, happy that she didn't have to wrestle the girl down. Lance and Rain once again found themselves alone.

"Rain, I think Johnny would be pretty upset to hear he lost you, too," Lance said gently.

"He's going to kill me!" she replied.

"I kind of doubt that," Lance informed her. "He didn't shoot Tommy to save your life just so he could do the honors."

She was trying to think of a good comeback, but another nurse informed Lance that his brother was awake. He was gone before she could say a word, thinking if he made a fast exit, he would leave her with something to chew on.

Lance snagged the doctor at the nurse's station and talked to him briefly, making sure he knew that Rain seemed to be bent on killing herself and that she needed close watching. The doctor nodded, telling him they would keep an eye on her, but Lance knew that sometimes patients like Rain slipped through the cracks. He would check on her later, but now he had to find Bryan. He headed to the room where he was told he would find his brother.

Bryan felt groggy but aware of the pain in his side. His memory flashed back to the events of the evening before. Images of the party, the girl, the explosion of pain and Lance's horrified face flashed in his mind. Now as Lance entered the room, he was glad to see a smile.

"Finally awake?" Lance asked, forcing himself to look positive.

"If you guys weren't such slave drivers, maybe I wouldn't need so much rest!" Bryan shot back.

"You have no idea how glad I am to be able to joke around with you!" Lance said with tears in his eyes.

"How bad is it?" he asked. "I'm sure they've told you more than me."

"The bullet lodged in a bone and that stopped it from doing more damage. As it is, you'll have to heal up from a broken hip but that's doable—more doable than damage to the liver, kidneys or heart."

"Easy for you to say!" Bryan shot back. He knew it was only the IV dripping the meds into his veins that was keeping the pain at bay. "How's the girl?"

"Physically, she took a bullet in the shoulder and some big lug fell on her, so she's hurting. But it's her mental condition that has me worried."

"Who is she?"

"She's Lori's brother's girl. He's a pimp."

"Lori's brother's girl?"

"A long story."

"Who did the shooting?" Bryan asked, still confused how this all happened. He never saw it coming.

"Listen carefully cause this is complicated and I know how hard complicated things can be for you!" Lance smirked before continuing. Bryan shook his head at his brother. "The girl was planning suicide, but the top man had ideas of taking her out. The boss got smart to the top guy's plot and went to warn the girl. Just as the boss is trying to tell the girl, he sees the top guy aiming. He goes for his gun and the girl thinks he's going to shoot her. She pulls a gun and shoots the boss. The top guy gets off a shot and hits the girl but she runs right into you. The top guy aims for another hit but at that moment, the boss takes him out but he hits the trigger and the shot hits you. The top guy is dead and the boss is injured, as are you and the girl. That's how I'm putting it together."

"That's just too weird!" Bryan replied, shaking his head.

"I agree. That's why I really think God has put these two in our path and we have to help them."

"Maybe we just have to let Lori reconnect with her family."

"Yeah, right!" Lance laughed. "I don't think this is going to be quite that easy! For one thing, this girl does not like Lori. Somehow Lori is connected to this girl's mother. That reminds me—our parents should be here pretty soon."

"Good change of subject! Are you avoiding talking about something here?"

Lance smiled and was saved from having to discuss this further when Dottie and Arthur walked in.

"How's my baby?" Dottie cried, moving to the bed to wrap her arms around Bryan.

"I'll be fine. Don't start crying."

"If your mom wants to cry after her baby's been shot, that is her prerogative!" Dottie scolded him, brushing the tears off her cheeks.

"How did this happen?" Arthur asked.

"Ask Lance and he'll give you all the details." Bryan replied, turning his gaze at Lance.

Lance obliged, starting right back at the beginning again. Maybe if he told the story enough, he'd understand it himself.

Lori took a deep breath before entering Rain's room. The girl sat on her bed with her eyes closed.

"Excuse me?" Lori called softly

Rain's eyes popped open. She was on overload with all the people coming to visit her and, to her, they were all enemies. This one was the least welcome of all of them so far.

"I'm Lori, Johnny's sister. I just thought you might like to know he's doing fine. At least, he keeps asking about you, so I'm guessing you might be curious about him."

Rain relaxed a little, talking about something she actually wanted to know something about.

"How bad is he?"

"It was a serious wound that could've been fatal, but because there were so many trained people on the scene, he'll be fine. I'll have to make sure to thank my husband for insisting that every one on his staff take that emergency medical course."

"I'm glad he's okay."

They both fell silent not sure how to approach the subject they both knew needed discussing.

"They all tell me you've been looking for me." Rain finally said, interrupting the silence.

"Yes, I have. I guess you've already heard about your mom?"

"How did she die?" Rain asked, while playing with a small fuzz on her blanket.

"She had cancer and it spread throughout her body. She phoned me, hoping I would know where you were, and I tried real hard to find you. I didn't even know which city to start at. I'm sorry."

"I was at your brother's. That doesn't sound that hard to locate."

Lori ignored the comment.

"I still wish you could've said good-bye. She left a few things for you and I had them put into a safety deposit box. I also have a letter. I'll bring it tomorrow."

"I don't want it!" Rain told her harshly.

"Rain, my dad disappointed me, too. I know how you feel, but maybe things weren't quite like you thought and this letter might help you understand."

"And what if it just confirms everything?"

"Then it does and you start from there."

"I was going to kill myself. Your dad and brother made me want to kill myself."

"My dad?" Lori questioned, feigning complete ignorance.

"Oh, Daddy's little girl is in the dark about it all," Rain scoffed. "They have more in common than just their names. Johnny Jr. took over where Johnny Sr. left off."

"My dad never made you prostitute yourself," Lori declared.

"No, he didn't," Rain allowed. "He just sold me to someone he knew would."

Lori could feel the hate inside this girl or was that the little girl inside of her crying? She hated Rain but smiled.

"I know you may not believe this, but you have people around you right now who will care for you in a way that you never knew existed. Let them love you."

She was glad to watch Lori scurry out of the room. Oh yeah—she felt the love! Rain shuddered at the idea of any more love in her life. She'd had more than enough of it. She was ready for solitude and the sweet peace of death.

Dave walked into the room where his brother-in-law lay. He took a deep breath before going in to meet the man he didn't know existed until a few short hours ago and act like he cared enough to save him from a situation he brought on himself.

"Johnny, I'm Dave Evans," he said, once he was sure the man was awake.

"Do I know you?" Johnny asked. For him, this had all been rather harrowing. Somehow, he had never before really had any run-ins with the law and now his game was up in one great event. No small charges—murder right off the bat.

"No, but I'm married to your sister, Lori."

"No kidding? She never mentioned she was married but then I guess it's been a few years."

"She didn't mention you either, or Rain, before this all happened."

"Lori isn't exactly thrilled with her family roots. I hadn't seen her for five years before Pop's death and haven't heard from her in the two years since."

"Two years? Your dad only passed away two years ago?" Dave couldn't believe it; the man had passed away while he and Lori were married.

"That a problem?" Johnny asked, noticing his reaction.

"Lori and I've been married for fourteen years," Dave said quietly, hoping he wouldn't topple with the shock. Obviously, his marriage wasn't the marriage he thought it was.

"Really?" Johnny said, considering all this. "I guess big sis really didn't like us cuz she's never worked too hard to keep in touch; and we weren't good enough to mention, even to you."

"I guess there's nothing much you can do about that," Dave replied, still trying to get all his emotions back in check. "So what's the deal with Rain?"

"Is she okay?" Dave didn't miss the concern in Johnny's voice.

"She's fine from what I hear. My colleague is on her case."

"You a lawyer?" Johnny asked, narrowing his eyes at Dave.

"No, I'm a counselor or a social worker if you like that term better."

"Rain's really delicate. I hope that colleague of yours realizes that."

Dave couldn't stop from staring at this man—a pimp who just described one of his girls as delicate. It was almost like he really cared.

"I think he's capable of handling the situation," Dave said after a moment, trying to recall the question. "Think you can fill me in on what brought us here?"

"Yeah, I can do that," Johnny agreed. He told the story as best as he could recall.

"She works for you?" Dave stated.

"Rain works and she gives me the money so I guess she works for me. She isn't like the rest of my girls though."

"She's special?" Dave said, tongue in cheek. This he had heard before.

"Very."

"So you save her for special clients?" He couldn't keep the icy tinge out of his voice.

"I know what you're getting at and you couldn't be farther off the mark. Rain has received special treatment and cost me more than you can imagine. I haven't knocked her around like some of the others even though she deserved it."

"Deserved it?" Dave could feel his anger rise.

"You think you know, but let me fill you in on the antics of the lovely Miss Rain. She's smashed me in the head with lawn ornaments and cut me with a razor, and she even locked me out of my own bathroom for four days. I've put up with it all and lost the respect of my other girls, let Tommy take over my business and now killed him; all because I promised Pop I'd look after Rain. If you don't believe me, I still have the scars from her attacks!"

Dave stared at him. "And you're telling me after all that, you didn't hit her?"

"Once, and I got a little rough in the bedroom, but if any of the other girls tried even half of what Rain tried, I'd have had them floating down river. I don't know why she's become so lost in herself, because I treated her like a princess."

"I'm afraid I can't give you that answer either. We always just assume the girls have been abused and broken."

"Rain was broken long before she came to me. I'll admit I destroyed her spirit, but she was messed up before I ever met her."

Dave had a torrent of emotions vying for attention: Lori had a brother that was a pimp, his father-in-law's death two years earlier, and this girl named Rain that didn't fit the picture at all. Add all this to a wife desperately wanting him to be her brother's savior. He needed some space, some time with Lance. He headed out of Johnny's room feeling like he was now ready to be the counseled instead of the counselor.

Lance sat in the cafeteria filling out forms that he should have finished a week ago. He felt that Dottie and Arthur needed time with Bryan, and he would wait for them so he could get them to his apartment where they would stay for the next couple of days until they felt it was safe to leave Bryan. He knew them well enough to know that was the plan even though nothing had been discussed. His ribs were sore and he was exhausted. Spending the night in the waiting room hadn't done him any favors.

He didn't notice Dave eyeing him from across the room or he would have seen the worry creases forming. Dave relied heavily on Lance and seeing him looking so tired scared him. Lance couldn't burn out. He was needed.

"Catching up with office work?"

Lance looked up and smiled. "No time like the present to do the job you dread. So what's up?"

"I'm that transparent?"

"Oh, yeah."

"I just talked with Johnny and he tells a very interesting story about the girl."

"He didn't hit her and she's not a user!" Lance shot back without looking up.

"How did you know?"

"I saw her chart and she's clean. She talks about Johnny with a fondness and lack of venom that tells me he didn't dog her too badly. She's suicidal and lost but not like most of the others. Taking her out of the business isn't going to fix what's wrong."

Dave slumped in his chair. Here he was a major mess and Lance was right in there fighting again.

"Why didn't Lori ever mention all this to me?"

"In all fairness, you knew that Lori had a history," Lance pulled his eyes off his work and grabbed hold of Dave's full attention. "Does this really surprise you?"

"I guess it shouldn't, but man, it hurts. I just can't believe after knowing her for fourteen years, she never said a thing. Her dad died two years ago and I had no idea."

"I think you're going to have to swallow it right now. Lori needs some time to come clean. She's ashamed and feeling guilty about things she really shouldn't. I think you need to just be there for her until some of the dust has settled here."

"You're right. You taking the girl on?"

"I think so. I have to talk to her again and make sure she doesn't belong in an institution where they can protect her from herself. It's going to be tough getting close to this one. She's not overly fond of men—or anyone else from what I can see."

"Johnny tells me she's got a mean streak—attacked him a few times. Sounds like she hit a few clients, too."

"Oh great! She's sounding like more fun all the time! I don't know if I have the energy for a girl like this!"

"But you are going to take her on?"

"I feel like God really wants me to."

"Lance, get some rest before my right-hand guy gets himself burned out. If she's too much, let someone else take her on—she sounds like a fulltime job!"

Lance smiled. Dave shook his head, knowing the chances of that actually happening were slim to none.

Bryan was going to be okay and now that he was sure of that, Lance had to get back to the office. He left his parents sound asleep at the apartment and went to the center. He prayed as he drove the short distance, using this quiet time to fuel up for the day ahead.

It didn't take long to see that the effort wasn't wasted. The center was going crazy! Both he and Dave had been gone all weekend and with all the excitement with the shooting, the phones didn't stop ringing. Even girls from Johnny's organization were calling looking for drugs that they felt the center should provide, having been deemed responsible for Tommy's demise. He patiently listened to messages in between calls and smiled with relief when he heard Dave's chair creak in the next office. Help had arrived.

A total of five counselors worked at the center but only Dave and Lance worked fulltime on payroll. The others put a day a week in while maintaining offices in the more wealthy parts of the city. Some people thought all five should be there fulltime but the budget would not allow that, so everyone worked with that reality.

Lance pulled himself out of his chair, shocked to find he had already been here four hours. He went to see if Dave was ready for a coffee break.

"This is why I don't need birthday parties!" Dave exclaimed, as he dropped the phone back in its cradle. "Are you going crazy, too?"

"Now don't blame the party!" Lance smiled. "The shooting is to blame for this!"

"I guess! I'm really sore at Lori and I guess I'm slamming everything she's ever done that I didn't agree with."

"I think you enjoyed the party!" Lance said, leveling his glance on him. "The issues between you and Lori run a wee bit deeper!"

"I still can't believe she lied to me about so many things for so long!"

"Have you talked to her?"

"She's spending every minute at the hospital or working at getting him off easy. It's almost like she's in complete denial about what this guy does for a living and the fact that he shot someone!"

"Well, I was going to ask if you'd like to have coffee but I think we just talked ourselves out of time!" Lance said, glancing at his watch.

"We are taking the time today!" Dave declared.

Lance shook his head knowing this coffee break would be a session for Dave! Oh, well, at least one of them would get a break.

CHAPTER 21

Rain didn't like the hospital. There was no place to escape the questions and no lock on the door. The cop had come back several times always with more questions that she dutifully answered, never trying to hide anything but hating the attention. The nurses and doctors always came carrying a syringe, pouring enemies into her body, ignoring her protests. By Monday evening, she wished she could vanish from sight and just be alone, but it wasn't happening. She audibly groaned when the door opened and the guy she rescued once again dropped by for a visit.

"Hi, Rain," Lance greeted, sounding weary. He had forced himself to leave the office to make visiting hours, but he was exhausted and hoped she would be cooperative. He still had a pile of paperwork to push through.

"Go away!" Rain demanded.

"Can't do that. It's my job to talk to people like you and if I don't do my job, I don't eat. I like eating."

"So do I!" Rain retorted. "I like eating alone in my house away from people who bother me!"

"That's hard to believe! You look like you could blow away," Lance smiled, ignoring the less than subtle hint. "I just can't see you as a closet eater!"

He wasn't leaving. Rain decided to try a new tactic.

"Johnny says that, too. Says the clients like a little meat so it's not like sleeping with a stick. I think he doesn't like sleeping with a stick."

He listened carefully for any clue into this girl's life. She just gave him something very key—she was Johnny's girl, but more importantly, his main girl.

"So you feeling a little better now?" he questioned.

"I don't know."

"Don't know if you're feeling better? Seems pretty basic—do you still hurt or not?"

"They keep me so drugged up I wouldn't know if you jabbed a knife into my heart."

Lance could hear the anger in her voice and it was the second time she complained about getting meds. He'd have to talk to the doctor about it.

"It must have been pretty scary getting shot."

"Not really."

"Well, you must be a lot braver than me."

She didn't reply.

"Rain, have you been made aware of the fact that you most likely aren't going to be facing any charges?"

"So?"

"So you won't be going to jail. Do you have a place to go when they release you?"

"I have nowhere to go and no need to go anywhere. What does it matter?"

Lance wanted to swoop her up and hold her, tell her it did matter, but knew he couldn't do that—she would get it all wrong. His gears went into overdrive! He had to find a way to reach this girl. How could she care so much about not getting addicted to painkillers and yet not want a future? There was life here; he knew it.

"Do you have any family we should be contacting?"

He saw the tears in her eyes but also the anger.

"I don't have family. None that care anyway."

The last part of the statement suggested something different than the first. Lance felt at a loss as to how to convince her anyone could care. Then an idea came to him.

"I'll be back," he promised.

Dottie stared at her son in disbelief. Lance could come up with the zaniest plans!

"You want me to go in a stranger's room and hug her? Have you lost your sense, Lance?"

"She won't let me touch her without misconstruing it. I talked to Dave and we agree that she needs a mother figure. I think her Mom hurt her and she's been searching for a mother's love for a long time from what I can ascertain."

"I'm not her mom and I don't see how me going in there and hugging her is going to make a difference," Dottie laughed. "I know some of you think my hugs hold some special magic that makes people feel good, but they're really nothing special."

"Mom, she will not survive a psych ward and that's where she's headed if a doctor sees her in her present state of mind. Lori is on me, begging me to take this one under my wing and I can't reach her—her view of men is a bit tainted. Just go in and see if she'll even talk to you." Lance put on his special begging face that always melted Dottie's resolve.

She stared at him. Usually he used Mel or Bryan in his schemes but rarely even approached her. But there was a lost child that needed help and because of that, she couldn't say no to him. He knew he had her hooked, flashing her a big smile.

Dottie still couldn't believe she had given in to this, but here she was pushing the door open to Rain's room. The girl in the bed looked so tiny and frail that it broke her heart and reminded her of Mel. Now she knew why Lance was getting so involved with helping this girl. He always had a soft spot for broken things, and this girl was broken.

Hadn't he been the one to bring every hurt living thing he found to the house for her to bandage? But this was not a bird or a butterfly, this was a person. She would have to tell him how many of those creatures he had brought she had killed, trying to be merciful. She couldn't just kill this girl.

"Hello," Dottie said, moving toward the bed.

Rain opened her eyes. "Who are you?"

"My name is Dottie. I'm Lance's Mom."

She squinted at her trying to put a face to the name. She couldn't.

"He's the one you rescued."

Oh, him again! Rain thought. He was becoming a pain!

"He thought maybe you and I could talk."

Rain looked the woman over carefully. She was a pretty woman with a carefully kept appearance. She was petite with a slight stomach, probably from having children, and nothing like her son in build. She appealed to her. This woman's whole being said 'mom.'

"I'm Rain," she said, almost bursting into tears with that simple statement.

"Yes, Lance told me. That's a nice name."

"I don't think it's a name at all," Rain scowled. "I've always thought that if my mom really loved me, she would've given me a real name."

"I can remember when I was in school and everyone called me Dottie, I had the same kind of thoughts. My name is Dot. Talk about a lack of a name. A dot is like the absence of everything. Most people think its short for Dorothy but it's not—I'm just Dot!"

"So did you think it was a mean name?" Rain asked, never before having met anyone with a name that meant less than hers.

"I've learned to live with it. My husband says I fill the world with dots of love. He says those dots are like spots of light in a sea of darkness."

"That's nice. No one can think of anything like that with Rain."

Dottie could but she moved on. The name thing was just a symptom of a deeper hurt.

"Lance tells me you are a bit sad?" Dottie said gently. Like Lance, she found herself wanting to wrap her arms around this girl and take her home and love her to death.

"I'm not sad," Rain declared as if that was a ridiculous conclusion to come to about her. "I'm cold."

Dottie looked deep into the face of the girl, trying to decide what she meant by the word 'cold.' She could see pain but there was also a detached look in the girl's eyes. Like she couldn't dare to feel anything, so great was her fear of daring to love and not getting anything back.

"Rain, would it be alright for me to hug you?" Dottie asked, fighting back the fears that the girl might refuse her.

Rain looked at the woman like she was crazy while two other things went through her mind. The first was that she was definitely out of her element and the second was she had no idea what planet she was on. People didn't just hug strangers. For that matter, they didn't talk to them either. Could she refuse? She had no idea if she was a prisoner here who had to do what she was told. What would the result of that be? In her world, to refuse things was a bad idea even when they were offered with a choice.

"I guess," she relented, thinking she would just cooperate and maybe that would make things go better. None of the girls ever talked about anything like this happening when they got caught by the cops!

Dottie had her permission but the task seemed undoable. She had expected the girl to lean forward to receive the hug but she, in fact, remained rigid on the bed as if challenging her to perform this task. She was not defeated that easily. She carefully worked her arm behind the girl's head and pulled her cheek against Rain's.

"Rain, you are very precious!" she whispered softly into the girl's ear. "I want you to know you are loved, because I love you."

Rain felt the arms close in around her and felt the warmth of Dottie against her. It was a hug that only a mother could give—at least, that's what Rain imagined when she watched mothers on TV. A hug she had longed for so long she was beginning to think it didn't exist. Rain slowly let her good arm move around the woman. She closed her eyes and just remained there in a place that seemed so unreal she thought she must be dreaming. Dottie moved her hand, stroking her head gently, each stroke like a match to the flint. At last, the flame took hold. Sobs erupted and a dam of emotion broke loose. There was more! Love was more than satisfying a customer or avoiding a beating. People could feel more, be more just like she always dreamed.

"Oh, Rain," Dottie said softly, "let it out. You've been hurting for a long time and you need to let someone else help you carry it all."

Rain hung on, afraid if she let go, it would be over, never to return.

Lance walked into the room wondering what was taking so long. He stared at the scene and smiled. He knew his mom's hugs were amazing. He watched the two women embracing, so lost in the moment that they didn't even take heed of him. He could see his mom falling in love in front of his eyes. When they finally pulled apart, he knew he had to save this one—no matter what it took. What had he done, bringing his mom into this fight?

Rain stared into the woman's eyes, wishing she could stay forever in her arms. But she knew life was never that simple and she was never that lucky. Dottie stroked her cheek gently.

"You just call me if you need me! Even if all you want is a hug and don't want to say a thing! You just tell them to call Dottie and I'll come. Do you understand?" Dottie ordered. Rain nodded, wanting very much to believe that was what would happen, but she had her doubts.

Dottie turned to see Lance standing there. He shuffled nervously, not liking the glint in his mom's eye.

"You get this girl to my farm!" she ordered. "You hear me now! You get it done!"

"I'm trying real hard, but it isn't quite that simple!" Lance informed her.

"Make it that simple!" Dottie ordered.

"Mom, Rain isn't helping herself here! She has to want to come to the farm as much as you want to get her there!"

"Look at her!" Dottie objected. "She isn't up to making these decisions. What does she know or understand when you tell her these things?"

"That's why I asked you to come in here. Now she has a better understanding but it doesn't mean the law will see it that way."

"Lance, you can't put her in my arms and then take her away."

And they were always accusing him of wanting to adopt everyone! The apple didn't fall far from the tree on that one.

"I'll try, Mom. I'll try harder than I've ever tried before."

"You'd better do better than that. Now you stay with her while I go light a fire under Dave and your dad." Dottie gave him a peck on the cheek as she left the room.

Now he was afraid—she was good at lighting fires. He was afraid this fire might get out of control and everything and everyone would burn down before it was over. He looked over at Rain.

"She likes you," he smiled, trying not to look as nervous as he felt.

Rain nodded, fighting back the tears. She wished Dottie could stay with her forever. Lance brushed a tear gently from her cheek.

"She won't stop until she's got you under her roof you know. What do you think of that?"

"I like her, too." Rain squeaked. She tried to imagine what 'under her roof' meant but she couldn't let herself go there. She looked up at him. "You're very lucky to have a mom."

It didn't escape Lance's ear that she said 'a mom' not 'her for a mom.' It all seemed so simple with this one but something told him it wouldn't be. She had definitely responded to his mom, but Johnny's warnings to Dave still echoed in his head about her being delicate and explosive.

"How old were you when she abandoned you?" he asked.

She looked at him—how did he know?

"She left me with Johnny Sr. when I was twelve as a payment for her drugs."

"And he made you work for him?"

"Not like you think!" she replied, once again letting her eyes fall in a blind stare at the wall. "I sold drugs for him but the cops were on to me so I had to leave—I was too much of a liability. I always am."

"So he sent you to Johnny Jr.?"

She nodded. "I always said I'd never be like her, but here I am."

"You don't do drugs!" he pointed out quickly. "I know your tox screen came back clean. Rain, that's an incredible accomplishment in the world you come from."

He knew it went completely against his policies, but he had already done that when he brushed the tears away. She hadn't pulled away from him when he made that contact so he was going to push it one step further. He took her face gently in his hands and looked at her. It was easy to see she didn't like looking him in the eye—probably didn't like anyone doing the same to her. He pushed her hair back gently.

"I heard what you said to Officer Coop and I know you want out. I can help you out but you have to want it. You're in charge of what the rest of your life will look like. Rain, if you want a happy life like the one you've imagined must be there somewhere, you have to grab on now! And don't tell me you don't want this. You had a stash of cash and a gun. You wanted out."

Tears shone in her eyes. "What can you do? You just told her it wouldn't work."

"Mom tends to want things to happen yesterday and the system is slow. She means she wants you to go from this hospital bed to her house and that won't happen without a miracle!" Lance made sure she was listening as he spoke, searching out her gaze. "We're still waiting for them to decide if you are being charged and with what. The arrest part doesn't worry me that much—we can get you out on bail and it's actually easier to get you in the program that way. I'm not worried about that! What I'm worried about is all this talk of dying. The program is for the ones who want to live. Do you think you could maybe want that if you knew Dottie would be there to give you a few more hugs?"

Rain struggled now. That was a dream she had long since abandoned. He seemed to be able to see into her soul.

"You said you wanted to dress nice and go to the bank and be somebody. Why?"

"Cuz I am!" she responded through the tears that had once again gathered.

"Of course you are!" he replied, making sure to catch her eyes.

He liked this eye contact stuff, she decided. She looked into his face—he looked kind even though at times he seemed harsh. There was something in his expression that told her he could be mischievous but not malicious. She desperately wanted to trust him but that was not easy.

"I've heard that from a lot of guys and then they use me like a dog!" she spat at him.

"I haven't!" he defended, keeping his voice gentle.

She narrowed her eyes at him. She wanted to push him, make him angry. She knew what he wanted, what every man she'd ever met wanted.

"I bet if you could afford me, you would!"

He laughed. "You'd lose! I'm not into using women for a few moments of pleasure. I'm not buying it from you or anyone else."

He knew what she was thinking; he had to be a queer! He'd had this conversation before.

"I am not queer! Is it so hard for you to believe I really want to help you?" he didn't let her answer. "I'll take you to the bank, open that account with a check from an actual job—a respectable job—and you can walk out of there with your head held high."

"I've learned nothing in life comes without strings!" Rain informed him.

"And neither do I!" Lance admitted. "Only I come with a different kind of string. If I fight for you, **you** have to fight for you! How come you robbed the cop and went back?"

"I've tried to get away so many times but I never had anywhere to go."

"You ran and went back—that's a bad sign," Lance didn't realize he was thinking out loud. He took a breath. "It means you weren't ready to really fight to get out. Had you been, you could've showed up at the center, found me or one of my colleagues and we would've helped you!"

"How was I supposed to find you?" she argued.

"People who really want something, find it."

"How dare you!" she cried. "You think I wanted to stay? I looked and never found this place you talk about!"

He didn't want to upset her but he did want to know if she really wanted out. She glared at him with a spark in her eye. There was some fight still left here if you dug in the right place. Today he was not going to dig any further so he changed the subject.

"Rain, are you Johnny's girl?"

She hung her head. "You already know the answer."

"I know he took care of you but are you his main girl?"

"I guess," she said, feeling dirty even talking about it.

He stared at her. He'd swear she was embarrassed by it. Most girls were proud to announce they were the boss' main squeeze.

"I have to tell you, you don't fit the picture of the main girl of the boss. You are much too together. You aren't on drugs and you don't look like he beat you into submission. What did he take from you?"

She looked at him. Johnny really didn't take anything she didn't give him.

"I thought he cared!" she whispered.

Lance nodded—now that was familiar. He pushed himself off the bed and headed toward the door.

"Can you really help me?" she called to him.

It was a cry that sounded just before death in most cases. If he made one wrong step, she was done.

"I can only do as much as you do for yourself," he replied, before slipping out of the room.

She let her head sink back onto the pillow. Then there was no hope. She had never been able to do anything before to help herself. What had changed? She shook the thought from her head, choosing to dwell on the hug she had received from Dottie. She decided she didn't like Lance, but his mom was wonderful!

CHAPTER 22

With budget meetings eating up every spare moment, Lance found it impossible to get back to the hospital. One of the center's biggest supporters was pulling out and had everyone scrambling. The staff cuts followed and now Dave and Lance found themselves very short staffed, with more calls coming in than ever. Lance's shoulders slumped in defeat when the phone once again demanded his attention.

"Hello. Lance Hawkins," he answered, with a total lack of enthusiasm.

"Hey Lance!" Brad Coop greeted him on the other end. "You sound awful!"

"Thanks! That should cheer me up!"

"Well, I didn't really call to cheer you up!" Brad laughed on the other end. "I think the news I have will be another dose of spirit dampening."

"Hit me fast before I decide I can't take it and hang up on you!"

"Rain Patterson is not being charged with anything! They're letting her off. The guy she stole the money from is seeking public office and not willing to blemish his image with charging her and dragging it through court. Johnny's saying she acted in self-defense when she shot him, and the PI feels if he can slide this under the rug, he's happy. She's getting off free!"

"I can't believe it!" Lance cried. "I'll never get her into the farm program now!"

"Sorry, I know you don't want this one falling through the cracks. I gave her the news about half an hour ago."

"Thanks for calling, Brad. I guess I'd better get to the hospital and see what's up."

Lance hung up the phone, closed the file he was working on and jammed it into his brief case. He would be busy with paperwork again tonight! He stood, taking time to stretch. His ribs caught him and he gasped in pain. Would they ever heal? He almost made it out the door before the phone rang again. He debated just letting it ring but he finally picked it up.

"Hello, Mr. Hawkins!" a familiar voice greeted him.

"Maggie!" Lance sang, trying to sound happy to hear her voice.

"I thought you should know the doctor is discharging Rain today."

"Discharging her?" Lance asked like that was not possible.

"Yes. I thought I'd better let you know before she escaped on you."

"I'm on my way!" Lance said. This time he was out the door before the phone could summons him again.

He didn't get far, stopping to talk to Dave. Rain would need clothes and Lance didn't have the money to buy an outfit, but Lori would be about the same size. Dave was more than happy to help out.

"Just don't pick any of Lori's favorites!" Dave told him, handing him the keys to his house. "Are you coming back here?"

"I hope to," Lance sighed. "I guess I have to if you want to get back into your house—unless things are better between you and Lori?"

"Make sure you come back!" Dave replied grimly. "She's still not talking to me, and now she's working a big case so she's putting in a lot of overtime. Of course, if she does find a free moment, she's at her brother's side."

Rain stared at the doctor. He wasn't just releasing her from the hospital, he was kicking her out. She had no idea what to do—everyone she would call was dead or in the hospital.

"But where will I go?" she cried.

"Well, you can't live here!" the doctor informed her.

Rain knew where his head was—she could turn a few tricks and be as warm as a bug in no time. No one would ever see her as anything else.

Maggie wished she could kick that doctor in places that weren't ladylike at all. She put her arm around the girl who was now sobbing. The doctor ordered her to give Rain instructions on caring for her wound. He had no time to spend on this patient.

Lance pushed the door open and found them like that—Maggie with her hand wrapped around the sobbing Rain. He rolled his eyes. What now?

"You and my mom!" he whispered to Maggie.

She looked up, relieved that he had arrived.

"I hope you remembered some clothes?" Maggie questioned.

"I think I know the routine here!" he laughed, handing her a bag. "I had to rob Lori's closet for these, so I hope they fit."

Maggie smiled. She knew Lori's closet often got raided and wondered how the woman kept herself dressed. She helped Rain put the clothes on after chasing Lance back into the hall until she was proper.

"Is it safe?" Lance asked, sticking his head carefully through the opening between the door and frame. If she wasn't, Maggie would catch his nose if he wasn't quick.

"Come on in!" Maggie announced.

Lance pushed his way into the room, smiling his approval at Rain. There was no denying her beauty that shone through even with her pale pallor. Maggie hurried passed him to get him the information he would need to keep up the girl's care.

"Don't you leave until I've talked to you!" she told him. "Rain is a little stubborn about taking pain meds."

He nodded and then turned to Rain. "So tonight we'll stay at my place and then figure out how to get you out to the farm, if that's okay with you."

"Why can't I stay in my house?"

"I guess, if you want to go back you can," Lance said slowly. "Johnny won't be there. I'm guessing with him gone, the other girls will rule the roost."

"How much longer will he be here?"

"Until he's better and then I think his sister has plans for his life. Am I to understand that you don't want my help?"

She bit her lip to stop it from trembling. She was scared—scared to go with this man and scared not to. Either way, her life had changed in ways that she couldn't understand and no place was offering security.

"I guess I'll go with you," she whispered.

"I know we're pretty much strangers, but don't forget, I owe you. You saved my life, so let me help you find yours."

She nodded, trying to be brave.

"Would you like to see Johnny before we head out of here?"

She nodded. "I would like that very much."

They stopped at his room but Johnny was sleeping. Rain let her hand run through his hair, tears filling her eyes as she took him in.

"I'd let you stay longer but we have to get going," Lance said, interrupting the moment.

He didn't know what to do. Rain looked exhausted after the move from the hospital to the car, and he had to get to the office where he had clients waiting. He didn't really want to leave her alone at the apartment with all her talk of killing herself. Maybe he should have left her at Johnny's side but that didn't seem wise either.

"Do you feel up to sitting around the office for a couple of hours?" he asked, knowing it wasn't even fair to ask.

"Sitting around?" she questioned.

"I don't want to leave you alone and find you dead when I get back."

"Oh," she sighed, glancing out the window as she spoke.

"So do I trust you alone or do I take you with me to the office?"

She hid her face from him not wanting him to see the tears. He didn't trust her and for some reason that hurt.

"I guess I'd better go to the office then," she complied.

He nodded. He could hear the huskiness of her voice and knew she was crying. He prayed that softness of heart would survive. It was another reminder that she was inside there somewhere.

Rain stared at the dilapidated building he pulled up to and cringed. No wonder she never found this place! He assisted her out of the car, hoping he wasn't adding to her discomfort instead of helping. He invited her in for her first look at Lance's world.

He pulled open the heavy glass door, knowing exactly how heavy it felt with broken ribs so thought he'd save her the pain on the gunshot wound. He pushed her inside.

Through the glass panes of the second set of doors, she could see hallways heading both directions with two doors directly in front of her. She could hear people but it didn't sound like talking.

"Those lead to the gym," Lance explained, guiding her into the hall. "My office is on the third floor. The gym kind of takes up the first two."

He led her to the staircase where he patiently waited for her to make her way up, knowing again how she felt—this hurt. He held open every door along the way, much to Rain's surprise.

"This is my office," he announced, as they stopped to unlock the door. "Now what are you going to do while I go to my meeting that I'm already late for?"

She stared in horror around the small room. Paper seemed to cover every inch of the space and where it didn't cover things, coffee cups did.

"If you want, you can put away some files for me but if you don't feel up to it, there's a couch in the lounge down the hall where you can relax."

"Files?" she asked.

He pointed to a stack of file folders on the corner of his desk.

"I arrange them alphabetically in that filing cabinet right there."

She nodded and he was gone. She took a deep breath and tried to decide if she wanted to even touch anything in this room. She finally grabbed the file on the top of the stack—this mess was unbearable!

Lance stared at the clock tapping his pencil nervously on the desk. This meeting was lasting forever!

"So," Lance finally interrupted, unable to listen to any more, "we're in big financial trouble?"

"Very!" Max, the center's head administrator nodded.

"Is there any hope?" Dave asked, running through the numbers in his head one more time.

"We need to find a corporate sponsor willing to pour some money into this place, but like I've said, they'd rather support something like an animal rights group than this. We don't throw good parties or attract the same crowd."

"It's so much easier to close our eyes and look at something else than look at the truth about humanity!" Lance sneered.

He left the meeting feeling frustrated. They couldn't find funding while people like Rain fell through the cracks everyday. He vowed not to lose this one. He was fire hot angry at it all and suddenly felt the need to prove his cause as worthy.

Rain bit back the tears as the painkillers seeped from her body and the true nature of the injury set in. The pain was incredible! She sat down in Lance's chair fighting to regain control.

Lance opened the office door to find Rain bent over his garbage can. He should've taken her to the apartment.

"I take it you're hurting?" he greeted, when she pulled herself up.

She nodded ever so slightly, afraid any movement would set her off again. He grabbed the package Maggie gave him and pawed at the contents until he found what he was looking for: painkiller. But could she hold it down?

He had no choice but to hope she would. He guided her to the lounge and grabbed a glass of water. She didn't argue, taking the pill.

"You'd better just sit for a bit," he advised her. "I have a couple of people to meet with, but it shouldn't take more than twenty minutes. Then I'm taking you home."

She waited, hoping the pill would stay down. It seemed like forever before he came back, but he was pretty proud to have finished in seventeen minutes instead of twenty. It didn't seem like a great accomplishment to her.

"Ready to go home?" he asked.

She nodded.

It turned out home was another dilapidated building. She hugged close to him as he guided her to the door. Two women standing on the sidewalk waved at him.

"Tuli?" Lance called, admonishing a woman standing on the sidewalk.

"Hey, Mr. Hawkins!" the girl replied.

"Please tell me you aren't working?"

"Ah, Mr. Hawkins, you know I gotta eat!"

"We all do, but some of us get paid for doing jobs that don't cost more than they pay!"

"I made more than you today!" she shot back.

"Yes, but I can sleep with myself at night!" he called, unlocking the outside door to his apartment building. "There are more ways that a job pays than money!"

Rain shivered. She couldn't stand to think about the woman's life.

"See why I want to help you?" Lance stated, guiding her up the stairs. "Her pimp was arrested and she refuses to let me help her. She's got no one to get her back onto the good streets, and she'll die if she doesn't get help, but she's a stubborn one!"

"I've never been that kind!" Rain said in her defense.

"Rain, they all end up there," Lance replied harshly. "As you get older, you lose that beauty of youth and suddenly you fall out of favor, and next thing you know, you're doing exactly what she's doing."

Rain wished she could hit him, but she hurt too much to even try. How dare he assume she would go to that level! But then her thoughts went back to Sissy and she knew he was right. They arrived at the door and Lance breathed in deeply.

"Mom's here already!" he smiled, opening the door to the smell of fresh buns. "Hi, Mom!"

"Lance, where have you been?" Dottie demanded. "Maggie told me you took Rain out of the hospital and I thought you must be here. Where have you been with this girl?"

"I had a meeting," Lance explained, grabbing a bun off the counter.

"You had a meeting?" Dottie said back to him, mocking his tone. Then she let go, revealing her true feelings. "Let me tell you, Lance Hawkins, this young lady does not have the strength and energy to sit in that dingy place and wait while you go to meetings!"

Rain listened, looking from mom to son. She wondered how Lance would respond.

"I thought about bringing her here but she hasn't exactly been stable! I didn't need her killing herself in my apartment."

"You could've called me. I was in the hospital!"

"I know, but Mom, Bryan needs you, too. Anyway, she's here now so why don't you go do your mom thing, and I'll go to the other room and try to catch up with some of my work!"

Dottie wasn't done with him and he knew it, but Rain would come first now. She turned to the girl and gave her a gentle hug.

"How are you feeling?"

"I'm fine," Rain mumbled.

Dottie pushed her toward the next room—the living room that bore a striking resemblance to Lance's office. Papers covered the whole room! She was beginning to think his name should be Clutter!

"Now would you like a bath?" Dottie offered.

"That would be nice!" Rain nodded.

Much to Rain's surprise, the bathroom was spotless and almost nice. It didn't compare to Johnny's place, but she could handle this. Dottie ran her a nice warm bubble bath.

"Now don't get your dressing wet!" the older woman warned, pulling the bathroom door shut so Rain could enjoy her privacy. She played with the bubbles.

Rain thought about her life. She had never before in her life had another woman draw her bath that she could remember. Did she even bathe as a child? She couldn't remember, but she must have.

"Lance!" Dottie called, heading from the bathroom to the kitchen. She found him by the table.

"Okay, Mom, let me have it!" Lance smiled.

"She's not well enough to be sitting in that place!"

"I gave her a choice and she chose the office."

"And you didn't influence her?"

"I guess maybe a little!" Lance admitted. "Mom, what am I going to do? She's not being charged at all so she won't qualify for a program. There's no way she can handle being set free and left on her own. She'll be back at her old life in seconds. I can't take her in. Not only does it violate my own rules, I just took another pay cut today."

"Oh, Lance!" Dottie said quietly, knowing very well the boy couldn't make ends meet as it was.

He shook his head in frustration. "Mom, I can't pay the bills anymore. If Lori and Dave didn't feed me, I'd be starving."

"You know Ricky is looking for some help at the farm," Dottie reminded him.

"I don't want to have to make the trip back and forth. Mom, I work twenty hours a day now. I don't think I can put any more time in."

"Twenty hour days?" Dottie cried, staring in disbelief at her son. "Lance you can't do this! Your body won't last at that rate!"

"What do I do? They call and call. Mom, what if I don't answer and the person on the other end kills herself because I don't work extra hours?"

"You can't carry that!" she told him. "Son, you've got to slow down. A dead Lance won't save any lives at all!"

"I know!" Lance said, dropping his head into his hands. "I don't know what to do. We started with five counselors working fulltime and now, there's me and Dave and one other who volunteers there one day a week. Most of those who were laid off keep volunteering some time, but it's not the same. They have jobs—we're lucky if we can get eight volunteer hours a week right now."

"Lance, take the job at the farm at least for a little while!" Dottie ordered.

"And where does that leave Dave?"

"Is he putting in those kinds of hours?"

"Not quite. He usually puts in ten-hour days. He does have a family. The center is my family!"

Dottie shook her head. She would talk to Arthur about all this. He had much more success talking to this son than she ever had.

"Do you have an extra tee shirt?" she asked, realizing none of this would be solved tonight.

"Yeah, in my drawer. I take it Rain needs it?"

"Yes."

"I guess I might have to take her back to her house even though that may have very bad repercussions, but she needs clothes and I can't afford any."

"Lori was saying Johnny wanted some things from there, too. Maybe the two of you could make sure Rain doesn't stay behind?"

"Isn't Johnny still in the hospital?"

"No—he got released, too."

Lance shook his head, thinking that was even worse than Rain getting the boot.

"I'll think about it," Lance replied, draining a cup of milk. It was so nice to have Mom around. "I think Lori might like Rain staying behind."

Dottie ignored him, heading to his bedroom to find a shirt for Rain but the comment nagged at her. Why would he even say something like that about Lori?

Rain accepted the towel that Dottie wrapped around her, only a little embarrassed to have the woman see her naked. She didn't protest the help with the shirt either. Finally, Rain found herself wrapped in the thick warmth of Lance's housecoat.

They headed to the kitchen, going passed Lance who was now buried in the papers. Rain didn't like the way he worked, but she had no time to dwell on it. Dottie led her to the kitchen and bid her sit by the small dining table.

"I hope you like chicken noodle soup!" Dottie smiled, setting a steaming bowl of the wonderful smelling broth in front of her. "And if Lance didn't eat all the buns, you can have one or two of those too!"

Rain ate, not sure if she would hurt Dottie's feelings by refusing, but the amount of food in front of her scared her. She never ate this much in a day.

"Mom," Lance laughed, walking into the room, "you've fed too many boys!"

He grabbed one of the buns from Rain's plate and it disappeared into his mouth.

"That's not good for you!" Rain informed him.

"Really?" he smiled at her. "So you're a health nut?"

"I kind of have to stay in shape for my . . ."

"Job?" he asked, finishing the sentence for her.

She looked down, ashamed of that truth. He felt bad but knew all these things had to be faced, and there was no time like the present to start.

"So what happens now?" Rain asked quietly.

"My mom and dad have agreed to let you stay at the farm with them. Now the thing is getting you some help, and I haven't solved that problem yet."

"I must really look like I need help the way you always bring it up."

"You aren't alone. Lots of people need help."

"So why me?"

"I don't let anyone who wants help slip through the cracks if I can possibly help it; and with you, I can help it. I just have to decide how it will all work."

Rain nodded but really didn't understand what he was talking about. Her shoulder was again hurting and she could feel her body starting to tremble.

"You need to get to bed!" he ordered, deciding all this could wait.

He helped Rain up and guided her to a bedroom that had to be his. She looked at him questioningly.

"I'll be in the other room," he said, with a wave of his hand. "Normally, you wouldn't even be staying here but Mom offered to stay. I won't stay alone with a girl under any circumstances."

She nodded, trying to decide why that would be. Whatever the case, with Dottie here, she would be safe—that she was sure of.

CHAPTER 23

In the morning, Rain woke up feeling disoriented but soon remembered she was at Lance's place, and she could smell something cooking. She pulled herself out of bed carefully. She vaguely remembered Dottie coming to her in the night with medications, but she took them without even really waking up. She headed to the bathroom first and then passed the living room. She stared in amazement—the room that yesterday looked like a paper storm had hit it was now tidy with a neat pile of file folders stacked in the middle of the coffee table. Lance lay sprawled on the couch, still sound asleep.

"Good morning!" Dottie greeted.

"Good morning," Rain responded with little enthusiasm.

"Now, would you like some breakfast?"

"I guess."

"Rain, if you don't want to eat, don't!" Dottie told her. "That guy in there will be waking any second now and he'll inhale any leftovers!"

Dottie finished setting the table, letting Rain sip her coffee. She gave Rain a wink. "Watch this."

Rain stared at her confused.

"Just watch!" Dottie said with a nod.

Rain didn't know what she was watching for, but like magic Lance appeared in the doorway. He looked ragged and worn but ready to eat.

"He can always tell when I have the meal ready!" Dottie laughed.

"Yes he can!" a very tired sounding Lance responded. "I can also tell you didn't wake me at six like I asked you to. Now I'm two hours late for work!"

"Sit down!" Dottie ordered. "The last time I looked at the clock it was four in the morning and you were still at it! There's no way I was waking you at six! Now eat."

Lance knew better than to argue and hurriedly ate. Rain shook her head.

"That's not good for you!" Rain told him once again.

"Neither is being late!" Lance replied, downing his coffee. He hurried out of the kitchen to get ready to go.

"Lance," Dottie called after him. "Dad's coming today. I think we're all meeting at Dave and Lori's. I want to spend some time with Bryan. Is there anything you want me to do for Rain?"

"Just bring her to the office around four. I have to get some forms filled in," Lance was still pulling his shirt on when he headed out the door. "Bryan's car is outside. He wants you to take it to the farm. I guess he doesn't trust my neighborhood!"

He was gone. Dottie sighed and looked at Rain.

"He's killing himself!"

Rain didn't have anything to say in response.

"I think maybe you have what we need!" Dottie smiled.

"Me?"

"Rain, if he has to come to the farm for you, he can take the job there."

"I don't think I'm much of a drawing card," Rain said, with a shake of her head.

"I don't know if much can get him to pull back from that job of his, but you have as good a chance of accomplishing that as anyone." Dottie sighed again. She would have to pray for an answer.

Dottie dropped Rain off at the center at four like requested. Rain found Lance about an hour behind schedule, but he still had a smile for her. She wondered how he could look so alert when she knew he had to be exhausted. He led her to a waiting room.

"I'm with a client right now so is it okay if you wait here for just a second?"

"I guess," she sighed, looking around the room. It wasn't clean in her estimation but she could probably survive here for a moment or two.

"Great!" he said, heading back toward his office. "I'll make this quick."

An hour past before she saw him again. People wandered in and out of the room, making her very nervous, but no one seemed to want to bother her so she just tried to make herself invisible. She was creeped out by this place. When Lance finally appeared, she ran to greet him.

"Miss me?" he asked.

"I don't like new places, especially ones where I don't know anybody."

"How did you ever do your job?" Lance laughed at her as he guided her back to the office.

"Johnny would threaten to kill me," she replied honestly.

"I guess that worked!" Lance acknowledged as they entered his office. He bid her take a seat. "So we need to get an action plan worked out here. Could you fill in this form?" he asked, showing her a piece of paper.

She looked at it and then back at him. "I've never been taught much about reading and writing. I know my alphabet and numbers."

"And you put all those files away for me?" he said, his face beaming with pride. "That had to be a pretty big job for you."

"I know my alphabet!" she repeated.

"I wondered why you left the files you did. You didn't know what to do when the letters were so much the same in some names!"

He hadn't realized he was thinking out loud until he heard the quiet muffled sobs. He knelt in front of her, handing her a tissue.

"Hey! It's okay. I don't expect you to know stuff you've never learned. Ask me to make a martini and I'm lost, but I bet you could do it."

She stared at him. Of course she could do that!

"Well," he said, returning to his chair, "this just changed things a bit."

He rubbed his temple trying to figure a way out of this new development. This would make almost every program out of reach, but he was not giving up on this girl. She had way too much going for her.

"I guess I'll have to think this over, but right now we need to get to the house where Johnny and Lori are meeting us."

"Johnny?"

"Yeah. He's out of the hospital. Speaking of which, how are you feeling?"

"Sore."

"We'll try to make it a short stay. I'm really hoping you have some clothes there."

"You mean we're going to my house?"

"Didn't I just say that?"

Rain smiled. It was the first time Lance saw the girl smile and he had to admit, she really was very beautiful, and the smile did something wonderful to her whole being. He wrapped his arm protectively around her as he guided her out of the office.

"Dave, I'm leaving!" he called.

Dave watched them walk away, surprised to see Lance Hawkins looking so happy with a real woman in his arms. And he was heading out of the office early, too. He'd have to rib him about this at supper tonight!

Rain's excitement as they pulled up to the house was almost palpable. Lance couldn't resist smiling at her, thinking she looked like a kid with a ten-dollar bill in a candy shop. He was glad Lori pulled up right behind him or he'd have had to prevent Rain from breaking down the door.

"I can't believe it!" Lori commented. "Lance, you're actually on time!"

"Hey, I want to eat tonight!" Lance replied. Lori laughed.

"If it's not too much for your ribs, can you help me get Johnny into his wheelchair?"

Lance helped get Johnny out of the car and then they headed to the door. Brad Coop pulled up and joined them.

"Caught a couple of girls trying to break in here this morning. I need Johnny to tell me if they took anything."

Lance could see the weariness settle on Johnny's face. It had to have been a tough week. Dave had told him that it looked like they would drop the charges down to self defense but that would be decided by a judge.

They made their way inside where Lance stared in complete shock. No wonder Rain struggled with staying with him! This place was a palace.

"You live here, hey?" he said, his mouth still gaping.

"Well, I used to!" Rain said. "Now I'm staying with you!"

Johnny smiled at Rain and she looked at Lance, her eyes pleading for permission to go to him.

"Sure!" Lance smiled. He really couldn't do anything to stop her but she didn't seem to know that.

"Hey, Babes!" Johnny greeted her. "They taking good care of you?"

"I guess. It ain't like livin' here!"

"Yeah, I'm guessing that boy is poor as a church mouse and probably a work hound just like Dave."

"His mom is real nice," Rain allowed. "She takes care of me like a mom even though she hardly even knows me."

"I'm glad!" Johnny sighed. "Look, Babes, I'm still hurting here so I thought maybe you could help my Sis pick out some stuff I could live with wearing?"

"Of course, Johnny," she said, more than ready to be a help. "What's going to happen to you?"

Johnny hung his head. He didn't really like to think about it and he didn't want Rain worrying.

"I'm facing some charges!" he said, trying to laugh it off. "Lori's helping me; she's a good lawyer."

Rain saw through the brave face and bit her lip nervously. She should be the one facing charges, and she was getting off and heading to a place that would treat her like a lady. She couldn't hide the guilt she felt.

"Aw Rain," Johnny sighed. "Look, I can handle this but you—you couldn't—and you know I couldn't stand to think I sent you to a place like that. You're my girl! Maybe if Lori can get this all worked out, you and I can do this thing up right and really get married like you want."

"Serious?" she asked while she still had breath.

"Serious. Mind you, we'll see where you are when I finally get out of this mess. Probably be married with five kids by that time."

She laughed. "Johnny, we've been together all these years and never had any kids!"

"Yeah, well, you never know—it might be me. Now go up there and get me some clothes—I think these are Dave's and I can't stand them."

"I can't say Lori's fashion sense excites me either," she replied.

"I'm guessing they'll make me buy new clothes," Johnny sighed. "I won't look holy enough in any of my things."

"What about me?" she questioned. "Do I even have any money to buy some new things? What about stuff I need?"

"Why? I thought you had these people helping you?"

"Lance doesn't have much money and I feel kind of bad spending what he does have."

"Are you staying with him permanent like?" Johnny asked, narrowing his eyes at Lance in a wave of jealousy.

"I stayed there last night with his mom. I don't think he likes girls."

Lance saw Johnny staring and had to know what they could be talking about. He wandered over.

"You better not even think about doing my girl!" Johnny whispered to him.

"I wasn't!" Lance smiled. "I have another mistress actually!"

"Oh you do, do you?"

"Yes I do—I spend twenty hours a day with her—it's called my job."

"You're just like Dave!" Johnny sneered. "You have to be a queer not to see this girl ahead of a job!"

"She *is* my job!" Lance smirked. Johnny's lip curled in anger. "Calm down, Johnny. I'm a social worker—a counselor. I help people you mess up make some sense out of the mess you made. Rain is very pretty, but I'm a little short on time and energy—thanks to guys like you!"

Rain blushed. Johnny calmed down but he was going to keep tabs on this guy. If he was really working with Rain, the girl would cast her spell, and Johnny wasn't about to lose his girl to this social worker.

"Johnny, do I have any money?" Rain repeated.

"Sure, Babes. I'll make sure you get some living funds. I'll get Lori to handle it."

Rain smiled, completely satisfied, but Lance wasn't quite so sold on the pledge.

"Johnny, how much money does Rain have and why doesn't she control it?"

"Why don't you mind your own business?"

"I am minding my client's business and I want to know why Rain has money but doesn't seem to know that?" Lance demanded. He wasn't buckling under Johnny's threatening looks.

"I take care of Rain!" Johnny informed him coldly.

"She doesn't need you for that anymore!" Lance replied with an equal coldness. "In fact, when I'm done with her, she won't need you for anything."

Johnny stared at this man with loathing. He was messing in a place Johnny didn't want anyone messing. Rain was exactly the way he wanted her.

"I'll go get those things!" Rain announced, grabbing Lance's shoulder gently. "You will help me, right? I mean, my shoulder still hurts too much to really do this myself."

Lance let his gaze go back to her and she led him to the stairs. Her heart was pounding in her chest, having never in her life seen anyone stand up to Johnny like that, and she feared for his safety if he didn't back off. She knew Johnny's temper and didn't want to see Lance hurt.

The bedroom was huge, like everything in the house.

"So this was your room?" Lance asked.

"Mine and Johnny's," Rain replied. She wished she could stay and enjoy just one last bath but she knew that wouldn't be happening.

"He won't be using his methods on me," he informed her.

"You don't know him," she replied.

"That's were you're wrong. I know him and a hundred more like him."

They quickly chose her clothes. This was an easy job, since she didn't want anything she had ever worn for work. Lance was pleasantly surprised with her choices, thinking they would even be practical for the farm.

Lori joined them and Rain told them which clothes Johnny would want. These were much more what they expected.

"Have you and Dave had a heart-to-heart yet?" he questioned while Rain busied herself with packing.

"We haven't had much of a chance to talk," Lori whispered back.

"You have to stop putting this off!"

"Can I take my jewelry?" Rain asked quietly, feeling she was interrupting them.

"Is it yours?" Lori asked with an edge of disgust in her voice.

"It was given to me!" Rain stated, feeling Lori hated her, but she wasn't sure why.

"I'll ask Johnny!" Lori announced. She didn't want this prostitute who got her dad's love to get anything she didn't deserve.

"Why does she hate me?" Rain asked Lance once Lori was out of the room.

"I don't know, but I think it has to do with her dad. You were pretty close to him, right?"

"He took care of me until he sold me out and sent me with Johnny."

"Yeah, well, he had a habit of selling people out. Lori was really disappointed with her dad after she learned about his career."

"That's not my fault."

Lance thought about responding, but Lori returned. He would finish the conversation later.

"Johnny said you could take it all. It's yours." Lori announced.

Lance helped Rain finish packing. He could see her pallor whitening with each passing moment.

"I'm going to be in such trouble!" he said, looking at her. "You look ready to melt down. I'd better get you to Lori and Dave's."

He guided her down the stairs where Officer Coop now had two women standing in front of Johnny.

"You!" one shouted when she saw Rain. Brad held the woman back so she couldn't attack.

"Sissy!" Rain cried, hiding behind Lance.

"Leave Rain alone!" Johnny ordered. Sissy shrank back.

"Let's get out of here!" Lance said, gently guiding Rain passed Sissy who was still glaring at her.

Rain didn't dare breathe until she was back in the car heading away from the house with Lance.

"I don't ever want to go there again!" she cried. "Sissy will kill me!"

"And exactly who is Sissy?"

"She was Johnny's girl until I came, and then she got kicked out of the house—not just out of his bedroom. She became Tommy's girl, and I think they were planning to get rid of Johnny and take his place. I guess I ruined the whole plan."

"I see." Lance felt everything she said made it clearer—she needed to get out of this place.

They pulled into a driveway that led to a modest house.

"This is where Dave and Lori live." Lance announced.

"He lives a lot better than you!" Rain said, raising her eyebrows.

"He has a better wife. She works for the prosecution side of the law—government payroll."

Rain nodded, trying to understand and hoping he'd explain more, but he didn't. They headed to the door where Lance told her to knock while he hid behind the door. A child opened the door and looked around. He saw Lance's car but this was not Lance.

"Hello!" he said quietly. "Can I help you?"

"I think I'm supposed to be here for supper," Rain replied.

The boy eyed her carefully and then Lance jumped out and the boy screamed, running back full speed into the house. Lance followed while a completely stunned Rain stood frozen to the spot.

"Come on in," Dave invited as soon as he heard the call of battle. "I'm Dave, by the way."

"Hi! I think I met you at the hospital," Rain acknowledged.

"Yeah, I guess you did."

He led her to the living room where she sat down, glad to get off her feet. Lance came charging in, followed close behind by two boys now. He grabbed a cushion and held it in front of him while grabbing a second in the other hand, using them to pummel the boys if they dared come into range.

"We'll get you, Uncle Lance!" the smaller boy threatened.

"Just try, Carter!" Lance smiled.

"Let's get him, Cody!" the brave boy said, charging ahead.

Lance dropped his cushion and substituted the child for a shield instead. Carter laughed, trying to break free.

Somewhere in the house, the doorbell sounded. Dottie and Arthur walked in and heard the noise. Dottie hurried to the living room.

"Lance Hawkins! No wonder those ribs won't heal!" she scolded.

"Aw Mom! The boys would never forgive me if I didn't do battle!" he sighed, now holding a boy in each arm.

Arthur smiled when he walked into the room. He grabbed the smaller boy and sat down with him. Soon the tickling started.

"No! Grandpa Arthur!" the boy squealed.

Dottie threw her arms up in frustration as she watched Cody wiggling and kicking in an effort to get free and help Carter.

"Okay guys!" Lance smiled, releasing Carter, fearing a hit to the ribs that were indeed still tender. "We don't want to get in trouble with Grandma Dottie!"

The boys looked at each other and ran off.

"They'll be back!" Lance announced, taking a seat beside Rain. "So Dad, I hear Ricky might need some help at the farm?"

"He's been indicating things are getting a bit busy," Arthur nodded. "Mom said you weren't considering it."

"And I wasn't until this afternoon."

"Oh? What changed?"

"Rain doesn't really read and write so she's going to need some extra tutoring. I know things are already hectic down there so I was planning on teaching her. My only concern is that there's no room at the farm right now."

"It's full but I think Mom has a plan. I do believe she's hoping to give Rain the spare bedroom at the house."

"Mom doesn't like the idea of me keeping her in my apartment?" Lance questioned, knowing very well that would not be happening.

"I think she'd better come stay with us!" Arthur smiled. "My understanding was that she would be returning with us to the farm tonight."

"What?" Lance questioned. "Dad, I don't even know if Rain is stable enough to be in that environment."

"Talk to Mom," Arthur said with a shrug of his shoulders.

Lance was angry. His mom was getting too involved with this one, but he had no time to consider it. The boys, as predicted, were returning to continue the fight, and Lance spent the rest of the time playing with them until they were called to the meal. Rain felt awful but obediently made her way to the table. Lori seated her between Dave and Johnny who sat at the end with the wheelchair. Dottie sat across from her with Arthur beside her. Cody and Carter squeezed Lance between the two of them. It was obvious the boys both needed to be beside 'Uncle' Lance to keep peace at the dinner table.

"So Lance," Dave smiled, with a twinkle in his eye. "You and Rain seem to get along well! Aren't you afraid being that close to a breathing woman might upset your mistress?"

Rain looked over at Lance. What mistress?

"I don't think my mistress needs to worry!" Lance laughed.

"If your sister were here," Arthur joined in, "she'd be asking how you could compare a warm body to a file folder!"

"And I would tell her she should try it sometime. A nice thick file can be amazing company some nights!"

Everyone laughed except the boys, Johnny and Rain. They didn't get it.

"I guess I had better explain," Dave said, still chuckling. "Lance here is married to his work."

"So am I!" Johnny quipped back.

"But you're getting a divorce!" Lori chimed in sharply.

Lance and Dave couldn't help but laugh at Johnny's contorted face. Even Rain smiled.

The mood lightened during the meal. Then Arthur rose.

"We've got a long drive ahead of us and, from what I hear, our passenger isn't up for a late night." He winked at Rain.

"I didn't exactly tell her all the details," Dottie stated. "Rain, you're heading out with us tonight."

"Why?" Johnny demanded. "My girl doesn't need to go anywhere. She can come stay here with me."

"She's isn't your girl," Lance growled, having heard him say that once too often. "And in case you forgot, your freedom is temporary. Rain needs a stable environment." He turned to his mom, "So what program is Rain going to be on?"

"You know as well as I do that this child needs a solid base right now. Dad and I can offer that."

"Mom, she's not Mel. She's got issues that I'm not sure you're up to dealing with. I know Dad can, but the house is not the same as the dorms. Can you really handle this?"

"I think I can," Dottie said, indignant at what he was insinuating.

"I'm just a little worried that you're getting in over your head. I can't argue that Rain needs placement, but I don't want to hear any complaints when she turns out to be a little more difficult than expected."

"We'll handle it," Arthur assured him.

Lance nodded, knowing they had made up their minds.

"Well, let's get her stuff transferred to your car," he sighed.

Dave stood. "It was good you could come." He took Arthur's hand. "Dottie, you take care not to overdo it now."

Lori pulled Dottie aside, handing her an old looking box. "Rain's mother wanted her to have this."

Dottie stared at it. "So give it to her."

"She doesn't want it or anything from me. I thought maybe in time—if you keep it for her."

Dottie nodded, tucking the box under her arm.

Rain was glad to be on her way. Her feelings were up and down about everything. It would be nice to have a place to just think. In no time, she was curled up in the back seat, fast asleep.

Johnny didn't say anything more, choosing to pout in a corner while they headed out the door. Lance found himself wondering about the two. It seemed like an unusual relationship. He went over to Johnny while Lori and Dave said their farewells to Arthur and Dottie.

"I don't want to talk to you," Johnny declared.

"Well, that's too bad, because I need to talk to you."

Lance knew the man was trapped and now leaned in to take in every word.

Lori headed to the kitchen to start the dishes as soon as Arthur and Dottie left. Having gained all that Johnny was willing to give up, Lance followed her to the kitchen.

"I know dishes aren't the top priority in your coming in here," she told him. "I know this is a counseling session."

"So when are you going to talk to him about all this?" he stated, confirming her thoughts.

"I haven't got this all settled in my brain yet."

"That's an excuse," he accused. "Talking this out with someone would probably help get it straight in your brain."

"That's pretty easy for you to say," Lori shot back. "You have a nice neat little family!"

"With a former prostitute for a sister," he reminded her. "Lori, I don't get the way you're acting here. You can't choose the family you're born into."

She didn't say anything more—Dave was coming with some of the things from the table. She did see Lance roll his eyes at her but chose to ignore it.

CHAPTER 24

Rain remembered being tucked in the night before and now here she was in a bedroom that only existed in her dreams. The walls were painted a pale pink and the whole room seemed fluffy with lace. This true little girl's room was something Rain had never had before. Dottie poked her head in the door to see if she was awake.

"Oh, you are up," she smiled. "Are you feeling up to having some breakfast?"

"I think so," Rain nodded.

"Let me help you up!" Dottie offered.

Rain sat at a table that once again she really couldn't believe existed: the lace tablecloth, the vase of homegrown flowers in the center—movies come to life. The blooms weren't perfect but the whole thing went beyond perfection for Rain.

"Do you always live like this?" she asked.

"Pretty much!" Dottie smiled. "In the summer, I just enjoy the flowers outside, but Ricky has been working on a greenhouse with grow lights so we can have flowers all year round. We sell bouquets to locals who want something for a special occasion. Once winter sets in, we didn't have a lot of work for the boys so we started this."

"I can't really imagine men enjoying growing flowers."

"They don't, but it fits with their program. Once the men realize that the flowers, like people—especially women, are delicate, they do okay. They don't have to like it as long as they learn from it."

Rain nodded. This place was very strange—the men had to do things they didn't like! She wondered what the women did.

After breakfast, Dottie led Rain to the bathroom and drew her a lovely bubble bath. Rain watched, wondering why this woman would do this for her but didn't say anything. Then Dottie helped her get her shirt off, fearing she would hurt her shoulder.

"I don't like anyone seeing me naked!" Rain protested to deaf ears.

Soon Rain was sinking into the water. Even Dottie's help seemed normal and wonderful. Rain couldn't help but think this must be what a home was like.

Dottie reappeared at the door about twenty minutes later carrying shampoo and conditioner.

"Now let me wash that hair!"

"I can do it!" Rain replied.

"Nonsense! You have a gunshot wound and a couple of broken ribs. I don't think you even realize how hard it would be to wash your own hair!"

It was becoming very clear that it was pointless to argue with Dottie! Rain let her wash her hair but she wasn't letting her wash anything else!

"You have such beautiful hair!" Dottie exclaimed, rinsing the last of the conditioner out.

Rain remained silent.

"You're such a beautiful girl!" Dottie continued.

Rain sniffed at that!

"You don't agree?" Dottie questioned.

"I do not agree!" Rain replied in a very certain tone.

"So how would you describe yourself?"

"Ugly."

Dottie was taken aback! How could this girl not see the beauty she possessed?

"I don't know how you can describe yourself as anything but lovely! How can you not look in the mirror and see that?"

"I don't look in the mirror!" Rain mumbled.

Dottie didn't say anything. The girl always looked groomed so she had assumed a mirror was involved. She finished her hair and hurried to fetch a housecoat. She stared at the room—something was different and then it hit her; the mirrors were all covered. She'd have to mention this to Lance.

When Rain emerged from the bathroom, she discovered her day was just beginning. Dottie had a full morning planned that would start with joining the woman in the kitchen.

"Rain, I would like you to meet Mia," Dottie smiled.

The girls took one another in carefully, mumbling a quick "hello."

"I have to give Mia this cooking class today so I thought Rain, you should join us."

Rain tried not to let her distaste at the thought of cooking show. She could see Mia was looking just as excited as she felt.

"Mia is joining us because cooking involves math and she has some difficulty with that subject," Dottie rambled.

"I don't have any trouble with math," Rain declared.

"I didn't say you did," Dottie explained. "I think you are here more for the cooking end of this."

Rain listened to the instructions and did as she was told. She didn't want to have to leave this place, and she felt not doing as she told would get her a one-way ticket back to the street.

Lance was up at five. He had wasted enough time lately and it was time to get back on track. He was out the door by six after a time of prayer and Bible reading—something he desperately needed. He knew his spiritual food was more important than his physical needs and yet this past week, the first had suffered. He felt renewed and ready to do battle as he entered the center.

He was the first to arrive and headed to his desk. The front doors didn't get unlocked until eight so he had two hours to get things ready for the upcoming storm. And it always was a storm. Lance couldn't remember a day when this place didn't become insane at some point—usually five minutes after the doors opened until they were closed at nine in the evening. Rain's presence had left him with the same workload and less time. He hated playing catch-up!

He sat down and started looking at his appointments for the day, going through the files and making mental notes of what issues to discuss with each client if nothing tragic had occurred since the last time he saw them. Then he checked his messages—all fifty-three of them. He quickly deleted the four from his Mom knowing those were just going to involve pet projects he didn't have time for. He wrote down the numbers, putting stars behind the most urgent ones knowing he would have to try to get back to most of them at some point in the day. One thing stood out on his day planner—a meeting with a new potential supporter. It was Dave's scrawl. He would have to ask Dave why he had to attend.

Dave came in about fifteen minutes after Lance arrived.

"I see you're getting back to normal!" Dave smiled.

"I sure hope so! I'll have to get to see Bryan sometime today or Mom will let me know she won't put up with my shirking family duties."

"I hear ya!" Dave agreed, making his way into the office and taking a seat. "I need to talk."

"Okay," Lance replied, settling in to listen.

"I'm having a lot of trouble with this one! I mean, Lori never tells me about this brother and now he lives in my house with my kids. Lori is in some kind of la-la land, acting like this guy is some sort of prince. I mean, she's in total denial of what the guy is! She won't talk to me about anything even though right now I need her to talk. I love her, but I can't help but be hurt by all this."

"This isn't good," Lance said. "Maybe once Johnny is positioned by the court's decision, she'll begin to deal with some of these things."

"I'm hoping, but why does she protect him? I can't say a thing to this guy!"

"How do you mean?"

"I don't like his language, but if I reprimand him, she tells me to back off. Says he wasn't raised in a good home like me and doesn't know any better."

Lance furrowed his brows with this news. This didn't sound like Lori.

"I'm living with a complete stranger," Dave responded, knowing what Lance was thinking, "but that's how it is. I know he was shot and everything but he's not hurt that bad! He does nothing all day! I'm not even sure he isn't still managing his girls from the house, because he always has the phone with him."

"You need him out of there!" Lance declared. "I can make some calls and get him temporarily placed."

"Maybe if you do it, Lori will accept it, but if I do it, she'll hit the ceiling. How am I ever going to get to the place where I can talk to her about how I'm feeling about all this? I almost walked out this week. Lance, how can a marriage that was doing fine a week ago be this close to falling apart seven days later?"

Lance didn't know but he would do all he could to not let that happen. He checked his watch.

"I know you've got stuff to do," Dave said, standing.

He watched Dave head to his office, knowing he hadn't solved anything but, at least, he could be a sounding board. Sometimes that's all that was needed.

Lance sat in the meeting that Dave informed him was on his schedule for a reason, but Lance still didn't know why. He didn't handle this stuff! It was a long two hours before they finally ended the ordeal.

"So why did I have to attend this?" Lance demanded later in Dave's office.

"They've laid off everyone except you and me. Everyone else that still comes to help does so as a volunteer."

"I know that already," Lance declared.

"Well, Max has to pull back, too. He has a family to feed and he's not on the payroll anymore either. He'll still help out when he can, but in reality, we are the whole team here now."

"Oh man, Dave! I just took a job at the farm to supplement my income and make it possible for me to work with Rain. How much extra work is this going to involve?"

"I didn't know that!" Dave winced. "We're in for some very long hours around here!"

"Dave, I put in twenty hours a day now! I can't put in any more."

Dave stared at him. Twenty hours?

"I take work home!" Lance informed him, seeing the bewilderment in his face. "I don't do my files here for the most part, I do them at home."

"You take your files home? Lance, how many people do you see a day?"

"I don't know. I usually do about fifty call backs a day and try to fit in at least sixteen appointments."

"What? That's insane! You can't do that and go to the farm and keep up with everything else around here!"

"I know that!" Lance cried in frustration. "That's why I couldn't believe you had me going into that meeting." He glanced at his watch, "and now I have to run and go see Bryan or face Mom's wrath!"

Dave watched him go, still stunned. Lance was handling double his own workload and he was swamped! No wonder the guy called this his mistress—it owned him. Suddenly Dave was filled with fear—how long could he maintain this schedule? He decided he was going to have to make sure that he could because he could not lose

Lance. All his thoughts of getting Lance to handle some of the financial end of the center flew out the window. He'd have to find another solution.

Lance hurried down the hospital corridor toward Bryan's room, checking his watch and knowing he had to keep this visit down to ten minutes! Then a sound hit his ears and for a moment, he debated turning around but pushed himself forward.

"Lance!" Mel cried when she saw him.

"Hey Mel! What are you doing here? I thought we were taking turns at this visiting thing?"

"Oh, I'm so sorry! I didn't know we were working on a hard rigid schedule here!"

"Hey guys!" Bryan called from the bed. "I think I'm the one you two are supposed to visit!"

"Hey Bryan!" Lance greeted, handing his brother a book he had picked up a month earlier and hadn't even cracked open yet.

"Thanks!" Bryan said, paging quickly through the book. "I need this in here!"

"So when do they think they'll let you out of here?" Mel asked Bryan.

"They think next week Saturday but they aren't making any promises. Why?"

"I want to celebrate Dad's birthday on the Wednesday after that, but I want to make sure you're going to be home!"

"You want to know if I'll be home?" Bryan smiled. "I think you had better ask this other brother if he can make it. Even if I'm still in here, I can probably get a pass, but this guy is a whole different matter!"

"Lance will be there!" Mel declared.

"I will, will I?" Lance said, shaking his head. "Mel, my schedule right now is insane and I can't see me getting more time off—I can't see me getting any time off!"

"I've already talked to Lori and she promised me she would get you there!"

Lance laughed. He wondered when she talked to Lori because he was pretty sure Dave wouldn't be any more excited about going to this party than he was. And wasn't Lori working a big case, too?

"Lance!" Mel said in a scolding tone, reading his thoughts, "you will be at Dad's fiftieth birthday party or you will die trying to get there!"

Lance knew there would be no negotiating this and he would have to decide if skipping this party would be worth the fight with his family. He looked at his watch.

"Well, I only had ten minutes and I have now spent most of them talking to you, Mel!" he turned to Bryan. "How are you feeling anyway?"

"I'm good as long as I don't breathe!"

"That good, hey?" Lance laughed. "Yeah, you sound totally ready to party hard!"

"Lance!" Mel warned.

"Sorry, but you drop these things without warning!" Lance complained. "Why can't it be on the weekend when I'll already be at the farm?"

"Because Paul works."

"I work on Wednesdays!" Lance countered.

Mel could see her brother wasn't very pleased but she wasn't giving in on this.

"Dad's actual birthday is Wednesday!"

"Okay, you two! I'm not saying this again." Bryan interrupted. "Remember this guy in the bed?"

Lance sighed. "I gotta go. Bryan, I really hope you get better real soon. I can't fight Mel alone!"

He gave Bryan an affectionate squeeze on his shoulder and Mel a quick hug. He knew he was stiff with anger and that it had flowed between them as they made contact.

CHAPTER 25

Lance arrived on Friday, actually glad to be at the farm and away from all the decisions being made at the center. He was weary of budgets and supporters who all looked down on him for needing their money.

Rain was waiting for him, and he smiled at her when he saw her.

"So are we going to have a good day today?" he asked.

"I was," she responded.

He pulled out the books and they started working on reading, writing and arithmetic. Rain breathed a sigh of relief that this session seemed friendly. She held her shoulder the whole time and, by the time they were finished, she was almost crying with pain.

"Rain, is your shoulder sore?" Lance asked, knowing he was stating the obvious.

"I'm fine!" she responded sharply.

Denial. He heard it a lot and understood the primal defense mechanism all too well. He knew she was hurting and that in all likelihood needed to go back to the doctor.

"Let me look at your wound," he ordered.

She narrowed her eyes at him. "I don't think so!"

Denial very quickly graduated to hostility and Lance knew the fight was on. This was not what he wanted on this first day.

"Just let me look," he said, making sure to keep his voice gentle.

She didn't protest, but she didn't move to reveal anything either. He shook his head in frustration but decided he would just take a look—the wound wasn't in an area he would consider off limits. He gently pulled back her shirt only to find the wound was bandaged.

"Could you by any chance help out here a little?"

She remained rigid.

He carefully pulled the bandage back to reveal an ugly wound that was oozing puss and blood.

"That's very infected!" Lance said, looking at her with worry written all over his face. "I think we'd better go to the doctor."

He looked at his watch. "He should still be in his office. I'll go see if you can get an appointment."

Rain let the shiver of disgust run through her body after he left. The feel of his fingers on her skin was a painful reminder of everything she identified men as being—dirty. She shook off the feeling when she saw him returning with her jacket in hand.

"I'm not going!" she declared.

"Yes you are!" he replied. "Mom's coming along and we're going to go see the doc. He's a good guy."

She shook her head and sat with her arms crossed in resolve. Lance shook his head and went to find Dottie. Dottie soon came with a sympathetic look on her face.

"Oh, Rain, it will be fine!" she encouraged. "Now let's get this done and then we can enjoy life again."

"I'm not going!" Rain replied remaining firmly planted on the couch.

"Honey," Dottie said, gently taking Rain's hand in hers, "if the wound is infected, it needs to be looked at by a doctor, and Dr. Martin is the gentlest man you'll ever meet."

Rain remained frozen. Dottie turned to Lance.

"Maybe she'll let me clean it." she suggested.

"Not on your life!" Lance replied, knowing he was sounding a little harsh. "Mom, Rain is a spoiled brat who isn't getting away with this."

"Lance!" Dottie protested. "How can you say such things to this girl?"

"Mom, Miss Rain has had a hard life but in some sick twisted way, she's been spoiled rotten!"

"How?"

"Well, she totally took over the house with Johnny and changed the whole system there. She somehow got away with things that would've gotten any other girl there beaten to death. I mean, locking Johnny out of his bathroom for four days? Rain is lucky to be alive. Do you have any idea? Then there's the little incident where she cut him with a razor, and slamming things over his head?"

Dottie looked at Lance questioningly. This girl was not capable of those things.

"Who told you that?" Rain demanded.

Lance raised his eyebrows in the most annoying, teasing manner. "Who do you think?"

Rain glared at him. How could he talk to Johnny behind her back? A shiver of fear ran through her—Lance had no problem standing up to Johnny, so what would he do with her?

"Now you either get up and we go to the doctor or you get up and walk out that door, because you are not staying here unless you are cooperating with the program!" Lance said in a no-nonsense tone, turning his body toward her.

Rain looked at Dottie for support.

"Surely you can be little more pleasant." Dottie chastised her son.

"Mom, she goes by my rules! We agreed to that and if you compromise that agreement, I'm done here!"

Dottie bit her lip. She had agreed to that and now it was crunch time. She left the room, knowing she could never hold her tongue and not interfere if she watched.

"Okay, Rain, what will it be?" Lance demanded.

Rain looked into his face, still trying to figure out how to manipulate this guy, but nothing was coming to mind. She finally got up, thinking she had the whole way to town to figure out a plan.

"How many painkillers have you taken?" Lance asked her when the town came into view.

His demeanor was soft again. She hated this Jekyll and Hyde act.

"I don't know," she sighed. "I think maybe three today."

"And are they helping?"

"Not much."

He looked over at her. He knew the pain had to be bad for her to take any painkillers, so she really was in pain but yet so reluctant to seek out help. He couldn't figure this one out at all. She was writing a whole new chapter in his book of experience.

They arrived at the doctor's office and Rain still needed a plan. She watched as Lance hurried to open the door on the passenger side to let his mom out of the truck. Next she would have to follow. She froze in fear.

"Okay, Rain, let's go!" Lance ordered.

"Please!" she pleaded with him.

"Rain, you are going in there and you are going to make this very pleasant!"

She wanted to cry but knew the tears would be wasted on Lance Hawkins! The man had no heart. She slowly made her way out of the vehicle and onto the sidewalk where, for one moment, she considered bolting but couldn't face the consequences she knew he would level on her. He guided her into the building, instructing Dottie to get her comfortable in the waiting room while he went to talk to the receptionist.

"I think it feels a lot better!" she whispered to Dottie.

"Rain, this isn't going to be that bad!" Dottie told her. "But if you leave it and let it get worse, this will be a place to fear!"

Rain sank into her chair.

Lance took the seat beside her, holding a clipboard.

"We have to fill this in," he told her, already letting his eyes scan the questions even though he was very familiar with this procedure. "Do you want to do it?"

"No!" she told him.

"Okay. Then I'll read the questions and you tell me the answers."

They took a few minutes to fill in the form, getting stuck on the question about Rain's birth date and age.

"How old are you?" Lance droned. He had skipped the question initially, knowing it was a touchy subject with most women, but now it was all that was left on the form.

"I don't know!" Rain replied flatly.

"Just tell me!" Lance demanded.

"I really don't know!" she repeated, frustrated that he didn't seem to believe her.

"Okay," he sighed, "when is your birthday?"

"I don't know that either," she said, tears now forming in her eyes. "See, I'm a nobody. I don't even have a birthday!"

Lance looked at her, feeling bad that he had pressed her on something that obviously was a very deep hurt.

"I'm sorry, Rain. I just find this is a question most women don't like to answer—I thought you were being difficult." He grasped her good shoulder gently. "You are a person and not the only one who doesn't know when her birthday is."

She leaned into him just needing someone, even him, to hold her.

"Now that is a pretty picture!" a voice scoffed from across the room. "Saint Lance daring to feel the skin of the opposite sex!"

Lance looked at the man speaking to him—Andy Pottman. He graduated with Lance.

"She's a real pretty one!" he continued, his eyes dripping with lust. "I bet she's one of them whores you guys have up at that farm!"

Rain could feel her anger building. She hated men, but men like Andy who felt so superior got a special dose of loathing.

"Leave her alone!" Lance growled in warning. He turned back to her. "Stay close to Mom. I have to go give this to the receptionist. I want to see if Dr. Martin has time for a physical since it seems you've never had one!"

"What is that?" Rain asked, not liking the way it sounded.

"How about we let them surprise you?" Lance smiled, making a quick getaway.

Andy watched him leave, thinking this would give him a chance to snuggle one of these women in a way that Hawkins wouldn't even understand. He took the seat Lance just vacated. Rain grabbed Dottie's arm nervously. Dottie didn't know what to do—the man had a right to change seats if he wanted. Andy smiled at her in a most perverted way.

"Why not let me calm those frazzled nerves!"

"Get away from me!" she whispered.

"Oh, come on!" Andy said, not believing this woman could be upset about him just wanting a little attention after all the things she had done in her life! He reached out to touch her hair.

Rain lost it. She pulled away from him.

"Get away from me, you pervert!" she shrieked.

Lance came running. "What's going on?"

"Get him away from me!"

Andy stood and grabbed her, pushing his lips hard against hers. Rain let her nails slide down the man's face, leaving deep jagged lines down his cheeks. She pushed him hard, causing him to fall against a chair. Andy grunted but wasn't about to let her go. He moved in again but this time Lance got between the two of them. Dottie stared on in horror.

"Back off, Andy!" Lance ordered.

"She's a whore!" Andy spat at him. He swiped his face with the back of his hand only to find it covered with blood. He gazed at the red stain for a moment before reacting.

"I'll kill her!" he declared.

He lunged at her again pushing past Lance, but Rain wasn't letting this guy touch her. She grabbed a plant from the corner of the room and brought it down hard onto Andy's head. Dottie gasped, Lance sighed and Rain ran. Luckily, Lance caught her, pulling her, kicking and screaming, toward the examination rooms.

"Just take her to room two!" the receptionist instructed, hurrying to see about Andy.

Lance pulled her into the room and slammed her onto the bed.

"What was that?" he cried out.

"He attacked me first!" she defended.

"I know that, but I wouldn't have let him lay another finger on you!"

"I don't need you protecting me! I can do it myself!"

"Rain, he'll probably charge you!" Lance said letting his voice get louder than he intended.

He stopped himself, taking a couple of deep breaths. Losing his cool would not work in this situation. He made sure to push down the anger that was bubbling inside of him before he spoke again.

"Let me tell you how it works. It doesn't matter that he made the first move. They look at you and your history and somehow, they'll make it look like you enticed him. If you want out of that mode, you have to behave above reproach. I know that isn't fair, but that's what your lifestyle has earned you."

"I don't care! If some weirdo plants his lips on me, I am not taking it." Rain said, wrapping her arms tightly in front of her.

He smiled. He realized here was the Rain he had been waiting to meet—the one Johnny spoke about. It was nice to know she was still alive somewhere inside this lost being. Now he needed to see how much of Rain was really this person and how much was the quiet, calm person.

Dr. Martin arrived, much to Lance's relief. Andy was fine, but then as Dr. Martin put it, he had a very thick skull! It also seemed that he would not press charges.

"What if I want to press charges?" Rain reminded him.

"You won't!" Lance declared.

Rain glared at him, but decided this was not the time to argue this out. She still needed to get out of this place before this doctor got his paws all over her. She was surprised when Dottie came into the room and Lance left. She didn't want Dottie to not like her. The doctor got right to the examination.

"So Miss Patterson," he said, taking a seat beside the bed, "how are you today?"

"Don't touch me!" she warned.

He smiled, "I see or I'll get the same thing Andy just got?"

"He deserved it!"

"Can't argue with that." Dr. Martin agreed. "Lance says he hasn't been able to dig up much for medical records on you."

"Probably because I don't remember ever going to the doctor before I got shot."

"Did they do a physical then?"

"Just looked at the shoulder," Dottie informed him, having already been briefed on all this by Lance.

"Well, then it's about time you had one, young lady. I'll let you get changed." He stood to grab a gown for her.

"Why do I have to change?" Rain demanded.

"So I can examine you."

"I don't think she knows anything about what is coming," Dottie said quietly.

"Oh!" Dr. Martin smiled and added under his breath, "I'm going to get Lance for this one!"

Lance listened for the screams, and he wasn't disappointed. Andy, with an icepack against his forehead, stared at him from across the room, wondering why he didn't warn him.

"She not what she looks like?" another man asked Lance, not trying to be mean with the question.

"She's not what she looks like!" Lance agreed.

Dottie emerged, waving Lance to come join them.

"How bad was it?" he asked, standing to join her.

"I have no idea how you do this day after day!" she declared.

"Trust me, Mom, they aren't all like Rain!"

They rejoined the doctor and Rain in the examination room.

"I'll start with the basics," he explained. "I won't get some of the test results for about two weeks, but the shoulder definitely has problems. She needs surgery."

"No way!" Rain protested.

"Shut up, Rain!" Lance ordered. "What exactly is the problem?"

"The bullet has severed a tendon, and she won't have full mobility with the arm unless she gets it repaired, and she needs it done now. I'm booking her in for Monday. We already took blood and all that, so I'll send the information we've collected to the hospital. She looks good—how long has she been in the life?"

"She was born into it, believe it or not!" Lance informed him.

"Wow! You are one very lucky lady!" Dr. Martin stated, shaking his head in disbelief.

"Oh, I think she's one very mean lady, and her johns learned it the same way as Andy," Lance responded.

They all chuckled except Rain. Maybe Mr. Hawkins needed a dose, too, if he was going to keep up this kind of talk.

"It's day surgery," Dr. Martin continued. "It would be better for her to stay in the city the first night, but I'd understand if you see that as a problem. It's a touchy procedure and the pain involved with the recovery can be intense."

"I'm not doing this!" Rain cried.

"Okay," Lance nodded, ignoring her protests. "You can fax anything else up to my office if I need to see it and I'll make sure she gets there on time!"

Back at the farm, Rain locked herself away in her bedroom to cry. Lance was so mean, and all she wanted was to get back home where she could control her life. When Lance pushed her door open around two in the morning, she wanted to greet him with a flying object, but she was too upset to find ammo.

"Hey Rain," he said softly, taking a seat on the bed. "I really am not trying to be cruel."

"Go away! I hate you!" she hissed.

"I know, and you know what? It doesn't matter because I still care about you. Rain, I know this is going to be incredibly hard, but it will change everything for you. Being spoiled is a bad thing, and you've got this really sick, spoiled, used thing going on. What am I going to do with you?"

"If I'm such a burden, why don't you just go away? I get along fine with Dottie."

"You get along fine because she hasn't challenged you yet. I'll let you know, this pity party thing will only go so far and then, reality will hit. My mom honestly did not think you were capable of the things she saw today, but now she knows. There is a reason why I do this for a living and she lives here!"

"Well, I don't like you!"

He smiled, letting his hand fall onto hers. It didn't matter, although he did wish she would like him a little.

"I'm here to offer you an olive branch."

"What's that?"

"I'll arrange it with Dave and Lori for Johnny to be with you when you wake up from the surgery if and only if, you go quietly to the hospital with no tricks."

She eyed him over carefully, not trusting him. He could trick her and have his way, and she'd be left on the wrong end of this deal.

"Think about it," he shrugged. "We'll head out Sunday."

She didn't like this olive branch deal.

CHAPTER 26

Johnny sat beside the hospital bed waiting for Rain to wake up from the anesthetic. Lance sat beside him.

"So is she doing okay?" Johnny asked, gently holding the small hand in his.

"Well, she's had a few problems. How about you?"

"I'm going crazy at that house!" Johnny admitted like Lance had just given him permission to bear his soul. "Dave and Lori fight all the time, and those boys drive me around the bend. I'm not much for kids, you know. I feel like a dog—you know—a pet that one person has brought into the house without the permission of the rest of them. Lori's so insistent that I stay there, and I know Dave doesn't want me there. I don't want me there! I don't know what's gotten into Lori. We never got along that well. Dad told us about his lifestyle when I was about twelve and Lori was about twenty. We didn't have a clue—even Mom didn't know, or so she said. She moved out and I stayed with Dad. Lori went to the university, hating Dad and vowing to stop him. Dad got me started in the business, so when I first ran my own place, I was about sixteen—I wasn't allowed in my own club! I wanted more, so I headed across country, bringing me here to run a club. Dad warned me about staying close to legal but I knew better. I wish I had been satisfied, but I met Tommy and we went into business together. Lori still thinks Tommy dragged me into it all, but that isn't true. I liked the perks until Rain came along. She messed up my whole world."

"That baffles me!" Lance admitted. "She's so difficult. Can't figure out why you'd keep her around."

"She is that!" Johnny admitted. "If you could see her like she was . . ."

Johnny felt the emotion rising in his throat. He pushed it down.

"She was so full of spunk. I can remember the day she died. I killed her, and she was everything to me. That's the day I realized I made a very big mistake—I chose the wrong thing. I put business ahead of love and I'll pay for that forever."

"She still loves you," Lance said, trying to picture this man fighting Rain and losing.

"I know but she's not herself. I was going to cut her loose. I was going to give her some money and tell her to find something else to do with her life."

"Johnny, you know she couldn't have found anything at that point." Lance was beginning to understand these two better. "You do know that I arranged for you to go from the hospital to the farm?"

He nodded but Rain stirred and interrupted them. Lance leaned over to see if her eyes were opening.

"Hey there!" he greeted. "If you can focus, you'll see I made good on my promise."

Rain tried to make sense of his words but it didn't register until she heard the voice.

"Hey, Babes!" Johnny said, pulling her hand to his lips.

"Johnny!" she murmured. "Oh Johnny, it hurts!"

Lance didn't want to hear that. He went to fetch a nurse. He returned shortly, finding Johnny kissing Rain on the cheek.

"Hello!" the nurse greeted, ignoring the pair. "I hear you're feeling some discomfort?"

"It hurts!" Rain moaned, still not completely aware of her surroundings.

The nurse injected something into the IV and then checked the vitals before leaving the room. Lance followed her.

"How long can she stay here?"

"We usually let them wake up fully. By the way, Bryan is being discharged today, too."

"What?" Lance cried.

"The bed is needed by a more urgent case. He's being kicked out! You're supposed to phone your sister."

Lance sighed heavily. He had such a crazy day already! He reluctantly went to the phone and called Mel.

"Hey, Lance!" Mel greeted. "I'm guessing the nurse told you that Bryan is going to be released and I can't get there to pick him up—Paul and I have prenatal tonight. Now I can probably drive him out to the farm and Mom mentioned Rain will need a ride back, too? I won't be able to pick them up until after nine though because I have a doctor's appointment in the morning, so I'm really hoping you can rearrange your schedule."

"Oh yeah," Lance mocked. "I can just rearrange my whole life to fit you. Are you crazy? Mel, I can't look after two sick people! It took me a little figuring to handle one and that was just for until she left the hospital!"

"And you call yourself compassionate? Lance, I'm willing to get them to the farm! Can't you meet me halfway?"

Lance rolled his eyes. "I guess I have to."

He went to check on Bryan, only to find he was already dressed and waiting in the hallway. He felt overwhelmed but had no choice but to make this work.

"I promised Rain that Johnny would be here when she woke up, and I'm not breaking that promise," he explained to Bryan, pushing his wheelchair toward Rain's room. "I can't do everything so I'm leaving you with Rain to make sure Johnny behaves himself. Call me when they discharge her, and I'll come and pick you guys up and take you to my apartment. Sounds like we're having a slumber party,"

Bryan looked from Johnny to Rain and then back at Lance.

"It won't be long. I have to check in at the office."

Lance left quickly so no one would offer protests to the plan.

Bryan decided they would have to make the best of this.

"Hey, Johnny, sounds like we're getting to know each other!" he greeted.

Johnny nodded, thinking this was going to be a long day.

Lance arrived at the office to find a line of people waiting at his door. He sighed, knowing he was at least an hour behind in his appointment schedule and hadn't found a second to even listen to his messages. He prayed for mercy and a short message list.

"Hey, Lance!" Dave called, catching him before he hid away in his office.

"What's up?" Lance replied letting his tone say it better be nothing.

"I need to talk before you take off, okay?"

"Okay," Lance sighed. Another thing to do! He called in his first appointment.

Lance glanced at his watch and looked out of his office. He had managed to get his appointment line down and he should be leaving for the hospital but he needed to talk to Dave. He knocked on the door.

"Is Johnny behaving?" Dave asked as soon as Lance entered.

"I think so."

"Lance, I've got to get him out of my house or I'm not keeping my marriage."

"I already talked to Dad and he's on his way to the farm today." Lance explained. "I'm going to let Mel take him along when she takes Bryan and Rain back."

"That would be wonderful!" Dave smiled back. "Are you sure you want Mel on that?"

"Oh yeah!" Lance nodded thinking it was just too perfect a job for her. "So how bad is it between you and Lori?"

"I don't know. I hardly saw her all week, with that big case she's on. It's when she's there that things are bad and mostly it seems to be because of Johnny. I can't figure out anything between those two."

Lance took it all in. He would pray, but now he had to run. He refused to take the hint and make this a counseling session.

Lance made his way to the hospital after making a couple of calls on his cell phone—he confirmed Johnny's move to the farm. He felt good, like things were looking better now than he could have imagined a couple of hours ago. His smile vanished as soon as he walked into the hospital where he was immediately confronted by a client's boyfriend.

"Mr. Hawkins," Leroy wept, "she tried it again!"

"Oh no," Lance sighed.

"Lakita done try to get herself killed again! Used razors this time! Just lucky I got off work a little early and found her."

"Where is she?" Lance asked.

"They just moved her upstairs and I was going to call you, but here you are."

Lance followed Leroy to Lakita's room, where he met with the girl for a moment. She was a little dopey from whatever they had given her, so Lance promised he would drop by a little later to check on them. He glanced at his watch and groaned; he was a whole hour late now. He hurried to Rain's room where three anxious people waited.

"Where have you been?" Bryan demanded. "You know I can't handle this sitting stuff too long yet!"

"A few things came up," Lance explained, glad to see Rain was ready to go but still looked pale. "How are you feeling?"

"Not so good," she sighed. "This hurts more than I thought it would."

"And the doctor said if you had pain you should take something."

He helped Rain into the wheelchair provided and stared—he had a train—three wheelchair patients to transfer to the van! He looked at Johnny.

"Can you walk?" he begged.

Johnny shook his head. He did walk around the house, but he wasn't sure he could make it through the hospital. Maggie showed up and laughed at him.

"You know, I've seen you get yourself into a fix, but this is really something!"

She grabbed control of Bryan's wheelchair and pushed him out of the room. Lance debated and decided to take Johnny first. Rain would need the front seat of the van. He was very glad he borrowed the center's van. He would have had to make a couple of trips with his car!

Security met him at the door, wondering how long he thought he could take up the prime parking in front of the hospital.

"I have three wheelchair patients to transfer and I've already loaded two. I can get out of here in a few minutes if you let me go get my last patient."

The guard smiled when he saw it was Lance. He waved him off. Lance hurried to get Rain. At last, he was on the road.

Johnny stared in complete disbelief at the apartment building Lance pulled up to.

"We're staying here?" he questioned.

"Yes!" Lance replied, no longer having the patience to deal with any complaints. He had other problems—the stairs. "Johnny you're going to have to walk up the stairs!"

Johnny glared at him but decided the guy really did have enough to deal with. Lance called over a teenager who was hanging around on the street.

"Louis, would you help me? I'll pay."

"How much?" the boy asked.

"How much you got on you?" Lance asked Johnny.

"I don't know—about fifty bucks."

Lance nodded. "Fifty bucks!"

Louis' face lit up with delight as he hurried over. Lance loaded Bryan back into his wheelchair and they started their trek to the door.

"Mr. Hawkins!" a heavily accented voice called, "I see you busy but can you watch Chris for just one minute?"

The chubby child in the woman's arms reached out for Lance.

"Oh, Meiling," Lance replied, straightening up from the job at hand. "I guess. You're just going to pick up Guy?"

"I'll be right back!"

Johnny stared in disgust as Lance took the child into his arms. The child smiled at him with familiarity.

"Hey, Bry, can you watch him?" Lance pleaded.

Bryan shook his head but took hold of the child's suspenders so he couldn't escape. Once Johnny got up the stairs, Lance grabbed Chris and dropped him on Johnny's lap. Soon they had the men in the apartment and had only Rain left to lift.

"You took long enough!" she cried when she saw him.

He lifted her gently out of the van and into her wheelchair. He locked up the van and they started the trek to the apartment. Again, they strained up the stairs. Both men were relieved when the job was done. Johnny reluctantly handed over the fifty and Louis smiled, giving the bill a quick kiss before disappearing out the door. Lance pulled it shut, locking it securely. Chris wasted no time sliding off Johnny's lap and crawling to Lance.

"Hey, Buddy!" Lance smiled. Rain watched him curiously. He obviously had no fear of handling children.

"I'm really tired!" Rain informed him.

"I'll get you to bed," Lance assured her. "You can sleep in my room and Bryan can have the spare room and Johnny and I will take this room."

"This room?" Johnny complained. "How about I just sleep with my girl?"

"I don't think so," Lance laughed as he moved to push Rain into the bedroom.

Soon he had everyone comfortable and he took the moment of peace to sit down on the couch. He had almost sunk down into the cushions when the door bell rang, followed by the thumping of urgent knocks. He found Tuli, a neighborhood street girl standing there, crying and bleeding.

"He's going to kill me!" she wept.

Lance pulled her inside quickly, making sure to lock the door behind him.

"Look familiar?" he asked Johnny, who was watching this whole scene with interest. "I'm guessing a few of your girls felt the wrong end of your anger, too."

Lance grabbed the phone in one hand while still holding Chris in the other. He led Tuli to the bathroom. Upon his return to the living room, he dialed the phone.

"Lance Hawkins here, I got some trouble at the apartment." He listened for a moment. "Yeah, but hurry. This guy can take a door out without breaking a sweat!"

As if on cue, a knock sounded on the door, followed by yelling and cursing.

"Her pimp?" Johnny asked.

"Yeah. Can you hold Chris?"

Johnny once again found himself holding the child just as the door began to shake with the force of the pounding on the other side. Lance braced himself for the worst.

"Brock, I'll open the door but only if you agree to stay outside!" Lance called through the door.

"Where's my girl?" an angry voice demanded.

"There's no such thing as a girl who belongs to you!" Lance shot back.

"I don't need your smart mouth!" Brock declared. The door was beginning to creak with the force being asserted on it.

"Brock, I've already called the cops," Lance informed him. "Now why don't you calm down?"

Brock didn't want to calm down, hitting the door hard. It flew open and a giant of a man came tumbling in behind it. Lance jumped back, staying out of his grasp.

"Where is she?" he growled.

"She's not going with you!" Lance told him.

Johnny stared, thinking this guy would break Hawkins like a matchstick. Lance ducked as the large fist came at him. Sirens sounded outside. Brock swung again, and this time Lance caught the fist with one hand while slamming the man hard in the gut with a blow of his own. The man grunted with the force.

"Back off!" Lance warned.

Officer Coop was moving up the stairs, already hearing the fight. He hurried.

Brock swung again, this time catching Lance on the chin but he stood the blow, returning the hit. Coop was there, pulling Brock down before he could slam Lance with a chair. Soon Brock was being escorted to a police car.

"You are so stupid!" Johnny declared to Lance. "That guy could squish you like a bug!"

"I know!" Lance said, still catching his breath. "So think about what a man like that can do to a woman."

Johnny blushed. He too was a large man and understood the underlying meaning of Lance's words. The worst thing was that he couldn't deny the truth of it! He was really starting to get scared—Lance Hawkins didn't run from a fight and threats didn't make him pull back. How was he ever going to get Rain away from him?

Everything took longer than he wanted it to and by the time the police had their statements and the ambulance had come for Tuli, Lance was again far behind schedule. Sometime during the chaos, Guy had come to pick up Chris, much to Lance's relief, having totally forgotten about the child. He left Johnny in charge of the patients and hurried back to the hospital to check on Lakita. She was very upset and it took a while to talk her into at least a state of calm, but the main issue still remained—she wanted to die. Lance left her, making a mental note that he'd have to keep in close contact. He hurried to the center where Dave waited, looking like a mad bull.

"You missed the meeting!" he snorted.

"Meeting?" Lance questioned, swallowing hard.

"You know, the budget thing."

"Oh man!" Lance sighed. "I completely forgot."

"It's on your schedule. I wrote it in there myself."

"Dave, this has been a crazy day!" Lance said, hoping it would offer some defense.

"Oh, and my day has been one of those where I get to smell the flowers? Lance you have to get to these things! These guys come in here and see a poorly run business and don't even take a second look. We need these sponsors to keep things going."

"I know," Lance sighed. "I'll try not to miss any more meetings."

"You'd better do better than try."

Dave stormed off, leaving a very distraught Lance standing alone in the hall but he had to suck it in. He had appointments to keep and he still hadn't got back to his messages.

Dave headed home after the blow-up with Lance, only to walk into another disaster. The house looked like a tornado had blown through it.

"Lori?" he called but got no answer. He headed to the kitchen to see if there was anything there to eat. Nothing.

"Dad?" a voice called and Carter emerged from the bedroom.

"Carter? Are you here alone?" Dave couldn't believe what he was seeing.

"Cody is here with me," he replied.

"Didn't you get the message to go to Mrs. Heimarks?"

He shook his head.

Dave hid the anger he felt from his son. The child didn't need that falling on him, but Lori wouldn't get off that easy.

CHAPTER 27

Lori was engrossed in the case file in front of her. She was going to make sure the man in question never hurt anybody again. It wasn't often she was given one of these flesh sellers on a platter like this. She stopped herself—what was she thinking? Her brother was going to be facing the same charges—did she want him to get the book thrown at him? She glanced at her watch and gasped. It couldn't be that late.

She grabbed her purse and hurried out of the office, calling the pizza place as she went. She jumped into her car and was on her way but in her haste, neglected to look both ways. She heard the crunch of the metal followed by a shooting pain in her neck. The air bag hit her. She had no idea what had happened.

It was only in the ambulance that she remembered about why she was in a hurry.

"Someone has to call my husband," she pleaded. "My boys—someone has to call them."

Dave sat alone in the living room. His boys seemed to have the good sense to know he needed a little space. The phone interrupted his thoughts.

"Hello," he answered.

"Dave Evans?"

"Yes."

"This is Officer Campbell. I'm calling you to let you know your wife has been in an accident."

"What?"

"Nothing serious—just a fender bender but she's at the hospital."

Dave felt his lungs empty of air. How bad was it?

"Thank you for calling," he managed.

He hung up and hurried to gather his boys.

"What's wrong?" Carter cried.

"Mommy's had an accident, but the Officer said she wasn't hurt bad."

They arrived at the hospital where the nurse showed him right to her bed. He hurried to her side.

"I'm sorry," she cried. "I lost track of time—I wasn't paying enough attention."

"We've all been running too fast to nowhere lately," Dave soothed. "What are they telling you?"

"It's just whiplash. The doctor said I'd probably feel it more tomorrow—they gave me something, so I'm not really sure how bad it is. He just went to get me a prescription and then I can get out of here."

Dave nodded. He was relieved, but he knew there was much more that they needed to discuss.

They got home where Lori seemed to be looking around for something.

"He's not here," Dave announced.

"Where is he?" Lori demanded.

"You know he was sitting with Rain today."

"Yes, but she was only in the hospital for a few hours. Where is he now?"

"He's being taken to the Hawkins' farm."

"What do you mean?"

"I mean, I can't have him here, Lori. I can't have that man around my children."

"He's not that bad," Lori defended.

"How can you not see the truth here?" Dave demanded. "He's a pimp with no desire to make a career change. I hate the way he looks at our boys—I bet you a thousand dollars, he'd have them on the street if he thought he could get away with it."

Lori's eyes flashed with anger. "How dare you!"

"How dare I? Lor, listen to yourself!" Dave begged. "Johnny isn't a saint and he needs a program. He's at the Hawkins farm where he belongs."

Dave escaped to the bathroom, pulling the door shut before she could respond.

Lori followed him, knowing exactly what he was doing.

"David Evans, we've been married for too many years for you to think I'm going to stand for this. Get out here right now."

"I'm going to the bathroom," he replied.

He could here her tapping her toe on the floor outside the bathroom. He put her out of his mind, choosing to study his sock instead of dealing with what awaited him. He saw a hole that he was sure wasn't there that morning. He studied it, finding it most fascinating. Lori pounded on the door, pulling him back to reality. He took a deep breath and headed out to face the monster.

"You have a lot of nerve," she accused. "I just had an accident and you have me standing out here waiting for you."

He hung his head.

"So just what possessed you to get Johnny placed without his lawyer's knowledge?"

He pulled her into the living room.

"You should sit down and relax."

"Don't you dare avoid the issue here!" she demanded.

He sat down, taking a deep breath before saying anything. "Lori, I can't have him around. He's a pimp."

"He's my brother," she retorted.

"How can you not see the truth here?" Dave sounded as defeated as he felt.

"He's not a pimp. He runs a service," Lori explained.

"Are you ever going to face the truth here?"

"That is the truth!"

"Whatever," Dave scorned. "How come the boys were here alone when I got home?"

"Because Johnny was supposed to be here."

"I told you this morning he'd be with Rain."

"And I thought that was just until she got released."

"I thought I made it clear I do not want him around my kids!"

"You've already stated that quite clearly!"

"How can you defend him?" Dave bellowed.

The boys huddled in fear in the bedroom, listening to it go round and around. They both prayed the fight would stop.

"He would never hurt the boys!" Lori stated.

Dave stood. He needed space and time.

"I can't do this," he told her. "I'm going to get out of here tonight and get this figured out in my head. I hope you do the same. Lori, I love you and I don't care about your family's past, but you have to deal with it—accept it. We can't live pretending this isn't affecting us."

Dave gave each of the boys a hug before grabbing his coat and walking out. It wasn't the first time he had spent the night away from home, but this time felt different. He would have to spend a lot of time in prayer before going back. He didn't want to go back to the stranger who called herself his wife.

Lori headed to bed where the boys tended to her every need. Once she was sure they were asleep, she wept. She grabbed the pain killer the doctor had prescribed and took two pills, even though she was only supposed to have one. At this point, she hoped they would help her sleep and maybe even more.

Lance worked until the sun was coming up on the horizon before finally closing the last file. Johnny lay on the couch snoring. Lance leaned back in his chair but a sound caught his attention before he could fall asleep. He stood slowly, forcing his weary body to move forward. He checked Bryan first, but he could see he was sound asleep. He slowly made his way to Rain and knew this was where the sound was coming from. He sat down gently on the bed beside her.

"Hey, Rain, you're supposed to take your pain killers if you start hurting!"

She looked up at him. Her face was pinched with pain and a tear rolled down her cheek. He offered her the medication and she gratefully accepted. He slid down onto the floor and joined her in returning to the land of dreams, too exhausted to make the move to the living room.

Johnny thought the whole apartment would give with the pounding on the door. That pimp guy couldn't be back—he couldn't be out of jail already. He looked around but couldn't see Lance so despite the warnings not to, he opened the door. Mel stared at him.

"Where is my brother?" she demanded.

"I'm not sure!" Johnny replied. "He was here when I fell asleep."

Johnny was given no chance to refuse her entrance as she pushed passed him. He watched her make her way around the apartment calling for Lance. She got to the bedroom.

"Lance Hawkins!" Mel howled.

"What?" a half-awake Lance cried, bumping his head on the night table in an attempt to sit up. This woke up Rain.

"What?" she moaned.

"What are you doing in a room with a woman?" Mel demanded to know, her eyes ablaze.

"I—what?" Lance asked not even sure he understood the question. "What time is it?" he asked. "What are you doing here, Mel?"

"I think I'm saving your reputation!" she informed him. "If Mom and Dad knew you were sleeping on the floor in a room where a woman was being housed, they'd lock you up!"

"I—I—oh man, I must have collapsed or something. Mel, you know me better than this!"

"I thought I did!" Mel responded. "You look like crap, by the way. Looking for a quick death these days?"

"I've just been a little busier than usual. What time is it?"

"About nine."

"Oh no!" Lance groaned, pulling himself onto his feet "I'm late and Dave's going to kill me! Look Mel, we need to get these three loaded into your car and then I have to get to work."

"Three?"

"Yeah. You'll have to grab them some breakfast at a drive thru."

"What? And who is going to pay for that?"

"I'll pay when I get paid. Johnny can probably snag some cash of his own if you talk to him."

"Who is Johnny?" Mel asked.

Lance pretended not to hear, hurrying to wake Bryan who was still sound asleep.

"Hey Bro, you need to get up and we need to get you on your way home. I'm running late, so Mel will have to help you."

"What?" Bryan asked, still yawning, but Lance was gone.

"Hey Guy, can you help me out?" Lance asked, pounding on the neighbor's door.

Mel didn't have a chance to argue as Lance dropped Chris into her arms, telling her she needed the practice. Soon Bryan and Rain found themselves in a car. Johnny took the seat beside Bryan in the back while Rain sat in the passenger seat in the front.

"Who is that extra guy?" Mel asked her brother, who was very much trying to slip away before she could ask.

"That's Lori's brother. He needs a ride to the farm."

"The pimp? The pimp that murdered that other guy?"

"Look, Ricky knows he's coming and Bryan and Rain will be with you. I'm sure you can handle it."

"Lance!" Mel said, her anger starting to get the best of her. "How dare you? You're sending me to the farm with a resident that would be delivered by armored vehicle. This is your pregnant sister here!"

"Mel, it isn't that big a deal. Johnny is harmless enough. You know that Ricky wouldn't ever have agreed to this if he thought you'd be in any danger!"

Mel narrowed her eyes at him but finally agreed to take Johnny. Lance looked sick and she didn't want to make it worse.

"Just remember when they find my body dumped on the side of the road that this was your idea!" she pouted as she climbed behind the wheel.

Lance waved her on. He had one thing done—now he just had to make the meeting on time.

Dave woke up wrapped up in his coat on his chair in the office. He slowly worked the kinks out before heading to the bathroom. At least the center had showers so he could get cleaned up. He stared at his beard and shrugged. Maybe it was time he just let it grow. He heard the front door. He smiled—it was nine fifty and that had to be Lance. At least he was on time for the meeting. He hurried to meet him at the office door.

Lance stared at Dave. "Something wrong?"

"I just got a new address," Dave said, shrugging.

"Oh?"

"Lori wasn't too happy about Johnny being placed without her express approval."

Lance could see there wasn't going to be a lot of talking about this now, so he grabbed the files he needed for the meeting and they headed to the conference room. At precisely ten, the newest in a long list of possible supporters sat across from the two men.

"I don't see either one of you as business people!" the man declared after only five minutes of looking at the books.

"That's probably because we aren't!" Lance informed him. "I'm a social worker. I work with people. I don't even know why you guys come down here. Doesn't anyone explain what we do here?"

"Lance!" Dave growled, kicking him under the table.

"I'm sorry, but I'm tired of guys like this looking at me and expecting superman!"

Lance left the room, leaving a very angry Dave to deal with the man. He headed out the door and to the hospital, knowing to stay around the office would be taking his life into his hands.

Mel stared at her passenger, watching his every move. Johnny found the whole thing irritating, to say the least, and was beginning to wonder how long he would be trapped in this car with this paranoid woman.

"So you're that Lance guy's sister?" he finally asked. He knew Bryan and Rain were happily asleep.

"Yes, I am. I still can't believe he thought I'd appreciate doing this for him! He's so dead when I get a hold of him!"

"Look lady, I've heard getting upset when you're in the family way can sometimes bring on early labor, and the last thing I want to do is deliver that baby!"

She laughed. He sighed with relief to hear the sound but felt slighted. He was, after all, a guy who owned women for a living and he knew how to make them do his bidding—he was still a predator of sorts. He realized what he thought was fear was more likely anger at her brother. He stared angrily out the window that he could so easily be shaken off as harmless.

Ricky sat beside Dottie, taking his turn at pushing aside the curtain to see if they were coming yet. He wasn't worried, but Dottie had been anxious for hours already.

"Mom, she'll be fine!"

"He's a murderer!" Dottie exclaimed. "He's a cold blooded murderer and my daughter is transporting him like he's some old acquaintance!"

Ricky pushed the curtain aside again, more to hide his smile than check the road. He felt the relief when the car pulled up at that moment, not because he was afraid for Mel but because he was running out of encouraging things to say to Dottie!

"They're here!" Dottie cried, rushing to the door.

"Hey Mom!" Mel called. "I hope Ricky is here to lift these invalids into the house. Can you believe Lance sent me with this pack and he didn't even feed them? That's why we're late. We had to get some money and then there was a line at the drive thru and then Bryan didn't get what he wanted and complained until I got him something else. I don't think Rain ate anything but this other guy, that I did not know was coming with me, ate all the leftovers."

Ricky hurried to the door and helped Johnny to the house, knowing he was still hurting from a gunshot wound—oh, yeah, he was a real threat! Dottie threw her arms around Mel, pulling her close like she had just escaped from a berserk elephant!

"These other two need help getting to the house," Mel told Ricky, pulling away from her mom. "Rain has been moaning in her sleep, and Lance gave very strict instructions about not letting her be in pain. I have all the doctor's sheets for the three of them. Bryan has slept the whole time! So much for protecting his sister!"

Arthur came in just in time to hear his daughter's lament.

"Will you need help?" Arthur asked Ricky after he gave Mel a hug.

"I think I will. I can probably handle Rain, but that other lug in here will need a couple of us."

"Lance put them into their wheelchairs," Johnny told them. "It wasn't so hard to lift them then and we didn't hurt them."

"Good idea!" Arthur agreed.

They brought the chairs out and soon a groggy Bryan and a quiet Rain were sitting in the Hawkins' living room.

Johnny found himself escorted to the dorm. Ricky looked him over closely.

"So Johnny Ross, the law finally caught up to you!" he smiled.

"You know me?"

"Do I know you?" Ricky laughed. "Tommy waited for years for me to get caught—I think he's the one who put the cops on me so he could take over my territory! Yes, I know you, and for a long time I was going to kill you, but things change and now I'm going to reform you!"

"Yeah, whatever!" Johnny said, giving Ricky that defiant look he knew all too well. A look he invented for this place.

"I guess you can have that attitude for now, but I know that by the time you leave this place, you, Johnny Ross, will be a different man. You know how I know that? Because I was you and you are a very special case, not only because of Dave and Lori, but because you took my girls and my territory."

"That was Tommy!" Johnny said, glaring at Ricky.

"Don't give me that! He worked for you and I know it. I've already seen some of my girls come through here after the two of you got to them and Johnny, I would remember that when dealing with me!"

Johnny backed down. Ricky Belarus was well known in his neighborhood and he wasn't about to cross him even if he no longer played the game. He went through the rest of the introduction to dorm life in silence. He had to get hold of Lori and get her to get him out of this place.

Lori didn't get out of bed until noon, having cried the night away. She called in sick and then laid her head back on the pillow to cry some more. The boys got themselves ready for school and caught a ride with a neighbor. She could hear them and knew she should get up and help them, but there was no strength in her to face them. She knew things had gone way past were she ever thought they could. They had a good marriage, didn't they? She pulled herself out of the bed, knowing she had to talk to Dave. She loved him.

"Hello!" Dave said into the phone receiver, not trying to hide the weariness he felt. It was almost closing time and Lance still hadn't showed, and he didn't know where he was spending the night.

"Dave!" Lori greeted him knowing the moment she heard his voice she would lose it.

"Lori," Dave replied, closing his eyes with relief.

"I'm sorry." she whispered and then hung up.

The tears streamed down Dave's cheeks. For some, that would have seemed very rude but with Lori, it was all he needed. He wasn't wasting another minute here. He walked into the hall, only to find himself face to face with Lance.

"You sore?" he asked, kicking at a crack in the floor.

"What do you think?" Dave demanded.

"I can't do the budget stuff, Dave! I have no time for it. I'm not an accountant."

"Maybe then you need to start looking for a new job!" Dave replied coldly. "This place needs someone who can do both."

Lance stared at the man that he had always looked up to, a man he thought of as a mentor and now a friend. Was he really being fired?

"Look, Lance, you do awesome work with the people, but you have to do the whole job here. Now I know when you started, that didn't include the budget stuff, but now it does. Can you handle this or not?"

Lance couldn't believe what he was hearing. His whole life was this place.

"Dave, I'm the one going out there while you sit in your office all day! I put myself in the risky places, and now I have to spread myself a little thinner. I work twenty-hour days—can you say that? No—you go home to your wife and boys and eat a meal every night! You can have your job if you think I'm not putting enough in here. Just try to replace me!"

Lance threw his key to the door down on the floor and left, obviously very angry. Dave sighed, realizing he hadn't quite handled this like he should have. He grabbed the key and hurried after Lance, knowing all too well no one would even apply at this place.

"Come on, Lance! You know what I'm saying!"

"I'm, done!" Lance announced, throwing his arms in the air.

"You know I need you!" Dave pleaded. "I just need you to at least cooperate at these meetings."

"I'm done. You fired me, I quit, however you want it!"

"I won't let you!" Dave told him, grabbing his hand and sticking the key into it. "Lance, you are good at this job and I know you don't like budgets, but this is our new reality and we both need to cope with it."

The sight of Lakita in the hospital crossed through his mind and he reluctantly took the key. He loved the people too much to quit, but he really was starting to feel the exhaustion factor weigh on him. He needed some sleep. He watched Dave pull away as he made his way back into the building where he would stay until the sun disappeared from the sky.

Rain watched Bryan as he tried to get comfortable with no success in the endeavor.

"Moving hurts!" she finally said after watching him for several minutes.

"Yeah, but sitting in a bad position hurts more!" he said, trying to laugh it all off. It didn't work.

Bryan let his body relax and the pain seemed to relax with him. He looked over at Rain. She was a very pretty girl who had few of the outward scars of a girl from the streets. She turned away from him, and he knew she didn't appreciate the scrutiny.

"Don't like being admired?" he questioned, knowing the answer.

"There's nothing here to admire!" she responded.

"Really? Funny, my eyes tell me there's plenty of good stuff to look at here—very pleasant and comforting!"

She raised her eyebrows at him. This guy was crazy.

"You are Lance's brother, right?" she asked.

"Yes, I am and I know we're nothing alike. That brother of mine isn't normal, especially when it comes to women! I think he's either dead or blind!"

She turned his words over in her head and suddenly felt a lot better about being in Lance's care. If he didn't like women, then she was completely safe from advances she didn't appreciate. Dottie came into the room.

"So son, are you ready to hit the bed?"

"Oh, yeah," Bryan replied.

Dottie soon wheeled him down the hall, leaving Rain by herself. She looked around the room. This place was so much the place she wanted all her life to call home she had to pinch herself again and again to believe this was real. Dottie returned for her.

"How are you feeling?" she asked.

"I'm okay. I feel pretty dopey, but everyone tells me that's how I should feel."

"Are you ready for bed?"

"I could probably handle that."

Arthur helped Rain into bed and then they both tucked her in. She shivered with joy. Dottie left, but Arthur sat down beside her.

"I guess Lance must have told you some of the things we do around here. I've discussed some things with him, and we both feel a Bible study would be a very good thing, and he wants you learning to read and write better. Bryan has offered to help with the reading and writing and I'll be doing the Bible study."

"Bible study?" she asked, totally unaware of what that might be.

"We're Christians and run this place on those principles. We believe in God and Jesus Christ is our Savior. Maybe we'd better begin at the beginning." Arthur smiled, pulling out a large worn book. "I read this to our boys when they were younger, and I find it really helps people like you with no understanding of our faith."

She looked at the title: *Stories of Jesus*. She had never had a bedtime story read to her before, but there's a first time for everything. That night she learned about a man who could do wonderful things, a man she couldn't imagine existing, but Arthur assured her He did.

CHAPTER 28

Mel stared at the clock and then back at her Mom.

"Where is he? I told him about the party and he knows how important it is to me that he comes!"

"He'll come" Dottie assured, giving her a loving rub on the shoulder. "Dave said he mentioned it to him today and he was coming. I think he was catching a ride with them."

Mel glared at the clock again, unable to believe they were all so inconsiderate!

Dave and Lance watched the clock while trying to keep their attentions on the speaker. The man was a new supporter who seemed to think he needed to discuss every detail before signing the donation check.

"Mr. King, we very much appreciate your support, but to be very honest, Lance and I have another important appointment."

Lance was glad Dave took the initiative. He was tiring of listening to the nonsense that came from the man's ignorant lips.

"Of course!" the man smiled. "I guess we have run a little long here."

Thankfully, the man soon bid his farewells.

"Mel is going to kill us!" Lance groaned, looking at the time.

"You got that right." Dave nodded in agreement. "Let's get out of here and try to at least get there for the cake!"

They stopped to pick up Lori, only to find her high on pain killers.

"Why is she on pain killers?" Lance questioned.

"She had a car accident," Dave declared.

"A car accident?" Lance said. "When?"

"It wasn't that bad—just a fender bender, but Lori got a whiplash out of it."

Lance shook his head as he helped Dave get Lori into the backseat of the car where she fell asleep. He hoped she was a little more with it by the time they got to the party. He didn't want to say anything, but he was pretty sure he could smell alcohol on her breath.

"Dave, how bad are things between you and Lori?" Lance asked as they drove.

"I don't know," Dave sighed. "This whole thing with Johnny has brought a lot of stuff to the surface."

"Is she dealing with any of it?" Lance demanded to know.

"Not with me," Dave admitted. "It's so easy at the center but how do you confront your own wife?"

"I would think your love for her would make that a no-brainer!"

He could feel Dave glaring at him, but it was the truth. At least, it would be for him.

Mel stared at her brother with a look that couldn't quite be called angry—it was so much more, but that was the closest he could come to describing it as he approached her.

"I couldn't help it!" he explained.

"You couldn't help ruining your Dad's fiftieth birthday party!" she shot back. "All you had to do was walk out of that place a little early for a change!"

"We couldn't get out of a meeting! Believe me when I tell you I would've gladly been here instead of there, but I couldn't get out of it any more than Dave could. I'm here now."

Mel glared at him, knowing at this point she would have to make the best of it or have Lance's behavior ruin the party for the whole family. She turned away from him, forcing a smile on her face.

He watched her go, feeling bad but knowing he'd done his best. She'd get over it.

The party went on and on and soon Lance found himself fighting to stay awake. Arthur pulled him aside.

"You look ready to hit the hay!"

"I am, but Mel's already angry with me," he said, looking down at his feet. "Dad, I'm so tired some days, I don't know if I have the energy to breathe."

"Then you're working too hard!" Arthur informed him. "You know when you were little and I warned you about the creek?"

"Yeah."

"I think you're in the creek, and a rescuer that ends up in the creek with those he's trying to save drowns everyone!"

Lance knew he was right, but he had no idea how to get out of the water that was swirling all around him. So many people counted on him.

"When the people look to you," Arthur told him as if reading his thoughts, "instead of the Creator, you have established them on the wrong God!"

Lance stared at his dad who didn't wait for a reply but moved back into the crowd of people. The truth had hit home, but he didn't know how to fix the problem.

Lance decided to do what he did best—turn his attention on someone else. Lori was up and moving but everyone could see she wasn't herself. He watched her. He knew that the accident wasn't bad enough to justify the level of high he was witnessing.

He prayed this wouldn't turn into another huge problem—he didn't have the energy to rescue anyone else.

And now he saw the remainder of that energy being sapped—his mom was headed his way. He tried to focus on her words as she updated him on every one of Rain's little personality quirks.

They got back to the city around two in the morning. Lori and the boys slept in the back of the car while Lance helped Dave stay awake in the front.

"Seems like we might as well skip the resting part of life and go right to work!" Lance sighed.

"I don't think I recommend that!" Dave smiled. "Lance, I'm really worried about you. You lose your train of thought and forget things. I think you need to slow down and smell the coffee for a little while. I don't mind you coming in at eight you know. That is when your shift actually starts."

Lance nodded in agreement but knew better. If he did that, he would never catch up.

Thursday he actually did only get there at eight. His body refused to listen to the alarm that told him it was five thirty and time to get up. He finally woke up at seven thirty and rushed to the office.

"I see you took my advice!" Dave nodded at him as he hurried toward his office.

"I slept in!" Lance growled back.

"Oh," Dave replied, biting his lip. Lance was definitely in a bad mood. "Are you heading back up to the farm this weekend?"

"I have to. I'm going to do Ricky's appointments tomorrow and then handle Rain on Saturday."

"You have something special planned for her?"

"Oh, yeah!" Lance nodded.

"Is she ready?"

"I have no idea. All I know is she's gotta face some things, starting with herself. Now I have a very busy day ahead!"

"Lance, just don't overdo it the first time—she's a little skittish."

"I know how to do my job," Lance barked back.

Dave left. Lance knew his job and he wasn't about to interfere. At least not today.

Lance made his way to the center Friday morning, hoping to get a couple of appointments in before he had to head out to the farm where Ricky had a full day scheduled for him, not including his time with Rain. In the last month, Rain had made many improvements where he seemed to be fading away.

He looked at the girl sitting across from him, trying to remember her name, knowing he had already asked her for that information twice! He listened intently, trying to digest the words, but it wasn't happening! He stood and asked her to give him a moment. He went to Dave's office.

"Something's wrong," he said, looking panicked.

Dave looked up at him. A flash of worry ripped through him.

"I can't seem to understand anything!" Lance looked confused even as he spoke.

"Are you okay?" Dave asked, rising to take a closer look at him.

"I don't know!" Lance said, shaking his head. He strained to think. "Her name—her name is—I know this—it's Molly."

"What?" Dave asked.

"It's okay, I remember now!" Lance said, nodding his head and turning to head back to his office. Dave followed him, watching him seat himself across from the young girl. "Okay, Molly, I think you need to move on. Forget this guy you're dating."

If this was a one-time incident, Dave would have shrugged it off, but this was becoming normal. He had lost it three times the week before, shouting at clients. He got impatient with a young woman who came in wanting to kill herself, telling her she needed to get a life. Dave pulled her into his office. And then there was the mumbling to himself like he had to repeat everything ten times or he'd forget. Lance needed help, but Dave was afraid to approach him.

Lance hit the highway, hoping it was indeed Friday and only became sure it was when he arrived and Ricky was waiting for him. He got through the appointments and then he had to face Rain.

"So how are things?" he asked, taking a seat across from her. They always met in the conference room.

"I'm fine."

"Looking in mirrors yet?"

"Not yet," Rain admitted quietly.

"Okay."

He left the subject and they chatted for a few minutes before he led her back to the house. He stared longingly down the hall toward the bedroom. All he wanted was sleep.

"Are you okay?" Rain asked.

"Tired."

"Then go to sleep!" she said with a shake of her head.

"And you'll tell Mom I was too tired to eat the supper that I know she's gone to extra lengths to prepare for me in hopes to fatten up her boy who is, as she puts it, 'wasting away where he stands'?"

"How about I wake you so you can eat?"

It sounded so good and he needed the rest—he couldn't resist the offer. He kissed her on the forehead, mumbling something about her being an angel before he hurried to the bedroom. He pulled the door shut and two minutes later, was sound asleep.

Dottie was surprised to hear Lance turned in for a nap before supper, but she wasn't blind. She could see her son was pushing his body to the end of his strength. Rain helped her with the meal, smiling at the many comments Dottie made about the meal that was indeed a work done with Lance in mind. Bryan rolled his eyes over and over again, wondering when he would get a meal like this. Then he remembered all the special things he needed lately and thought maybe Lance did deserve this. He helped with what he could.

Rain knocked on the bedroom door five minutes before it was time to eat but there was no answer. She opened the door slowly, afraid he might not be decent. He was sound asleep, tucked in under the blankets.

"Lance!" she called, shaking him gently. He didn't move. "Lance!" she repeated. After five shakes and no response, she went to fetch Dottie.

"He won't wake up," she said, shrugging her shoulders.

Dottie went in and, after several minutes, managed to get Lance to groan. Arthur finally came in and got him up by pouring water on his head until he opened his eyes, sputtering for air. He shook the sleep off.

"What?" he asked, glancing around trying to get his bearings.

"It's time to eat!" Arthur announced.

"Oh! I'm coming!" Lance announced, really wishing he could just stay right where he was.

Lance ate like a robot, knowing he had to or his mom would get upset, not noticing the effort was in vain. Her motherly senses were already honing in on him.

"Lance, I think you need to get a little more rest!" she chastised.

"I know," he sighed.

"Man, you look like you're more dead than alive!" Bryan informed him.

"Thanks for telling me what I already know!" Lance said, giving Bryan a dirty look. "Are you ever planning to get back to school?"

"My therapist says I should heal up before getting back."

"Therapist?"

"Debbie. You know her."

"Yes, I do and she's not a therapist!"

"She's training to be one!" Bryan defended.

Lance laughed. "Oh, I just bet she is! And you're her test subject?"

Rain listened, enjoying the family dynamics that were so foreign to her. She felt like such an outsider to everything.

"You like Debbie, don't you?" Bryan asked, looking at Rain.

"Yes, she's nice," Rain said, hearing the quaver in her voice. "She spends more time with you than me."

"See what I mean?" Lance smiled. "I really should sit in on one of these so-called sessions and make sure they aren't lip exercises."

Bryan blushed but didn't deny there might be some of those kinds of lessons occurring. Dottie and Arthur laughed, glad to see their boys being the boys they knew and loved.

Bryan obediently headed to the kitchen after they finished eating followed by Lance, but Dottie redirected Lance to his bedroom.

"I'm fine!" he argued.

"Go to bed now!"

Lance knew better than to argue and turned toward his bedroom where he quickly fell asleep, but not before he formed a plan in his mind about how to get Rain moving ahead in her treatment. She was doing well, but he had no illusions that she would be able to remain free of her old bondage if left on her own. Next time he met with Miss Rain, they would be facing some reality!

CHAPTER 29

Lance always tried to fit a couple of appointments in on Friday morning before heading out to the farm. On this morning, he found himself meeting with the center's volunteer board of directors once again about budget changes. He was getting very weary of these discussions. Dave looked over at him with the same thoughts. He should've just headed to the farm.

But ignorance was bliss as the employees at the farm struggled with all kinds of extra stresses. Boy scouts were exploring the creek with their squeals of delight wafting up the slopes, compounding the drudgery of weeding endless rows of garden. Then the college students arrived to do workshops with the dorm residents.

"Dottie, we have a problem!" Kelly, the girl's dorm mom, announced, showing up at the house where Dottie was working on teaching Rain about doing laundry.

"A problem?" Dottie asked.

"We have one extra student and I know they don't like doubling up counselor trainees with clients. It makes the client feel ganged up on. I was wondering if Rain could take part?"

"I don't think so!" Dottie replied, shaking her head at the thought.

"Why not?" Kelly argued, thinking it was the easiest solution to the problem.

"She's not ready to deal with that!"

Kelly wasn't giving up. "She's recovering from the same things as the dorm residents. These kids are going to ask standard questions—Lance has probably already asked all of them. I don't see any reason why Rain can't help out with this."

"I don't think she's ready," Dottie sighed, but looking at Kelly, she realized the girl really was in a bind. "I still think it's a bad idea—Rain isn't really a resident. Make sure she gets someone with a gentle way . . ."

"Thank you!" Kelly sighed.

Dottie didn't think to pray before making her decision, and now that she found time to do just that, her whole spirit regretted allowing Kelly to include Rain. She tried to contact Lance with no luck. She wrung her hands in fear of the fallout her rash decision would cause.

Rain stared at the pompous young man who stood before her. She could see that every cell of his body felt superior to her, and she hoped this interview would be over quickly. It never occurred to her that she could have refused to meet with him and even now felt totally out of control of the situation.

"So you are Rain Patterson. Quite a name!" the young man laughed at her.

Rain hadn't felt the way she felt this moment since the last time she spent time with a john. This guy had all the trappings in her mind. She narrowed her eyes at him, but he missed the warning.

"So Rain Patterson," he said, still snickering at her name. "How does your family react to you being here?"

The question brought on a rush of emotions and Rain had no idea how to deal with them all. She needed to have someone here to let her know if she had to answer. She got up to seek out Kelly.

"Where do you think you're going? You haven't answered any of my questions!" he declared. He didn't relish the idea of having her run off saying something to her superior that in some way might poison his clean cut image. He blocked the path to the door.

Rain sat back down, swallowing hard as the old feelings gathered in her mind. No man was controlling her—she would die before any man did that to her ever again! She wrapped her hands around the small glass container that held the pens on the desk. He didn't notice as he browsed his notes trying to decide how to continue.

"So you're a real hooker?" he finally said, shaking his head and once again laughing. "You must have been one hot honey!"

That was it! Rain let the small glass tumbler crash on the boy's head with amazing force and bolted from the room. Kelly saw her run and groaned. The boy emerged from the room, blood spewing from the cut on his forehead.

Kelly moved quickly to the young man with a first aid kit. She apologized over and over again as she worked to stop the bleeding on the cut. As she listened to his ranting, her compassion soon vanished and she felt like adding a second lump to his skull.

Dottie decided to recant her earlier decision to let Rain participate and now headed to the conference rooms where the interviews where being held. She heard the cries for help and intuitively knew it had to be Rain—she was too late. She pulled the cell phone out of her pocket and dialed Lance one more time, praying that this time she would get him on the line.

"Lance Hawkins here!" a voice said, sounding far away.

"Lance! Thank God! You have to get down here. It's Rain."

The hour drive took just forty minutes. Lance hurried to the conference room where the boy stood, still enraged about the 'crazy woman.'

"Where is she?" he asked breathlessly.

Johnny had warned him about her sudden outbursts but what could've brought this on? Who could have provoked her? Why was she in the conference room?

"Oh, Lance," Dottie wailed. "Thank heavens, you're here. We can't find her. Dad and Ricky have been looking, but she's nowhere."

"Get Johnny," Lance snarled, glaring at the young man. "He'll find her faster than any of us."

Kelly nodded, hurrying to find Ricky to fetch Johnny. She really didn't want to be around when Lance found out exactly how this happened—he'd have her hide for this!

Johnny saw Ricky coming toward him, making him drop the hoe he was holding, feeling like he was about to be executed. He hadn't done anything—he was sure he hadn't.

"Johnny," Ricky explained quickly. "There has been an incident with Rain. Lance thinks you'll be able to find her and bring her back faster than any of us."

Johnny was surprised but quickly agreed to help out. He and Lance walked out toward the creek, and by the biggest tree, Johnny pointed out the small ball. Lance let out a sigh of relief.

"There she is," Johnny sighed. "You want me to get her?"

"Could you please?" Lance begged.

Johnny headed to the tree slowly—very slowly. He didn't speak until he was right beside her.

"Rain, its Johnny. What you doin'?"

She uncurled her limbs and stared in surprise at Johnny who now stood directly over her.

"Johnny?" she said quietly. "Why are you out here?"

"Finding you," he replied, holding out his hand to help her up. "What did I tell you about hitting people with stuff?"

She got up only to fall against his chest weeping. He pulled his arms around her and held her—he could see this had been a pretty tough transition for her.

"I'm sorry," she said between sobs. "He's just such a jerk. You'd have hit him, too. You know I don't like those kind!"

He bit his lip. What were they doing to her? He knew they'd never send her out. He tried to figure out what exactly she was talking about. A voice behind him spoke up.

"I don't think he was looking for favors, Rain. From what I hear, he's just a kid that thinks he knows everything because he's read some books—you can't go hitting people that bother you." Lance kept his tone soft and gentle even though Johnny knew he wasn't real happy at the moment.

She looked over at Lance and she knew she had failed—failed to qualify for the role of being normal, failed to think before she acted, failed at everything.

Lance ignored her downcast face and had Johnny escort her back to the conference center. Ricky then escorted Johnny back to his chores, much to Rain's horror. If he could stay, maybe she could handle this. Lance watched her eyes follow the man until he was out of sight and then he pulled her to the side of the man who now sported a white bandage on his forehead.

"You are the young man who conducted this interview?" Lance asked.

"Yes, I am," he admitted, still cocky, letting his eyes gaze coldly toward Rain.

Lance took the boy and Rain to an office and closed the door. He bid them take a seat while he bowed his head. He prayed, needing some very special guidance on this one. He could hear Rain and the boy squirming uncomfortably on their chairs. Finally, he spoke.

"Rain, what's this young man's name?"

"I don't know," she stammered, not looking up from the floor. She felt awful about the incident and wished it could just be forgotten.

"Oh, what is your name?" Lance asked, letting his gaze shift to the young man.

"Darrel," the young man replied, still not giving up his defensive edge.

"Hi, Darrel, I'm Lance and this is Rain. Now, you didn't bother to introduce yourself, so what did you do?"

Darrel shifted uncomfortably in his seat, upset that this man had the nerve to question him! Why not question the girl who bashed him over the head?

"Shouldn't she be somewhere else for this?" he replied.

"No, she should be right here so she can see what I think of your interview methods. Now answer the question."

"I asked the questions that we went over in class."

"Which were?" Lance asked through clenched teeth.

"I looked at her file and saw her name and asked her about her family."

"You asked Rain about her family?" Lance repeated, shaking his head.

"He forgot the joke he made about my name!" Rain cried in frustration that he wasn't telling the truth. "And he didn't ask about my family he asked how my family liked having a whore for a relative."

"Whoa, Rain, calm down." Lance ordered.

"But that's what he said!" she argued.

He looked her in the eye and saw the plea for him to believe her. He turned back to Darrel.

"Darrel, is Rain telling the truth?" Lance said, looking even more disgusted with the young man.

"She is a whore!" Darrel defended. "I wasn't doing anything but confronting the truth."

"Ouch," Lance winced like Darrel had said something painful to him instead of Rain. "Darrel, don't go into counseling. Rain is a person, usually a very quiet person. She's here trying to work her way out of a life that she was born into. You just made it very clear that you have no intentions of letting that happen. What life were you born into?"

"Uh, my dad's a doctor and my mom's an accountant," Darrel replied, not seeing any reason he needed to answer the question but couldn't see any harm in it either. He was proud of his upbringing.

"Silver spoon boy," Lance said, shaking his head. "So what do Mommy and Daddy think of their boy going for a career that's going to put him in contact with druggies and prostitutes?"

"Excuse me?"

"You asked her, I'm asking you."

"They're proud that I want to make a difference in people's lives."

"Well, let me tell you something. Rain hasn't got much family, but she does have me and I'm very proud of her because she's coming from nothing and fighting her way to make a life for herself. She has courage, where all you have is good intentions and trying to make Mommy and Daddy proud. Next time you think about doing an interview, remember that the files represent living, breathing, feeling people; not just paper and names with a case history. You can leave now."

Darrel stood to leave but turned to get the last word. "I did things by the book. My professor says I'm good at this and I don't know who you think you are telling me anything different."

"I don't know what book you're working out of but find a different one. I find the Bible to be a good text to use in context with the career you've chosen."

"You've got to be kidding," Darrel scoffed.

"I most certainly am not!" Lance shot back. "I am definitely contacting your professors and letting them know you are one student that is not ready for this career!"

Darrel's eyes shone with anger as he turned once again to leave. This time he made it pulling the door shut hard as he went. Lance took a deep breath glad he was gone but now had another situation he needed to deal with: Rain. He turned to her trying to decide what action he needed to take.

"So what do you have to say for yourself?" he asked her, trying to imagine what response she would have.

"I'm sorry, Mr. Hawkins, I really screwed up," Rain said, looking hopeful that it would cover it.

"I don't think so. And stop calling me Mr. Hawkins—it's Lance unless you want me calling you Miss Patterson."

Rain shook her head. She tried another excuse. "He made me mad."

"People do that. He made me mad, too, but I didn't hit him in the head."

"You did, just not with a glass!" she argued.

"Okay, I reamed him out and I bruised his tender ego, but I didn't physically attack him. You can go to jail for behavior like that! What were you thinking?"

"I got up to get Kelly and he blocked my path. He made me feel like he owned me; he treated me just like one of them."

"One of them?" Lance asked, not taking his eyes off of her.

"You know what I mean."

"Say it Rain. He treated you like . . ."

"Like the men that used me. Happy?"

"No, and he shouldn't have treated you like that. But Rain, you can't hit everyone who acts like a jerk. Society doesn't accept that!"

"I'll never be a part of society!" she wailed in frustration. "I'm useless."

"Yes, you will and you're not useless," he said, letting his demeanor soften. "Why were you being interviewed in the first place?"

"Kelly said they had too many students. She didn't want any doubling up so she asked if I could participate. Dottie didn't want to and she tried to call you but she couldn't get a hold of you. Kelly convinced her."

Lance let out a heavy sigh. They wanted him to do these things, but then they interfered with his program and undid months of work in one moment of impulsive action.

"I'll talk to them," he promised. "Rain, we have to get to the issues here so the next time you run into a Darrel, you're prepared. How about meeting me at three tomorrow?"

What choice did she have? "I'll be here."

Bryan watched Lance curiously as he put together his props for his meeting with Rain. He had spent more time with Rain than Lance and he didn't think his brother was really thinking her reaction through on this one.

"Don't you think this might be a little harsh?" he asked as Lance worked.

"She's spoiled and used to getting her way," Lance replied, making sure all his props were in just the right place. "She manipulated Johnny and his dad into making them go easy on her. She wasn't always one hundred percent successful, but she had it pretty easy in comparison to many girls. I asked Ricky and he agrees with me on this one. I've watched her weave her spell over Mom, and I'm hoping she hasn't got to you!"

"Got to me?" Bryan declared. "She's pretty ordinary when I'm around her. She does what I ask her to do and when she has trouble, she asks for help. I don't see this conniving manipulator you seem to see."

Lance shrugged. Bryan could have his opinion.

"I'm not naive!" Bryan defended, knowing his brother's thoughts. "You think she's got me in her web?"

"I do."

"Oh, so I'm not suave enough to avoid it, but you won't fall into this trap," Bryan said shaking his head. He hated it when Lance got arrogant.

"I will not."

"Women can be pretty tricky!" Bryan smiled, shaking his finger at his brother. "You know, Lance, dating would be a great asset to you at times like this!"

"Thank you for your input!" Lance droned. "Yes, she's tricky but this one knows only one place to use these skills and I'm not biting."

"Do you have any normal urges?"

"Yes!" Lance said, giving his brother the evil eye. "You don't have to be insulting."

"I just wondered because you're so set on not getting married, and all these beautiful girls don't seem to have much effect. Rain is exceptionally pretty and you seem to think that won't be a problem."

"Rain is pretty, isn't she?" Lance remarked as if he just realized this fact.

"He is human!" Bryan cried, raising his arms to the sky. "If I were you, I would watch myself with that one."

"I still don't think it will be a problem," he replied, heading toward the door. "Miss Rain's number has come up and I know that number!"

Bryan followed Lance out of the room toward the office where Rain was waiting.

"Take it easy on her!" Bryan warned as he watched Lance enter the office. "Mom has a soft spot for her that she'll use against you!"

Lance nodded, knowing on this occasion, Dottie would have to back off even if she was his mom. He had to do this his way.

"Sorry I'm late," Lance apologized, hurrying into the room. "Bryan and I were having an interesting discussion and I lost track of time."

"It's only two minutes," Rain replied.

"So I'm two minutes late and I apologize. Now, we have a lot to accomplish so let's get started," he said, leading her out of the office and to the conference room door. "Can you please close your eyes?"

"Close my eyes?"

"And don't open them until I say you can."

Rain didn't like surprises, but she decided she'd better humor him. If she didn't like where she saw this going, she could bolt. He took her hand in his and led her into the room, making sure she kept her eyes closed. Finally, he sat her down in a chair, taking a position behind her.

"Open your eyes!" he commanded.

Rain obeyed the order, slowly pulling her eyes open. She gasped. Everywhere she looked there were mirrors reflecting back the truth she feared. She threw her hands in front of her face, only to have Lance pull them away. The fight was on! Lance ordered her to open her eyes, and she responded with screams of protest.

Ricky and Bryan sat outside the room, waiting for the protests to sound and they weren't disappointed. Ricky shook his head, knowing Lance and Rain both had strong wills that would be doing battle, with neither able to accept defeat.

"I just don't know if he's going about this in the right way," Bryan sighed.

"Lance will handle it. Your brother is very good at what he does and I trust him to know how far he can go," Ricky assured. "I was instructed to get involved only if he sounded like he was losing control."

Bryan nodded. Lance did seem to have a way of understanding people that he didn't but this seemed too harsh.

"Look in the mirror, Rain, and tell me what you see." Lance ordered, trying to remain patient and kind in his delivery of the order, but it had been an hour of fighting with her now.

"I won't! This is cruel!" she cried, trying to pull out of the chair and, with any luck, run out of the room.

"Look in the mirror!" he ordered, now holding her hands firmly on the armrests on the chair.

She managed to work her hand loose enough to dig her nails into his skin, hoping this would loosen his grip and give her a chance to escape, but he held her fast in the chair. He knew this would anger her, but now that the challenge had been wagered, she had to look in the mirror. She could not have the victory this time.

"I'll kill you before I look in those mirrors!" she shrieked.

"Look in the mirror!" he repeated, not reacting to her threats.

She tried to squirm free but he wouldn't have it. Three hours into the session, Rain realized this guy was not leaving until she did as he asked. She let her body go limp, giving up the fight. Lance held on, waiting. She opened her eyes slowly, glancing at the reflection that greeted her but turned her head back to her toes quickly. He rewarded the effort by releasing her hands that were now sore from his hold on them. He spoke very softly to her.

"Rain, I want you to look in the mirror and tell me what you see."

She felt the grip release and took her chance. She leapt off the chair heading toward the door, averting her eyes away from the images that jumped out from every corner of the room.

"Where are you gonna run to?" he asked, taking a place between her and the door.

"I can't do this," she wept, trying to fall against him, but he held her back.

"Answer the question."

"I have nowhere to go and you know that!" she swore at him.

"We have some place to go, and the journey starts with that image in the mirror." Lance told her firmly.

"Why are you being so mean?"

"I'm not," he said, hating to have to upset her like this. "Rain, this is what love does."

She let him believe that the words had touched her and let herself go limp. He wasn't that easily fooled and stood on his guard.

"If I look, is that enough?" she asked, sounding as sweet as an angel.

"No!" he said, shaking his head.

The anger flickered in her eyes. She hated it when it had to be all his way. This meant war. She shoved him hard and pushed passed him out the door. He shook his head—he had expected this. He played the game running after her, catching her on the front step. He lifted her, kicking and screaming, and carried her back into the room. Ricky smiled at him Bryan didn't know what to make of it.

"How come he can get her branding iron hot under the collar and that guy yesterday got in trouble?" Bryan asked.

"What happened yesterday was very different," Ricky explained. "That guy wanted to prove his superiority over Rain, where Lance is trying hard to show her she's no different than the rest of us. See the difference?"

Bryan nodded. He wondered if he had it in him to do this job. He knew he couldn't ever confront anyone the way Lance was doing right now.

"You get to realize when they're conning you," Ricky explained seeing the doubt on Bryan's face. "Darrel didn't prepare a new foundation to build on. I realize with houses, you tear down and then rebuild but with people, you have to start laying the new before completely tearing down the old. You have to give them something to hold onto during the transition. Lance has shown Rain he cares about her and that this place cares about her. She can let go of the old and have a safe place to land while she figures out the new."

"I think I get it," Bryan stated. "I guess I'm just more of a take one brick at a time kind of demolition guy."

Ricky laughed.

"I hate you!" Rain screamed when he set her back on the chair.

"That's fine, but you're still looking in that mirror." Lance replied, preparing himself for a fight.

Rain raised her eyes, not to look at her reflection but his. There was a stubborn line of resolve on his face and she knew she would not wait him out. Escape was futile so she was left with knocking him out or complying. There was no way for her to reach any object with which to strike, and he stayed behind her, making it hard to attack. She swallowed hard, realizing she was defeated.

It angered her that he had gotten the better of her, and now she needed to figure out the most graceful way to accept the inevitable. She slowly turned her eyes to her reflection. He prayed a silent 'thank you' to the air.

"What do you see?" he whispered.

"You know very well what I see!" she replied angrily. This was just rubbing in the victory from her vantage point.

"No, I don't, because what I see may not be the same as what you see."

"I see ugly, used." The tears came, racking her small frame in sobs.

He caressed her shoulders, gently encouraging her to say more. She wanted to break those fingers at this moment.

"What else?" he asked.

She remained silent.

"Rain, tell me what you see?"

"I see my mom. I see failure, nothing."

"Rain, look at the person, not at the feelings."

"What do you want me to say?" Her voice was rising again.

"Tell me what you see!" he said, the words coming out as softly as the movement of a butterfly's wing.

"I see a blond, brown-eyed girl with a tear stained face."

"Thank you," he said quietly. "Now I know we at least see some of the same things. Rain, people can't see the feelings when they just look at you, but you think they do. You think they see the ugly you feel, but they don't. I see a beautiful girl who seems very sad."

Lance stood and mercifully took down the mirrors. She breathed easier, thinking they were done. She glanced at the door but Lance had other ideas. He called Bryan in to join them.

"I want you to look at these pictures and tell me which one you think is the prettiest," he instructed Rain.

She sighed but did as she was asked. The pictures all looked like fashion models and, after much consideration, she picked one.

"Sam," Lance said, picking up the picture and admiring it before turning it back to her. "Yeah she is very pretty and this is a professional photo and she is a fashion model. I don't know if you noticed but she has a lot of the same characteristics as you."

"No, she doesn't."

"She's blond with brown eyes. She's a graduate from here and lived on the streets for ten years."

"That's not fair!" she cried. "You didn't tell me they came from here."

"So, she's not pretty anymore?" Lance asked, staring at the picture as if he were looking for what had changed.

"I know what you're doing and you can't do this!" she declared.

"What can't I do? Show you the lies you keep telling yourself? You live in a world of self-pity, and Johnny fuelled it by spoiling you rotten. You are a spoiled brat who really had it pretty darn easy in comparison to many of your fellow workers. Johnny told me how he had to make other girls make up for your lapses."

"Johnny told you that?" she questioned, hating him more every second.

"Yes."

This changed the whole thing for Rain. Now she decided to work from a new angle. She was making this stop!

"Why should I sleep with some old guy?" Rain defended. "They enjoyed it and I hated it. I did what they wished they could do—I refused."

"So why do you hate yourself so much? I mean, you accomplished quite a feat getting Johnny to care about you. You manipulated everyone around you and are still trying very hard to continue to do so!"

"He betrayed me and made me become my mom. If he cared, he wouldn't have done that and if I had any self purpose, I wouldn't have done it even if he had killed me."

"You compromised your standards!" Lance said, pointing his finger at her.

"Yes!" she cried in disgust and anger. "Yes! I sold myself out."

"Then why do you blame Johnny? He loves you; he doesn't see you this way at all!"

"What do you care? You don't know anything!" Rain yelled. "He was supposed to take care of me and he hurt me. He used me when I was hurting. He took my compassion and turned it against me."

"I know you're a spoiled brat who managed to upset a household where a common whore doesn't do that too often! He did his job or at least he sort of did it," he said, knowing she wouldn't like the words he was using. "So why don't you like to look at your reflection?"

"Because I see her and I hated her!" Rain wept, just wanting this all to stop.

"Her, you hated her?"

"My mom."

Lance backed off, softening his demeanor. He leaned back in the chair, giving her a moment to get her emotions back in check.

"Do you want a hug?" he asked, throwing her once again off balance.

"Not from you."

"From her?"

She laughed in disbelief that he would suggest such a thing. He didn't know anything at all about her.

"I want to spit on her and hit her and bash her head. I want to rip out her hair and make her see that I am right there seeing her. I'm hungry and cold but she just keeps them warm and fed. I don't want to eat the crumbs that fall off the bed anymore."

"Your mom failed you. But Rain, she didn't send you out."

"I didn't know anything else."

"You could have learned."

"I never even saw a tree before I went to Johnny's," Rain said quietly, avoiding his question.

Lance fell silent, looking at her. Rain's anger had very little to do with prostitution. She was suffering from abuse of a totally different nature, and her soul had somehow been misplaced. He glanced at his watch, shocked to see it was past supper.

"Was this exercise really necessary?" Bryan asked, taking in Rain's flushed face.

"It was," Lance replied. "I now know the root of Rain's situation. I can now move forward in a way that will be directly set for her. I think that's a lot better than thinking she's simply a prostitute and that's the end of the story. What do you think?"

"I'm confused."

"Rain's problems stem from a different place other than just prostitution. She's a hurt little girl needing her mom's love. Most prostitutes have abuse issues and once you find that source of pain, you can help in the healing process."

Bryan nodded. He still didn't like the method but it was all clear to him now. He'd seen this but never understood it as clearly as he did this moment.

"Thanks for the lesson," he stated, rising to leave.

"No problem," Lance replied. "It was my big brother duty."

Rain wished Bryan would stay but once again it was down to the two of them.

"You ready to quit or do you want to talk?" Lance asked her.

"Are you really giving me a choice or is this another trick?" she asked. "You've been so mean! Why do you make me remember all these things?"

He was ready to stop, but he would answer the question.

"Because I want you to live and be happy. I want you to forgive because until you do, you'll live as that little girl eating the crumbs."

"I can't do this! I won't and you can't make me!"

He let his gaze go to the window. They had been at it for hours already. He was hungry, as she must be. If he kept going, she would seal her hate toward him.

"Do you like pizza?" he asked.

She wasn't ready for the offer and eyed him carefully before answering.

"If I say yes, what will that mean?"

"It means we'll have pizza before we continue!"

She wondered what the trick would be behind the offer. She was hungry and tired and the offer of food was just too inviting. He ordered the pizza.

Much to her surprise, Lance did a hundred and eighty degree turn when the pizza arrived. He talked about growing up at the farm and getting into trouble—things that had nothing to do with her. She laughed at his stories but never totally let her guard down.

Then the pizza was gone and it was time to return to the business of the day. He led her out of the conference room, knowing the dorms would be full soon. He didn't think Rain would want to face the other residents today. He took her out to the trees near the creek.

"What did you think the first time you saw trees?" he asked when they had seated themselves on the grass.

"I thought it was amazing. I lived in a place where there was barely a blade of grass that dared to grow. I really didn't get outside very much anyway. That trip to Johnny's was my first trip away from that ratty shack. We went to Johnny Sr.'s. You know, I realize now she went there all the time because she was his. He owned her. It was such a nice house with beautiful furniture. It was all like a dream and in the end, that's all it was. But it was the trees that amazed me the most—they were so big. So strong and big and rooted down so it was hard to hurt them or move them."

"I don't get why you would like the rooted down part," Lance said, shaking his head. "It seems you didn't like being rooted down."

"But they could be beautiful where they stood."

"Okay," Lance said, thinking about that carefully. "Do you like it here?"

"I like Dottie and Bryan. I like talking to your Dad."

"And me?"

Rain bit her lip. What should she say?

"I don't know."

"Yes, you do. Rain, I'm not going to be terribly hurt if you don't like me. It's not my job to make you like me—it's my job to try and help you."

"You can be nice," she whispered. "Sometimes you almost have fun but usually you're too tired to care."

He smiled. "I guess I don't see much 'fun' in my job. If I could get some sleep once in a while, I might not be tired all the time. So what about me makes me different from the others?"

"You're mean sometimes."

"Because I challenge you," he added. "How do you feel about Johnny?"

"I love him," she said, not looking at him as she spoke.

"That was convincing!"

"We've been together a long time. In a way, we've been married for a long time," she looked at him. "Do you understand?"

He understood—she was settling, but what he didn't know was why?

Bryan and Lance shared a bedroom on these weekends just like old times. For both of them, it was kind of nice to be able to rekindle their old traditions, one of which was talking deep into the night. Tonight Lance was tired but Bryan had a lot on his mind.

"So she handle it okay? You had her trapped all day!"

"She was fine. You seem a little more than interested!" Lance said trying to sound tired so Bryan would shut up.

"I got my eye on someone else, thanks!"

Lance was suddenly wide awake. "Who?"

"You really are so thick when it comes to women and relationships! I'm dating Debbie! I'm planning to ask her to marry me."

"Debbie? Marriage?" Lance shook his head.

"Where have you been?" Bryan replied. "Mom and Dad have talked about it with me in your presence."

"I don't remember—I wouldn't forget anything like that."

"I'm hoping to ask her tomorrow night."

"As long as you're happy, I guess, but really, Debbie?" It bothered him that he couldn't remember anyone mentioning this.

"I think you're jealous," Bryan announced.

Lance laughed.

Bryan threw his pillow across the room, hitting his target dead on. Lance grabbed the pillow and tossed it back with more force than needed. Soon they were deep in a pillow fight. Arthur came to see what was going on. The boys quickly quieted down, knowing they couldn't get away with a second warning, even at their age.

"So you really aren't going to ever get married?" Bryan asked once he was sure Dad had gone to bed.

"You know Bry, I can't see how a woman could put up with my schedule and I really am married to the work. I'm always on duty."

"But Dave's married."

"He is, but he'll tell you how hard it is. I don't think I could make the sacrifices it would take to make both work."

They fell silent. Bryan wasn't finished with his schooling and hearing Lance talk so candidly and honestly about his life made him wonder if he had chosen the right major. He would have asked more about it, but Lance was snoring.

CHAPTER 30

Morning came and Arthur had his family out of bed in plenty of time to get ready for church. It was a place that Rain had not yet experienced because of the pain her shoulder was causing. Lance had determined today to change that.

"What do they do at church?" she asked.

"Sing, pray and listen."

"Listen to what?"

"Other people sing, pray and talk."

Rain scrunched up her nose, thinking this didn't sound like much fun, but she didn't think she had the right to say no to the invitation. Lance and Ricky escorted her to the car while the others went with Arthur.

The church was a very simple building—nothing that seemed grand or special. Rain let Lance guide her through the door and that's where the differences between this place and any other place she had ever been became clearly evident. People welcomed them—even her—with open arms. It seemed to take forever to get seated, but eventually things quieted down and a man took his place in front of the people. He greeted everyone warmly, smiling broadly as he spoke. Rain examined the smile. It was a pure expression of what the man seemed to feel: rare.

The service moved to the singing. Lance heartily joined in, obviously enjoying the songs that Rain had heard at the dorms but didn't feel comfortable trying to sing along with. It wasn't nearly as bad as Rain thought it might be, and the sermon even held certain comments that caught her attention—words she had heard at the farm. Lance smiled at her, glad she looked comfortable with the whole experience.

Lance had to head back to the city right after dinner, giving Rain no chance to talk to him about the church service. She was disappointed that she couldn't talk to him about it, so she did her best to jot down her questions so she could ask them next time he talked to her.

On Monday, Arthur had a surprise for her. Johnny sat in the kitchen waiting for her. She squealed with delight.

"I missed you, too!" he smiled, when he saw her. He had been very nervous waiting, thinking she had probably moved beyond him, but the look on her face settled those fears.

Ricky sat on the other side of the table and Rain only took note of him after she gave Johnny a hug.

"I'm sorry!" she said, biting her lip. "It is okay for me to hug him, right?"

"Fine!" Ricky smiled. "Actually, I want to talk to both of you. I thought we might as well have breakfast together while doing it. Dottie's cooking is so much better than anything we get in the dorm!"

Dottie swatted him gently. "You know very well I cook breakfast there, too!"

Ricky let a mischievous grin cross his face as he heaped the food on his plate. "I know, but here I can get seconds and thirds!"

Johnny shook his head, laughing. Ricky seemed to like food a lot!

"So," Ricky continued, "part of the program for Johnny includes being confronted by some of the people in his past. Now there are two girls here who worked for Tommy, but we know that equals working for Johnny, too. We really would like someone who worked a little closer and that leaves only you, Rain."

"What does it mean?" Rain asked, not fully understanding what he was trying to say.

"It means you confront Johnny with the things he did that hurt you. He has to listen and apologize but he can't argue. The other two girls will be doing it, too, but like I say, Tommy is really the guy they learned to hate."

"But I love Johnny!" Rain said, looking at the man who was in very many ways, her husband.

"I know. Lance told me. He still thinks there are issues you could confront Johnny with."

"So I have to be quiet through all this?" Johnny asked.

"You get to apologize."

"Why are you here telling me this?" Rain asked.

"I'm not going to force you to do this. Lance isn't going to force you to do this. We both think it would be a good thing for both of you, but we are giving you the final say."

"Oh," Rain said, thinking hard. Why would Lance want her to do this? He didn't do things unless there was a purpose.

"You can call Lance and talk to him about it," Ricky offered.

"Do I have to give you my decision right now?"

"No. Actually, Lance will be here when we get this thing going. I just wanted to let you have a chance to think about it, and I brought Johnny here so you would know he's in on this."

They finished breakfast and then Ricky led Johnny out the door. There was work waiting in the form of endless rows of weeding. Rain watched them leave, thinking hard about this new twist in her existence.

Lori sat at the table sipping her coffee when Dave finally emerged from the bathroom, his hair still dripping wet from the shower.

"You're running very late!" she told him.

"I know. Lance will let me know it, too. I talked to Ricky today and it seems Johnny is already heading into the confrontation program. He must be doing real well."

"He hasn't even had his day in court yet!"

"Lori, you know he pleaded guilty and the judge has okayed the farm. I don't think we're going to be in for any surprises on this one." Dave was getting frustrated as he spoke.

"I still feel like he was cornered into that plea!" Lori replied, letting the disgust drip from her voice. "If you and Lance had stayed out of it, I could've got him off with nothing! That shooting was clearly self defense."

"He's a pimp!" Dave said, making sure to clearly enunciate each word.

"He runs a club!" Lori defended.

Dave rolled his eyes as he headed back to the bedroom to get out of the line of fire. This conversation always led to the same place, and it was never a good place. She slammed her coffee cup onto the table in frustration, hating it that he believed the worst about someone she loved so dearly.

He re-emerged from the bedroom carrying a half-full pill bottle.

"Are you still taking pain killers?" he questioned.

"My neck still hurts," she told him.

"Then you should go back to the doctor," he advised. "Lori, you've been under a lot of stress and these things can be addictive."

"Are you calling me a drug addict now?" she snarled. "I was in an accident, and those have been prescribed to me by a doctor!"

Dave shook his head. He couldn't win—everything with his wife was an argument as of late.

When Lance arrived late at the office and Dave wasn't there, he knew he had to brace himself. Dave being late meant a fight with Lori, which ensured his boss' mood would be bad. He unlocked the front door and headed to his office. He said a quick prayer, knowing he didn't have the strength to deal with it all.

The center was a hub of activity on any given day, providing teens with a place to come and relax, play some basketball or talk to Lance or Dave. Because most of the clientele was in school, the place was usually quieter during school hours and then insane until they locked the door at night. Volunteers ran programs after office hours when Lance was supposed to go home but it never seemed to work out that way. Mornings were usually very busy with appointments, and this morning was like any other.

Dave rolled into work around nine-thirty—two hours later than usual. The fight with Lori took his energy down to zero, and showing up at this place without any energy was an exercise in danger. They saw far too many strung-out people to risk looking uninterested in what they had to say. He leaned into Lance's office to let him know he had arrived.

"Let me guess," Lance said upon seeing him. "Johnny and pleading guilty and you not caring about the people she loves."

"Bingo!" Dave smiled grimly. "If I had a million dollars, you would've just won it! But today a new twist was added to the plot."

"A new twist?"

"How long should one be on pain killers after an accident?"

"Depends on the injury."

Dave nodded. "I better let you get back to work and I am way behind."

Lance didn't have peace about the conversation, but he knew they'd talk more later in the day.

The day seemed endless, but finally Lance was with his last appointment. It was a new client that he knew very little about so he was on his guard.

"Hello, Mr. Reed," he greeted. "I'm Lance Hawkins. How can I help you?"

"You can help me by getting my brother back to me!" the man snarled.

Lance's senses tingled—this guy was looking for trouble.

"Who exactly is your brother?"

"Leroy Reed! He was talking about you and how much you helped him and the next thing I know he's arrested!"

Lance turned the name over in his mind for a moment. So far, the guy was definitely upset but not violent, so maybe this could be reasoned through.

"He came to see me?' Lance repeated. "Would you by any chance know what he saw me about?"

"I really don't know!" the man stated, his voice staying even. "All I know is after seeing you, he got arrested."

Lance couldn't recall the name and didn't know if this guy would let him grab the file. He prayed, begging God to bring back the name.

"Just get him back and we'll call this even!" the man said, now rising from his chair.

Lance swallowed hard, wondering what he was up to but much to his relief, the man walked out the door. Lance took a deep breath gasping for air. That could have turned very ugly!

By Thursday, Rain had decided that she would do the program with Johnny but didn't think it would help him much. She really didn't know what she would have to confront him with. Lance turned up on Friday, glad she was willing, and the first meeting was set up.

"So you two understand what we do here?" Ricky stated as they took their places around the table in the conference room.

"Oh, yes we do!" the one girl named Wanda declared.

"We can hardly wait!" her friend Bernice said, glaring at Johnny.

Rain came in with Lance, looking nervously at the others in the room, but trusting that Lance would keep her safe.

"Okay," Ricky sighed. "Let's begin—Bernice?"

"I just say what I think of him?"

"You relate an incident to him and he apologizes."

Bernice recounted a scene that Rain knew all too well and knew the girl wasn't lying. Johnny could be very cruel.

Johnny wanted to run. He hated having Rain listen to these things even more than he hated having to apologize for them. He knew he was guilty as charged.

"Johnny?" Ricky asked.

"I am very sorry!" he said with a total lack of enthusiasm.

Then it was Wanda's turn and, once again, the story spoke of a level of cruelty that disgusted even Ricky who usually didn't get too disturbed by these things. It too was followed by a half-hearted apology. Then it was Rain's turn. Wanda and Bernice looked at her, wondering what she could possibly say that would even come close to the stories they just told. Rain looked at Lance, knowing she didn't have any stories that could come close to the things she had just heard.

"Just share your own experience," Lance said, encouraging her with his eyes.

"Well, um," Rain stammered, trying to think of something. "I, um remember one incident that really bothered me."

"Okay," Ricky said, looking at her kindly, "share that with us."

"It was after Johnny Sr.'s funeral and we got back to the house," Rain said slowly, looking down as she spoke. "We sort of had this bet, I guess you'd call it, that if Johnny took my virginity, I would be his. But that night it wasn't about bets or anything. We both needed someone, someone to love, to feel."

Rain fell silent, letting her gaze move directly to Johnny who had dared to let his gaze lift to her.

"It wasn't about the bet, not that night!" she stated.

"You gave in!" he whispered.

"Not that way!" she said, pushing back the tears. "I had nobody else. I was hurting and needed someone to love me just like you did. It wasn't fair for you to take . . ."

Johnny looked at her, knowing very well what he took; knew she was right. He had needed her and used the love she gave him to destroy her.

"I'm sorry," he whispered. "Tommy was laughing at me already and then came that night. I am so sorry."

Lance and Ricky watched them. Johnny had no emotional attachment to these other two girls and would do as he was told as far as they were concerned, but Rain would be the one to break him. They could see the anger in Wanda's eyes as she realized the same thing. This would be a very interesting process.

CHAPTER 31

The weekend behind him, Lance sat at his desk, feeling like he was coming down from a high. The farm provided him with a chance to remember what it was like in the beginning of his counseling days—he loved the in-depth work he was able to do there. He felt alive when he worked with Rain. Seeing her realize her value as a person was like watching a rare flower open to show its beauty for the first time. In contrast, here they simply put bandages on gaping wounds in hopes that their patient would seek out a place like the farm. He sighed, feeling all his efforts here were futile. His office door swinging open brought him out of his train of thought as he found himself once again facing Mr. Reed.

"You ain't done nothin' to help my brother!" the man slurred, falling into the chair across from Lance.

"I looked at his file and the reason he came to see me was personal—nothing that would involve police. I have no idea why he was arrested." He had a feeling nothing he said would help.

"It was you!" the man bellowed, pulling a large knife out of his belt.

Lance said a quick prayer, preparing for the worst.

"I'm sorry, but I didn't have anything to do with . . ."

The man slammed the chair back, standing like an angry bear over Lance's desk. He let out a primal shout, and the knife cut threw the air, directed toward Lance's chest. Lance reacted, quickly deflecting the blade that sliced away at his arm. The man stared in disbelief. He could see the man wasn't used to being challenged. He wasn't about to die quietly.

"I didn't have anything to do with your brother!" Lance repeated, hoping the man would come to his senses, but the blade was again moving.

Lance pushed his chair back hard, knowing it would hit the wall and hoping it would alert Dave. Now if he could just avoid the blade that Reed was waving wildly at him.

Dave heard the hard thud against the wall and something inside told him Lance needed help. He hurried to the next room where he found Reed still slashing violently at Lance whose arms were bleeding profusely from deflecting the blows. Dave saw the knife plunge just as he moved to grab the man from behind. Not even considering his own safety, he joined in the fight. Others in the building heard the ruckus and came running. It took three men twenty minutes to subdue Reed, and then their attentions went to Lance who was gasping for air in the corner of his office.

"Oh man!" Dave cried. He turned and shouted to the other helpers, "Get an ambulance! Now!"

Dave waited in the hospital for any word on Lance's condition, but there was none coming. With each passing minute, he got more worked up that maybe Lance was dying.

"Heard anything yet?" Lori asked, taking a seat beside him.

"Nothing," he replied, taking the coffee she offered him. "I guess I'd better call Arthur and Dottie. I was kind of waiting until we got some word, but he might not even make it. I don't want to have to make the first call that call!"

Dave got up to make his way to the phones.

Dottie and Rain smiled with satisfaction at the row of pies that now stood on the table, ready for that day's noon meal. The phone rang.

"I'll be right back!" Dottie said, turning to answer the call.

Rain listened to Dottie's tone change as the conversation on the phone progressed. She called Bryan, fearing the news was very bad. Soon Rain, Bryan and Debbie were crowded around Dottie waiting to hear the news, but Dottie didn't explain. Instead, she sank to the floor, looking deathly pale.

"Mom!" Bryan cried.

"Get Dad!" she wept.

Bryan headed out the door to find his dad, not sure if Dottie was having a heart attack or what. Debbie hurried to the woman's side.

"What is it?" she cried.

"Lance!" Dottie managed to say before the heart wrenching sobs took over.

Arthur hurried to the house, dirt from the garden still clinging to his clothes. The phone still hung from its cord, swinging in the air. He could hear Dottie's sobs from somewhere within the house.

"What is it?" Arthur demanded.

"Lance," Debbie said, shrugging her shoulders. "That's all she said. She's in the bedroom changing."

Arthur grabbed the phone. "Hello?"

"Arthur, its Dave. Lance has been hurt and it's bad. I mean, I'm not sure he's still with us!" Dave felt his throat closing.

"We're on our way!" Arthur announced.

"What is going on?" Bryan cried in frustration.

"Lance has been hurt, maybe killed," Arthur replied, not truly understanding the words he was saying.

"No!" Rain cried. How could this be? Lance was trying so hard to do good things!

"Mom and I are going up."

"I'm coming!" Bryan declared.

"No," Arthur said gently. "You stay here and be with Rain. Tell Ricky."

Bryan didn't argue, suddenly not wanting to be that close to anything this bad. He couldn't face watching Lance die. He started to pray.

Dottie and Arthur found Dave still waiting when they arrived at the hospital. Things still looked bleak. Lance was still alive but his exact condition was not known.

"What happened?" Arthur asked.

"A guy came in and stabbed him. He fought, Arthur. The guy had him trapped, but he managed to signal me. The guy got him at least three times that I saw. I told them this would happen! We're so putting our lives in danger in that place. If he dies, I'll forever blame myself—I knew the way things were set up that this kind of thing could happen. He was caged in there with the monster."

"Dave, he's still alive!" Arthur stated, trying to think of something encouraging to say. "Problems at the center can be fixed before the next incident."

"Arthur, he looked bad. I mean far worse than Bryan."

They fell silent, each one petitioning the Father for help.

Rain cried, leaning on Bryan and Debbie for support.

"I think I'd better go tell Ricky," Debbie said, still in shock. She moved like a robot toward the door.

"Okay," Bryan replied, also still spinning from it all.

"I don't understand why people would do this!" Rain lamented. "Lance just wants to help people! Why would they hurt him for that?"

"I don't know," Bryan said quietly, but then he did know. "Dave and Lance work with a lot of people, and I'd guess this will be traced back to some person who was unhappy with the work they do. It's a risk they take, helping those who don't always appreciate the help."

"Your dad would pray," Rain said, biting her lip. "Could you and I do that?"

"I think we can; in fact, I think we'd better."

"Bryan," Rain said, her mouth going dry. "I'm not a Christian. I hear your dad talk about it in the Bible studies, and I know the people in church have something I don't. I'm not even sure if I can talk to God."

Bryan looked at her. He had never before had a conversation like this with anyone. Why couldn't Lance be here? He was no good at these things.

"We can change that real quick if you want," he stammered. "I mean, you can talk to God even if you aren't a Christian, but it's better if you are. You can be one."

"Are you sure?"

"Positive."

"I don't know if I want to take that step. What difference does it really make?" Rain asked.

"Praying without knowing God . . ." Bryan said, trying to think of how to explain this, "is like throwing a ball into the darkness and hoping you hit the plate. But when you know Him, the plate is all lit up."

Rain didn't really understand.

"Okay, I can see baseball isn't your sport," Bryan stated, trying to come up with another good analogy. He wished Arthur was there! "When you go out to meet your dates—escorts, whatever you call them, if you walk into a room with two hundred people with no idea what this guy looks like or what he should be wearing, you'd have a hard time getting to that one person. Now if you knew that person, you could get right to him. If you know God, you don't have to guess where He's at."

"I think that makes sense," Rain said quietly. "Bryan, will God accept me?"

"Why wouldn't He?" Bryan asked, taking her hand. "We all come to God in the same condition—fallen short of God's glory."

"I want to be able to pray!" Rain pleaded. "I want Lance to be okay."

"That's the easy part!" Bryan responded. "Living the life is the hard part. When you pray, God gives answers that sometimes involve action on our part. Rain, I want you to pray and become a Christian, but not just because of Lance. It's something you have to want to do with your life."

"I see all of you and I know you have something I don't. Something I want to have. Lance getting hurt just makes me see how much I'm missing in my life."

Bryan smiled as he took her hands in his.

"Well, then repeat after me," Bryan instructed. "I Rain Patterson."

"I Rain Patterson."

"Accept that I am a sinner."

"Accept that I am a sinner."

"I need the forgiveness that only Jesus Christ can offer."

She repeated the words.

"I believe He died on a cross for my sins."

"I believe He died on a cross for my sins."

"And that He rose again. He is the Son of God and my Savior."

Rain repeated the words, each one becoming a cleansing balm, washing her clean. When she raised her head, she knew something inside had changed; she wasn't sure what it was but it felt good.

The doctor finally emerged from the operating room looking tired but hopeful. He recognized Dave and could see the family resemblance of his patient to the elderly couple sitting near him.

"Dr. Wallace!" Dave cried, hurrying toward the man.

"He's alive!" Dr. Wallace announced.

All four of them sighed with relief but knew there was much more the doctor needed to tell them. They had been waiting for three hours since Arthur and Dottie arrived.

"How bad is it?" Arthur asked, bracing himself for the news.

"It's not good!" Dr. Wallace informed them. "He was stabbed four times and cut all over his arms. I think we put at least two hundred stitches in his arms alone! That's probably a good thing—it shows he defended himself well! The problem is, he didn't deflect every blow and one wound was very much life threatening. The knife went into his chest, punctured a lung and then angled downward and caught his kidney. This guy was using a serious weapon here!"

"He was!" Dave nodded.

"He's lucky to be alive!"

"Can we see him?" Dottie asked, wiping the tears from her eyes.

"I'll get a nurse to fetch you when he comes to."

Ricky and his wife Sarah had joined Rain, Debbie and Bryan in their prayer vigil. They sat with heads bowed as they each poured out their cares and concerns. Then the phone interrupted them. Bryan hurried to answer it.

"That was Dad," he announced, after he hung up. "Lance made it through surgery, but he isn't out of the woods yet."

"What are the injuries?" Ricky demanded to know.

"How long will he be in the hospital?" Rain asked.

"Is he talking? Did the guy do anything to his head?" Debbie inquired.

"He just got out of surgery," Bryan repeated. "They don't know much else except that it's pretty serious."

They decided to go back to praying—it was easier than just waiting.

CHAPTER 32

A week later, Lance closed his eyes, praying they would soon be at their destination. The trip to the farm was almost more than he could bear.

"Are you comfortable?" Dottie asked, seeing him pale once again. She knew he was hurting and felt angry that he was being sent home when it was so obvious he needed hospital care. "We'll be there in a few minutes!"

"Just get me there!" Lance pleaded.

His arms were still wrapped in bandages so he couldn't see the sutures, but his imagination had filled in the blank spots. His chest hurt, his back hurt, his shoulder hurt—everything hurt, but he was still happy to be leaving the hospital where rest didn't seem to come. The man who did this was in jail and he had to say that gave him peace of mind, but he still couldn't understand the man's radical behavior. He had only met Leroy Reed once and that meeting lasted all of ten minutes. He saw the farm come into view and his mind switched gears. He was thinking about the transfer from vehicle to house. He was not looking forward to that!

They were all there to greet him, staring at him like he was some prize jewel. He hoped they treated him in a manner that reflected that sentiment.

"So how do you want to do this?" Ricky asked, knowing they had to get him inside.

"I don't," Lance admitted, "But since that isn't an option—gently."

Ricky did his best, but Lance couldn't stop the groans of pain.

"Sorry, Man!" Ricky said when the ordeal was over.

Lance let his head sink into the pillow, glad to be on his bed.

"I know you're feeling awful but I need to know if you want Johnny and Rain to meet when you aren't there to referee?" Ricky asked.

"U-hhhh," Lance sighed, leaving Ricky to wonder if it was a moan of pain or an indication that he was thinking about it. "Probably we should skip this week."

"Okay," Ricky agreed. He wasn't going to argue! "We'll just let things go for a bit here."

Lance tried to nod but the slightest of movements caused spasms of pain to ripple through his being.

"Hey, Ricky, can you make sure Rain is getting some counseling? I don't want to lose the work we've done."

"No problem. Bryan's working with her schoolwork every day, so I'll make sure he makes the sessions a bit more in depth."

Lance blinked his acknowledgement before giving in to the exhaustion. He closed his eyes. Ricky said a quick prayer over his friend before going to find Bryan.

Rain sat by Lance's bedside praying. She had pleaded with Bryan and Ricky to be allowed this luxury for just this one day—she had something she had to tell him. He looked so pale and hurt, and she felt he needed her even though he hadn't even once asked for her. Bryan was with Debbie so she knew she could sit and gaze at this man's sweet face without interruption.

"Staring at me?" he asked in nothing more than a whisper.

She blushed. He caught her.

"Sorry!" she admitted. "You looked so peaceful."

"What time is it?"

"About one in the afternoon."

"What day?"

"Monday."

"That sounds bad to me."

"Bad?" she asked, cringing at the comment. Even in all his discomfort, he didn't seem to forget things. Things like the fact she should be working with someone at this moment.

"Rain, why is Bryan not working with you?"

"He's with Debbie right now but don't worry, we'll make up for it later on today. Lance, I have to tell you something!"

"And what is it that you have to tell me?" he asked, sounding weary.

"I did something."

"Did something?"

"I," she looked him in the eye, "I asked Jesus into my life."

He couldn't help but feel her excitement. "That's great!"

"When I heard about you, I was so scared!" Rain continued, once she was sure he was glad for her. "Bryan and I were here waiting for news and I wanted to pray for you but wasn't sure I could. Then Bryan said I could pray and more—I could be a Christian like you! I feel so different inside!"

"I'm happy for you!" Lance said, tears in his eyes. He was truly happy for her but also sad that he couldn't have been the one.

"Lance, I've been reading the Bible, and I need to ask you something if you're not too tired?" she asked, biting her lip. She knew Lance's lack of energy and that he slept more than he was awake these days.

"What?" he asked, giving her the permission she sought.

"Johnny and I have known each other as man and wife for a long time, but he's not a believer, and as I understand it, I need to be with a believer."

"That's ideal," Lance agreed. He searched for words. "I don't really understand you and Johnny, but it seems like there are deep feelings between the two of you. You've come into this relationship with Christ with your past like we all do. That means there are going to be things that don't fit the picture, so we need to carefully consider and pray about these things before we jump into making radical changes to our lives. Until we seek His will, we can't know for sure what plan He has for us."

He leaned back looking very tired.

"I'd better go and let you rest," she said, thinking about his words. "You answer my questions better than anyone else. You can be very mean, but you're very good at what you do."

He smiled with the compliment. He closed his eyes to go to sleep but his dad's words rose up in his thoughts—as much as he enjoyed having his clients depend on him, he had to start pushing them out of the nest.

Ricky brought Johnny to the house on Wednesday at Rain's request. They sat in the living room, neither saying a word to the other for several minutes.

"Is there a reason I'm here?" Johnny finally asked.

"I have something to tell you," Rain said, taking a deep breath. She was excited and scared about how he might react. "I became a Christian."

He'd been hearing all about religion since he got here and hadn't paid much attention. He looked into Rain's face—something was different. Suddenly he had a million questions in his head.

"I've always wanted to know love," Rain explained. "I finally do."

Johnny couldn't deny the joy in her face.

"So what you think?" Rain pleaded.

"That's great," he stated, trying to reflect some of her joy back at her. "That's great."

The next Friday, Lance had Ricky push him into the conference room to continue the meetings between Johnny and his girls. Wanda and Bernice glared at him and Rain. They had enjoyed her absence.

"Okay, let's get this going before I fall asleep!" Lance ordered, letting everyone know he wasn't accepting any pity.

"We let these two talk last week so maybe Rain can start today." Ricky suggested.

Rain bit her lip. She didn't really like this.

"Go ahead!" Lance instructed.

"I wanted you to see me as a person," Rain said, looking directly at Johnny. "All I ever was to you was an investment. I held income earning potential, but you needed to kill my spirit, and you did. You've told me you love me. You've talked about marrying me. Johnny, why did you kill me if you loved me like you said?"

"Ah Rain, I had to keep the business running. Tommy was taking over and these two along, with most of the others, had already switched allegiances," he said, waving his hand at Wanda and Bernice. "I don't know why you presented such a threat, but you did. I do love you and pray every day that when I'm done here, you'll take me back and we'll do it right. I'm sorry I hurt you—killed you as you put it. I knew it was happening and you know, until that day in that restaurant, I refused to see it. If that whole thing with Tommy hadn't happened, you'd have been free. I was going to cut you loose."

"And what then?" Rain cried. "Johnny, I couldn't be free. I didn't know how to live without you."

He looked down, not sure what he was supposed to say.

"This is making me sick!" Wanda cried. "This little weasel put Tommy out there so he would keep his precious name clean. Tommy took care of us!"

Johnny stared. "Tommy beat the crap out of all of you!"

"Whoa, boy!" Ricky warned.

Johnny scowled but fell silent.

"You beat us, too!" Bernice said, getting very quiet. "Rain's the only one we never saw you hit."

"We all know she was too delicate!" Wanda scorned.

"He did hit me!" Rain defended. "And I had other things to contend with!"

"Like what?" Wanda cried.

"He used me in ways that would've made a physical beating seem like a treat!"

Ricky looked at Lance to see if he should intervene, but Lance didn't indicate anything. Johnny sat listening, glad that the conversation no longer seemed directed at him.

"How about letting him take a round right now?" Wanda suggested.

"I don't think so!" Lance interrupted. "You know this whole group is so weird! Who are you two really mad at—Rain or Johnny?"

Wanda and Bernice sat silent.

"Look, Johnny ran the business," Lance explained. "He ordered the beatings by Tommy and he knows it. Yes, Tommy was working at a takeover but that never had a chance to happen. Rain worked like the two of you."

"She had special clientele!" Bernice sneered.

"Did she have to sleep with these guys?" Lance asked.

They glanced at each other before nodding.

"Then she did the same job as you," Lance repeated. "If you're selling yourself, you're selling yourself. Johnny sold all of you."

Johnny hung his head. Pop's words rang in his head—protect her, protect her.

"I sold her!" Johnny said quietly. "I broke my promise to Pop."

"I think that's it for today," Ricky announced, glancing at his watch. Lance nodded in agreement.

Ricky escorted Johnny out of the room. Kelly came for Wanda and Bernice so that Rain could wheel Lance back to the house.

"That didn't go like it should," she said.

"It went far better!" Lance told her. "I think Johnny is finally getting this! The truth is finally sinking in!"

Rain wished she could see that!

They were just about to the house when Bryan relieved Rain of the job of pushing the wheelchair. He made sure she was ahead of them as they entered the house. Rain stared at the banner on the wall that read, "Welcome to the Family!" She looked around the room, and there sat Ricky and Sarah, Arthur and Dottie, Debbie and a confused looking Johnny.

"What is this?" she asked, her legs hardly holding her.

"You can't possibly think we wouldn't celebrate your new birth." Lance declared.

"My new birth?"

"Becoming a Christian—we're celebrating your spiritual birth!"

Dottie moved to the kitchen, emerging with a cake with a single candle.

"Welcome to the family!" she declared.

They all ate cake and celebrated. Rain's face shone with joy as Arthur spoke a blessing over her. Johnny took it all in but didn't quite get it.

"What is this?" he finally asked Lance.

"This is a celebration of Rain finding what was stolen. You can't take her soul anymore."

Lance smiled, knowing Rain was on the road to recovery in a big way. This time, he was sending his charge to the right source of healing.

CHAPTER 33

Johnny sat in his dorm room thinking about his latest talk with Ricky. These talks were straight up 'rubber meets the road' type of sessions that left him hating the image in the mirror. Today Ricky had been relentless, dogging him on every angle, and the guy knew where it hurt! But it wasn't really Ricky—it was his guilt. But having lived the life himself, Ricky got into places Lance and Arthur didn't know existed. He lay his head down on his pillow and closed his eyes, praying for sleep to come.

The images were vivid! Johnny pleaded for mercy, but there was his dad standing over him, accusing him again and again—you didn't keep your promise! He saw Rain's face as she celebrated her 'spiritual birth.' She'd never looked so happy, so alive. Then the image of her dying face came to him, the knife dripping with her blood still in his hand.

Johnny woke up gasping for air, relieved that it was just a dream, but this wasn't the first time the dream haunted his sleep. Rain always got to him. Every dorm room was fitted with an emergency button and Johnny pressed it now.

"Problem, Johnny?" the worker asked, opening the door.

"I need some air!" he stated, knowing the rule was once in the dorm, you stayed.

"Sorry, Man, you know the rules!"

Johnny nodded. "Could I get something to help me sleep?"

"Come on, Johnny!" the worker scoffed, but Johnny's eyes were pleading. "I can get you some warm milk."

Johnny didn't want warm milk but accepted it, watching the door once again shut. He drank the milk slowly, wishing Rain were there to talk to. He missed her so much!

Ricky pulled Johnny out of his room early after the worker told him about his restlessness during the night.

"Have a problem last night?"

"Yeah," Johnny sighed.

"Want to talk about it?"

"It's kind of complicated," Johnny replied.

"We have some time."

Johnny took a deep breath. He didn't really want to talk about this at all but knew that he was already in too deep to let it slide. Ricky would hound him until he spilled his beans.

"I'm having some trouble with nightmares," he said, looking away from Ricky to avoid the humor he was sure he would see etched on the man's face.

"What kind of nightmares?" Ricky asked, not finding anything to laugh at.

"Well, it has to do with a promise I made to my Pop on his deathbed," Johnny sighed. He decided Ricky would get this out of him anyway. He always did! "I promised him I'd protect Rain, and I failed."

"And that gives you nightmares?"

"There's more, but I really don't want to get into it."

"Let me guess—it's the other side of legal?" Ricky said. He had gotten to know Johnny very well over the last few months and knew he would talk about anything unless he felt guilty about it or it wasn't exactly legal.

"No, this is about Rain," Johnny explained. "This is about who I am. Ah Ricky, this is so bad! I did something really bad."

"And it will haunt you until you until you fess up."

Johnny took a deep breath. He knew Ricky was right.

"You see Pop had a real soft spot for Rain and that made me mad. I didn't think this girl—a common hooker's daughter—deserved the attention she got from my Pop. Then Lori and I get to the reading of the will and Rain gets a huge chunk of change from my Pop. My Pop! Well, then I find out because she's still a minor, I get the job of being her guardian. I never told her about the money and still haven't."

"Johnny, we all mess up our lives," Ricky explained. "You and I come from the same backyard, played the same games, but there's one big difference between us."

"And what would that be?" Johnny scorned.

"I've been forgiven by my Heavenly Father."

"Religion," Johnny scoffed. "That's the answer to everything around here!"

"No, it isn't," Ricky replied. "Religion gets you trapped, but a relationship with Jesus Christ gets you freedom."

"Freedom?"

"The guilt is eating you up and that's what's bringing on the nightmares. When Jesus died on the cross, He took away all that guilt and dirtiness that we brought on ourselves. You get a new start. All is forgiven and the slate is clean. You can make it up to your Pop."

Johnny hung his head.

"No one is beyond the forgiveness of Jesus Christ!" Ricky assured.

Johnny broke down. Ricky led him in a prayer of salvation followed by a time of confession on Johnny's part. Finally, they both leaned back in their chairs, smiles spreading across their faces.

"How much money?" Ricky asked, more out of curiosity than his need to know.

"Enough that she could live very comfortably."

Ricky fell silent. He could've spared Rain; could have spared her but he didn't. Why? Why risk the wrath of his father?

Ricky sat in the bedroom where a very frustrated Lance lay. Dottie seemed to always have someone that needed Lance's expertise.

"How can she think I have the energy for all this right now?" he lamented.

"You know Mom! She knows you have a way with people."

"I'm hurting here," Lance said. "Ricky, I can hardly sit up and Mom's bringing me people to talk to about their problems. I have problems here right now! I have nothing to give."

"And I'm here with a similar mission!" Ricky admitted.

"Not you, too!" Lance said, near his breaking point.

"I'm here about a client I know you're still seeing," Ricky smiled.

"Rain?"

"Johnny made a commitment to Christ today."

"That's great—those two really have a chance now."

"Yeah well, I would agree if he hadn't followed that up with a rather startling admission."

Lance once again buried his own discomfort and settled in to listen. This sounded worth his attention.

"Johnny's father had a very soft spot for Rain and actually left the girl a hefty sum of money in his will, but Rain knows nothing about it," Ricky explained. "Apparently, Lori and Johnny decided because Johnny was also named as Rain's guardian, they wouldn't tell Rain about this inheritance."

"Lori knew about this?"

"Sounds that way. Johnny had his reasons—obvious reasons—but Lori baffles me. Anyway, the money is in a trust."

Lance closed his eyes, trying to imagine why they wouldn't want Rain to have this money. Like Ricky, he could understand Johnny. He knew this was a new can of worms that could put all the work they'd done with both of them back at square one.

"Johnny was having nightmares about some promise he made to his father," Ricky continued. "Last night it got real bad and he even called the attendant. He came clean about everything this morning."

"Ricky, can you get me a copy of that will?"

"I'll see what I can do."

Lance leaned back, feeling angry on Rain's behalf. She could have escaped—she did! How could they keep her when they both knew what the life would do to her? Why did Lori do this?

Johnny sat quivering with nerves in the living room of the main house, wondering what event could have gotten him summoned here. He never desired a summons to this place without good reason, and he couldn't think of any good reasons, but bad ones were creeping out of every thought.

"Hello," Lance greeted, letting Rain wheel him into the room.

"Hello," Johnny said, avoiding eye contact.

"Let's get right to business!" Lance said. "I got some very interesting information dropped on my lap earlier today. Actually, it all began with a visit from Ricky yesterday. I think Johnny has something to tell you, Rain. I believe there was a certain event that took place."

"What is it?" Rain asked, shifting her eyes from one man to the other.

Johnny smiled—of course, it was a spiritual birth celebration.

"I became a Christian," he declared. "I couldn't stand the guilt any more, and Ricky helped me see how to fix it."

"Oh, Johnny!" Rain cried, throwing her arms around him.

Lance gave them a moment to celebrate before moving to the next part of the meeting.

"Johnny," he stated. "I think there's a bit more you need to talk to Rain about."

Johnny felt his heart go wild in his chest, suddenly realizing it would all be coming out at this meeting—all his secrets would be exposed. The door by the kitchen opened and everyone's eyes moved to the sound. Lori walked in, being led by Arthur, still not sure why she had been summoned to the farm. She couldn't see anything that would be that urgent that she couldn't deal with on the phone, but the request was made for her to appear in person.

"Good!" Lance greeted, pushing himself out of the wheelchair and to the table. "Lori, come join us! Rain, Johnny, let's have a seat here."

Lori slowly moved to the table, her mind cascading questions that avalanched through her brain, freezing up everything.

"Lance," Rain finally said quietly, "what is this about?"

Lance let them all sit for a moment in silence until he was sure their minds were focused on what he was going to say. He wanted their attention.

"I'm guessing that at least two of you are wondering why I wanted to meet and why today. As we all know, Johnny is only here for one more month. With some luck, Rain and I will be headed out this week. Now something has come up that very much needs to be settled before any of you move on."

Lori was baffled, as was Rain, but Johnny hung his head.

"I wanted Ricky to be here, but he has other duties that need his attention, so he's left this in my hands," Lance explained. "So Johnny, Lori, does one of you want to begin?"

Johnny looked at his sister, hoping maybe she would do the honors, but he could tell she still hadn't caught up with what was even going on here. He took a deep breath.

"Rain, Honey," he said, pleading with her with his eyes, "there's something I never told you."

She couldn't imagine what he was going to say. Her mind whirled out different possibilities, but nothing seemed to make sense.

"I don't want you to hate me!" he begged.

"What is it?" Rain asked, her eyes searching his face for a clue as to what was going on.

"When Pop died, he left a pretty large estate," Johnny said, trying to think of a way to drop this bomb and not destroy the relationship. "He left some to me and some to Lori and some to you—actually quite a lot to you."

"What?" Rain asked, now looking at Lance and Lori for an explanation.

"Good question!" Lance nodded, looking at Lori. "How could you?"

Lori felt the blood drain from her face. What could she say?

"He was my father!" she finally defended.

"It was his wish that Rain receive her share of the spoils!" Lance was angry and it showed. He expected this type of thing from Johnny but not her.

"Don't you sit there thinking you're better than me!" she cried, pointing her finger at him. "You have no idea how this happened."

"That's why we're here listening!" Lance reminded her. "Why don't you tell us how it was?"

"It was Johnny's idea not to tell her!"

"You're a lawyer, Lori!" Lance said, his voice rising in disgust.

"She's not my client!" Lori shot back. "She was his problem and I didn't want anything to do with any of it! The men in my family had their playthings—why should I interfere if these women are too dull to realize what this was all about!"

Lance worked his jaw, knowing if he let go and spoke at this moment, he would regret the things that came out.

"I don't understand," Rain said confused.

"You're a very rich woman!" Johnny explained. "If I had been honest with you, you'd have known that you didn't need to go out. I wanted you and as long as you thought you needed me, I thought I had a chance."

"How could you?" Rain cried as the truth hit her. "How could you?"

Rain rushed out of the room, running to the bedroom. Lance stared at Lori. Much to his relief, Ricky made his way into the room at that moment.

"I see things are a little tense!" he sighed.

"A little tense!" Lance nodded. "Why don't you talk to these two and I'll go check on Rain."

Lance headed toward Rain's room but stopped at the door. Leaning against the wall, he took five deep breaths, praying he could calm the angry storm that was flowing through him at the moment. Dave and Lori were his friends. He never imagined she could harbor secrets like this. But did he really know her as well as he thought? After all, she kept the fact that she had a brother from Dave. He winced as he moved to knock on the door. His body still complained about every move he made.

"Come in!" Rain said, knowing it would be Lance. He pushed open the door. "Why aren't you in your chair?"

"Forgot!" he smiled, hoping to relax her. "I knew this would be a shock."

She nodded—that it definitely was! He moved slowly toward the bed where he gladly laid down, letting his head rest on the pillow. She sat down beside him.

"He didn't quite come clean with everything!" Lance said quietly.

"What else could there be?" she cried.

"I read the will and the house you two lived in was actually Johnny Sr.'s house and he left that to you, too. I know that probably isn't helping with the pain of the lie, but I wanted you to know."

"I own the house?" she laughed at the irony of it. "I never had to be a prostitute at all! Why did he do this to me?"

Lance looked at her, wishing he had a good reason, but he didn't. He wasn't sure Johnny did either.

"Johnny liked the power and I think he was pretty upset when he discovered his father had stripped him of it. I have no idea how they did this—you should have been at the reading of the will. They both protected the empire their father had built, knowing if you got hold of it, you'd tear it down."

She leaned on Lance's shoulder and cried.

Ricky looked at Lori and then back at Johnny.

"You two have any way to explain this?"

"Lori didn't do this!" Johnny said, shaking his head. "I did this. Lori knew about it but what did she know of Rain? I hated it that this girl got my dad's love."

Ricky stared at the man, wishing words would come, but they wouldn't. He hardly dared to look at Lori.

"Can I please go talk to her?" Johnny pleaded breaking the silence.

"I guess," Ricky shrugged. "Don't expect Lance to let you be alone with her!"

Johnny nodded and rose slowly. He looked at the doors lining the hall, trying to decide which one was Rain's. He knocked lightly when he found the one with voices on the other side.

"Hey Rain," Johnny said, hanging his head. "Can we talk?"

She nodded, pulling herself away from Lance and taking a seat on the chair by the desk. Johnny shifted from foot to foot trying to find the words that would explain this away.

"He loved you! All I ever wanted was his love and you know when I was growing up, I thought I had it until the day he told us all about this other life of his. It was all an act! It hurt and then you come into his life and I see this sparkle in his eye. I wanted to destroy you, and I did. Rain, there was a war going on inside of me the whole time—why do you think I waited so long? You got to me but I didn't want to let you. I'm so sorry."

"I don't know if sorry is going to cover this!" Rain told, him shaking her head.

"I love you, Rain! I'm not that man anymore!" Johnny pleaded, falling to his knees at her feet. "We belong together!"

Rain creased her forehead, fighting with her logic and her emotions. She cared about this man, dreamed of being his wife, but this hurt.

"Johnny, I need some time!" she finally told him.

He stood, nodding his understanding. He headed out of the room, back to the living room where Ricky waited to take him back to his chores.

"She didn't hurt you!"

"I wish she would've!"

"Johnny, she's a smart girl. She understands what you did—she just has to decide if she can forgive you."

It was the first words of hope Johnny had heard all day.

Lance waited for Ricky to take Johnny back to the dorm and had his mom comforting Rain before he approached Lori.

"That was about as low as anyone could go," he informed her.

"Stop the saint act," Lori shot back. "Don't tell me you've never done anything you regret."

"Lori, you forced her into a life of prostitution. You knew what was going to happen to her."

"She already belonged to him," Lori retorted. "She still does! You know, if it weren't for stupid girls like her, there might even be a chance of stopping the pimps."

"Why didn't you turn him in?"

She glared at him.

"Why didn't you turn your dad in?"

She didn't need to listen to this. She stood to leave, but he grabbed her elbow.

"Rain isn't the problem here," he declared.

She pulled away and left.

CHAPTER 34

Lance was very happy to be heading home. He knew Dave was happy, too, but he hadn't had a serious heart-to-heart with him yet. But that would be happening soon.

"He's not at full steam!" Arthur warned, helping Lance into Dave's car.

"I know," Dave sighed. "I realize I throw too many things on him. I'll make sure to check myself whenever I say his name."

Lance waited until they were on the road before saying anything.

"Dave, has Lori told you about our little talk?"

Dave glanced over at him. "Nothing earth shattering."

"She and Johnny kept an inheritance from Rain that kept her from escaping the life."

"What?" Dave questioned.

"Johnny Sr. left a large sum of money to Rain, but your wife and her brother decided to keep it from her."

"Oh, no," Dave wailed. "Why?"

"That's something we'd all like to know," Lance grimaced.

For the first week, Dave and Lance were uncomfortable with each other. Lance wanted Dave to confront his wife, and Dave couldn't. He put in his time but nothing extra. He could see Dave didn't appreciate the effort. Then it happened. Lori called, dumping her duties on her husband, and he ran to Lance.

"Hey, Lance, could you take a couple of my appointments?" Dave asked sticking his head into Lance's office the day after Rain made her move.

"I guess," Lance sighed, finding it hard to say no to his boss. Lance got out of the office at nine that evening.

The next morning, Dave stared at his waiting room, knowing he had to pick his boys up. Lori was working on a big case. He walked over to Lance's office.

"Hey, I have to pick the boys up again today. Could you take a couple of my appointments?"

Lance stared at Dave. He had a full day himself.

"I know, I shouldn't ask!" Dave shrugged, backing away.

"I'll do it!" Lance sighed.

Lori and Dave sat at the dinner table two hours later. Dave had no thoughts about the office as he and his wife fought through another meal. To top it off, Lori seemed drunk as well as high. The boys once again hid in fear in the bedroom. She pushed herself away from the table to head back to the office.

"You need help!" Dave demanded.

"What for?" Lori said, turning sharply to face him.

"Lori, you're high. Is there even a case or are you going to get a hit from the local dealer?"

"How dare you!" Lori shrieked. "You've gone too far this time!"

He felt the door slam as the shock waves thundered through the floor. He bowed his head, needing some serious divine intervention.

Lance finally saw his last appointment at ten that evening, his whole body going limp with relief. Dave used a drop-in system to set up his appointments that usually left him overbooked. Lance had had it. From now on, he could deal with his own appointments! He wearily crawled into bed around four in the morning, knowing his alarm would ring at six. In one short week, he was again exhausted with a body that still needed to heal.

Mel dropped in the next morning with her daughter in her arms. Lance smiled when he saw her.

"You look terrible!" Mel cried.

"How's my niece," Lance asked, doing his best to ignore her.

"Not today," Mel announced. "Mom and Dad told me to check on you. Mom tried calling you last night and couldn't get an answer. Do you want to explain why not?"

Lance groaned. "I can't say no."

Mel stared at him. Lance never admitted anything, always just saying he could handle it.

Dave walked into the office, surprised to find Lance and Mel waiting for him.

"Something up?" Dave asked.

"Oh, yeah!" Mel nodded, obviously agitated.

"Okay," Dave sighed.

"Tell him," she ordered, gently pushing her brother.

"Dave, I have all the appointments I can deal with on my schedule," Lance explained, hoping Mel would be satisfied but one glance told him he needed to explain a little further. "I can't take on any more of yours. I have extra duties with Rain here in the city, and I can't ever get out of this place in the daylight."

Like Lance, Mel scared Dave. She had a way of making you feel the pain with the expression on her face.

"I'm sorry," Dave replied. "I shouldn't be leaning on you so hard."

"I'll be checking up on you two," Mel declared.

They nodded, feeling like two schoolboys caught throwing rocks. Lance waited for Mel to leave before confronting his friend.

"What is going on?" Lance asked Dave knowing his moods by the way he stood.

"It shows?"

"Yes."

"Lori—I think she's doing drugs," Dave said, shaking his head.

"Have you confronted her?"

"Ever since Johnny came back into our lives, all I've done is fight with my wife. I can't get her to admit anything. I don't even know her anymore and I'm giving up trying to communicate with her."

"I guess that's fine," Lance shrugged. "I'm sure she'll kill herself quick enough right in front of your eyes, and the eyes of your boys!"

Dave took a deep breath to stop himself from losing it. "It's not that easy. Just spouting off Band-Aid solutions doesn't work in the real world."

"She needs help. Yeah, we might hand out Band-aids around here but at least we do something! You're not doing anything! Has she even dealt with any of this stuff with Rain and Johnny yet?"

Dave shook his head. Lance rolled his eyes in frustration.

A week after the meeting with Johnny and Lori, Rain made the transition from the farm to the city. With her new-found wealth, the whole thing was a lot easier than she could have imagined. Her biggest obstacle was the loneliness of not living with someone. Lance smiled with satisfaction at her victory—she had come back from the dead. Something he didn't know if she would ever do the first time he met her. A soul had been restored.

Rain enjoyed arranging everything in the house. Mel helped her do the shopping and now she looked around with glee at the results. It was a home—her home. The doorbell rang. She swung the door open to find Johnny on the other side. She ran into his arms.

"I missed you, Babes!" he smiled, swinging her around before setting her down in front of him.

"I missed you, too! What are you doing here?"

Before he could explain, Ricky stepped into view.

"He's getting to the part of the program where we reintroduce him to real life," he explained. "No one leaves the farm without some classes on getting back into society."

"Hi, Ricky!" Rain said, giving him an affectionate hug.

"Nice to see this guy isn't the only one you missed!" Ricky smiled. "I was wondering if we could invite Lance over here tonight? I need to talk to that boy!"

"If you can actually reach him." Rain shook her head. "I don't know if he ever answers his phone."

"I know how you feel, but Dottie's telling me in no uncertain terms to get him to the tux fittings for Bryan's wedding," Ricky said shaking his head. "You know, usually the best man has to take care of the groom not the groomsman taking care of the best man."

Rain laughed. Lance wasn't the best man of anyone's dreams. She showed Johnny the main living area while Ricky made the call.

"He'll be here around six. Around six—he might as well have said sometime within the next twenty four hours!" Ricky complained after he dropped the phone back in its cradle.

"He's a hard worker?" Johnny questioned.

"Oh yeah!" Ricky sighed. "If we all had his work ethic, Rome would have been built in a day. Now, I have a few things to do and I'm guessing you two have some catching up to do so how about I give you two some quality time?"

Ricky headed out the door, winking at Johnny as he went. Johnny nodded and then turned to this girl who suddenly seemed very much a woman.

"Rain, I missed you," Johnny whispered. "I wasn't sure if you'd ever speak to me again!"

"I'm not that good at holding a grudge!" she smiled.

Suddenly he was on his knee in front of her, holding a small box that held the most beautiful ring she had ever seen. She gasped, her mouth going dry.

"I know I don't deserve you!" Johnny said, his voice shaking as he spoke. "Rain, you're the most wonderful, beautiful person I've ever had the luxury of knowing, and I'd very much like for you to become my wife."

She stared at him, taken aback by it all. It was all so unexpected.

"Oh, Johnny," she gasped. She licked her lips in an attempt to buy some time. Why did she have so many confusing emotions when this moment was all she ever dreamed of? She looked into his eyes and saw the pleading. "Of course I'll marry you!"

Johnny slid the ring onto her finger. He pulled her close and kissed her.

Lance arrived at the house around seven. He glanced around the room as he took his place at the table and knew something was up. Ricky and Rain couldn't believe how bad he looked, and Johnny was on cloud nine.

"What did I miss?" he asked.

"We're getting married!" Rain announced, taking Johnny's arm in hers.

"Really?" Lance replied, not looking very enthusiastic. "That's great."

"Boy, that sounds sincere!" Ricky ribbed.

"Lance, you knew this was happening," Rain said, becoming quiet.

Ricky froze. He looked from Lance to Rain, the bells going off in his head.

"I know. I guess it just seems to be happening sooner than I expected," Lance told her, not daring to look her in the eye.

The meal went on in silence for several minutes.

"You look awfully tired!" Rain told Lance.

"I am awfully tired."

"I thought you were working a light schedule for at least the first month." Ricky replied, creasing his brow.

"Didn't quite work out that way!" Lance replied.

"Well, I'm here to let you know that you must make the fitting on Friday. You think you can handle that?"

"Friday," Lance nodded. "What time?"

"One in the afternoon. Lance this is important!"

"I know," Lance replied, leveling his eyes on Ricky. "I will be there Friday at one!"

Lance left right after dessert. Ricky hung his head. Rain looked at him, knowing what he was thinking—Lance was in trouble.

"Dottie!" Ricky sighed. "Lance isn't up for anything these days!"

Dottie had just suggested her son help set up a new mentoring program they were working on for the farm. Since he would be around for the fittings, it seemed the perfect time to bring up the subject. She now gazed at Ricky, curious why he would say that.

"Lance is on an edge and he needs us to take some responsibilities away from him—not add to them!"

"Is something wrong?" Dottie asked.

"He's in trouble. I'm hoping he shows for the fitting today but honestly, I'm not sure his brain is working well enough to even let him know he's supposed to be there!"

"But you talked to him about it," Dottie replied.

"Mom, he's really in trouble."

Dottie didn't understand and he knew it. He would have to pray.

Lance walked into the office Friday morning looking over his schedule. He knew he had to make the fittings or he would be in deep trouble. He was just finishing listening to his phone messages when Dave stuck his head into his office.

"We have a meeting—some budget issues again!"

Lance shook his head, wanting with every fiber to refuse, but obediently followed Dave to meet with the three men waiting to tell them about the financial problems of the center. In his office, the phone rang.

"Mr. Hawkins, I need a reason to keep going!" Lakita begged on the answering machine. "I need a reason!"

Lance stood, heading out of the conference room, disgusted that his whole morning had been wasted. He glared at Dave.

""Dave, I don't do budget meetings anymore!"

"But . . ."

"I don't do them!" Lance declared again, turning sharply and leaving the room.

Dave bit back his anger. What was wrong with this guy? No one liked budget meetings but they were a necessary evil around here.

Lance moved to his office only to find himself engulfed by the arms of a large man weeping.

"She done succeeded this time!" he moaned.

"Oh, no!" Lance cried. "Not Lakita?"

Lance couldn't believe it. He tried his best to calm the man down before a family member came to take him to the funeral home to make the arrangements. It was only then that he noticed the red flashing light of his answering machine. He listened and as the words hit him, he collapsed. The sobs wracked his body until he could cry no more. Then he just sat, wondering why he even tried. Why he let himself care and how could he have failed this one?

Bryan waited for his brother while Arthur tried to reach the man on the phone.

"I can't believe he did this!" Bryan cried after they finished without Lance making an appearance. "He's supposed to be the best man at my wedding—how can I know he'll even show?"

"I'm sure he has a good reason!" Arthur said, sounding calmer than he felt. How could Lance miss this?

They pulled up to the center where Lance's car sat in the parking lot. Bryan fumed. They headed inside where they found Dave but Lance's office was empty.

"Dave, do you know where Lance is?" Arthur asked.

"Not really," Dave admitted. "He left here around noon. He seemed pretty upset about something."

Bryan and Arthur went from upset to worried by that evening when there was no sign of Lance. Ricky drove up to the city to help in the search, everyone remembering the beating. Lance wasn't healed enough to handle another round.

"The rehearsal is tomorrow!" Bryan cried. "My brother is missing, and I'm supposed to be thinking about my wedding!"

They had all gathered at Dave and Lori's except Ricky, who was still searching.

"He'll show up." Dave felt guilty. He knew he had put too much onto Lance's shoulders. In the weeks since Lance's attack, he found the whole center falling apart. Volunteers had taken Lance's appointments during his time off, but Dave had to carry his own load. It was so easy to give it to Lance when he returned—a habit actually. But now Lance wasn't carrying that for him, and he wasn't doing a very good job of carrying it either. He was exhausted and didn't know how he'd perform a wedding ceremony at this rate—the center was taking all his energy. And he knew if he was sapped of strength, Lance was ten times more sapped.

Lance spent the afternoon with Lakita's family, mourning with them. Like most of his clients, he had gotten too close. He felt the guilt acutely, knowing if he had just listened to his gut, he'd have been in that office. He wouldn't be here!

Then he headed out—he didn't care where. Just out. He walked down the streets, staring at the young girls and hating it all. People made this work! People who had the nerve to think they weren't hurting anyone.

Ricky had to think like Lance—a crazed, exhausted Lance. He drove down the streets, heading for his old area, realizing this would be the first time he had returned here since his arrest. He cringed.

After an hour, he gave up on driving and hit the pavement on foot. He talked to a few girls, finally finding someone who had seen a man fitting Lance's description. Ricky prayed.

He found him sitting on a bench watching the girls on the corner. Ricky sat down beside him.

"Tough day?" Ricky asked, staring out into the street.

Lance leaned over and wept.

Dave hung up the phone, relief washing over him.

"That was Ricky," he announced. "He found Lance."

"Is he okay?" Mel asked.

"He's with Ricky. He didn't say anything about his condition except that he was taking him to the farm."

They all said a prayer of thanks—he couldn't be hurt then. They didn't realize this was almost worse.

Lance sat beside his friend as they drove to the farm—the one place Lance really didn't want to go right now. He could feel Ricky's eyes on him. Lance had cried for half an hour before they even moved toward the car and they hadn't actually spoken much yet at all.

"What's up?" Ricky asked when he thought Lance was up to answering.

"You know when Mary went to Jesus at that wedding and more or less forced Him to perform a miracle and He did—he turned the water into wine?" Lance sounded disconnected from his body as he spoke.

"I know it!"

"I'm not Jesus, but I have my Marys who seem to think I am."

"Mmmm. I hear you. I don't suppose the word 'no' ever occurred to you?"

"It has, but at what cost? It's the clients that suffer and I don't think that's fair!"

"Lance, the clients are going to suffer if someone like you who really does care isn't around anymore." Ricky looked grimly at the young man who looked years older than he was. "Did you hear?"

"Hear what?" Lance sighed.

"Johnny has decided to keep his nightclub," Ricky said, turning the conversation sharply into a new direction, "Yep, he's going to turn it into a non-alcohol place with Christian groups to give the people of the area an alternative! What do you think?"

"Sounds good if he can keep his nose clean."

"That's what I thought!" Ricky smiled.

Lance didn't want to talk any more. He turned and stared out the window as they drove. He was glad Ricky had the sense to let him get lost in his thoughts.

Ricky got home with Lance sound asleep on the seat beside him. He shook his head, lifting the man into a fireman's carry and carrying him into one of the empty dorm rooms.

"What are you doing?" Lance demanded.

"Making sure you get some shuteye," Ricky replied. "No one will find you in here."

He secured the lock on the door before heading home for the night.

Rain was as relieved as everyone else when the news came that Lance was safe. She could now put her thoughts back onto the upcoming wedding. She was very shocked when Bryan asked her to be part of the wedding—she wasn't a part of the family. She suspected Arthur and Dottie had something to do with this. She thought about asking them about it on the way out to the farm but she was afraid they might see her as unappreciative of the gesture.

"Rain," Dottie said as they drove, "I found that box from your mom at the house and wondered if you had changed your mind about looking at it?"

"I forgot all about it!" Rain sighed. "I'll have to pray about it! I have many mixed feelings about that box!"

"Well, that's better than throwing it away!" Dottie nodded. She felt the girl should open it and would mention it to Lance and ask him to encourage her to do so.

Everyone was ready for bed as they arrived at the Hawkins farm and didn't waste any time getting there, knowing the next day would be a busy one. No one even thought to find out where Lance was spending the night.

CHAPTER 35

Dottie didn't know where Lance was the next morning and didn't have time to ask when Ricky and Sarah arrived. Sarah went right to work, helping get ready for the big event.

It had been decided that they would have the ceremony at the farm on the porch, but the porch had to be cleared before that could happen. With all the excitement with Lance, the job had gone unfinished but that had to change this morning. Bryan and Arthur were already busy transferring objects from the cluttered porch to a garage nearby when Ricky arrived.

"Good!" Bryan sighed. "Another set of hands!"

"In a while!" Ricky promised. "I have some very urgent business to attend to first!"

Bryan and Arthur couldn't imagine what could be more urgent but didn't argue. Dave and Lori should be here soon and Dave could help.

Dave went to the office around six to make sure there were no emergencies that needed attending to before he left for the farm. These days, all his emergencies related to keeping investors happy—not clients of the center. He smiled when all of his messages turned out to be fairly simple things that could wait until Monday. He headed out of the office but stopped—what about Lance's messages? He groaned and made his way into the other office. The red light flashed, telling him there were messages. He stared in shock when he found out there were forty-nine in total. He never got more than five or six! He listened and groaned—these were life and death situations! He jotted down numbers with thoughts of giving them to Lance so he could see to them. He felt he had done his duty as he went out the center door to get Lori and the boys and head to the farm. Lori—he hoped she would be sober today. Lately, she'd been drinking and he knew it and knew it had to be confronted, but not today. Today he just hoped there would be no alcohol available and he'd make sure her pills weren't available either.

Lance woke up in the dorm, glad to be there. He closed his eyes to go right back to sleep and was still asleep when Ricky showed up, waking him with the clanging of the door.

"Hey, Sleeping Beauty!" Ricky smiled.

"Let me sleep!" Lance begged, pulling the blankets over his head.

"Sorry, Bryan is getting a mite excited!" Ricky informed him, pulling the blankets away.

Lance groaned—he had totally forgotten about the wedding.

"Ah, he does remember what day it is!" Ricky nodded. He sat down on the bed. "I'm not pushing to hear the story today but Lance, you and I are going to have a heart-to-heart after this wedding!"

Lance nodded. After the wedding—he'd file it with all his other things to do.

Bryan smiled, overjoyed that this day had finally arrived while Lance did all he could to seem interested. The sleep he had gotten in the dorm had helped, but he was still hurting. Dottie fussed with their cummerbunds and tried making sure they were looking their best before stepping out onto the porch. It was a beautiful day—perfect for a wedding!

Soon they were standing on the porch staring down the aisle watching a radiant Debbie making her way to them. It seemed like forever before they finally got to the reason for them all being there—the exchanging of the vows. The vows were beautiful and Lance listened to the pledges of love and commitment closer than he ever had before. For the first time, he realized that a job could not be married to you or you to it. People died but work just went on and on. People cherished but work beat the life out of you. People loved but work just existed, never being completed. It never gave back; it just demanded.

The ceremony was done and Lance hoped he was, too, but soon learned that the reception held just as many responsibilities as the wedding. He was hiding in a far back corner when Bryan caught up to him.

"You are the best man here!" he complained. "People want pictures and I can't find you unless I look under the rocks."

"I'm right here!" Lance defended. "Why do I have to be in the pictures anyway?"

"Best men get that type of thing!" Bryan shot back. "Now get in here and let's get this done. My mouth is hurting from smiling and I want to relax for at least ten minutes here!"

Lance followed him to the room where cameras were being set up in rows. Lance didn't like the looks of this—he might be stuck here for hours!

Finally it was over! Bryan and Debbie were on their way to marital bliss and the rest of them were left with the clean-up. It was well past midnight when they all hit the pillow. Lance lay in bed trying to get to sleep, but his mind wouldn't let that happen. The vows Bryan and Debbie exchanged kept running through his mind for reasons he couldn't explain.

Rain watched the wedding, dreaming of her own special day. Johnny sat beside her.

"This is nice!" he commented.

"It is," Rain nodded, biting her lip.

It was only when his voice broke into her reverie that she realized her dreams didn't include him. She'd envisioned everything else—the cake, the dress, the location, even the suits the groomsmen would wear.

CHAPTER 36

Mel, Dottie and Rain sat in the living room the day after Bryan and Debbie's wedding looking at magazines to start planning Rain's nuptials. She had put aside the thoughts from the day before that had left her confused. Johnny's absence from her daydreaming was probably just because she was concentrating on the decorations. Now with Dottie and Mel, she was making sure to include the groom in the idea exchange.

"We'll make this the most wonderful day of your life!" Dottie smiled, leaning over to give Rain a hug. Rain hoped she was right.

Ricky still had Lance in his custody and wasn't releasing him without some explanations. He escorted his friend into his office.

"I told you we wouldn't get into this until after the wedding," Ricky told him as he sunk into his chair. "Now tell me what is going on with you!"

"Lots!" Lance nodded. "Ricky, I'm so tired I can hardly think. I forget stuff all the time that I shouldn't forget—like fittings and people's names. But this episode has to do with being asked to do things at the center that aren't my job. Dave insists that I attend budget meetings, and that's where I was Friday morning when a call came into my office. A girl that I've spent two years working with . . ." his voice trailed off as emotion choked off his airway. "Ricky I should've been there for her!"

"Oh, Man!" Ricky tossed the pen he was holding onto the desk. "She's been on the edge for two years and you're blaming yourself?"

"I should have been there for that call!" Lance argued.

"Okay—I agree you shouldn't have to be doing all this budget stuff but you can't be there all the time—you'd have missed her call sooner or later."

"Ricky, it's more than that one call. It's hundreds of calls. It's Dave shoving his workload onto me. It's working impossible hours. I've officially gone from the rescuer to the one needing rescuing."

"I know the story!" Ricky smiled. "I think everyone hears it at least ten times if they work here! So if that's the case, let me help you!"

"You gave me a couple of days rest here without Mom hassling me—she's another one! Always pushing someone on me to help." He couldn't keep the bitter edge out of his voice.

"Lance, you have to learn the word 'no'!"

"Yes, I have but if I say 'no', who's going to say 'yes'?"

"Oh, are you in deep!"

"I'm just trying to do my job," he defended.

"No you're trying to be God. You can't save anyone—just point them in the right direction."

"I know!" Lance sighed.

He knew all this in his heart but in his mind, things didn't settle out as well. These people were looking for a savior and they saw him as it. He glanced at his watch.

"I have to get to the office."

"I guess I can't stop you, but I can get you there. I have to take Johnny up anyway. He's headed out on his own today, so I get to get him settled."

"He's getting married! He'll have a wife to help him with that!" Lance said, not able to keep the sarcasm out of his voice.

"What is it between you and Rain anyway?" Ricky asked. "If I didn't know you were this 'married to his work' kind of guy, I'd say you have some feelings for this one."

"I think she's settling out of guilt. She's slept with him so she has to marry him."

"Uh-huh." Ricky said thoughtfully. He thought there was more here but he wasn't going to push. At least, Lance had started a dialogue and Ricky would make sure to keep the line open.

The week at work proved to pull Lance further down than the week before it. He was weary! He couldn't help these people. Dave was falling into the same wave of futility now that Lance had left him with all his own appointments. Two exhausted social workers headed home at midnight Friday, hoping to sleep the weekend away.

Mel was more than happy to check on her brother when she got the worried call from her mom. It was what she found that upset her. The apartment was a mess, and one glance told her Lance was eating junk food and bringing too much work home.

Lance sat up straight, all of his senses aroused to a peak with the noise coming from the other room. He didn't know what day it was as he glanced out at the sun shining brightly through his bedroom window.

"Lance!" her familiar voice called. "Are you home?"

He sighed with relief—it was only Mel.

"Hey, Mel," he called from the bedroom, not making any effort to get out of bed. He knew she would come through the door just as he tried to get himself dressed.

"What's going on?" she cried, bursting into the room just as he thought she would.

"Could you fill in a few more details as to what we're talking about?"

"Mom has been trying to call you since Friday afternoon."

"She has?" Lance questioned. He hadn't heard the phone. How many times would she try before calling Mel? Lance had a bad feeling. "What day is it today?"

"It would be Sunday—my one day with Paul and here I am, trying to make sure my brother is still alive!"

"Sunday?" Lance couldn't believe that.

"Yes!" she cried but then looked into his face and softened. "You've slept right through, haven't you?"

"You woke me up for the first time since I laid my head down on Friday around one or maybe it was two."

"Okay!" Mel said, suddenly feeling very scared. "I can't take any more of this! You're killing yourself!"

He couldn't deny anything. How could he have slept for two days?

"I'm calling Mom and getting you locked up somehow, somewhere!"

"No!" Lance begged. "I'll get help, Mel—I promise, but don't get Mom into this."

Mel stared at him, trying to decide if he was being straight with her.

"You tell me what exactly you plan to do and I'll see if I'm satisfied!"

"I'm going to quit," Lance sighed, hanging his head. "I'm going to tell Dave tomorrow and give him two weeks notice. Is that good enough?"

"Are you serious?"

"Yes!"

"So what then? You quit and then find another job just like it somewhere else?"

"I don't know!" Lance cried, raising his hands in frustration. "Maybe find a nice padded cell!"

Mel bit her lip. Every time she saw Lance he seemed to be less and less like the brother she knew and loved. He looked so old and tired.

"I'll tell Mom you're okay, but you make sure to get some rest!"

Mel left Lance to consider his life. Today, even two weeks seemed impossible, and he prayed something would make it shorter.

Rain was excited with the prospect of her upcoming wedding and couldn't believe how much Dottie was helping. Now, she was putting on a shower for her. Rain called Johnny with the news, even though she knew he didn't really care much about the details of these things—all he cared about was what time he needed to be at the church. Rain hung up and thought about who she could tell that might show some sort of joy with the announcement.

"Rain, what are you doing here?" Lance smiled, when she stepped into his office. It was Monday morning and this was a good way to start the week—a client that was actually doing well.

"I had to tell someone my news who would actually react. Johnny just acts like it's all nothing!"

He leaned back in his chair to listen.

"Your mom is throwing me a shower!" she said, her eyes sparkling with excitement.

"That's sounds nice."

"I think the men are supposed to be there, too."

"Knowing Mom, that sounds right."

Rain bit her lip, shifting her eyes to the floor. Lance raised his eyebrows, curious what could be going through that busy mind now. He waited.

"Lance," she said, taking a deep breath. "Lance, would you be willing to give me away?"

He stared at her. This was not the question he had anticipated.

"Um, uh," he wet his now dry lips. "I guess if I'm still around."

"Are you going somewhere?"

"I'm quitting here. I've thought about taking a job in a nice office where my wage is a little more regular."

"Oh." Rain stared at him. "So if this happens, I can't see you any more?"

"You can always come see me!" Lance smiled, even though inside he hurt.

"You'll come to the shower?"

"I can't," he said, truly regretting that he couldn't. "I only have two weeks here. I'll be swamped trying to get all my files up to date and ready for the next sap that takes this place on."

She nodded, feeling disappointed but understanding his point. She turned to leave.

"Rain," he called, "I would be honored to give you away!"

She turned back and smiled at him. He shook his head in disgust, watching her go—the last thing he wanted was to give Rain Patterson to Johnny Ross! She deserved so much more.

CHAPTER 37

Rain ran to Dottie's waiting arms, the excitement of the coming evening showing in her lit up face. One of Dottie's famous hugs was a welcome gesture for the young woman.

"Now come inside!" Dottie ordered, guiding her inside the house where Mel and Debbie were still busy at final decorations in preparation for the event.

"Do you think anyone will even come?" Rain asked Dottie, gazing around the room that had been prepared for a large number of guests.

"We'll have a houseful!" Dottie assured. "Now let's relax and talk about some of these final wedding plans!"

It was all too much to be real, but it was. Rain felt like she was floating most of the time these days, and she wondered when she would return to earth.

"These napkins are so lovely!" she heard Dottie say. "You know, I love the colors you chose!"

Rain smiled, fingering the napkins gently, letting her finger trace the names— names she had put together for so many years. A shiver ran down her spine—this was real and she didn't know . . . Rain shook it off—just last-minute jitters.

The house did indeed fill up with guests. The men gathered in one room while the women gathered in the other, finally coming together for the gift opening. Lori and Dave sat together, putting on a good front for everyone. Lori still didn't want this woman in her family, but it didn't seem possible to stop it from happening. Dave shot her a warning glance as she tensed up with the thought. He was glad they'd decided to let the boys stay with friends for the night.

"I know!" she sighed, looking over at him. "I will remain silent!"

Rain and Johnny opened the gifts, surprised with everyone's generosity. They said their thanks and then the people dispersed. It seemed the evening was over until Dottie pulled out one last box with only the family, including Dave and Lori, still present.

"I know you once told me to throw this away, and you are free to do that if you want, but I think your Mom wanted you to open it."

Rain stared at the familiar box. Johnny didn't know anything about it.

"What's this?" he asked, taking the box that Rain still had not accepted from the hands holding it out to her.

"Star gave me this!" she explained, letting her hands run over the top of the worn box. "I've always been afraid of what this might contain."

"Babes, you can't fear something you don't know!" Johnny cried, unable to believe Rain could stand the mystery. "Open it!"

Rain took the box in her hands, trying to stop her trembling. She pulled gently at the string that held the box shut.

"Hurry up!" Johnny cried impatiently.

"It's my box!" Rain defended. "I'll open it at my speed!"

Rain pulled the cover off and found a yellowing paper on top of the contents that were all carefully wrapped in tissue paper. Rain grabbed the letter and read it out loud.

"Dear Rain: I know this might be too little too late but I wanted you to know I think about you all the time and now how I wish I could see you again. I can imagine your beauty and so long to hold you but it doesn't seem to be possible. My time is running short. I love you so much, baby, and wish I could have been the mom you deserved."

She took a break, wiping the tears from her eyes. Dottie and Mel did the same; it was such a touching letter. Lori rolled her eyes—this was emotional dribble! Rain cleared her throat and continued:

"I know, baby, how scared you were that day I left you with Johnny and how Johnny made it look like I didn't care—you were just payment for a fix but there was more to it than that. I knew I had a problem and knew it was going to keep me in that life forever where Johnny could do you better. You probably know now that I was Johnny's girl and I liked being his girl—thought I had a special bond with him. He even let me meet his kids at one point although they wouldn't have had any idea who I was exactly. I thought he must really love me to bring me into his home like that! I thought I could trap him. I had you—me and Johnny had you and he knew it, but it didn't quite excite him the way I had hoped. He beat me so bad and pushed me into that place we lived, telling me that's all he would ever give someone that tried a stunt like that. He didn't love me at all—said I was nothing like his wife, and I was dreaming if I thought I was anything more than a business project. Told me I wasn't a lady like her—just a used up whore. I should have run then but I wasn't that bright! Rain, I hope you got out—I hope Johnny didn't sell you out, too, but that man could! He could even sell his own flesh. If you read this and are still in the game, get out! Rain, this life has no happy endings!

To say I love you now beyond the grave seems too little too late but that's the best I can do. I love you, baby! Love, Your Momma, Star."

Rain looked up at Dottie, her eyes pleading for help to make sense of it while Dottie and Mel stared back in shock. Dave watched his wife freeze in time like the world had stopped for a moment. He wrapped his arm around her to be there when the storm hit. Johnny grabbed the letter to reread the words, not believing any of them.

His father wouldn't do this—he would have told him this was his sister. He wouldn't die without saying something—he had every opportunity. The reality of the contents of the letter was hitting them all like a bird hitting a glass window.

"Johnny, we're brother and sister!" Rain cried.

"This is wrong!" Johnny growled. "This is a lie!"

He tossed the letter down on the table in anger. This had to be a trick. Rain wanted to hide, but let her attention go back to the box where she pulled out the first object—a silver cup with her name and birth date engraved on it. Lori and Johnny gasped. Rain stared at it. She didn't remember this! She pulled out a spoon and a rattle to match, all engraved with a familiar inscription—Johnny's Sr. insignia accompanied by the word 'Rain' and a date.

"Oh, my God!" Lori screamed. "No, no, this isn't right! He wouldn't do this to us!"

Dave held her. Johnny looked from Rain to Lori. It hit him! The resemblance was there, but he had never taken note of it before. Rain looked like Lori—looked like their dad. This was all real!

"I guess we finally know your birthday," Johnny shrugged, not knowing what else to say.

Rain could see the expression on the faces and knew the contents of the box had confirmed the words of the letter. She ran from the room, choking back sobs until she was hidden behind the door.

"What a mess!" Bryan sighed, just as lost as the others.

"Lori, look at these!" Johnny said, picking up the objects gently. "We have the same set!"

"Don't say it!" Lori pleaded. "This can't be! It can't!"

"I think it is!" Dave said quietly.

"Lor, you can't deny it!" Johnny said, still staring at the cup in his hands. "She looks like us! I don't know how I never made the connection before!"

"Forget it, Johnny!" Lori yelled as she fled the room. "I will never accept that, that whore is not my sister!"

Dave sighed, getting up slowly. He would have to do damage control, but he really didn't want to—he was tired of Lori's unreasonable dislike for Rain.

Dottie knocked softly on the door before entering to find Rain still crying uncontrollably. She went over and wrapped her arms around the girl.

"It's okay!" Dottie encouraged. "You didn't know—none of you knew!"

"I slept with my brother!" Rain moaned. "I almost married my brother—oh, my goodness—all the stuff!"

"Rain, it's okay! We can deal with all of this later!"

Rain wiped the tears away, relieved to have someone there ready to take control of the situation. Another knock sounded on the door.

"You okay?" Johnny asked, sticking his head into the room not sure if it was safe to enter.

"I'll live," she sighed, putting on a brave smile.

"I didn't know!"

"I know. I just can't believe . . . how could he not say anything? I feel so betrayed."

"He always told me to leave you alone," Johnny confessed. "He always said I needed to take care of you."

"We have so much to do—cancel everything," Rain stated, her mind frantically trying to deal with the emotional overload.

"We'll get it done," Johnny assured. "I'm guessing you'll need a ride home?"

Rain nodded and pulled herself up. Dottie hugged her once more and then Rain and Johnny headed home. Mel and Paul sat in the living room with Arthur, Debbie and Bryan, talking in hushed tones.

"Is she okay?" Mel asked Dottie.

"I think so. You know, she didn't seem as upset as I would have been, but then Rain sometimes reacts to things in ways I don't understand."

"What happens with all these presents?" Bryan asked, looking around the room.

"We'll figure this out tomorrow!" Arthur announced. "Tonight we pray and go to bed!"

They all knew the boss of the house had spoken.

Dave found Lori in the car, pawing through her purse in a desperate search.

"They aren't in there," Dave informed her. "Lori, this cannot continue. Rain can't help the love she got from your dad. She can't help being your sister. She needs you right now."

"Give me my pills!" Lori growled, "I'm in pain."

"No way," Dave replied. "You either go into treatment for drug addiction tonight or you don't need to come home. I can't keep living like this and neither can the boys."

Lori glared at him. If she could have killed him with her eyes, she would have.

CHAPTER 38

Lance didn't know anything about the shocking discovery at the bridal shower when he arrived at work on Monday. He had five days left at the center and he had so much work to do. Dave stuck his head into the office that morning to see if Lance was in.

"Hey Lance, can we talk?"

Lance looked up from the file he was working on and smiled. It had been a long time since Dave stopped in to talk.

"What's up?" he asked.

Dave moved into the room and took a seat. He looked at Lance, sighing heavily.

"I'm sorry. I've been a jerk about a lot of things around here. If you'd consider staying on, things could change."

Lance laughed.

"I take it that's a 'no'?" Dave said.

"Dave, I'm burnt out! I'm no good to you or anyone this way! Let me get back on my feet and I'll consider coming back."

Lance waited as Dave sat rubbing his hands together staring at him. He seemed awful nervous about something.

"Something else?" Lance asked, knowing he had too much work to spend so much as a minute on a staring contest.

"At the shower on Saturday, something happened," Dave said, trying to find the best words to use. "It turns out that Rain and Johnny are brother and sister."

Lance choked on his own saliva. He suddenly found himself bent over coughing uncontrollably. Dave ran around the desk and patted his friend on the back.

"You okay?"

"Fine!" Lance grunted, still feeling the tickle in his throat. "How did this come to light?"

"The box from Star—Rain's mom."

"Wow! How is Rain?"

"I don't know, but Johnny is pretty upset. Lori's nuts! She won't accept any of this and is demanding DNA testing to prove Star wasn't just blowing smoke."

Lance nodded.

"I confronted her about the drugs—gave her an ultimatum and she left. She packed her suitcases and left."

"Oh, man, I'm sorry."

"I love her and I can't help her."

"Did she explain any of this to you?"

"Not really, but somewhere inside her head I think she feels her dad didn't think she was good enough to be one of his girls. She, in some sick way, wanted to be Rain. She wanted that relationship with her dad."

"I guess we can convince ourselves of a lot of things if it means feeling accepted, especially by a parent."

Dave agreed. Lance promised to pray.

Lance debated calling Rain but decided he'd let her contact him. He needed to get some work done so he could devote his complete attention to her when she did connect with him.

Rain spent the morning staring out the window, wondering what she ever did to deserve the twists that seem to follow her around. Just when she felt life was going okay, someone derailed her and she was left tumbling in space with no idea how to get back on her feet.

By four, she knew she was spiraling in a bad downward direction that would lead nowhere good. She called for a taxi to take her to the center, knowing that trying to phone Lance was pointless—she had tried that before.

Dave sat at his desk looking over his files, glad to see the clock making its way to three. Soon he could head home and face explaining to his boys that their mom wouldn't be there—now that was just what a guy wanted after a day at work! Dave bowed his head and started to pray. Knowing the center was almost empty except for him and Lance for a change, he could have the moment. Then the door flew open. His eyes looked up into the face of a very large man. The man glared at Dave through drug hazed eyes that burned with anger.

"Can I help you?" Dave asked, swallowing the fear he felt.

"You can bring me back my girl!" the man howled, slamming his fist hard into his door.

"Yo—yo your girl?" Dave questioned but it wasn't the right question.

Before he could blink, the man's face came to within inches of Dave. The man wrapped his hands around Dave's collar. He felt himself being lifted off the chair in one smooth motion, moving through the air where the man held him, his feet dangling inches above the floor.

"Where is she?" he screamed, his face contorted with rage.

"I, I don't know!" Dave stammered, having no idea who this guy was.

Sparks flew from the man's eyes as he slammed Dave into the wall. Then he twisted the shirt in his hands closing off Dave's airway. Explosions were going off in his head as he fought to keep his brain continuing to function. If he would just say a name or something! The room was beginning to spin as Dave fought to stay conscious.

"Talk or I'll kill you!" the man continued to demand.

Dave couldn't breathe much less talk, frustrating the man further. The hands loosened their grip on the shirt and he felt himself falling. His legs were like rubber, and he felt the hard edge of the desk catch his forehead. Giving no thought to the blood now dripping down his face, he concentrated on getting his breathing under control when the man moved in for a second attack. 'React or he'll kill you!' Dave's mind told him. He grabbed his chair and managed to put it between the two of them. The man let out a horrific roar as he wrenched the object from his grasp, swinging it across the room. The air by his head made a swooshing sound as the chair hit the wall, just missing him. He soon followed the path as he struggled helplessly against the brute's strength. He hit the wall like a fish being slapped against a rock!

Lance heard the noise and hurried to Dave's office, sensing something was very wrong. He stared, his mouth gaping in shock as he watched from his vantage point at the office doorway. He had never witnessed such force and strength before and somehow he had to stop this monster! He was frozen to the floor as he watched the man turn and move toward him.

"Where's my girl?" he questioned, growing more agitated with each passing second.

"I don't know!" Lance replied, trying to avoid the man's grasp but failing. The hands of steel had him.

Lance felt his feet leave the floor as the man heaved him into the wall beside Dave before he had a chance to react. He crumpled like a rag doll, dazed by the force.

Dave was still trying to regain his bearings from his flight when Lance came crashing down beside him. Dave had no other weapon but prayer, and he used it now. It was answered as the man gave them an ominous smile before tossing something into the room. He pulled the door shut, shaking the walls to the foundation three floors down and leaving his victims to their fate—a fate he had already determined.

Dave and Lance unwrapped their bodies from the floor and took stock of their injuries. Lance could feel his body argue with every movement, but something else had taken control of his senses—a new enemy!

"Fire!" Lance cried as the smell of smoke permeated his nostrils.

Fear crossed Dave's features as he hurried toward the door—it wouldn't open. The flames were spreading quickly, fueled by the paper strewn on the floor.

"He's locked us in." Dave said, the fear quickly turning to panic.

"We have to keep our heads!" Lance said more to himself than Dave.

"Didn't you hear me?" Dave screamed back. "We can't open the door. We're going to burn in here and we can't get out."

Lance ignored him, choosing rather to put his effort on the fire. Ripping off his shirt, he began batting wildly at the flames. Dave only needed to be shown the effort to join in, and soon the flames were nothing more than dying, smoldering embers. They sat back to catch their breath.

"He must have barred the door!" Lance said, still breathing hard from the exertion of putting out the fire. He picked up the phone—it was dead. "My cell is in my office."

"Mine is out of battery power," Dave said. They both looked at the window.

Every office had a large window overlooking the hall that now seemed to be the only means of escape. Lance grabbed a large book and heaved it forward, covering his face until the sound of shattering glass stopped. Both men looked up only to be greeted with smoke billowing in through the broken glass—the whole place was on fire!

They both gasped, giving in to the feeling of panic but looking at each other they knew—panic and die, think and live.

"We need the cell!" Lance cried, jumping through the window followed closely by Dave. They hurried into Lance's office and pulled the door closed. Lance searched for the cell. He couldn't find it.

"We have to get out of here!" Dave announced, looking through the hall window only to see a sea of orange glow coming their way. "I think we're too late to take the fire escape!"

"Then were going out the window!" Lance replied, looking at the small window that adorned one corner of his office.

"We're on the third floor!" Dave argued.

"We can burn alive or we can jump," Lance explained as if Dave didn't already know that.

Dave and Lance hurried to the window and used another chair to break it, watching the shards of glass tumble to the sidewalk so far below. By some miracle, Lance remembered an old volleyball net someone had dropped off for the center earlier that day. It wouldn't stretch to the ground but it would make the jump a lot shorter. Lance went first—Dave decided he was the senior counselor and the captain of the ship.

Lance didn't take time to argue or they wouldn't get out at all! He lowered himself out the window, carefully grabbing hold of the net and quickly lowering himself down to the end. He stared down at the distance still between him and the ground, swallowing hard. He could feel the heat of the fire inside grabbing at him even out here on the outside of the building. He let go of the net, not giving himself time to think about the pain he would feel when he landed. Dave needed to get out of there. He closed his eyes and let his body fall, pain shooting in every direction on impact.

Dave watched and winced as Lance's body hit the ground. He didn't even want to think about how much it was going to hurt! He lowered himself quickly, following the same path as Lance, but now the fire licked outside the walls of the old building. Dave felt like he was being cooked alive as he worked his way down to the end of the net. He whispered a quick prayer and let go. He hit the pavement hard, feeling the impact in both legs. Lance looked on in horror—Dave's tee-shirt was on fire. He moved quickly, rolling the man over, ignoring the agony in his own body.

The flames were out. Both men lay still, completely spent.

Rain stared at the sight that greeted her eyes a block before the taxi even arrived at the center. She gasped. The next light was red, and now she could see the body dangling from the outside of the building, making its way to the ground.

"Oh, my God!" Rain cried, jumping out of the taxi and running the last hundred feet to the building. "Lance!" she yelled, not sure if he was dead or alive.

"Rain?" he moaned.

"The building—it's going to fall!" she cried, grabbing him under his arms and pulling. He screamed in agony, but she knew it was do or die.

The taxi driver acted fast, dialing 911 before hurrying to help the pretty young lady in her rescue attempts. He assessed the scene quickly and now lifted Dave into a fireman's carry and hurried across the street. Seconds later, the building collapsed into a ball of flames.

"Call an ambulance!" Lance moaned.

"It's done, sir!" the driver informed him. "Just lay back and help will be here shortly.

"Dave?"

"He's fine!" Rain lied. She could see the fire had torn away Dave's shirt and scorched his exposed chest. She hurried to the pizza place nearby and got wet rags to apply to the burns—it was all she could think of to do.

The firemen and EMTs arrived in about ten minutes after they got the call but it was too late. The center was gone. They searched for the victims they were told had been pulled from the area.

"Over here!" the attendant yelled at his partner upon seeing Lance and Dave.

They worked fast, making getting both men to the hospital a priority. It was only after they were loaded that the EMT turned to Rain.

"Looks like you have a nasty cut there, too!" he remarked, looking at the blood soaking through Rain's shirt.

She looked over at her shoulder and stared. She hadn't even felt a hint of pain until that moment. The EMT pulled back the shirt to reveal an ugly cut.

"That needs stitching. Hop in and they'll help you at the hospital."

She took a seat near Lance who was now moaning in pain. She stroked his hair, praying as she waited for them to get going. At last, the attendant joined her.

"How bad is he?" Rain asked, fighting back the tears.

"We'll know more when we get him to the hospital, but I think he'll be okay."

Rain nodded. She wondered if Lance ever would get healed up at this rate.

The farm was quiet with Arthur and Dottie gone to a seminar leaving Ricky in charge. Bryan and Sarah sat in the living room talking about budgets while Ricky hunted for a snack in the refrigerator when the phone rang. Ricky answered. He listened as Rain recounted what she knew about what had happened.

"Bryan, we have to go!" Ricky announced when he hung up the phone.

"Go where?" Bryan responded.

"Lance and Dave—a fire at the center. We have to go!" Ricky responded, already headed out the door.

The word fire was all that they needed to hear to get them moving. Sarah and Bryan rushed out the door to join Ricky who already had the car running.

Officer Coop stared at Dave, not sure who he was even looking at. Dave's eyebrows were singed off and his face was covered with ugly burns. The doctor had mercifully sedated the man. He decided to see if Lance could give him some information. He found him much more alert.

"What happened?" Brad asked.

"I heard a noise in Dave's office and ran to see what was up. I saw this huge guy throw Dave like a stick. I knew we were in serious trouble, and quite honestly, I thought he would kill us but then he tossed in a fire bomb and left." Lance stopped to take a breath. Brad could see he was in pain, so he waited patiently even though he knew they needed to get this guy fast. Lance knew that, too, and pushed himself to continue. "He was a white guy with lots of tattoos on his arms. Greasy, long, thinning, brown hair. The tattoos—I think I saw a dragon. I wish I could give you more."

"Can you remember anything else?"

"Locked us in the office to burn. We smashed the inside window and that's when we realized he had set the whole place on fire. We escaped out my office window." He took a moment to take a breath. "I think it said 'Blow' on one of his arms."

A light went on for Officer Coop. He was pretty sure he knew who they were dealing with and Lance was right—this guy was a giant—a very mean giant that he had dealt with before.

"He was asking about his girl," Lance continued.

Brad now knew. They had arrested Burt Gallows' girlfriend a week earlier!

"Thanks, Lance. I'll let the doctor finish up with you."

Lance was glad he seemed to have satisfied the officer. He leaned back and prayed that the pain would go away.

Ricky found Rain in the waiting room of the hospital sporting a sling. He hurried over, and Sarah and Bryan followed close behind.

"What happened?"

"The center burned down," she announced.

"Are Lance and Dave okay?"

"Dave got burned pretty bad—I haven't heard what they're doing with him. Lance just re-injured himself."

"And you?"

"I don't even know what happened to me!" Rain declared. "I guess something must have hit me when I went to pull Lance away from the building. You should have seen it! The taxi driver just pulled Dave away from the building when the whole thing just went poof!"

"Wow!" Bryan whistled. "Was the guy hurt?"

"No—I don't think so!"

"Well, let's see if we can find the guys!" Ricky sighed.

Lance didn't want to stay but the doctor wasn't listening. There was no way he could leave—at least, not on his own steam. He let the nurse make him comfortable in his room for the night.

"You know, I didn't have a reservation!" he complained.

"Good thing we had a vacancy!" she shot back.

"You must be new."

"Started this week."

"Oh, great!" Lance sighed. "I hate it when anyone breaks their skills in on me."

"How did you know I was new?"

"I know everyone here. I'm a social worker who spends an exorbitant amount of time here!"

She smiled, heading to the door. "Just buzz if you need me!"

"I know the drill," Lance said.

The door opened a minute later and Lance wondered what the nurse had forgotten until he saw Ricky. It was too much. He fought to keep his emotions intact.

"Oh, we're doing well!" Ricky sighed. He moved over to set his hand firmly on Lance's shoulder. "I think the time has come to tell you, my friend—you are officially off duty! We are going to do some serious intervention with you, boy!"

Lance didn't argue.

Arthur and Dottie were three hundred miles away when they got the news, but Ricky downplayed it all, knowing Lance needed a little space between him and Dottie. Dottie was a wonderful woman but she was too caring at times. Lance needed to feel his hurt and let his body speak to him. He convinced them everything was under control and they decided to finish the seminar. Ricky smiled.

Mel and Paul showed up, looking very worried.

"Ricky, is he okay?" Mel asked her eyes filled with anxiety.

"He's fine. Dave's the one who took the worst end of this."

Lori hurried into the hospital just as Ricky spoke these last words.

"Oh, no!" she cried, her boys under her arms. "Is he alive?"

"Lori!" Ricky sighed when he saw her. He didn't want her to hear that! "Dave's alive. He suffered some pretty bad burns, and he's in the burn unit now."

"Oh, no!" Lori cried.

"He'll be okay!" Ricky said, putting his arm around her.

She collapsed against him. Rain and Bryan hurried to wrap their arms around Carter and Cody. Lori sprung out of Ricky's arms like a fish out of a net.

"What are you doing here?" Lori demanded upon seeing Rain.

The girl sat speechless. She was here to offer support and even now, Lori hated her too much to accept her. She hurried to find somewhere, anywhere where her sister couldn't hurt her. She ended up in Lance's room, and even though he slept, found comfort just being near him. She curled up on the chair into a ball and wept.

Lance woke up, surprised to find Rain on the chair, curled up so tightly that he couldn't figure out what part went where.

"Hey, Rain!" he greeted, glad the painkiller was doing the job.

"Hey, Lance!" came the muffled reply.

"Something wrong?"

"I'll handle it!" Rain answered.

"Do you think you can sit up and we can talk like regular human beings?"

"Why?" she asked.

"Because I like talking to faces!" Lance replied, making sure to sound calm. "It's just one of my little idiosyncrasies."

"I don't want you to see me!"

"We've been through this!" he said, feeling too weary for this discussion.

Rain unrolled herself and gazed at him. He knew why she didn't want him to see her—Rain had been crying.

"Why does she hate me?"

"I take it the 'she' is Lori?" Lance sighed. "Don't let her upset you like this. You're not what she makes you out to be and, honestly, the issue is Johnny Sr.'s behavior toward his kids. But he's not here, so you're an easy target for her to throw her anger at."

Rain looked at him and knew he was very tired and hurt. She forced a smile.

"I shouldn't be bothering you! You've been through this horrible ordeal and here I am, selfishly hiding in your room."

He smiled back. "Rain, you're not that hard on these old eyes! Just let me sleep and you can sit in here all night if you like."

She moved beside him, gently pushing his hair out of his face. He closed his eyes allowing her gentle touch to woo him back to sleep.

Rain went home around midnight, glad to be able to leave Lance sleeping comfortably. He woke up several times, moaning in pain, but she knew he had a new dose of painkillers to carry him through the next few hours. Ricky was there to drive her home.

"How's Dave?" she asked after inviting Ricky and Sarah to spend the night at her place, an offer the couple didn't refuse.

"He's got some pretty bad burns and both legs are broken. He's in a lot of pain, but his worst pain is the fact that his blood, sweat and tears is a heap of rubble. That's all he kept bemoaning!" Sarah said, shaking her head.

"I've seen how much these guys put into their work!" Ricky countered. "I can see why he's crying."

"I thought Lance was quitting." Rain said quietly.

"He was—I guess now he has. I'm going to do some work with him!"

Rain stared at him.

"Don't panic. He knows all about it. Rain, I know you're pretty fond of him, so I'm letting you in on this—actually only the three people in this room can know about this!" Ricky stated, giving each of the women a hard stare as he spoke. "Lance has been sharing some things with me—struggles that he hasn't shared with anyone else. I don't think anyone has any idea how bad it is with him. I mean chronic pain, trouble sleeping, often not even laying down at night, memory loss, chest pains, trouble putting sentences together—I mean he's a mess!"

"Surely we'd notice this!" Rain protested.

"I don't think so—I mean, I have when I deal with him one on one, but he hides stuff real well. He couldn't remember being at Bryan's wedding two days after the event, but he thought he recalled the vows. After talking for a little while, he was certain he had to have been there—that's how he put it."

"But he's always so clear when I talk to him!" Rain argued.

"I know he seems that way, but he stays away from stuff that comes out fuzzy. I force the issues."

Rain was baffled. She would have noticed!

"Rain, he's burnt out!" Sarah explained, realizing the girl wasn't sure what to make of this revelation.

"And his family isn't seeing it—actually Arthur does; the rest know he's tired but have no idea how tired," Ricky explained. "Rain, we want to help him. That's why I'm taking him away from the source of the problem until he's back on his feet—firmly planted."

"Why are you telling me this?"

"Because," Ricky stopped to make sure he worded this right, "because I think you care very deeply for Lance. I know you won't tell anyone what's really going on when they all go crazy when he isn't around to pick up the pieces of everyone's lives. I also think you can help calm them."

Rain didn't know how she would accomplish that but felt very honored to be trusted with this secret. Even with that, she didn't understand anything Ricky was going to do.

CHAPTER 39

Lance stared at the small lonely cabin he and Ricky had arrived at ten minutes earlier, wondering how he would handle being here. Ricky had told him he needed some 'alone time' but this was completely isolated.

"I didn't know I'd be a hermit," Lance complained.

"This will be good for you," Ricky assured. "You'll have your Bible."

"And all the chores that come with this place. I don't know if you've noticed, but it gets cold at night in the mountains and that's a fireplace—I don't think I can do this."

"I'll chop enough wood and make sure you have lots of easy-to-cook items around here for the first little while. I'll be up every weekend."

"How long do you think I'll be here?" Lance cried, hearing this.

"Lance, you're not getting out of here until I see the guy I love and adore back. And no visitors! I want you to soak in the Word and prayer and relaxation."

Lance took another look around and wondered if he was up to this. This place was sparsely furnished with none of the conveniences Lance felt he needed.

"I won't have power or running water," Lance said, more to himself than Ricky. "I don't know if I'm up to roughing it right now."

"Don't worry!" Ricky laughed. "I'm not abandoning you forever! You'll have a cell phone with a charger, the truck is just down the path about a mile, and I'm leaving you well stocked so you won't need to get water. Keep the fire going and you'll be as snug as a new batch of puppies!"

"I guess!" Lance sighed, still feeling very unsure about this. "Now, you aren't telling Mom and Dad anything?"

"I'll deal with that end!" Ricky said with a wave of his hand to let Lance know he wasn't even letting him think about it. "Is there anyone if something comes up that you'd be able to see without going squirrelly?"

"I'm not squirrelly! Lance defended. "Just tired. I can't really think of anyone—wait—maybe Rain unless you can handle that situation. What about all my other clients?"

"Since the fire, they have an abundance of volunteers and Max is helping out to arrange schedules and stuff. You forget all of them and work on number one." Ricky headed toward the door. "I'll make the judgment call if something comes up with Rain."

Then he was gone. Lance wanted to run and get him to take him back but knew that wasn't happening. He let himself slide onto the worn couch and take it all in.

Dave was in agony even though he had already spent a week in the hospital. The burns and the broken limbs seemed to work directly against each other. Because of the burns they hadn't put casts on his legs, but that made every movement excruciating as the broken bones shifted. The burns were itchy, making holding still hard. Lori stood at her husband's side and did everything she could to keep him comfortable. Johnny took his turn, but Rain found that a cold shoulder greeted her every time she tried to visit her brother-in-law. Today she got lucky: Lori wasn't there, and Johnny wasn't standing guard, having gone to find something to eat.

"Hi, Dave!" she greeted. "I just wanted to make sure you're okay."

"Rain!" he said, surprised to see her. "I've been wondering why you hadn't dropped by."

"I have," she said, her brow furrowing in question. "Lori won't let me in."

"What?" Dave cried. "Why wouldn't she let my rescuer come to see me? Lance told me the story before he left on his intervention adventure!"

"You know about that?"

"I know he's gone and that he doesn't want me contacting him. We had some issues between us, but I guess they're neither here nor there now! The center is gone!" Dave choked back the tears. "I guess a friendship for the center is a good trade. I'm not sure the friendship would have survived otherwise."

"Dave, why does Lori hate me so much? She's even got Johnny hating me!"

"It's really not you. I'll try and talk to her."

"Don't!" Rain begged. "If you defend me, she'll have another person to pour her anger out on, and I don't want to come between you two."

"Rain, Lori and I were in big trouble before all of this. We've put on a good face but behind closed doors, it's unraveling. She won't forgive, she won't forget and someone has to pay. I thought it was my job and the hours, so I dumped a bunch of stuff on Lance and almost destroyed him and our friendship, but nothing at home improved. She's here but she rants on and on about her childhood and all she was robbed of. She does try to make me comfortable, but I can't listen to much more. I made her mad when I told her to get over it today—that's why the guardian isn't here. You know, now I'm wondering if I'm the reason she's here or keeping you out!"

"I think she's here for you!" Rain laughed nervously.

"You don't know your sister, but you do know Johnny—Johnny Senior! I have a feeling they both fell pretty close to the tree!"

"I'm totally shocked!" Rain said, shaking her head. "I thought you guys had a good marriage—a Christ based relationship."

"We did and she is a believer, but all this stuff has embittered her. I keep praying for the Lori I love to return."

"I'll pray, too!" Rain promised just as Johnny walked into the room. He looked at the two with worry written on his face.

"Johnny," Dave said harshly, "how could you keep Rain away from me? The girl put her life in danger to rescue us!"

"Lori . . ."

"I don't want Rain kept from seeing me! You understand."

"I guess, but you get to deal with Lori on that!"

She turned to leave. Johnny followed her out the door.

"It's not personal," he told her, taking her hand in his. "I just feel like I have to be there for Lori—I never have been."

"I'm your sister, too."

"Must you remind me? It almost kills me with guilt to know what I did with you, to you."

"I know all about it."

"He tried to tell me," Johnny sighed. "Pop tried but I didn't understand. I still love you—and not the way a brother loves a sister."

Rain hung her head. She felt guilty that she didn't have those feelings—she was more than happy to just have Johnny as a brother.

"Johnny, I'll always love you," she told him.

He nodded, trying to hide the tears. They embraced before Rain hurried down the hall.

Ricky had practiced his speech over and over before he finally found himself confronting Arthur and Dottie. He had to stick to the plan no matter what!

"Where is Lance?" Dottie asked when she didn't find him on the farm.

"Dottie, Arthur," Ricky started, taking a deep breath before continuing, "Lance needs some downtime and is in a facility that will allow him some time to regroup."

"What?" Dottie cried.

"He's in serious need of some counseling. You have to have noticed that he's been a little stressed lately?"

"I have," Arthur nodded gravely. "I guess we just didn't think it was this bad. Did something happen that we should know about?"

"Nothing really. He just couldn't cope anymore."

"I want to see my son!" Dottie demanded. "I can help him more than any psychiatric facility!"

"Dottie, leave it alone!" Arthur ordered.

Ricky was relieved to have Arthur on his side, but Dottie could prove to be a problem. He hoped Lance got better real quick.

CHAPTER 40

It amazed Lance what four weeks without people demanding things of him could do to help the healing process. His body felt strong again—alive. Ricky's visits had been the hardest part of this deal; forcing him to pull the emotions out of the place where he had buried them. He remembered the episode of making Rain look in the mirror and realized he was now doing the same thing. He would have a lot more compassion for anyone he ever had to counsel with that method again! His biggest problem now was that he loved it here—he didn't know if he ever wanted to return to civilization again.

Lori had been around on and off to help Dave with the boys, but he didn't consider it being married. He had the boys at the house and looked after their needs as best he could. He was glad his mom came to help out for the first three weeks after the fire, but now he was on his own. He still had some healing to do and the boys needed care. At least, his mom had stocked his freezer with frozen food that simply needed to be heated up in the microwave. The phone rang.

"Hello," he greeted.

"Dave?" Lori questioned on the other end.

"Lori, what's up now," Dave replied, letting bitterness edge his voice.

"She's really his daughter," Lori said, her voice giving away the feeling of defeat.

"You knew she was," Dave said, softening his tone.

"I don't understand," Lori cried. "Why did he love her more than me?"

"What makes you think he did?"

"She lived with him—she saw him every day. When did I see my dad?"

"He used her!" Dave declared.

"He included her!" Lori responded.

Dave took a deep breath. "Why don't we meet somewhere and talk about this?"

The phone went dead. Dave Evans bowed his head and wept.

Johnny got the next call. He listened as Lori cried about it all.

"Lor, you got this all wrong!" he declared. "Rain was a scared little rabbit around Dad. He sold her to me, knowing very well what I'd do. I pushed my own sister into sleeping with me and prostituting herself. Lor, I almost killed her. Stop holding this against her—me and Pop are the bad guys."

"But she . . ."

"Listen to me!" Johnny ordered. "She paid a very high price without a choice. You're throwing everything away!"

Lori couldn't think it all through; she was too high. Everything she was hearing was tainted into fuzziness from the drugs, but she knew she hated what he was saying.

Dottie still hadn't managed to secure the location of her son, but today she was changing that. She marched into Ricky's office with a determination that told Ricky he was in trouble.

"Hi, Mom!" he greeted.

"Don't 'hi Mom' me! You tell me right now where he is!"

"I can't, Dottie," Ricky sighed, hanging his head.

"Why not?"

"I don't want to hurt you," Ricky said, praying that this woman would understand, "but Dottie, you're part of the problem."

"What problem?"

"Lance's problem."

Dottie could feel the anger surge through her. She loved her son! How dare he say this!

"I know this hurts!" Ricky continued, "but honestly, he needs to be away from here, away from you—all of you."

"I can't see any time when a mother shouldn't be with her son!"

"Dottie, he can't be your Jesus—performing miracles at your command," Ricky tried to explain.

"What?" Dottie cried. "I've never . . ."

"Yes, you have," Ricky interrupted. "You have someone here that's difficult and you pass him on to Lance. You have someone that needs individual attention—call Lance. Dottie, he can't do it anymore."

"I don't know where you get off, but let me tell you Mr. Belarus, you have a lot of nerve!" Dottie stormed from the room and back to the house to talk to Arthur—they didn't need this kind around this farm!

Ricky waited for the visit from Arthur he was sure would follow, and he wasn't disappointed. He hoped Lance appreciated his sacrifice here.

"Hello, Arthur!"

"Ricky."

"Can I help you?"

"I'm guessing you know that Dottie has already come to me and that's why I'm here. Ricky, how bad is he?"

"Arthur, he's burnt out. He didn't want to see you—he doesn't want to see anyone. I have to admit that, at this stage of the game, I thought he might be ready to get back into living, but he's not. He was so run down and with all the physical injuries—it's taking a little longer than I expected."

"You've seen him?"

"Yes, I have."

"Ricky, I'll talk to Dottie and when Lance is ready to come back, he can talk to his mother. I would advise you to avoid her!" Arthur laughed. Then he grew serious. "Things between Lori and Dave don't seem to be getting any better."

"I heard things were bad."

"He's at his wit's end as to what to do. He phoned to tell me Lori has finally had to face the fact that Rain really is her sister. Seems she's having a hard time facing that."

"Where are the boys?"

"With Dave."

"I'll go up and see him when I can get away."

"I'm going to go talk to him this week, too. Of course, now I'll have to work on Dottie, too. Maybe seeing Mel and the baby will take her mind off Lance."

Ricky nodded. This place was becoming a zoo! The scary thing was that just having Lance out of the picture for such a short time seemed to be throwing them all in the creek.

Rain tried phoning Dottie, but she was upset about Lance. Then she tried Dave, but he was upset about Lori. Johnny proved to be too busy—she knew he didn't work evenings very often. He had converted the strip-club into a non-alcoholic club offering an alternative to the area. The place was filled to capacity every night, but Johnny had staff to handle that. He usually only went in during the day to do the books and put in orders. She recognized it as a brush off.

Loneliness was the one thing Rain had to cope with, and she was struggling. She had never expected all those she had surrounded herself with to reject her. She looked out the window and for the first time since her deliverance out of the world she hated, Rain longed for the company of anyone; even a john. The thought scared her.

Sarah opened the door, shocked to see Rain on the other side.

"Hi, Rain," she greeted. "Would you like to come in?"

"Is Ricky home?" she pleaded.

"No, but he should be in a few minutes. Come in and make yourself comfortable."

Rain warily entered the Belarus home, feeling guilty about the interruption. She watched as Sarah moved around the kitchen finishing her dishes. Funny, she'd never noticed her swelling belly before. The truth hit her—if she really was as much a part of the family as she thought, someone would have shared this with her. She was just another resident of the farm! And then there was that wretched box—she and Johnny might be expecting too if not for that! The sound of a car pulling up shifted her thoughts just in time to stop her from getting worked up yet again.

Ricky was weary. Working around Dottie this past week had been miserable, to say the least. He just wanted to sit down with his wife and have a quiet Friday night eating popcorn and watching an action flick. He walked in the door and pulled his wife into his arms.

Sarah smiled at him, pointing him in the direction of Rain. Ricky rolled his eyes.

"What's up?" he whispered.

"She hasn't said a thing."

"Mmmm!" Ricky sighed, heading toward Rain. "Hi."

"Hi!" she squeaked back.

"Something wrong?"

"Please take me to him!" Rain cried. "I need him."

Rain burst into a torrent of tears, leaving Ricky at a loss. He wasn't sure Lance was ready for anything like this, but Rain was the one person he did clear as okay for a visit.

"I'll take you to him!" Ricky announced.

They were in the car ready to go.

"What?" Ricky cried out.

"I didn't say anything!" Rain replied.

"Sorry," Ricky apologized. "Sometimes God speaks to me so clearly, I forget people around me can't hear Him."

"So what did He say?" Rain asked, suddenly wondering if hanging around Ricky was a safe thing to do.

"I'll be right back," he replied, hurrying out of the car.

Right back turned out to be a half hour, and Sarah was with him when he finally returned, carrying an armful of stuff.

"Okay, let's try this again," he stated, taking his place behind the wheel once again.

Sarah took a place in the back. Rain didn't even want to know what the plan was as long as she got to see Lance somewhere in this.

Rain would have been spellbound by the view around her had her thoughts not been so heavy. Ricky didn't talk much, sensing the girl's lack of desire to share things with him. He took the time to pray. Sarah slept in the back seat.

"What?" he cried out, suddenly making Rain jump.

"I didn't say anything!" she cried. "God talking to you again?"

"Yeah!" Ricky smiled. "He seems to have a lot to say to me tonight."

Rain shook her head.

CHAPTER 41

They stopped in an area that didn't seem to be anywhere. There were no houses, and the road ended with nothing but forest beyond it.

"We walk from here!" he announced. "Actually you walk from here!"

"Walk where?" Rain asked, looking around her, surprised to find they were in the middle of a forest.

"There's a cabin up there," Ricky replied, pointing into the trees. "You just need to follow the path about a mile and you'll find him. Sarah and I will gather up the stuff and be right behind you."

Ricky had spent the drive praying and listening. He knew he had heard the voice tell him to let Rain go up the hill by herself and confront Lance. It wasn't the way he would approach this, but he felt very strongly that they needed a little time alone. He and Sarah wouldn't be that far behind.

"You want me to walk through the forest?" Rain questioned, feeling scared at the thought.

"We'll be there just as soon as we can get this gear packed on our backs," Ricky promised.

She glanced up the path and then back at Ricky.

"You can do it," Ricky encouraged.

She nodded and headed down the path.

"Why did you do that?" Sarah demanded.

"I don't exactly know except it feels like what God wants."

She nodded but didn't really know about this feeling as being good.

Lance soaked in the tub that he finally worked up the energy to get ready. It had been a big job, heating the water and filling the tub, and now he let his head fall against the back of the tub to enjoy the fruits of his labor. Situated in the middle of the room near the fireplace, it was like a scene out of a western movie. He smiled at the thought.

"I guess I should maybe do a little scrubbing before the water gets cold!" he said out loud to himself.

He lathered his hair with the shampoo, enjoying the feel of it on his scalp. The past five weeks, bathing had been a quick wipe with a wet facecloth. He knew he had never enjoyed a bath this much before. He let his head sink underneath the water.

Rain saw the cabin and sighed with relief. She knocked but there was no answer. Was this the right cabin—she looked around thinking it had to be—there was no other cabin to be seen. She pushed the door open and glanced inside. She broke into laughter when she saw him.

Lance stared at her, more than a little surprised to see her.

"Rain! What are you doing here?"

"I'm sorry!" she said, still laughing. "Ricky dropped me off down the hill by the road and here I am. I knocked but you didn't answer."

"I was under the water." He explained. "You definitely caught me with my pants down!"

"How about I go back outside and give you a chance to get out of there?" she offered. "Ricky and Sarah are on their way, too."

"I just got in here!" he argued. "How about you put on another pot of water for me so I can warm this up and stay in a little longer?"

"Not on your life!" Rain said, shaking her head.

He laughed. She listened, realizing it was a sound she had never before heard.

"Okay, I'll get out, but I'll have you know you're interrupting my first bath in five weeks!"

"Five weeks?"

"Yep, but that's okay. I'll cut it short for you."

She felt the guilt that he was laying on her, but she was not heating up any water—she didn't even know how or where to start! She backed out of the cabin to wait for his signal that she could enter.

Lance smiled and then laughed at the situation. It would figure he would get company in the middle of his bath. He washed off quickly and pulled himself out of the now tepid water. He looked at the door, debating what to do next. He really needed to wash his clothes and he had planned to use his bath water for just that but what would he wear? He shrugged, tossing the clothes in the water. He would wear his towel until Ricky arrived—he would have something extra along.

"When is Ricky arriving?" he called, sticking his head out the door.

"I don't know," Rain replied. "They said they'd be right behind me, but they were bringing some gear with them.

"I have to wash my clothes," he explained. "I didn't know I was going to be here this long and I didn't know I'd be getting company and I don't have anything clean."

"I don't think I should be here!" she said, wondering exactly what he was wearing behind the door. She turned away to stop her mind from going there.

"I think you've seen it all before," he smiled with a mischievous glint in his eye. "Granted, no woman has ever seen this particular body that disrobed, but you know, it's all very much alike—you've seen one, you've seen them all!"

"I don't want to see you naked," she announced.

"Well, it isn't exactly what I desire either at this moment in time. What brings you here anyway?" he asked.

"I was having a crisis!" she told him, not looking his way as she spoke.

"Crisis?"

"I thought about going back," she said quietly. "I'm so alone!"

The tears came—she didn't want them to, but nothing would hold them back. He closed his eyes and said a quick prayer. He knew if she was here, Ricky felt she needed help. He waited for her sobbing to subside before speaking.

"I'm guessing you didn't take that route," he replied. He was stabbing in the dark, having no idea what was going on in the world these days.

"Lance, I thought I had friends. I thought I was more than just another girl who needed help at the farm, but that's all I was."

He knew that wasn't true. What had happened since he left anyway?

"How do I make friends? My family doesn't even want anything to do with me!"

"I don't think it's that they don't want anything to do with you, but I would like to have this conversation somewhere other than in the doorway with me standing here wearing a towel. Give me a couple of minutes to finish up in here while you enjoy the scenery. Ricky and Sarah are coming—right?"

"He said they were."

He ducked back into the house, leaving her to wait for Ricky and Sarah. They arrived a couple of minutes later.

"What are you doing out here?" Ricky demanded.

"He's having a bath and washing his clothes," she shrugged.

"Oh," Ricky replied, his face showing his disappointment.

"I think he said he would need something from you to wear."

Ricky nodded, heading into the cabin.

"There you are," Lance greeted, still bent over the tub scrubbing his clothes.

"What a time to decide to get all dolled up!" Ricky replied.

"Well, to be honest, I'm kind of glad I had the bath. So what is going on here?"

"Rain wanted to talk to you and she seemed upset."

"I got that part."

"I don't know what the issue is."

"I got that, too. I want to know what everyone has been doing about it."

"What is it?"

"She's feeling unwanted, unloved."

"I don't know," Ricky sighed, taking a seat on the rocking chair. "It seems like you're the glue that holds things together some days."

"Man, are we in trouble if that's the case."

Ricky laughed. "Here's some clothes. Get dressed and have a talk with the pretty lady. Sarah and I will get the tent set up. I figure you and I can sleep in there and the ladies can take the cabin."

"I'm getting pushed further down the social scale all the time," Lance sighed, taking the clothes. "Just let me hang these up."

"I'll do it," Ricky offered. "Daylight is fading fast and I really think she wants to talk tonight."

Lance nodded.

Soon he was stepping outside wearing Ricky's much-too-big clothes. Rain ran to him, throwing her arms around him.

"Oww!" he cried out as she hit his broken ribs.

"I'm sorry!" she cried, pulling away quickly.

"It's okay!" he said, gasping for air. "That area still hurts."

She turned to look at him. She could still see bruising on his face and could imagine what his body felt like. Neither noticed Ricky and Sarah slip away to get the tent set up.

"I'm so selfish to even be here," she sighed, letting her hand gently trace the bruises on his face. "You don't need this."

"Actually Rain, I'm glad you're here," he replied. He felt something he never thought he'd let himself feel—a tingle deep inside.

"But you came here . . ."

"I know why I came here," he interrupted, letting his hand fall around her shoulders. "I needed to work out a lot of things. You know, my time with you has given me many insights during my time here. I'm not that much different than you."

"You aren't?" she questioned.

"Rain, I prostituted myself."

Rain stared at him in shock. He laughed at her reaction.

"I didn't sleep with anyone!" he explained quickly. "I sold myself out—isn't that what it's about? I had my standards and I bent them and forgot them in an attempt to please everybody. I let Dave and Mom take over my life—I sold out."

"I think that's a little different than what I did!" Rain said, feeling the rush of shame with the memories that surfaced.

"The Bible says to obey God ahead of men. I didn't do that—I sold out. If anything, my crime is worse than yours. You didn't know better and I did. Acting out of knowledge is far worse than acting out of ignorance. Did you know that the church is the bride of Christ?"

She shook her head.

"Well, we are. I let people convince me that I was Jesus—well, I know I'm not, but for a while I let myself believe that I could save them. A prostitute offers men pleasure that isn't real, and I offer solutions that aren't going to last unless I'm turning them to God."

"But you were trying to do something good."

"I knew I was doing things that would give momentary pleasure but the end result would be negative. I took the quick fix."

"Well, I don't think you did, and I'm glad you took the time for me."

"I am, too!" he smiled.

She stared at him. She didn't know if she had ever seen him smile this much, and she definitely had never seen him in Ricky's clothes before.

"Am I funny looking?"

"No," she said, embarrassed he had caught her. "You're very pleasant to look at, even dressed like a clown."

"I guess that's a compliment," he smiled again. He looked at her. "I'm going to kiss you."

She had no chance to say anything as his lips surrounded hers in a kiss as soft and gentle as she had ever felt. She felt the tingle in her being and felt herself returning the pleasure. He pulled away.

"We had better stop that!" he said, looking like he would very much like to continue. "I don't think this is a good counseling method."

"I kind of like it," she replied.

He blushed and she smiled with satisfaction. He knew she knew she was getting to him.

Rain smiled at him and he grinned back like a schoolboy in love. In love—she stared at him and knew—his face, it was his face in her dreams of the perfect wedding.

"I think I'm in love with you!" she announced.

"I know I'm falling in love with you!" he responded.

She swallowed hard. It wasn't what she expected him to say.

"But you have a mistress," she argued.

"We broke up. She wasn't very loving."

Rain didn't know what to say. She hadn't come here for this, or maybe she had.

Dave looked at the architect's drawing of the new center and smiled. This place would be great! The fire seemed like the worst thing until the phone started to ring. Now he had supporters and money pouring in. Everyone was singing the praises of the work the center had done in the past, and the fire was not going to end the dream of the community to continue to help those who needed it.

The phone rang. He picked it up, thinking maybe it was another supporter.

"Lori?" he questioned when he heard the voice on the other end.

"I can't quit," she sobbed.

"Where are you?"

"I need help," she cried.

"Honey, where are you?"

"I'm at Dad's."

"I'm coming," Dave promised.

As soon as she hung up, he picked up the phone and called in a few favors and soon knew where she was. He debated going himself but realized he wasn't the one for the job. But the guy he needed wasn't among the living these days. Dave bowed his head and started to pray that Lance Hawkins would heal quickly.

CHAPTER 42

Ricky didn't say anything the first night he and Lance spent together in the tent while Rain and Sarah enjoyed the comfort of the cabin. Lance was glad for the silence. He and Rain had enjoyed each other's company, and he wanted to reflect on all these new feelings inside of him. He had known for a long time that he didn't want her with Johnny, but he had never let himself consider that it was because he wanted to be with her.

Morning came and Lance found himself still thinking the same thoughts as the night before.

"You scare me when you wake up smiling," Ricky announced.

Lance turned to him. "I didn't realize you were awake."

"I am and wondering what we're having for breakfast."

"Well, it all depends on what you are willing to catch."

They both smiled.

They could hear the girls talking when they arrived back at the cabin carrying a dead rabbit.

"What is that?" Rain asked, grossed out with the sight of the dead animal.

"This would be breakfast," Lance announced proudly. "I caught it myself!"

"I'm not eating that!" Rain protested.

"Why not?" Lance asked.

"It's horrible!"

"It's meat! You know everything we eat comes from living things. How do you know when you pick those little berries off the branches, the tree isn't screaming 'not my baby, not my baby!" Lance challenged her. "It could be."

Lance wasted no time getting to work at skinning the rabbit while Rain looked on.

"I don't know if I can ever eat again!" Rain moaned.

"I think you'll do it!" Ricky smiled, approaching them.

"Hey Ricky!" Lance said, looking up from his task. "How long are you and Sarah staying?"

"I have to get home to build a nursery! Our house doesn't have a real good space to make into a baby room, so I'm rearranging some walls."

"If you released me from my prison, I'd come help!"

"That's very tempting, but I think you need to stay here a little longer, although I think I'm seeing the guy I love returning."

Rain knew what he was talking about. She didn't know the guy she was looking at which made her wonder what the real Lance was like. Right now, he was so full of life and mischief!

The rabbit was ready to cook—a job Rain decided Sarah could have and she would offer moral support.

"So you ready to get down and dirty?" Ricky asked, looking at Lance.

"I guess!" Lance shrugged. He couldn't say he liked this part of the deal. He turned to Rain. "I'm sure Sarah can handle the cooking if you want to go explore."

"I got this," Sarah agreed.

"I think I'll go find some flowers," Rain readily stated.

"Just remember those little screams as you pick off their heads!" he laughed at her as she left.

She turned just long enough to stick her tongue out at him.

"You two seem to be getting along!" Ricky commented as he took a seat on the porch.

"We are!" Lance nodded.

"So what can we talk about today?"

"I don't know," Lance laughed. "Can I just stay here forever?"

"No."

"Mom hassling you?"

"Yes."

"I think I'm ready to come home!" Lance declared.

"That's my decision!"

"Okay, so what do you want me to say? I let Mom and Dave dictate my life and I can't do that anymore, and they'll have to hear the word 'no' from my lips. Now can I leave?"

"Lance, they need to hear a whole lot more than no. You need to sit them down and confront them with all this stuff!"

"Why?" Lance sighed. This was the one stickler between the two of them.

"Because they need to hear it from you."

"I already told Dave all this!"

"Say it again!" Ricky stated. "And what about Mom? Lance, you told them all you would let them know when it was too much before, and how long did it take for you to be right back where you started?"

"Ricky, she's my mom! I can't confront her—the Bible says we need to respect our parents—honor them. As for the others, I do get what I need to do."

"And you'll be back in the same place you came from. Lance, you have to talk to her and be completely honest, telling her you can't do this anymore."

"She'll freak," Lance sighed, hanging his head.

"She'll get over it, and your dad will support you one hundred percent. He understands."

"And Mel and Bryan?"

"I think they understand, although Bryan seems a little upset. Lance, you want out of here, but you don't want to face anyone!" Ricky laughed. "How does that work?"

"I don't know!" he shrugged.

"Look, you're a people pleaser and that's okay as long as you understand that sometimes you need to say 'yes' to you first."

Rain returned, not sure if she should walk passed them or linger out in the forest a little longer. Ricky saw her.

"Come on up!" he welcomed her. "We're not getting anywhere with this anyway!"

She approached the men slowly, trying to decide if the session had gone well or not. It seemed the latter.

"I want to put my flowers in water," she told them, heading toward the door.

"Go ahead," Ricky said, moving out of the way. "I want to talk to you anyway."

Rain moved inside with Ricky on her heels.

"He's coming back to the land of the living, but not today. Are you okay staying out here one more day?"

"Are you and Sarah staying?"

"I'm not about to tempt him that much!" Ricky laughed. "We'll be here the whole time. Rain, you have to help him see that he needs to make a few changes in his life."

She nodded but had no idea what she could do.

Ricky and Sarah took the opportunity after breakfast to go and spend some quality time together, leaving Rain and Lance to fend for themselves.

"So what should we do, my Lady?" Lance asked.

"I don't know," she admitted.

"How about we do a little exploring ourselves?"

"I guess."

Lance took her arm in the crook of his and guided her outside. He took in a deep breath, closing his eyes as he did so.

"You like it out here, don't you?" she commented.

"Yeah. I miss being out in the country, not that I have had any time lately to contemplate the absence of it in my life."

"Why do you keep yourself so busy?"

He stopped short. It was something that had never occurred to him—he kept himself so busy. He was always thinking it was the rest of the world, but in fact she was right—he was the one who demanded it all of himself.

"I don't know," he admitted. "But I do know I'm not letting it happen anymore."

They had a wonderful afternoon. Rain picked flowers while Lance told her all the names of them. She was surprised he knew so much about them.

"My parents do run a market garden and a greenhouse."

"I didn't know you ever worked there."

"You have no idea!" he laughed.

They talked and walked, enjoying the time they spent together.

Rain sat across from Lance at the table for supper later that day. She managed to eat some rabbit. Ricky and Sarah had found some berries that helped get it down.

"I think I'm really ready to go," Lance announced.

Ricky looked up, his brow creasing with the announcement.

"I know you have your doubts, but I think I finally got something today—thanks to Rain."

"And what epiphany did you have?" Ricky questioned.

"It was me all along," Lance admitted. "I chose to let others direct my time. I chose to never say 'no.' I ran myself ragged."

Ricky had no response. He was in shock.

"I can face them all now," he explained further.

"Maybe you can," Ricky agreed.

But Ricky wasn't about to trust Lance's understanding that easily. He and Sarah packed up, taking Rain with them. Lance didn't argue about the decision to leave him behind, knowing that when he did leave here, he would have a lot of people to face.

It was two days later, after another visit, that Ricky decided he really could use help on the nursery and Lance could come back to his house with him.

Rain felt less lost when she got back, but she felt that she had a few things that needed to be dealt with. She went to Johnny's house first.

"Rain," he greeted, looking surprised to see her.

"Do you hate me?" she asked.

He was even more shocked with the question than her being there.

"No, I don't hate you."

"So why do I feel like you do?"

He hung his head. "Why don't we sit down and talk?"

She followed him into the house, taking a seat at the dining room table.

"Rain," he seemed to not be able to find the words. "Want some tea?"

"Sure," she answered, freeing him from the stress of the moment.

It was several minutes before he returned to the table. He set the tea down in front of her, already containing cream and sugar.

"We know each other so well," she said, looking at the cup.

"Sorry," he replied.

"I don't mind," she replied. "I didn't think you would remember."

"There's not a thing about you that I can forget," Johnny said, tears forming in his eyes. "I love you."

"So why make me feel like I don't matter?"

"Rain, I can't look at you without the old feelings and then I remember—that's my sister. And then I feel so angry and disgusted and dirty."

"Johnny, there's something I have to tell you."

"What, Babes?"

"I knew we shouldn't get married—not because of being related, but because I knew that I didn't love you as anything more than a brother."

"Why didn't you say something?"

"I felt so guilty about sleeping with you."

He pulled her hand into his. "Babes, you can't let me have that much power over you. How am I ever going to feel like you're safe?"

"I didn't think you worried about whether I was safe."

"Rain, I did not treat you the way I did all these years because I didn't care. I cared too much most of the time. Now that I look back at it all, I know somewhere in my being I knew the truth."

"I need a big brother," Rain told him.

"And I need a little sister," Johnny replied.

They embraced. They both still hadn't totally overcome the awkwardness of the situation, but they were at least starting to see the role they needed to play in the other's life.

Rain sat in her living room that night nursing a cup of warm milk in her hands, listening to some wonderful worship music. She was enjoying an alone moment for the first time in her life when the phone interrupted. She stood and reluctantly answered it.

"Hello," she greeted.

"Hey, Rain," a voice greeted back.

"Lance?" she said, a smile forming on her lips.

"I'm officially on parole and would like to celebrate with the most beautiful woman in the world."

"Is that right?" she asked.

"Yeah, but she wasn't available so I'm calling you."

Rain was silent.

"I'm joking," he added.

"It's not very funny."

"Ah Rain, you know I think you're beautiful—the most beautiful woman I've ever met."

"So how would you like to celebrate?"

"As I said, I'm on parole so my options are limited, but my guard has said I could come pick you up and bring you back here."

"Where is here?"

"Ricky and Sarah's."

She told him she would love to join him to celebrate. She hung up the phone smiling—she'd made her first real date!

Lance dropped the phone, wiping the sweat from his brow. He wasn't sure how guys did this all the time—he was shaking like a leaf.

A couple of hours later, Lance sat on the grass, enjoying the view. Rain looked so content.

"So how long will you be here?"

"Not long," Lance replied. "I just have to come up with an action plan for the future."

"I think you taught Ricky too well," she laughed.

"Do you want to go crayfish hunting?"

"Hunting?" she asked, scrunching up her nose.

"Not killing—just finding them in the creek."

They headed to the creek edge where Lance taught Rain the fine art of crayfish hunting. She refused to touch them, but he forced her to look at the ones he caught.

Dave knew that Lance would go to Ricky, and now that he knew of Lori's whereabouts, he just had to find Lance. He headed to the Belarus house.

"So where is he?" Dave demanded.

Ricky took a deep breath. "What is it?"

"I found Lori."

"He's not up to counseling yet."

"He's the only one who can talk to Lori and get her to listen."

"I'll ask and if he says he's willing to talk to her, I'll let you know."

Dave was livid, but had no choice but to accept that. Ricky wasn't giving Lance's location away.

Lance and Rain arrived at the house about an hour later.

"Dave was here," Ricky informed him. "He felt you were the only one who could talk to Lori."

"Did he now," Lance smirked.

"Yep."

"So he's a counselor—why can't he talk to her?" Lance stated, knowing this was a test.

Ricky smiled. "Exactly."

"I am her friend," Lance then added. "I can act in that capacity but I can't act as her savior. In fact, I think me acting in a professional capacity would be a negative in this case. I don't want to know the whole story."

Ricky nodded. He'd give Dave the message.

Lance sat back on his bed that night feeling ready to face life again. But for the first time in a long time, he was also ready to face death. He realized there would always be those who chose not to go on. He would love them all and let God have His job back; he wasn't doing any more saving.

The next two weeks went by fast. Ricky and Lance had many good talks—not just about his condition, but about his dreams and future plans. Rain became a regular visitor, and Lance found her company very relaxing. He noticed his dream of the future seemed to include her more and more.

He sat with Rain at the table finishing their dessert. Ricky and Sarah were in the kitchen doing dishes.

"So Rain," Lance said, sitting back in his chair. "When should we get married?"

She choked on her food. It came out of nowhere! He hurried over to pat her on the back.

"Sorry!" he cried.

"That's okay!" she said, still coughing. "What would make you ask that?"

"I've been thinking about it. I love you and you love me—this seems to be the next step."

"Lance, we've hardly even really dated."

"Oh—so what was the last two weeks?" he nodded.

"It's been nice," she granted him.

"So doesn't this seem like the next step?"

"I don't think so!" Rain laughed. "I can't believe you, Lance Hawkins, would suggest that I, a girl who just broke off an engagement, get married to my counselor."

He smiled at her. She wondered what was up now.

"I know you weren't in love with Johnny! You, Rain Patterson, had thoughts about me a long time ago!"

"Did I?" she replied, indignantly.

"Yes, you did!"

"Maybe I did!" she conceded, "but that doesn't mean you're ready. You might be on the rebound, too."

She gave him a smug look of satisfaction, daring him to think of a logical argument for that. He looked her in the eye, leaned over and kissed her passionately. It was a very good argument!

"Let me pray about it," she conceded.

"That's a very good idea," he agreed.

In the kitchen, Ricky and Sarah both gave each other a concerned look. It didn't seem to them that either one of these two people should be even using the M word!

CHAPTER 43

Mel held Baby Sadie in one arm and hurried around the kitchen fixing plates of finger foods with the other. She wished Debbie would hurry to help her with these preparations for Dottie's birthday party. They had been planning the party for weeks and had tried everything to convince Ricky that Lance should be in attendance. He didn't make any promises.

"Oh, good, you guys are here," Mel said when Bryan and Debbie walked through the door. "I need some help!"

"Sorry we're late!' Debbie said, washing her hands and diving right in. "Would you believe we had a flat tire when we got out to leave?"

"Figures!" Mel said in disgust. "Mom and Dad will be home any minute and I'm so far from ready. I've got guests working all over the place around here!"

The women hurried putting the plates on the buffet table that had been set up in the dining room where many people were still working on the last-minute decorations. The decision to make this a surprise party was being seriously questioned!

"We had to!" Bryan stated. "You know Mom would have done all the work if we had told her anything!"

A car was pulling up! Everyone rushed to his or her place, deciding whatever wasn't perfect now would just remain the way it was.

Dottie and Arthur drove into the yard suspecting nothing. Dottie had thought when her birthday so conveniently fell on a Sunday, her children would have done something special like they did for Arthur's fiftieth, but apparently she was wrong. She could hardly hide her disappointment when Bryan and Debbie gave her the certificate for a dinner out at a nice restaurant, good only for this day. Maybe they felt that with Lance still not around, she wouldn't want a party. Arthur escorted her to the door, fumbling for the key. They made their way inside where Dottie's mouth opened but no sound came out. The loud 'surprise' caught her good!

"Happy birthday!" Bryan and Mel shouted, running out to hug their Mom. Soon the room was overflowing with guests.

"How did you do this?" Dottie cried, still in shock.

"Believe me," Bryan said, shaking his head, "it wasn't easy!"

Soon the party was in full swing with everyone seated at tables set up in the backyard. It was a beautiful day—not too warm or too cold. Dottie sat at her place of honor enjoying everything with only one regret—Lance wasn't there.

Rain had let it slip that she still did not drive. Lance decided it was time to learn. He put her in the driver's seat and they were off—nearly off the road.

"You don't need to turn the wheel so much," he instructed, laughing at it all.

"We'll never get there at this rate," she scorned. "Lance, we'll miss the whole thing."

"We'll get there," he said, looking her in the eye. "It doesn't matter if we're a little late."

He instructed and soon she was at least managing to stay on the road. They were in sight of the farm when she stopped the car.

"Do you really want to marry me?" she asked.

"I don't usually ask for the fun of it," he replied.

"Will you be mean like you were in the beginning?"

"I never was mean," he defended. "But I hear where you're coming from. I haven't felt overly excited about some of the things Ricky and I have dealt with. If facing these things was easy, we'd do it all on our own. Love sometimes means helping someone even when it seems like you're hurting them."

"So does that mean yes?"

"No. But I do hope we can be honest with each other, even if we know the truth might sting."

She never thought about it that way before. "I guess you have a point with that. Lance, I can't imagine not being with you, but I like this you better."

"So do I and I mean it, if you ever see me slipping down that slippery slope again—stop me."

"Okay—and yes, I'll marry you."

Lance wanted to shout and holler but he decided that could wait. He bent over and gave her a kiss instead.

They pulled up to the house. Ricky had mentioned the party for his mom but this looked like a pretty big bash. He wasn't sure he wanted to make this his first trip back to the real world.

"Do we do this?" he asked Rain.

"I think we have to," she nodded. "I see faces staring out the window."

"Well, let's go party."

Lance pulled his mother's gift out of the back seat of the car and took Rain's hand gently in his. She smiled at him, reassuring him that they would be fine. They made their way through the house and to the backyard.

Dottie stopped mid-sentence, staring at the doorway where he stood. She was up, running, hurrying, afraid it was just an apparition. But he was real! She kissed his cheek gently, tears streaming down her face. Now everyone turned to see what the excitement was.

"Happy birthday, Mom!" Lance said, looking a bit guilty.

She held him at arm's length, looking him over carefully—he seemed so strong, so healthy. His face glowed with color, and she couldn't remember seeing him look so good in a long time.

"Welcome home!" she whispered.

Mel hurried over to give him a hug followed by a handshake from Bryan. Arthur held his son. Ricky gave him a wink from the corner of the room.

The party went on into the night and somewhere in the activity, Dottie lost Lance. He and Rain left as silently as they arrived.

She lay in bed with Arthur that night, unable to sleep.

"Did you see the gift he gave me?"

"Yes," Arthur said, really not wanting to discuss this tonight.

"What was that supposed to be?"

"Ask him," Arthur said quietly.

Dottie thought she would do just that if she ever got the chance—she had no guarantee she would be seeing him again soon.

Ricky stood in the doorway of Lance's room that night.

"Do you have any idea what you're doing?"

"I'm ready, Ricky."

"I hope you're right!" Ricky sighed. "Marriage is a big step."

"I thought you'd be happy that I was thinking about a real person instead of a file."

"I am, but it all seems kind of quick."

Lance had thought about that, too. He would keep praying, but this seemed to be where God was leading.

CHAPTER 44

Dottie was busy making bread when Lance walked into her kitchen once again with Rain at his side. She looked at him curiously.

"I'm going to go down to the creek," Rain announced.

Lance let his eyes take her in as she made her exit. Dottie knew what it meant—her son was finally ready to talk, but what was he going to say?

"I found your gift rather interesting," she said as she mixed her dough.

"I thought you would."

"I didn't know you did this type of work!"

"Mom!" Lance laughed, finding that hard to believe. "I've done this kind of work since I was ten!"

"Really?"

"Really. Where do you think all those wood figurines I had in my room came from?"

"You mean you carved them?"

"Yes! Did you think I stole them?"

"I guess I never thought about it," she said. "So why would you carve me a statue of a woman waving goodbye with her apron strings in hand?"

"Because I want you to let go of me!"

"You're a grown man!" Dottie said, hiding her tears in her work. "I've never stopped you from being one."

"Mom, I'm not doing it anymore. I can't help all your strays."

She turned to him, anger flashing in her eyes. "Is that what this is all about? Well, let me tell you, I never forced anyone on you!"

"Mom!" Lance said, holding his hands up in defense, "you pushed them to me and said 'fix.' I've tried so hard to please you, to honor you. I love you, but I can't take all your strays and help them and then take Dave's strays and then help Bryan and keep Mel happy. I'm quitting. I have to focus on Lance and what God wants for me."

Arthur walked into the room, having seen Rain outside. He now took his place beside his wife. Lance closed his eyes, praying they wouldn't gang up on him.

"So?" Arthur asked.

"Dad, I'm not helping out at the farm anymore."

"Figured that," Arthur smiled. "What are you planning?"

"I don't know. I have some ideas but nothing's finalized yet."

"Lance, the farm was my dream and you helped it come true," Arthur said, looking at his son, his very grown up son. "I spent years planning and praying before it ever came to life. Mom and I kind of threw it on your shoulders without ever considering it may not be your dream. Lance, you're a thinker, a dreamer by your own right. Bryan is a follower. Bryan will be very happy following in our footsteps and someday taking this place over but you, you need to discover your own path. You never played by the rules! We love you and we'll support you, but we won't try to stop you anymore."

Lance threw his arms around his dad's neck, relief washing over him. Arthur held him and knew—his boy was finally back on shore. Dottie stared at her husband in disbelief but knew better than to argue.

The whole Hawkins family was gathered, along with Dave, and the boys and Johnny. Rain and Lance had invited them all over and now the couple stood in front of them all.

"We," Lance started out, shaking as he spoke. "We would just like to tell you all that we're getting married."

The silence hung heavy over the room. Rain and Lance waited for someone to say something.

"File folder not doing it for you anymore?" Bryan finally smiled.

"There are no more file folders!" Lance responded, a grin spreading across his face. "I lost those in the fire, so I had to seek a new form of loving."

Mel got up and hugged both of them. The dam was burst and they all came to congratulate them. Johnny hung back. Rain approached him when the others had moved on to the food.

"It was him for a long time," Johnny sighed. "I knew that guy had you in his sights!"

"Then you knew more than he did!" Rain smiled.

"I have a little experience with these things. Rain, I'm really happy for you!"

"Thanks. Johnny, I really want you to give me away. You're as close to a father as I have."

"I'd be very honored," he smiled. "Is it okay for me to bring an escort to the ceremony? I've met someone."

She hugged him, overjoyed. She had wondered how he would deal with her moving on, leaving him behind, but it seemed God was taking care of that. They joined the others, both feeling content.

Dave felt the loneliness. Now even Lance was getting married, while he struggled to make things work in a household that seemed to be coming apart at the seams. Even thoughts of the new center weren't bringing him satisfaction anymore.

"Uncle Lance, put me down!" Carter insisted when Lance stopped the oncoming attack before the boy had a chance to execute his plan to douse the man with water. Lance laughed.

"That's enough now, boys!" he warned, setting him down and patting his bottom gently and sending him on his way to join his brother for what he knew would be another planning session. They hadn't got Lance all evening! He headed toward Dave.

"They seem to be doing okay," Lance said, grabbing a sandwich off a tray that sat nearby.

"With you," Dave sighed. "With me, they express their anger and disdain."

"Is she coming back?"

"I keep hoping, but this prescription drug thing has me pretty scared."

Lance nodded. "So get her some help."

"Sounds so easy," Dave replied, shaking his head. "It's what I do for a living and you know what, it's all just a big game. I don't do anything and can't do anything except spout off a bunch of bunk. Truly, it's only when people really want to change that anything happens. I just stand there and pat their backs for the results of their hard work."

"Sometimes that pat is very important," Lance insisted. "I know it made a big difference to me."

Dave nodded, wishing he could believe it, but the disillusionment was too keen. His cell phone rang. Lance watched Dave's face and knew the news was bad. Dave dropped the phone in shock.

"What is it?" Lance asked.

"Lori," Dave whispered.

"Dave?"

"She's in the hospital—she overdosed."

"I'll take you," Lance nodded, taking control.

The others were quick to offer support and soon the boys had a place to stay, and Dave and Lance were on their way to the hospital. The nurse escorted them to a room where Lori lay relaxed.

"Hey, Lori," Lance greeted, leaving Dave in the hall for the moment.

She turned to him. The eyes were glassy, but he knew she recognized him.

"So what's going on?"

"I hate her! She resisted what I was too weak to avoid. I hate him for giving so much to her."

"Lori, let's be honest with each other for a moment. You hate yourself for being his daughter. I don't know—maybe even in some twisted way, you wish he had put you into the business. That would have been acceptance from him, now wouldn't it? You have a husband who loves you and two great kids. Why wallow in the past?"

"Lance, I had everything and I blew it. I let it all eat me up until I felt so ugly, I couldn't stand to look anymore, so I started taking the pills."

"Because you wanted to forget what? Your dad's lies. What did Rain ever do to you?"

"She existed."

"That was not her choice. She needs her big sister."

"I don't want to be the big sister, I want to be Daddy's little girl. I want it back to the way it was before he told us the truth. I want him to be my hero again."

"People can't live up to hero worship—not even dads. The image always gets shattered somehow. But God—He is everything He promises to be. Lori, take your eyes off yourself and get off the pity pony. Look around and see all the blessings God has given you."

"Will you help me?" she pleaded.

"I'll always be your friend," he promised.

She nodded.

"So what do you think might be the next step here?" he inquired.

"Rehab," she stated, "followed by years of counseling."

"Let me share something with you," Lance said, "Get out your Bible and start reading. Start praying for healing—I think you'll find the process goes much faster."

He called Dave into the room. He watched the two of them embrace and knew this one would be okay. Lori wanted back into life, and she would have friends there to pull her through the hard times. Even Dave might figure it out—God was the Great Physician and they were only instruments.

Lance left Dave at her bedside and headed to the waiting room where, much to his surprise, sat Arthur. He took a seat beside him.

"Dad, how can this be? Dave is losing his vision and Lori has become an addict. I'm recovering. We all fell into the pit!"

"That's the risk of being a rescuer!" Arthur nodded. "Let me ask you something."

Lance leaned back in the chair to listen.

"What would have happened to Jonah if he hadn't turned back to God?"

"He would have died in the fish's belly!" Lance nodded.

"What if he had continued to live?"

"It wouldn't have been a very nice place to exist!"

"I think we all turn from God and find ourselves in the belly of the fish," Arthur said calmly. "Lance, it's at that point that we have to figure out if we want out or not. You wanted out! Lori's just realizing she's in the belly, but Dave hasn't figured it out yet that he's in the belly. But God works through people and when he sees Lori and you recover, he'll realize. When you refuse to live for God after you know Him, there are two places—serving Him on shore or living in the ugliness of the belly."

Arthur fell silent. Lance thought over the words very carefully, finding many truths in them. Yes, the person patting the backs was very important. Lance stood.

"Dad, I want to take you for a cup of coffee and thank you for being there for me." Lance couldn't hold the tears back.

Arthur got up and pulled his boy into a hug before they headed toward the cafeteria.

CHAPTER 45

The wedding day was perfect, but the bride was a mess. Johnny laughed at Rain, thinking Lance was a lucky man but he was luckier. Since meeting Sandy, he realized how much work Rain could be!

"You look perfect!" he encouraged.

"Do I?" she questioned.

"Lance will be blown away!" he promised.

He was relieved when Dottie arrived to convince her of the truth. She wrapped her arms around the girl and whispered something in her ear. Rain nodded and smiled. She took a deep breath and headed to take Johnny's arm.

"What did you say?" he demanded of Dottie.

"Something she needed to hear!"

Lance stared at his bride, still taking deep breaths to calm himself. He was getting married! He was getting married to Rain. Why was he marrying her? He let his eyes take her in and smiled—because he loved her!

Rain was glad to have Johnny there to hold her up and get her to the handsome guy that she still feared might flee at any moment. Sarah took her place and then it was Rain's turn to take the spot beside Lance. Tears filled her eyes—tears of joy.

Bryan stared at the woman coming up the aisle, still in a state of disbelief that this woman would be Lance's wife—living breathing wife! Others there felt the same way.

Mel nestled against Paul with Sadie in her arms. She couldn't be happier. She had a good family, a good husband, a lovely daughter, and now she could add a sister who she truly could share anything with! She loved Debbie, but she and Rain had so many common bonds. They both got out, they both overcame, but sometimes life had a way of stirring the residue to the surface and they would both understand when that happened.

Lori and Dave sat together. She had a new glow on her face. She'd taken Lance's advice and the healing was in process. Dave was starting to see the changes and she knew his healing would follow. Things would be different when the new center opened.

The ceremony was short and simple followed by a wonderful reception. At last, the couple left for the honeymoon with the words of wisdom passed on to them from all the others who had already taken this step—Lance couldn't remember anything they had said.

Rain fell asleep as he drove. He looked over at her and the nerves hit again and again—what if he didn't measure up? She knew so much more about this than he did. He was still a virgin.

"Lance?" she said sleepily. She had been studying him for about ten minutes and could see a storm was brewing inside.

"I'm fine!" he replied, sounding like he had a million frogs in his throat.

"Where are we going? It's our wedding night and it seems like you're planning to drive until morning."

"We're almost there!" he promised. "I wanted this to be perfect for you!"

She didn't pry anymore, knowing exactly what he was worried about. She remembered her own fears of being a virgin with someone of experience—even if she wasn't really the best example of experienced. She went back to sleep.

He shook her awake gently, his eyes smiling at her. She looked around to find herself surrounded by massive trees on every side.

"Where are we?"

"Redwood Forest."

"This is so incredible!" she cried, overwhelmed by these big majestic creations of God.

"Ready to see our accommodations?"

She nodded, following him up a path that led to the most amazing house she'd ever seen. It was all glass.

"Ricky's friend owns this. It even has a tree growing in the middle," he explained as they made their way inside.

"The bedroom is on the second floor."

She nodded, following him up the stairs. It was just like being in the branches. She gazed outside—it was amazing.

He pulled her against him, kissing her on the base of her neck. She turned to return the affection, surprised at the beads of perspiration on his brow.

"Lance, we'll take this at our speed okay?" she said, tracing his cheek lightly with her finger. His body tingled with her touch. "I've never done this either."

He gave her a quizzical look.

"I've never given myself to someone else, wanting to fulfill him."

He pulled her to him and suddenly all his fears melted away. He loved her and went with that. Rain never felt so cared for or complete before in her life. They remained in each other's arms, gazing out the glass walls, enjoying the full moon that illuminated the branches around them.

"You know, Rain, the only way these trees could become what they are was with good fertile soil and years to become all they are."

"We just made love and you want to talk about the trees?" she laughed.

"I want to talk about our future!" he smiled, nuzzling her in his arms. "I was trying to make it all sound romantic! Anyway, people are a lot like these trees. With good soil and the right raising, in time they become strong and good. I've been thinking we could create a place where those things could be found."

"What are you talking about?" Rain asked, confused where he was going with all this.

"I've thought about you and the way you had to live as a child and about my clients and how it always seemed that I got them when the damage was beyond repair. Rain, I want to run a farm, sort of like my dad's but different. I want the kids to come to our farm and find a place where they can grow."

"Our farm?" she questioned. "We don't have a farm!"

"I know. Rain, I was hoping we could sell that house where you and Johnny lived, because I really don't want anything to do with it, and buy a place. I thought we could have animals instead of gardens—I don't like rock or pea picking!"

"I love gardening!" she protested.

"Then have a garden!" he cried, laughing as he spoke.

Rain let the idea sink in. If someone could have rescued her . . . if someone could have rescued her! She knew she couldn't let another child go through what she lived without doing what she could.

"Let's do it!" Rain announced.

Lance smiled. "Now do you mean let's do 'it' or let's buy a farm?"

She punched him playfully in the arm. "How about both?"

He smiled, pulling her into his arms. He liked the way this wife of his thought! Together they would let God lead them down a very interesting path.

Note From The Author

Sometimes we all feel we're above people lost in worlds we deem as dirty and less than acceptable. In truth, we all sin and make mistakes. In the Bible, turning away from God is often referred to as harlotry or prostitution. Hosea's whole life was a symbolic representation of this. But we don't need to sit in the cesspool of physical or spiritual prostitution. God has offered us a way to Himself—His son Jesus Christ came and paid the penalty for sin once and for all. All we need to do is confess our sins, believe in the saving power of Jesus Christ and be obedient to the Word of God.

Many people try to sell the free salvation part of the deal but I challenge you to look at the Bible and the way Jesus dealt with salvation. He always made sure people understood the cost. Yes, salvation is a free gift but the life comes with a cost. Weigh that cost. I can tell you for me, the cost was worth everything I gave in return for the awesome blessings I've received.

If you want a life filled with excitement and wonder, let God guide you. I think Hosea ended his book with the same words I'll end this book.

"Who is wise? Let him understand these things. Who is prudent? Let him know them. For the ways of the Lord are right; the righteous walk in them, but transgressors stumble in them." Hosea 14: 9